DAISY DEAD

ALSO BY SUE WATSON

Psychological Thrillers

Our Little Lies

The Woman Next Door

The Empty Nest

The Sister-in-Law

First Date

The Forever Home

The New Wife

The Resort

The Nursery

The Wedding Day

The Lodge

You Me Her

Wife Mother Liar

His First Wife

Fiction

Love, Lies and Lemon Cake

Snow Angels, Secrets & Christmas Cake

Summer Flings and Dancing Dreams

We'll Always Have Paris

Bella's Christmas Bake Off

The Christmas Cake Café

Ella's Ice Cream Summer

Curves, Kisses and Chocolate Ice Cream

Snowflakes, Iced Cakes and Second Chances

Love, Lies and Wedding Cake

WANTING DAISY DEAD

SUE WATSON

This is a work of fiction. Names, characters, organizations, places, events, and incidents are either products of the author's imagination or used fictitiously. Any resemblance to actual persons, living or dead, or actual events is purely coincidental.

Text copyright © 2025 by Sue Watson
All rights reserved.

No part of this book may be reproduced, or stored in a retrieval system, or transmitted in any form or by any means, electronic, mechanical, photocopying, recording, or otherwise, without express written permission of the publisher.

Published by Thomas & Mercer, Seattle

www.apub.com

Amazon, the Amazon logo, and Thomas & Mercer are trademarks of Amazon.com, Inc., or its affiliates.

EU Product Safety contact:
Amazon Publishing, Amazon Media EU S.à r.l.
38, avenue John F. Kennedy, L-1855 Luxembourg
amazonpublishing-gpsr@amazon.com

ISBN-13: 9781662523861
eISBN: 9781662523854

Cover design by The Brewster Project
Cover images: © Olena / Alamy Stock Photo; © Mazur Travel
© bdvect 1 © New Africa / Shutterstock

Printed in the United States of America

*For my friend and reader Harolyn Grant,
Thanks for saving Daisy and me . . . or is it Daisy
and I?*

The Killer Question: Who Wanted Daisy Dead?

Podcast transcript, 2025

On a cold November night twenty years ago, in 2005, student Daisy Harrington left the house she shared with her fellow second-year students and went to meet a friend. She didn't want to share with everyone who she was meeting that evening, but her housemates were busy with their own lives, and she set off alone.

It was the next morning before any of Daisy's friends realised she wasn't in her room, so hadn't come home the previous evening. Assuming she'd stayed over at her boyfriend's, they continued with their day, expecting her to turn up later. But later, when Daisy still hadn't returned home, they called her and there was no answer, so they contacted some of her friends from her English lit course, who said they hadn't seen or heard from her either. Becoming concerned now, the housemates posted on MySpace and Bebo, the precursors to Facebook, asking if anyone knew where she was. But no one had seen her since the previous evening, and so they called the police and raised the alarm.

Over the next few days, the police began a thorough investigation, interviewing anyone and everyone who'd come into contact with the young woman. Friends and fellow students posted online, handed out leaflets and tied yellow ribbons around trees, all apparently desperate to find her. As Daisy's mother was too distraught to speak to the media about her missing daughter, the five housemates stepped in. In newspapers, TV news reports and soon documentaries, they pleaded for Daisy, or whoever had her, to contact them. 'We love you and want you back,' her friends cried. Their appearances went global, their crying faces were on all the front pages; the news on TV was filled with images of the concerned friends and the beautiful young woman who had gone missing. Tears on camera, wringing hands, running mascara, all of them begging for her return, and as fears grew of a killer on campus, there was concern for their own safety too.

It was a media frenzy, and the iconic photo of the five housemates – friends together in grief and fear – stayed with the nation for a long time to come.

The press hinted that each of those grieving housemates had a reason to kill Daisy, which was true. But only one of them had enough of a reason to actually kill her . . .

So who was it, and why did they want Daisy dead?

1

Now – Twenty Years After Daisy's Murder

Lauren Pemberton, Daisy's Best Friend and Housemate

I look across the table at the tiny woman who is smiling as she attempts to eat the minuscule starter covered in foam. She looks up from her herculean struggle, and our eyes meet momentarily, before we both return to the task at hand. Lunch with my agent.

'Do you like the new book?' I ask, toying with a small leaf on my plate. I'm so nervous that if I actually put anything in my mouth I may choke.

It's taken me a long time to write my second book – ninety thousand words containing my blood, sweat and tears. Not to mention the late nights and early mornings, the constant exhaustion resulting in vicious arguments with Richard and accusations of neglect from my daughter. If Finty says no to this book, then I have no future.

'Please just tell me the truth,' I ask her again, now putting down my fork, unable to even look at the oily leaves congealing on my plate. 'Finty, we've known each other for a long time. You plucked me from that slush pile and saw promise back then . . . What about now?'

Eighteen years ago, I was the toast of the book world, with a huge bestseller and a 'one to watch' label from all the critics. I was feted wherever I went: queues of readers lined bookshops and pavements, waiting for me to sign the precious hardback copies they clutched like Fabergé eggs. After all the horror and suspicion around Daisy's death, I believed this was what I deserved. It was a deliciously sweet – if short – respite from the darkness.

After the trial, when Daisy's killer was safely in prison, I finally found the courage to send the manuscript out to almost every agent in London. Finty was one of the first to get back to me. She hadn't long left Limerick, and her excitement for a bigger life made her Irish eyes sparkle. And all my doubts and fears disappeared in the champagne bubbles as she called me to say publishers were offering six-figure sums for the book.

It was like a dream – *A Day in the Life and Death* went on to sell millions, the film starring Scarlett Johansson was a box office hit, and for nearly two decades I've been living off the proceeds. But the tragedy is, I found myself unable to write a second book; readers clamoured for more, but writer's block, anxiety, panic attacks and guilt stopped me in my tracks.

But now the money has run out, and nothing focuses the mind like losing one's home. So I finally wrote book two, sent it to Finty, and I'm desperate for her to like it so she'll do her magic once more, sell it to a publisher, and I can keep my home. I'm waiting for the effusiveness, the glint of ambition and thrilling praise, just like there was for book one.

But instead of sparkly eyes in a thirty-something face, I'm looking across the table at a fifty-year-old woman with thin lips and too much Botox, whose accent has faded along with her enthusiasm.

'Your writing is . . . good,' she starts slowly, and for the first time I realise this may not be the meeting I've been hoping for.

'But?'

'I don't know, Lauren . . . It lacks something. Your first book had so much . . . *more*.' She gazes upwards. Is she searching for words? Or avoiding my eyes?

Inwardly, I writhe in agony as she returns her attention to her plate, nibbling at a leaf like a baby rabbit.

'Some people only have one book in them . . .' She stabs me with her words.

Holding my breath, I sip my wine self-consciously, vowing not to have another in her company. I might say too much. I'll have a large one on the way home.

This book is make-or-break for me. I haven't had any luck since those heady days of my debut.

When *A Day in the Life and Death* was released, Daisy Harrington's murder was still fresh in everyone's minds and the parallels were clear. Being her best friend and housemate, it was assumed I'd written it about her, but we avoided any legal problems by stating this was a work of fiction. Of course that wasn't strictly true – it was about Daisy, though not the Daisy we knew but another, far more complex one, working through the watershed before womanhood. There was no death in the original; Finty and I just cobbled that together at the end because the publishers were clamouring for a body count.

During my first lunch meeting with Finty all those years ago, she ordered for both of us – the most expensive things on the menu, including a bottle of pink champagne.

'Your writing is refreshing and raw and beautiful,' she said then, her eyes glittering. 'You are a rare talent, Lauren. Cheers!' And we clinked our champagne saucers, and she ordered a second bottle.

Today, we drink subdued white wine in a less expensive restaurant, and she talks, using non-committal phrases like 'okay' and 'not sure' and 'the market is flooded'.

'What are you saying, Finty . . . ?' I ask, crossing my fingers.

Now there's a buzzing in my head; it's getting louder and louder and suddenly her little voice is lost in the sound, and only then do I realise it's my phone ringing.

'Sorry, I have to pick up, it's Richard. Clementine's off school with a cold.'

'Of course.' She goes back to her foam and leaves.

'Hello, is she okay?' I ask, panic and fear pumping through me.

'Who?'

'*Clementine*, of course – isn't that why you called?' I try not to sound as frustrated with my husband as I feel.

'No, she's fine. She's definitely going back to school tomorrow, whatever she says.' My heart feels like it's beating in my head. If, as I suspect, Finty doesn't think the book is good enough to offer to publishers, then I won't have a second book deal. And we're careening towards financial oblivion.

'Richard, I'm with . . . Finty,' I say, like I'm trying to hide my irritation with a three-year-old.

'I know. That's why I'm calling. Does she like it?' Richard's been like this ever since he lost his job – bored and aimless. I feel like I have *two* children sometimes.

I try not to swear. I need to be at my very best, my most focused, in case there's a slim chance of saving this.

'See you later, have to go.' I'm about to put the phone down.

'Lauren, you've had a note through the letterbox,' Richard says.

'Okay, well, I can see it when I get home.' *Idiot, I think. Why does he want to discuss the bloody post now?*

'It's an invitation to a party – a fortieth birthday party. It's a whole weekend,' he continues regardless.

'Great, let's talk about it when I get home.' I smile and give Finty a slight eye-roll, but she doesn't bond over annoying husbands. She's enviably single, and doesn't bond over anything except deals and money, and she hasn't made *any* money with me for a long time.

I glance at the blue eyes and pencil-thin arms of the disillusioned husk sitting opposite me. I think the industry – and probably having me as a client – has sucked her dry.

I'm about to hang up so I can try to convince Finty that, if we did it once, we can do it again. But he's still talking.

'Richard, please . . .'

'I called you because I think it might be a scam.'

'Why?' I ask, irritated.

'Well, it's signed "*The Killer Question* podcast" but the party is for someone called Daisy Harrington. Isn't she . . . Isn't she the one who was murdered?'

My blood turns to ice. I can't speak; a panic attack is winging its way towards me. Any minute now I may have to take out the paper bag I keep in my laptop carrier and put it to my mouth and start breathing heavily in and out. And I'm not quite sure how Finty and the rest of the diners in the restaurant are going to feel about that.

'And there's something else,' Richard is muttering. 'Inside, it says—'

'*What?*' I reply, so sharply Finty's head shoots up from the thimble of seafood she's struggling to eat.

'Is everything okay?' she's mouthing.

'Fine, fine,' I mouth back, before attempting a beaming, lying smile.

'What does it say . . . ?' My voice is hoarse; my head is filled with Daisy. Today of all days I don't need this.

'Sorry, I had to get my glasses,' he's mumbling. 'You know what my eyesight's like, Lauren . . .' There's an infuriating pause while he must be putting his glasses on. 'So, it says: *Dear Lauren, you are cordially invited for a weekend to celebrate the fortieth birthday of Daisy Harrington. The birthday girl will sadly not be attending, but her friends will all be there.*'

He stops talking. I can barely breathe. What is this?

'Richard, does it say anything else?'

'Er, yes, it's at your old university, Exeter. St Luke's Campus?'

'Yes, yes, that's right . . . Okay . . .' I can't deal with this right now.

'There's more . . . Oh, it doesn't make sense, that's rather odd.'

Shit.

'What does it say?' I try to ask lightly, but it comes out as a squeak.

'Well.' He pauses, and I think I might die. 'It says, *We know why you wanted Daisy dead – and if you aren't at her party, everyone else will know too.*'

That's when I knock my glass from the table, sending shattered crystal all over the restaurant floor.

2

GEORGIE FRASER, DAISY'S FRIEND AND HOUSEMATE

I can't find my fucking phone. I left it here on the kitchen counter last night – I'm trying to detox and having it on my bedside table was making me really anxious. But now I'm even more anxious because I can't find it. One of the kids must have moved it, or perhaps *he*'s been trying to access it again? My stomach drops at the thought of him flicking through my phone, probing around in all my secrets. Ironic, because I use my phone to probe around in his secrets.

I have a really important meeting this afternoon with a potential new client, and need to get going. Dan did the school run like it was a big deal, but I packed the lunches and the sports kits and made sure they had all their books. Dealing with the detritus of everyone else's lives makes me late for my own.

The envelope is thick, white, embossed and damning. It keeps catching my eye from its place on the kitchen counter. My eyes are drawn to it, and I'm compelled to reach across and pick it up, wishing it didn't exist. This envelope contains a virtual bomb waiting to go off in my kitchen, tearing everything apart – my marriage, my long-hidden secrets, everything.

I found it on the mat earlier, with no stamp, no return address. Someone must have delivered it by hand, which gives me the creeps. How dare they just walk up to my front door and push their nasty little note through? It's opened up old wounds I never thought I'd have to deal with again after all these years. Daisy Harrington's bloody birthday. I presume Dan has one too – perhaps he picked his up when he left. I'm glad he's gone, I don't want to talk about it with him. I can't bear to dredge it all up.

Despite it being the most horrific thing that's happened since . . . well, since the murder, I must compartmentalise. For now I need to put it in a box in my head marked 'Later', and work out what I'm going to do about it then. Today is a big day: I have to pitch a glamorous, gourmet wedding buffet to a big new hotel.

I need to be at my best – smiley, shiny and sharp. So, hiding the envelope in my trouser pocket, I try to forget it for now and concentrate on what's ahead, but first I need to find my bloody phone.

'Where the fuck is it?' My head's starting to get hot, my chest is filled with rage; I need to calm down, but I can't. I was inexplicably angry from the moment I woke up this morning, which has been exacerbated by the bloody invite. I feel rage building, like an oncoming wave, and I know that once it hits I can't control it; I'll be drowning in fury.

I do another lap of the kitchen, searching frantically with hands and eyes. I start moving the coffee machine to see if my phone got stuck behind there. But nothing. *Fuck!*

I dash into the hall, still scanning all areas for the phone while grabbing my jacket off the coat rack.

And suddenly, weirdly, *there's* my phone, on the side table in the hall. Relieved but puzzled, I grab it. *How on earth did it get there?*

I didn't put it on the hall table, I just know I didn't. I stand for a moment trying to remember when I last had it, and wonder if I'm going mad. I mean, literally having a breakdown.

But I don't have time for madness now, so I push my arms into my jacket, and my phone into my trouser pocket next to the folded-up envelope. Then, with keys in one hand and handbag in the other, I let myself out into the freezing-cold day.

Work isn't exactly glamorous, a prefab near an industrial estate that's seen better days, but inside we have a great kitchen and all the latest equipment. It cost a fortune – I had to get a bank loan – but I know I'm going to make this work, and one day I'll be rich, even richer than bloody Lauren.

I find a discreet parking space and apply concealer to the emerging cracks around my eyes. All the while I'm aware of the envelope now lying on the passenger seat next to my phone and handbag. I feel like there's another person sitting there, and as much as I try to ignore it, my eyes and mind wander back to the envelope. It's addressed to *Georgie*; no surname. Whoever pushed it through my letterbox knows me and my address – and apparently so much more. The fact they stood on my doorstep, just feet away, feels so intimate. *Too* intimate.

I put another layer of concealer on, as if covering my wrinkles will erase what happened. My secrets have lived with me since I was nineteen years old; they were at my graduation, my wedding day – they were even there, in the shadows, when my children were born. Daisy never had kids, never married; she didn't even get her degree. And consequently, every golden moment, every defining life event, has been tarnished by *her*. I can just imagine her seething resentment – I have what she wanted. Wherever she is now, she must hate me. I doubt that she rests in peace.

I dared to hope this catering business would be a new beginning for me – that the past was buried now and I could move on.

Who was I kidding? I may have got what Daisy wanted, but I've paid the price, and it's been a living hell. 'Be careful what you wish for, love,' my nan used to say. I think about that every time I look at him.

Bang bang. I'm shaken from the past by a sharp and sudden knock on my car window, a face looming in the glass.

'Come on, you're gonna be late!'

Sam, my new catering manager, loves 'having a laugh'. I don't find her funny.

'I'll be with you in five.' I put five fingers up at the window, palm facing her, which a body language expert would correctly interpret as 'Go away!' I add a half-smile to soften this. I don't want to lose any more staff. Apparently, strong leadership is considered to be 'bullying' these days. It was only a plastic spatula that I threw . . . God, the fuss they made – anyone would think it was a carving knife. Fucking snowflakes!

I find people difficult to work with; I don't have time to micromanage their feelings. I just need to get the job done.

I wait until Sam's gone inside before I pick up the envelope. I take out the card. Her picture smiles at me – the penetrating blue eyes, the halo of blonde hair . . . I feel someone walking across my grave.

I've never said this aloud, but it was a relief when the police arrived to tell us she'd been found. After a week of searching, speculation, in-fighting and finger-pointing, Daisy's body had finally been discovered. She was in a brightly painted hut on Exmouth Beach, not far from the university. At first there was no obvious suspect, and with all the publicity, and the media parked outside our door day and night, everyone convinced themselves it was one of us, her housemates. There were six of us, including Daisy, and we'd lived together since halls at the start of university. We all got along, and when it came to finding a place to live for second year, we'd decided to move into a house near St Luke's Campus. We'd assumed the fun would continue, and the friendships we'd formed by living together in the first year would become stronger. But it wasn't to be. The second year was very different: the closeness we'd thought we all had turned out to be toxic, and bad things happened between us. By the time Daisy died, we were all so vulnerable and broken, we didn't trust ourselves, let alone each other.

As I sit in the car, the past holds me down – makes me feel trapped, isolated. I take out the invitation, holding it only with my thumb and forefinger. It feels dirty; I don't want to touch it fully with my hands.

Opening it, I read the words again, and wait for the rush of horror to overwhelm me, as it did earlier when I first read it at home.

Dear Georgie,

You are cordially invited for a weekend to celebrate the 40th birthday of Daisy Harrington.

The birthday girl will sadly not be attending, but her friends will all be there.

Please join us on Friday December 12th at St Luke's Campus, Exeter, for a weekend of memories.

Check in by 5 p.m.

We know why you wanted Daisy dead – and if you aren't at her party, everyone else will know too.

LOVE FROM

THE KILLER QUESTION Podcast

My stomach lurches, and I wonder again just what they know, and who *they* are. I don't listen to podcasts; I'm too busy cooking, cleaning, child rearing, building a business, and keeping my husband from other women's beds. I don't have time.

God, I can't face any of them. All those other students who pretended to know and love her will be swarming around. Ambulance-chasing bastards with their fake grief and fake memories – they never knew her like we did, they have no idea what she was really like.

I have no intention of going to this *circus*, this ridiculous birthday weekend for someone who's been dead twenty years. I mean, WTF?

But the other side of me, the one that holds the secrets, is less brave, and she's worried that it might all close in on her again.

Who the hell is behind this? And how do they *know*?

3

MADDIE PARR, DAISY'S HOUSEMATE AND FRIEND

I think it's a birthday card; I didn't get a single one this year on the actual day. My birthdays have been pretty solitary since Mum died, not that they were anything exciting before, just me and Mum with a candle in a Mr Kipling cupcake.

I open the thick white envelope, wondering who it can be from. I only moved here a few weeks ago – I don't know anyone here. Oh Christ, it's not one of the weirdos I've met through work, is it? I wonder if I should even open it, or take it straight round to the police station. I've had stuff like this before, and it's really unnerving when you live alone to know someone's been hanging around your door.

But as I slip the card from the envelope, I see her face and I can't help it – I drop the card like it's infectious. It lands on the kitchen floor, and now she's staring up at me, blaming, judging, taunting. I can't bear it. Who could possibly have put this through the door? And why?

With trembling hands I pick the card up and lean against the kitchen island for support. I open it, skim the words inside, and my blood turns to ice. An invite to Daisy's would-have-been fortieth? A birthday weekend for a *dead* person? Who *does* that?

I'm not going – it would be weird and horrible – but as I read on, I can't believe this is happening . . .

> *We know why you wanted Daisy dead – and if you aren't at her party, everyone else will know too.*
>
> *LOVE FROM*
>
> *THE KILLER QUESTION Podcast*

Somebody *knows* . . . and now I'm really scared. My whole body starts to shake as I realise that, after all these years of hiding, running away – someone knows what I did to Daisy. And now the horrible mess has caught the eye of some thirsty podcaster looking for a hit and planning a 'birthday weekend'.

I immediately call Alex. He'll know all about this podcast, I'm sure; he's a computer nerd, and an expert on digital and streaming and stuff. I'm pretty good myself, but not like Alex. He brought my computer back to life over the phone all the way from San Jose once. I had to tell him not to look at my files, told him my work stuff was extremely confidential – well, it is.

'Hey Alex,' I say as he picks up.

'Morning, gorgeous.'

'It's early evening here. You okay?'

'I'm good, babe.'

'Did you get an invite to Daisy's birthday weekend?'

'Yeah. What do you make of it?'

I take a deep breath. 'I think it's a bit sick.' I'm terrified, but I can't tell Alex that.

'Yeah. You are going, aren't you, Madds?'

'No, I can't. I'm busy. You?'

'But I thought we all have to go . . . ?'

'They can't force us. It's a podcast, not the police, Alex!'

I'm intrigued that he says we 'have' to go. Makes me wonder if his invite also includes a threat if he doesn't turn up.

'The wording is a bit weird, isn't it?' I offer, to see if I can tease it out of him and confirm whether he's going because he's scared something will be revealed.

'It's pretty straightforward to me. There's a party and you have to go.'

My stomach drops. 'What do you mean, I have to go?'

'Because it'll be a laugh and I'm going. It's our chance to see each other . . . and . . . Maddie, if they're doing a special podcast all about Daisy, it'll look bad if you *don't* go.'

I groan inwardly at this. He's right. If I don't attend, I'll look mean and uncaring – or worse. And if they make good on their threat, my life could be over.

'It's no coincidence that her murderer killed himself recently and now the podcast is sniffing around,' I say.

'I read that he used his own bed sheet to kill himself slowly. His cellmate was sleeping, happened in the middle of the night. The guy in the other bunk woke up and found him.'

'Ugh. I know. It's awful, Alex, but I can't feel sorry for him. He killed Daisy.'

'He never confessed, even in his suicide note.'

'He didn't need to confess, the blood was all over his hammer, along with his fingerprints.'

'Yeah, but his fingerprints *would* be on his hammer. Presumably he used it to hammer things.'

'Yes, he did. He hammered Daisy.' I cringe in horror at what I've just said. I have this image of what her body must have looked like, battered and bloody, lying there undiscovered for a week.

'He had another appeal coming up. You'd think he'd have waited until after to check himself out, wouldn't you?'

'Yeah, but he was guilty, and maybe the prospect of returning to a world where everyone knew he was a killer was too much?'

'I guess.'

'So, do you know anything about this *Killer Question* podcast?'

'Yeah, a bit. The podcast is true crime, but the difference is that they aim to get innocent people out of jail, and they do this over a series of episodes. So they question everyone connected with the case, the family and friends of the prisoner, and, if they can, they interview people connected to the victim too – it helps give a fair account of the story – and they sometimes get access to police files. So, while they're sifting through the evidence to do that, they also play detective, to try and find out who really did it.'

'Ugh, not *armchair* detectives?' My heart sinks at this.

'Yeah, kind of, but they're good. I think it's two sisters – the main host is a lawyer, and the other one is in TV and radio production or something like that.'

'I knew you'd know everything about it – even the hosts' life stories,' I tease.

'Not really. I happened to see an interview with them on YouTube. They basically combined their two careers and started a podcast. They don't always "get their man", but the success rate is pretty good, I think. They have a huge following – more than two million.'

I feel sick. Two million followers? I can only dream of that.

'Yeah, they've worked with famous cases. They got that guy they called the Southend Serial Killer out of prison.'

'Oh, *them*? Yeah, I read about that.' Now I'm *really* worried. 'Wasn't it his twin brother who was the real killer?'

'That's right. And he let his brother take the rap, until the podcasters started looking into it. Fascinating because, being twins, they had the same DNA. Anyway, the podcast know what they're doing – they drop weekly episodes and the occasional *Killer Question* weekend, a more extended podcast.'

'And that's what this Daisy birthday weekend is?'

'That's my guess. I presume they think David was innocent, and they want to find out who *really* killed Daisy.'

'Bit pointless. Everyone knows he did it.'

'I guess they're doing it for the family. He had kids, you know?'

'I heard his wife left the country, took the kids with her. Their dad was a murderer – I doubt they care about his *name*.'

'Who knows?' Alex pauses. 'So, go on, go to the weekend. I'm coming all the way from the US, and you're nearer to Exeter than I am.'

'I'll think about it.'

We say our goodbyes, and as I hang up I realise I might have no choice. If *The Killer Question* has more than two million listeners, as Alex reckons, I can't take the chance of *anything* being said about me. At least if I'm there I'll be able to stand up for myself, even if I have to hide some of the truth.

But why is Alex coming all the way from San Jose? I'm always suggesting he visits the UK, and he knows he can stay with me, but he says he can't leave his company. Did he get the same message as me on his invite? Is he scared of what might come out if he doesn't turn up? Did Alex want Daisy dead too?

I know they had their ups and downs, and he was always lending her money – quite a bit of money, as I recall.

But, more importantly for me, if he *has* had the same message, then whoever's running this podcast isn't just focusing on me. They might be bluffing and sending these messages to all of us, trying to smoke the killer out . . . At this prospect, relief floods through me – and regret too. I should never have got involved with Daisy Harrington.

Her death ruined my life, and robbed me of my future. I never finished my degree; I couldn't stay at university after what happened. I was too scared – we all were, for different reasons. But they all stayed on, and presumably *moved* on? I couldn't face it, and went travelling for a while. But that didn't work out, so I came home, and erased myself from my own life.

'You'll be famous one day,' Mum used to say. I dreamed of being a dancer, then later an actress. I wanted fame, I guess, and I also wanted a life away from mine and Mum's bedsit with the damp walls and dodgy gas heater. I used to imagine myself living in a big Victorian house in London and starring in West End theatre productions. But, instead, I'm almost forty and living in a new-build on a housing estate, starring in a warped version of my own sad life.

But I shouldn't complain. I have no mortgage, can work from home, and I earn in a month what most people earn in a year. The other nice thing is, I work alone – except for my cat, Minty. I love having another heartbeat in the house. Living and working alone with just a white Persian for company may not be everyone's cup of tea, but to me it's heaven. Because hell is other people.

It isn't the life I would have chosen for myself. I don't have friends, as they ask too many questions, and these days just the idea of leaving the house scares me.

Daisy's death affected all of us, but I imagine the others have their distractions. And at least they were able to stay on and finish their studies. Lauren cried a lot at the funeral, but she still managed to go back to her course, write a book and become this big hot shot. And Georgie has two kids – I can't remember how I know that, I think Alex told me. Yeah, they all cried for Daisy, said how much they loved her, but they still carried on with their lives. I couldn't. I never found love, never wanted children – I was too broken. I guess we're all different, and we reacted in different ways.

The trauma wasn't helped by all the attention we received at the time. We were young, and I'll admit strangely flattered that these newspapers and TV programmes wanted our stories. What did we think about Daisy? Was she kind, talented . . . promiscuous? They asked all kinds of questions, and we gave our opinions, our different perceptions of who she was. Daisy was seeing more than one person when she died, but I never told anyone. Daisy told me not to.

I feel a binge coming on, and try to remember what my therapist said. I have to ask myself *why, what, who?*

Why do I want to binge? *What* is drawing me to the saltiness of a pack of cold butter on a loaf of hot toast? And *who* is causing such emotional turmoil that I am compelled to consume enormous bags of crisps and chocolate bars the size of bricks, until I'm sick? *You tell me, you're my therapist.*

The minute I open the fridge, Minty comes padding across the kitchen, so I lift her up for a cuddle and we both stare at the calorie-counted meals neatly stacked on the shelves. I stay in the moment, remain mindful, and take out the chicken katsu. 'Mmm, almost good enough to eat, eh, Minty?'

I lower her on to the floor and put the food in the microwave for four minutes on high.

I hate to even think this, but I'm glad David Montgomery's dead. My only surprise is that he waited all these years in prison to finally kill himself. I do feel sorry for his kids, though. I lost my dad at a young age, and though my dad died and theirs went to prison, it's still a loss when you're young, and I know how hard it is. But back then they were kids and didn't understand. All the evidence was there, and the prosecuting lawyer was amazing, she took everything he said and twisted it back around. He was toast!

I wander impatiently around my little kitchen as the microwave hums, counting down my four minutes closer to death. I spot the card again, and my stomach lurches. The last twenty years have been devoted to hiding, and holding my secret close. Now suddenly there's this invitation with a threat. But they can't possibly know. No one can.

The picture on the invite is Daisy, her hair golden in the sunshine. I remember taking that photo; they used it for her funeral. She's smiling, her mouth is open, but her eyes are cold – she was angry with me that day.

It's hard to leave the house, my sanctuary, but sometimes, when I don't have what I need in the cupboards, I have to overcome my fear. Before the microwave has a chance to finish nuking the chicken, I grab my keys and purse and run out to the car. Then I drive as fast as I legally can to the nearest supermarket, and throw everything in the trolley: cake, cheese, chocolate, crisps. As I walk through the car park with a basket full of temporary happiness, euphoria and self-loathing fight it out in my head. And even on the drive home I start cramming food into my mouth and I won't stop until it's all gone.

4

Dan Levine, Housemate

When I get in from work she's in the kitchen with the kids – doesn't even look at me. Obviously pissed off because I was supposed to pick them up from the childminder's an hour ago.

'Sorry, I was held up at work,' I say, but she ignores me, and continues to chop up two apples for the kids. 'It's not the end of the world.' I walk towards her, both arms open, and she whizzes round, the knife in her hand. 'Whoa, watch that,' I warn, smiling.

'Not the end of your world, perhaps, but it's the end of mine!' she hisses. 'I had to cancel a really important pitch this afternoon.' She can't look at me, and goes back to chopping.

'I'm sorry! Something came up – a few million pounds, to be precise,' I mutter as an afterthought. 'Look, I had to be there. If the stock market crashes and I'm at the school gate, I won't have a *job*!'

'But I've worked so fucking hard on that client—'

'Don't swear . . . The kids . . .' I widen my eyes in Violet's direction, as our eight-year-old gasps theatrically at 'Mummy's swear'.

'Here, take these for you and Elspeth,' she says to Violet, handing her the chopped-up apple. 'You can watch TV.'

This is a source of great delight, as the girls scramble to get out of the kitchen to the sitting room. Like most things in our lives, Georgie has made watching TV into forbidden fruit, and in much the same way as I now hide my guilty pleasures from my wife, our daughters will learn to do the same.

As they leave, I turn to her. I'm too tired to argue, I just want to flop on the sofa and fall asleep. But her anger is palpable – it throbs in her veins, pulses through the air, creating this thick layer of tension between us. She scares me when she's like this.

'Couldn't you move your pitch meeting to another day, or get a sitter . . . ?' I suggest gently, but before I've even finished the sentence, I hold my breath. I can feel the blast of heat. My wife is breathing fire, which is soon followed by the familiar yelling and swearing, punctuated by crashing pots and pans. No wonder she keeps losing staff – I certainly couldn't work with her. She needs help, but now isn't the time for that conversation.

I wander into the sitting room to let her cool down, and even the kids seem to be giving me the silent treatment. Kids pick up on stuff like this, though fortunately they're still young enough to be bribed by chocolate, so I produce the Cadbury stash I bought from the petrol station on the way home.

'Do you want to poison your kids with sugar?' She's standing in the doorway, glaring at me.

'Has Daddy *poisoned* us?' Elspeth, the little one, lisps through no front teeth, her eyes wide in child horror.

'No, darling,' I say, before adding in a murmur, 'Not half as much as Mummy has.'

'Dan!' Her voice is raised. 'It's not okay to wreck my business then turn up late with bloody chocolate bars like Father Christmas.'

Accustomed to Mummy snapping at Daddy, our girls don't flinch at this, but I catch the look between them, presumably at 'Mummy's second swear'.

Georgie stomps from the sitting room, and the girls eat their chocolate in silence, mesmerised by the blue Australian dog on the screen. I go back into the kitchen, and my darling wife is holding another sharp knife. This time, she's chopping manically at a carrot. I'm sure she's wishing it was one of my fingers – or worse.

I know she's seen her invite to the Daisy thing – it's lying on the kitchen counter.

She hasn't mentioned it at all.

She says she can't trust me, but I'm not sure I trust her. She's been texting more than usual, and in the past couple of weeks her phone has rung and she's picked up and left the room. The other night I walked into the living room and she took her phone outside. I mean, what the hell?

'Who was that?' I asked casually when she returned from the arctic temperatures of the back garden on a winter's night.

'Just a work thing.'

'You seem to be taking a lot of work calls outside and upstairs recently. I didn't realise one had to sign the Official Secrets Act to discuss a finger buffet with a client these days.'

'Don't be so stupid,' she hissed, and stomped upstairs to bed.

Something's going on with her, and I know that's hypocritical coming from me, but I don't like how it makes me feel. This morning I tried to check her phone but she's obviously changed the PIN, and on the way to work I realised I hadn't put it back where she'd left it. She'd go mad if she knew, even though she's constantly trying to get into my phone.

But that's the least of my problems right now: the invite is swirling around my head constantly. Who could possibly know that I wanted Daisy dead? I'm really worried about what these freaks have on me. I need to mention the invite to Georgie, but daren't give anything away. I'll have to box clever on this one. Jesus, she's so contrary that if she thinks I *want* to go, she'll make it her mission to stop me, either by refusing to go herself or by kicking off if I try to go alone. But I *have* to go, because if I don't that podcast will tell everyone *everything*, and that would be curtains for me.

Whoever posted mine and Georgie's invites through the door did so last night. It was late, I'd been for drinks after work, and I opened the door to see two envelopes lying there. Neither of them had a postmark, or a stamp, and one was addressed to Georgie and one to me. This worried me, because why wasn't it one letter to both of us? So, I double-locked the doors and checked outside through the windows to see if anyone was standing in the garden. It wouldn't have been the first time we'd had a nocturnal visitor in the garden, but Georgie doesn't know about that. I'll be frank, I haven't been the most faithful of husbands, and there have been some slightly tricky moments as a result. And, seeing those envelopes on the mat, I thought they were from the woman I was seeing last summer, finally bringing the wrath she'd been threatening. I assumed the letter to me was an X-rated tirade of abuse, and there was a strong possibility that Georgie's might contain photographs of me and the woman in flagrante. It was a bad move even starting that affair – it had car crash written all over it – but what can I tell you? She was beautiful, with a great body. I had no idea she was a psycho.

To my horror, Georgie found out about my summer psycho when she spotted a message on my phone. It took months to convince her not to divorce me, and if this correspondence *was* from her, it could trigger Georgie into retaining a divorce lawyer all over again.

Anyway, I was standing in the hallway with these two envelopes, and as Georgie and the kids were in bed I locked myself in the downstairs toilet so I could read them. I opened my envelope first, but instead of the abusive letter I'd been expecting from my fling, another woman was suddenly staring out at me – Daisy. That angelic face, innocent and beautiful, peeling away time like it was yesterday. She was smiling, the sun was shining, and the future held such hope and optimism. Daisy's photo was so mesmerising, I didn't register at first that this was an invitation. I just drank her in, remembering the good times, the great sex. But even so, it was unsettling, and even the memory of her long legs, her full breasts and those come-to-bed eyes couldn't hold back the darkness. Everything I'd kept hidden for the past twenty years was now flooding back up my oesophagus, like a memory reflux.

The silver lining to this dark trip down memory lane is that Georgie's envelope was obviously an invite too, and not a series of scandalous photographs sent by my summer fling, so I left hers on the mat. She could find it herself in the morning, after I'd gone to work. I didn't want a conversation about it, I always find it very difficult, and I know she does too.

Georgie and I rarely talk about Daisy – we can't. There were things I didn't tell her then, and I know how distressing that was for her, but how could I confide in her without incriminating myself?

Georgie and Daisy had been friends – not best friends, but they liked each other – but then, after what happened between us, that changed. Georgie grew to hate Daisy. 'I wish she'd go away, far away,' she'd mumble through her tears. 'I can't bear to live in the same house as her anymore – I wish she was dead!'

Georgie didn't mean it literally; she says terrible things when she's angry and upset. It was one of the reasons I tried to keep them apart, because I was seriously worried that Georgie might lose it with Daisy.

I still think about her every night, still dream about her, and when she's drunk Georgie always asks me if I loved Daisy. I did. But I always say no.

In the week between Daisy going missing and her body being found, I was suspect numero uno. The press and public seemed to love the weird posh kid because I never said no to a photo or an interview. I was so naive, so stupid. I thought they genuinely liked me and wanted to hear what I said, but all they wanted was to poke fun at me and make me look guilty. And when they asked me questions about Daisy, I replied honestly. I didn't realise those comments, and my smiling photos, would be turned into something quite sinister.

'I Miss Her,' Says Lovesick Housemate Dan.

I can't deny I said I missed her, but 'lovesick'? It made me sound weak and pervy. But then, about a year after Daisy's murder, the court case finally took place and, despite everyone assuming David Montgomery was guilty, the press still kept me in the spotlight. I was photographed, quoted, and there was a documentary about Daisy that focused on her housemates, especially me. I thought that I was famous and that being on the telly would impress the girls. But Twitter had just started up, and when someone in my tutorial group gleefully pointed out that 'Dan the Pervert' was trending, I was mortified.

I admit that when I was younger I was probably too keen with the opposite sex, but in my defence I attended an all-boys school until university. Women had always been a mystery to me, and suddenly I was sharing a living space with these wonderful, enigmatic creatures who wandered around the place in flimsy clothes with their firm young flesh out for all to see. Who could blame a boy of eighteen with hormones raging for taking lascivious pleasure in rescuing girls from errant spiders camping out in their rooms? One hint of a scream, and I was the first at their bedroom door with my glass to catch whatever creepy-crawly was causing such distress. I could only imagine the delights waiting on the other side of that door: a terrified, half-dressed girl, crying in fear, begging me to save her.

'The other girls think you hang around outside bedroom doors trying to get a glimpse of them in their nightclothes,' Georgie told me after we started sleeping together.

'God, that couldn't be further from the truth,' I replied, feigning outrage.

'I know, but they're a bit paranoid. There are rumours about a bloke hanging around, stealing girls' underwear and peering into the windows at night. It's made them all a bit jumpy.'

'That's *all* it is, just a rumour. No one's stealing pants and peering through windows,' I assured her.

'I know, and I don't care anyway because now I've got you to protect me,' she said, all cutesy. Yes, she was like that once – vulnerable and girlish – but it was just a ploy to reel me in. Once I'd fallen for the kitten, I was stuck with the Rottweiler.

'Yeah, I'll protect you,' I said, stroking her head as we lay in her little single bed.

After Georgie told me that, I weaned myself off the underwear stealing and the voyeurism. I also got rid of the jar of spiders I kept to release in their rooms. But even now I can still get aroused when I think of Daisy terrified and screaming, begging me to save her.

5

Lauren

'So . . . you hate my book?' I ask, after the waiter has cleared the crystal detritus from my broken glass. I have to get this meeting back on track.

Finty looks down at the remnants of her foam and slowly pushes away the plate before resting her tiny chin on those tiny, perfectly manicured hands. 'I . . . don't *hate* it . . . I like it.' She's shaking her head in micro-movements; her body is betraying her. She *hates* it.

The ribbon of rejection slips painfully through my veins.

Did she just look at her watch?

I suddenly realise I'm on a fool's errand. I've spent a fortune on new clothes for this meeting, and planned my script for weeks, but it looks like she has no intention of trying to sell my book. This is a pity lunch. She just didn't tell me.

'Look . . .' She pauses, seeming to be working out what to say. 'I was thinking . . . What about writing a non-fiction book . . .'

'I can't write non-fiction,' I say, though it turns out I can't write fiction either.

'Hear me out. The public appetite for Daisy Harrington's tragic story is still strong. This year she'll be forty years old, just like you!'

'Yes, don't remind me.' I think of the invite Richard read to me over the phone and the dread in my stomach returns with a vengeance. My vision blurs, I can barely see Finty just inches away from me; she's morphing into Daisy, but a swirly, sinister Daisy, the one that screeched and fought and bit like a dog.

'Are you okay, Lauren? You're shaking.' Finty is staring at me.

I look down at my hand, resting on the stem of my fresh glass. She's right.

A waiter appears holding two plates, which distracts her, thank God. We both chose the lamb, which sits next to half a chargrilled baby gem lettuce, next to a circle of fondant potato. Decorated with delicate purple viola sprigs, it's pretty, but looks more like an ornament than something one would eat.

'What was she like?' Finty asks, picking up her knife and fork. They look huge in her tiny hands.

I shrug, feeling uncomfortable. I must be careful and not say anything that could be misconstrued.

'Daisy was like anyone else – she had her flaws. I remember one of our housemates, I think it was Maddie, saying, "Daisy's like the girl with the curl. When she's good she's very good, and when she's bad – she's horrid."'

Finty smiles and raises both eyebrows. 'How intriguing. Would you agree with that?'

'Yes, I would.' I ignore my food and continue to play with the stem of my wine glass. 'I remember thinking it was a perfect analysis. Maddie wasn't as close to her as I was. I suppose she saw her more objectively.'

'She sounds astute.'

'Maddie? Hardly – she's lovely, but astute is the last thing I'd describe her as. In fact, she was a bit slow. You had to explain everything to her. We'd all be laughing at a joke, and one of us would have to explain it to Maddie before she'd laugh.'

Finty giggles at this, and covers her mouth. Then she leans forward, and while still chewing she says, 'I'm fascinated by all this – the way you talk about them, you could write it. If not for me, think of Daisy?' she adds, turning her mouth down on both sides. It looks so ludicrous I want to laugh. But instead I just shake my head and down more wine. 'Your first book was magical, so you obviously have the talent – we just need to channel it. Why not use your gift to write this, the true *story* – the true *crime*.' Finty puts her arms on the table. 'You are one of the few people who can *tell* that story!'

'No.' I run my fingers along the linen napkin, which means I don't have to meet her eyes.

'You could offer an interesting perspective. You were there.'

'I *wasn't*!' I snap defensively.

'I mean, you *lived* with her. You were her best friend.' She's studying me, watching my eyes. Does Finty *know*?

'But isn't non-fiction something journalists write?' I ask, into the silence.

'Not necessarily, Lauren. Think of it as an autobiography. Write your story as you saw it through your own eyes. Who was she? What made her tick? There's still such an appetite for this girl, and you knew the *real* Daisy.'

I shake my head, and take another large glug of wine. It's cold on my throat, weakening my defences. When I drink wine I think I can do anything, and we do need the money.

'I also think there would be film and TV interest.'

She has me there . . . and I guess I could write it as a true crime, the way she's suggesting.

Three cups of coffee and an amaretto later, we're edging into the cocktail hour, still talking, and my initial horror at the idea is changing. The money would be amazing, but, more than that, I could be a *writer* again, only this time it'd be the truth!

'What happened to you guys was unique. Awful, yes,' Finty adds so she doesn't sound too thrilled about a nineteen-year-old girl having her head hammered in, 'but it's remained in the collective consciousness for twenty years. Daisy is the every-daughter, the girl going away to college with her life before her, slain by her lover on a lonely beach.'

'You're already writing the blurb, I see.'

She smiles. 'Guilty as charged! This story will write itself. People still can't get enough of Daisy Harrington. She's like Princess Diana . . .'

I look at Finty doubtfully.

'Okay, no, I'm getting carried away, but still – she's someone everyone loved, even though they'd never met her. She had youth and beauty, and there's real scope for a mixed readership too. Young girls, parents of older teens waving their kids off at uni . . . The story is their worst nightmare, but so relatable. And globally – I can see a lot of foreign rights sales, Lauren.' She sounds like a fortune teller.

I feel a frisson of excitement, not to mention relief at the prospect of money coming in again. I'm keen to tell Daisy's story, and it might be the wine, but perhaps it's time to tell all our stories. Obviously my story will be edited, by me. I have to erase what I did.

I try to convince myself that this will be how I make it up to Daisy. I don't believe it, but this way I can justify making more money from my best friend's murder. Just.

'Hard to imagine if you weren't there, but we were right in the middle of it. We were so caught up, we couldn't escape each other, or the story, and for me that's continued,' I say, almost writing the story as I speak. 'We were told to stay away from the press, and it wasn't safe to be around the uni because people saw us as suspects.

We couldn't go home because the police wanted to speak to us all, and we were so young and scared.'

'Scared?' Finty says, licking her lips.

'Yeah, we were scared of ending up like Daisy. No one knew why she'd been killed – was it someone she knew, or just a random attack, or a serial killer on campus? We were also scared of being accused of being involved. We all lived together, and sometimes things got heated. There might have been an incident or a quote from any of us that was innocent, but seemed incriminating. We were also scared of each other. Had one of us killed her? I remember being convinced that Alex Jones had something to do with her murder, and I avoided him like the plague.'

'Of everyone, what made you think Alex . . . ?'

'I can't remember exactly why now; it was more of a feeling. Alex always knew where she was, like he kept tabs on her. He'd go out in the middle of the night just to walk her home from a nightclub. The friendship – if that's what it was – seemed odd. He'd do anything for her, and she let him. It seemed a bit creepy to me.'

'What an interesting dynamic, and I suppose until David Montgomery was actually arrested it could have been any one of you.'

'Yeah, and of course it wasn't. But, stuck together for days in that house, scared and guilty and sad – we trauma-bonded.'

'It must have been such a febrile atmosphere, very raw,' Finty says, feeding me the lines.

'Yes, and though I haven't kept in touch with any of them, apart from one, I feel like we're all attached by an invisible thread. All connected because of Daisy. We all at some point had a friendship or relationship of some sorts, and we loved her . . . and hated her.'

'She was an enigma really, wasn't she?'

'In death we all become enigmas. And when you're young, beautiful and dead . . .'

'Hang on.' Finty is tapping something into her phone. 'That's the title right there – *Young, Beautiful and Dead*.'

'A bit much?' I query.

'Not at all,' she says, and I hear that lovely Irish lilt returning to her voice. Finty's back. We're both warming to the theme, and I'm excited at the prospect of holding this book in my hand. Then I remind myself through an alcoholic haze that I have to write it first.

'What if you can sell the idea, but I can't write the book?'

She shrugs. 'We'll cross that bridge . . .' She gazes discreetly around the restaurant. 'What was the worst part for you? Obviously her death . . . How did you feel? Set the scene for me . . .' She focuses back on me, resting her chin on her hands as she waits expectantly for my story.

'She'd been missing for a week when they found her, and by then everyone felt they knew her. People who'd never even met her declared their love for Daisy, and left flowers and soft toys by the oak tree outside our place. They sobbed at her funeral, wore black, made daisy chains out of plastic daisies. It was like they wanted to own a piece of her, a slice of grief that they wore like a fancy scarf,' I add sadly.

'Write that down,' she urges. Her pale-blue eyes are wide, thick black lashes like spiders.

I do as she says, making a note on my phone.

'Lauren, when you talk about this, your words are so . . . *evocative*. I know I'm right – you have to write this.'

'A part of me worries that I'd be inviting it all back again. The accusations that one of us knew where she was, the blame for not noticing sooner that she was missing . . . and finally that horrible, horrible guilt. We would go on and live our lives – but she wouldn't.'

'Yes, and writing it all down might *exorcise* all that,' Finty offers persuasively.

'The others would hate me if I resurrected it all. We've moved on, and they have their own lives and want to leave it all in the past, along with Daisy.'

'Fuck them.'

I look at her.

'I'm sure they'll be rightly pissed off if you write another book. They'll be jealous and wish they'd done it first. This is *your* chance to tell the story from *your* point of view. You'll be ahead of the wave, and lifting yourself up above the rabble. If you don't write it, be sure one of them will,' she says.

My stomach lurches. 'There's a party, a weekend being organised back at the university to celebrate Daisy's fortieth,' I blurt, knowing I might regret telling her this.

'Oh my GOD! And you're going, of course? What a great setting – the prologue is you all returning to the place it happened twenty years later.'

'I don't know if I'm going.'

Finty's mouth opens in horror.

'Thing is, I haven't seen any of them since our last day at university,' I lie. 'Besides, I imagine it's going to be a huge weekend party with everyone from the whole year. People who didn't even know Daisy will want to pay their respects, I'm sure. And even if they attend, I might not actually *see* any of my old housemates.'

'You can seek them out, surely?'

'I don't know, Finty.' Doubts are flooding in again. It's such a huge risk.

'But I thought you *wanted* to do this – you were Daisy's best friend.'

'Yeah, at first, until she started seeing David Montgomery. He changed her . . . but we were in the same tutor group.'

'Ooh, so David Montgomery, the one who killed her, he was your tutor too?'

'Yes . . .' I really don't want to talk about him.

'I always thought that other guy did it . . . You know, the posh pervert, always on the TV telling "his story"? I always felt he was fake.'

'Dan? No, I think he was pretty genuine, just loved the limelight. He wasn't a pervert.' I don't want to talk about him either.

'Wasn't he two-timing his girlfriend with Daisy when she died?'

Christ, I really don't want to get into this. 'His girlfriend?' I pretend not to know what she's talking about.

'Dark hair, brown eyes, very slim, wiry, but she was an attractive young girl.'

'Oh . . . Georgie – yeah, she went out with Dan.'

'I remember her in that documentary,' Finty says. 'Very intense, thin lips, arms folded defensively throughout the interview.'

'Yeah, that was Georgie. Permanently angry or anxious, and an obsessive clean freak, which was a gift to a bunch of messy students. She did business studies, and wore trouser suits in dark colours with neat little collars, like a contestant from *The Apprentice*.'

'And her boyfriend, the wannabe TV star . . . ?' Finty asks.

'I think he went into banking. Probably spends his lunch hours in dark clubs paying for lap dances from women young enough to be his daughter.' I snort at my own joke.

'Then there was Alex, who you thought might be the murderer?'

'Yeah. He's done surprisingly well for himself. He smoked far too much weed and took nothing seriously, but he was really handsome. Long dark wavy hair,' I add, smiling at the memory. 'All the girls had a soft spot for Alex, but, as I said, he seemed to have this thing for Daisy.'

Imagining these people in my book makes it easier to contemplate the awful prospect of seeing them in the flesh on the birthday weekend.

'And finally, Maddie, the dance and drama student who always wore ballet shoes. She'd been at ballet school since she was six. She was sweet, quite sensitive really, stunning to look at, long white-blonde hair and blue eyes. She left uni after Daisy died; she was very fragile. I heard she went to Dubai and joined a dance troupe.'

'Not ballet?'

'No.' I shake my head. 'She'd given up ballet dancing by the time she got to uni, but you could tell it was in her bones; she was always pointing her toes and doing ballet poses. I asked her once why she gave up, and she said because she got too fat. I thought she was joking, but she said, "No, I'm serious, Lauren, they threw me out," and there were tears in her eyes.'

On the way home, I feel positive about writing this book. It seems achievable. Yes, I need the money, but I also want to make amends with Daisy by writing her story, giving her back her voice.

But I have to be *very* careful. If the podcast were to reveal my secret on this birthday weekend, I'd have nothing. And Finty would have nothing to do with my book, or me.

6

GEORGIE

'Don't drive so fast, the roads are treacherous,' I say, gripping the car seat as Dan puts his foot down like a bloody idiot.

'Give it a rest, Georgie – stop telling me what to do.'

'I'm not. I'd just like to survive this journey,' I snap. London to Exeter is two hundred miles, and he's been speeding for most of them. 'It's dangerous in this weather.'

'Thank you for making the journey fun and reminding me of this fact every three minutes,' he replies sarcastically.

'You're welcome,' I mutter, and despite his erratic driving I close my eyes and drift off. I haven't slept much since this nightmare started. It's been a month since the envelope landed on the mat and resurrected the past, and I've been a mess.

I wake up after a short nap and, on opening my eyes, the tension and dread of the impending weekend floods back.

'Jesus, this doesn't exactly look like a party,' Dan's murmuring as we pull into a dark, empty car park.

'Where is everyone?' I ask.

'God knows, but this clearly isn't the happening place it used to be.'

'Are you sure this is the right car park? There are no other cars here.'

'Of course, I'm not stupid. This is St Luke's Campus, where we spent three heady years drinking, having sex, and doing a little academic work now and then,' he jokes. He looks happy to be here. I'm not.

'Don't you feel weird, coming back?' I ask.

'Yeah, a bit – but I had some good times.' Then he seems to remember why we're here – Daisy's would-have-been birthday. 'Apart from the bad bits, of course,' he adds. 'Look, I can see the halls of residence over there, through the mist.'

Without speaking, he opens the car door, letting a blast of freezing air in.

'What are you doing?'

'Er, getting out of the car. Unless of course you'd like to have the reunion *in* the car?'

'Your constant sarcasm wears me down, Dan,' I sigh wearily.

'Are you coming or what?'

'I don't want to do this. Please can we just go back home?'

'*No!* I've just driven for more than *four* hours. I'm not turning around and driving back now.'

'*I'll* drive,' I offer, terrified of what might happen this weekend, but also scared of the consequences if I *don't* turn up. I haven't dared ask Dan if his invite contains the same threat as mine, because then I'd have to tell him why *I* wanted Daisy dead. There's stuff that happened with Daisy that I can never tell anyone, not even him.

He's standing outside the car now, his door open, and he leans in, frowning at me. 'What's wrong with you, Georgie?'

'What's wrong with *you*, Dan? Couldn't wait to get here, could you?'

He sighs and, opening the rear door of the car, reaches for his bag on the back seat.

'So who is it you want to see this weekend?' I call.

He stands there for a moment, probably working out his lie.

'All my old friends, like a *normal* person,' he monotones, moving to the front of the car and slamming his door. Shutting me out.

'None of the girls?' I yell. I hear myself, and I hate myself. He pretends he can't hear me and moves away from the car.

I reluctantly clamber out and grab my weekend bag off the back seat while Dan sets off ahead.

'Wait for me,' I call after him, but he's disappearing into the darkness. I know I'm being paranoid, and I know he isn't interested in our old housemates, but I just have to test him. He says I'm unreasonable, but with his history I can never be completely sure.

'Wait, I can't see anything. *Dan?*'

He walks on purposefully like he's not even with me. It's as if he wants to turn up for the weekend as a single man. And by being jealous and immature I've given him a reason to wander on ahead, a reason to be with someone else. I wish I could let him go, and didn't care so much. But for some reason I love him as much now as I did then.

He doesn't look back to see if I'm okay, just keeps walking, like he can't bear to be near me. God, it hurts. And the more he hurts me, the nastier I have to be to make him think I don't care. Because when you love someone too much, you weaken yourself, and you give *them* all the power. I'm never doing that.

I watch him walk through the arches of the North Cloisters and up the steps of the old Gothic building. It's eerie out here in the dark, the mist swirling around. As a student here I always saw the place as old, but not creepy like this. I felt proud to be at a traditional university with history. My mother had been a student here too; it was in my blood. I vividly remember walking through the grassy quadrangle, waving to friends, playing frisbee or sitting in the sunshine. Those of us who attended St Luke's Campus at

Exeter were known as 'Lukies', and because Mum had had such a happy time here, it felt familiar, like home. But Mum was a brilliant scholar; she's a retired doctor now, and though I'm proud of her I've always felt in her shadow.

I'm not academically clever like Mum – or my brother, who followed our parents into medicine – and I guess I've never felt quite good enough. I tried to plough my own furrow by doing a business degree and talked vaguely about being an entrepreneur. 'I'll be a fucking millionaire by the time I'm thirty,' I used to say. But, like everything else, that dream died at the altar of Dan, and besides, I just wasn't smart enough. And after Daisy died I just kept my mouth shut, and tried to stay sane while wading through an ocean of guilt and grief. My degree suffered, and when I left university I spent the vital career-building years working in coffee shops, taking part-time jobs and staying close to Dan. What happened with Daisy made me insecure and paranoid, and threw me into an unhealthy co-dependency with Dan, who I couldn't really trust. Death made me insular. For me, the world became a scary place; I realise now that what I experienced the night Daisy died put me into shock for years.

I sometimes wonder if I imagined it, down there on the beach, but it's so vivid, so present, it's always been just under the surface no matter how hard I try to push it down. And now I'm back here, I feel like I'm walking into a trap. But as scared as I am, I *want* to finally face this, because after all these years, the truth has to come out.

I wait a moment before going after Dan, who's now disappeared through the archway. Half of me wants to follow him through the cloisters into the beautiful hall, to redemption – but the other half just wants to escape.

Despite the cold, I need a moment to take it in, to understand why I feel this way, and I put down my heavy bag. God, I was so young; this was the first chapter of my adult life, and I'm choked with silent tears as the past unfurls before me. I'm eighteen years old again, my chest tight with terror and excitement, being guided by older students to halls, where I'll meet the people I'll be living with.

The accommodation was old, but it had been modernised; the stone walls that had stood for hundreds of years had been plastered and painted over. Each student apartment in the halls of residence had five or six bedrooms, and a shared open-plan kitchen which opened out on to a living area with seating and a coffee table. Some of us had our own en-suite bathrooms, some didn't.

I'll never forget how the first person I saw in there was Daisy, stretched out across an old sofa in the corner of the kitchen. A shaft of light sliced through the blinds, striping her with late-September sunshine, and as she looked up, her lips moved, in a lazy smile of almost recognition. She was wearing a short silk robe, and her long legs seemed to stretch out forever. She was Kate Moss skinny, her hair was long and messy blonde, and she had a cigarette hanging from her mouth. She looked to me like an album cover.

The heroin-chic, fag-end waif look of the early nineties was passé even then, but she wore it well. And as an eighteen-year-old ingénue I thought she was the coolest thing I'd ever seen.

For the first time in my life I was embarrassed by my parents, and gave a slight eye-roll at Mum and Dad for just *being* there. Daisy and I hadn't spoken a word, but I needed this achingly cool girl to approve, and in her presence, parents were an embarrassment.

When I'd finally ushered them off the premises, Daisy gave me a cigarette and opened a litre of vodka, which we drank straight from the bottle. I knew she was wild and might lead me into danger, but back then I had no experience of people like Daisy, so when she put the bottle to my lips and urged me to 'drink', I did as I was told.

'Come on.' Dan's outside the main building, and I can see through the stained glass that there's a light on inside, but the double doors are closed and there's no one else around. 'Why are you taking so long?' he's grumbling. 'And don't tell me you're missing the kids. Usually you can't wait for a night off. You're running down the drive as soon your parents arrive to babysit.'

'Fuck off,' I mutter, shivering.

'Calm, Georgie,' he warns, reaching for the doors and pulling them open.

As usual, my self-obsessed husband refuses to engage with my anxiety, my reluctance to be here. He assumes it's about him, and that I'm being petty and jealous at the prospect of him talking to old girlfriends and one-night stands. He hasn't *seen* my fear in the terrible build-up to this weekend. He's been more concerned about what he should wear, what aftershave he should splash on. I know him too well; he'll be all over Maddie the minute we get inside.

I remember him hugging Maddie when the police came to tell us Daisy's body had been found. She was upset but I was upset too, and I was his girlfriend. Later I asked him why he'd made such a fuss of her.

'Maddie's sweet,' he said. 'She brings that out in me. Some women are just like that – you feel like you want to protect them.'

If Maddie's still a people-pleaser, she'll go along with the flirting and the hugs this weekend as she did then, while I pretend it's all fine. Until it isn't.

7

MADDIE

I don't think any of us had ever been as excited and happy as we were when we walked through those arches that September.

The first person I saw in the apartment at halls was Dan. He was with his dad, a posh old guy who never met my eye but gazed at my breasts. He called Dan 'son' but it felt like a reprimand; there was no affection in his voice. I'd turned up on my own, and everyone else seemed to have a parent, or two parents, to help them move in. Mothers fussing over duvet sizes and dads carrying boxes and checking electrics. I often wondered what dads did – I didn't have one, and it turned out neither did Daisy; we were the only two whose parents were absent. We moved ourselves in.

Daisy and I bonded so quickly. 'We're both orphans,' she joked, putting her arm around me. 'Come on, Baby Spice, let's get some breakfast while they play happy families.'

We went to McDonald's in Exeter town centre, and on the walk there we got to know each other a little. She was easy to open up to, and we shared our stories: both fatherless, and brought up by our mums. By the time we'd eaten our sausage-and-egg McMuffins and walked back to the apartment, I felt we had a real connection. But as soon as we got back to halls, she started drinking a bottle of vodka with Georgie, and ignored me, so I went to bed.

What I didn't realise then was that Daisy wasn't someone I could rely on. She picked people up and dropped them when someone new came along. We went on to spend freshers' week together, but soon after that she met Lauren, and though we remained friends, I felt like Daisy's second choice.

I often think about the randomness of who we lived with back then. We were an arbitrary list of students whose names had been thrown together and allocated – in our case to apartment number 101. The university housing office had set us all on a path, as they have done and will continue to do for all students. In those first few weeks I imagined we'd be in each other's lives forever. I guess we are, but not in the way I thought we would be.

I've arrived at St Luke's Campus a little later than I'd hoped due to the bad weather. I had to drive really slowly through the fog and ice and I'm relieved to finally park up. God, I'm dreading this, and I'm so tempted just to turn the car around and go back home, but I can't do that.

I gaze out into the dark, and see a faint light coming from the main building, where our apartment was. I take a deep breath, open the car door and, throwing my rucksack over my shoulder, make a run for it towards the archway entrance. It's too dark and too quiet. I know it's mid-December and the students have left for Christmas, but surely there must be some still hanging on – and besides, where are the other weekend party guests? Am I at the right place? Is this the right weekend? God, how typical of me to get things so wrong!

I finally get to the halls of residence, and peer through the stained glass before pulling open the heavy double doors. The old student café bar is just ahead, and as I walk towards it I'm amazed at the change. It used to be a bare room with twenty or thirty plastic tables, and a makeshift bar in the corner selling cheap cider, beer and watery instant coffee. But it's been transformed, and now a long table stands in the middle of the room, decorated with flowers and flickering candles. I walk slowly towards it, gazing around at the transformation. Gold balloons fill the archway windows, matching streamers and banners glimmering on the walls. I feel like I'm standing in a glamorous ballroom waiting for the music to start, and I turn around and around in the huge space. I still love to dance, and as I turn I lose myself in the moment, my eyes closed. Then I open them and look up to the ceiling: it's scattered with stars, and 'Happy Birthday Daisy!' is written in glittering letters emblazoned across the navy-blue painted 'sky'.

The hairs on the back of my neck stand up, tears fill my eyes, and I stop turning.

'Maddie?' I hear a woman's voice in the echoey silence. It's coming from the hallway, so I head for the door to see who's there.

'Lauren?'

We walk towards each other, and embrace awkwardly.

'Where is everyone?' she's saying, shaking the rain off her umbrella, opening her Burberry trench coat.

'No idea. You look well,' I add, desperate for something to say.

'You're looking fabulous yourself,' she exclaims. 'Wow, that silk scarf is divine.' She reaches out and lets it slip through her fingers. 'It's vintage Hermès silk – my grandmother had one just like it.'

'Oh . . . I didn't know.'

'It must be worth a fortune. It's Adolphe Mouron Cassandre.'

'I'm sorry?' Lauren can be a bit pretentious. Sometimes she'd just speak in French to annoy everyone.

'He was a famous artist,' she's blathering on now. 'Lots of graphic design and posters . . . Came into his own in the fifties?'

I'd love to say 'Oh, Adolphe – yeah, I love his work', but I've never heard of him, as I'm sure she knows.

'Where did you find this? It's exquisite,' she's asking, with her face almost pushing into the pale-turquoise silk.

'I've had it for years, no idea where I got it from,' I say vaguely. It was Daisy's, but I'm not telling her that. 'The last time I saw you was on the telly. You were talking about your book,' I say, to move on from the scarf.

'That was a few years ago now.' She smiles sadly.

'You did so well, didn't you? A bestseller, and a film . . . I couldn't believe it when I saw you walking up and down a red carpet with Brad and Angelina. I was like, "I *know her*!"'

I'm aware I'm probably gushing, but I need a friend and ally this weekend. Georgie will cling to Dan, and Alex is his own man; he's also a bit flaky and, despite encouraging me to come, might not even turn up himself.

'So there's only us here?' she says, without acknowledging my fawning remarks. Daisy said I used to irritate Lauren. Does she still find me annoying?

'Yeah, only us so far.'

She's looking around, then walks slowly into the old café bar, her high heels clacking on the stone floor.

'Wow! It looks so different. They've certainly made the effort,' she murmurs, as if to herself.

I follow her in, and notice for the first time that the table has place settings. But there are only four, and Lauren has clearly noticed this too.

'It doesn't make sense. Daisy had loads of friends at uni, she was really popular. I would have expected this place to be full of people wanting to celebrate— pay their respects,' she corrects herself. 'I thought that was the idea of the podcast. What's this all about?' She gestures towards the table.

I check the names on the place settings. 'It's just me, you, Dan and Georgie. There isn't one for Alex.' I *knew* it. I knew he wouldn't come.

'That's so odd. Why only us?'

I take a breath. 'I don't know. Apparently *The Killer Question* is a podcast that tries to help wrongly convicted prisoners.'

Lauren is nodding absently as she takes in the room.

'If they feel there's been a miscarriage of justice and the wrong person has gone to prison, they basically try to right that wrong,' I continue. 'They help find evidence for an appeal, but at the same time they also try and find the killer.'

Her head shoots round. 'What? So they're *still* trying to say he didn't do it?' She's shaking her head in disbelief. 'Is that what this weekend is about? You don't think they're going to try and pin it on one of us, do you?'

'How can they? We're all innocent. That was proven when they put him in prison.'

She nods slowly. 'David Montgomery *was* guilty.'

'Exactly. I agree, it's a bit much. He's suffered enough. They need to accept the verdict and let him rest in peace.'

'You'd think so, wouldn't you? But there's a lot of money in podcasting. It's always about the money, Maddie. I mean, look around you: this room alone must have cost a fortune to dress.' She points to the plates on the table. 'Look, Villeroy & Boch Artesano – I had that in my house in LA.'

I'm not even sure what that is, so I just keep talking. 'Well, whatever the podcast is planning, looks like it's just the four of us. I reckon it's going to be a quiet weekend.'

'Let's reserve our judgement until Georgie arrives,' Lauren jokes, rolling her eyes. I think of Georgie arriving at a hundred miles an hour, arms wrapped around herself, anxiety exuding from her like fumes from a cigarette.

I giggle, but then feel guilty for laughing at Georgie. She had a lot on her plate back then with Dan. She simply loved him too much, and I could relate to that. I've never shown my feelings, I've always kept things buttoned up, but Georgie didn't. Anxiety simmered in her eyes, it flexed her limbs, propelled her forward, and made her say things I'm sure she would often regret.

Her constant worrying over Dan kept her right on the edge, and it also kept her slim, I remember thinking wistfully.

I could just make a run for it. And even if these podcasters know what I did, by the time they reveal it I could be long gone. I could go back to Dubai; it's full of people like me escaping from all sorts of horrible stuff. I was there for ten years, and I can't say I was happy, but at least I felt hidden.

'I don't like this one bit, Lauren,' I say, looking at her for reassurance. Lauren was always the calm grown-up one who told us it would all be fine, and cleaned up the vomit after someone had drunk too much. But she seems as unsure as I am, which isn't the Lauren I knew. Perhaps the intervening years have changed her?

'I don't like this either,' she says. 'I feel like we're back in 2005, and not in a good way.'

'There was nothing good about 2005.'

'No – the only good thing that happened was when they jailed that monster. Until he was convicted, I felt like we were all under suspicion.'

'We were.'

'I hope this stupid podcast doesn't start it all up again – the accusations, the trolling, the sheer abuse from strangers in the street.'

'It was horrible,' I reply. 'Only someone who's been through it knows how terrifying it is to have a stranger scream at you that you're a killer.'

'Yeah, I was terrified to leave the house. But after all this time . . . I mean, the man's dead. And he was guilty as *hell*. Montgomery was her lecturer, and she was threatening to tell his wife *and* the university. There's the motive right there – an open-and-shut case.'

'They can't open it up again anyway . . . It's too late, isn't it?' I ask, falling back into my role of needy child to Lauren's calming parent.

'Who knows?'

'David Montgomery was really creepy, wasn't he?' I say with a shudder.

'Do you think so? I wouldn't call him creepy; I always found him quite charming, and very attractive. He was my lecturer too – he taught Daisy and me creative writing. He was a brilliant teacher.'

'I guess I find it hard to be objective about someone who murdered my friend.'

'Yeah, me too, of course.' Lauren seems to back down, remembering the crime he was accused of. 'I just mean that at the time I found him quite attractive – but when I think of how he . . .' She stops for a dramatic pause. 'How he bashed her head in with a hammer.' She shivers. 'The affable lecturer everyone loved was certainly hiding something very, very dark.'

'Ugh, you can tell you're a writer. The way you talk scares me.'

'This place is scaring me,' she says, looking up at the high ceiling, the ancient brick walls. 'It was creepy at the best of times.'

'Yeah, not exactly cosy, is it? But if these ancient old walls could talk, eh?'

'Yeah – the car park is where the old gallows used to be.' Lauren starts to smile. 'Daisy said they hanged witches there, and buried them there too.' She hugs herself protectively. 'God, that's just reminded me – if ever I was out late with Daisy, and we walked back this way, she'd say the ghosts of the people who were hanged were following us. She scared me half to death.'

I gaze out into the darkness through the big glass doors. She used to scare the hell out of me too.

8
Dan

I'm standing in the doorway of the cubicle that, as students, we used to call an en-suite bathroom. Being back here with all the memories of carefree student sex is making me quite hard. I push against Georgie from behind as she applies mysterious creams and potions.

'Da-aan, stop it!' she hisses. 'Sounds like someone else has arrived.'

'Remember when we made love in here? You said it was like a toilet on a plane. We reckoned we'd joined the Mile High Club.' I chuckle at the memory.

'Well, it *wasn't*, was it?'

'No, but we did join, a few years later, on that flight to Amsterdam.'

'Ugh, it was cramped and the floor was wet with piss.'

'Don't spoil a beautiful memory for me.' I can't help but smile, remembering the rushed lust against the tiny stainless-steel sink.

'Dan, *move* – I want to do my eyeliner.'

'No you don't, you want me to take you from behind over this tight little sink,' I murmur in her ear as I push harder.

'Dan, just *fuck off*,' she says into the mirror.

I step aside, defeated. 'I hoped coming back here might remind you of the good times.'

At this, she bothers to turn her head and look at me. 'No, darling, being here just reminds me of how the good times were outweighed by the bad times.'

'Why are you so angry, Georgie?'

'Because I don't want to be here, but for some reason, which I'm sure will become apparent, you *do*!'

I walk away, back into the little room where we both used to sleep, squeezed into her single student bed. I don't want to be here either, and I'm not convinced I can brazen it out. And talking of brazening it out, if Georgie spots me even talking to *her* this weekend, I'm in trouble. I thought having a fling with an old flame from university would be safe, but I never expected to be invited to what feels like a bloody reunion – with my wife watching!

I'm also trying to hide the fact that the podcast that's hosting this weekend knows I wanted Daisy dead. So, to put Georgie off the scent, I've pretended to be happy about coming back here because I don't want her to think I have anything to hide regarding Daisy's murder. But it seems to have had the opposite effect – she thinks I want to be here to meet up with one of the girls from uni and rekindle something. Little does she know that happened months ago.

I watch her now. She looks gorgeous tonight: her shiny dark bob is perfect, her make-up beautiful, and her body looks fabulous in that fitted dress. I wonder why I have this compulsion to be with other women. I know it's self-destructive, and I'm on my last chance with her. One more, and she says she's leaving and taking the kids. What she doesn't realise is the thrill for me is about getting caught, and by threatening this she's just upping the stakes.

She leaves the bathroom and wanders into the bedroom looking for her shoes.

'I'm going to see who's out there,' she says, unsmiling. I nod, feigning indifference so she doesn't think I want to see who's out there too.

The door slams, and I wish things could be turned around, but it might be too late. Georgie's asked me to sleep in *my* old room, and she'll stay here in hers. It's a punishment for the affair I had last summer, and a metaphor for our marriage. She told me she needs her sleep, and I snore, 'and we can't possibly *both* fit into a single bed' – as according to my wife I've got 'too fat'. I weigh the same now as I did when I was eighteen – I am not overweight, it's just classic Georgie. She's insecure, and wants me to feel the same. I sometimes wish I could tell her that the other woman says I never snore, and *she's* never complained about my apparent weight issue.

I wonder fleetingly if we'll have any chance to be together while we're here this weekend, or will Georgie be watching me like a hawk?

Joke is, I know my wife had a thing for Alex. I don't mind, but I'd hate to think of her flirting with him when I'm not around. Perhaps Georgie and I are more alike than we might seem?

I go back to my own room, pull on my trousers, fasten my shirt, and go out into the common area, a small kitchen where the six of us used to socialise.

'Hey,' I call as I walk into the kitchen. 'Hello, gorgeous!' I say to Maddie, who I think is sitting alone, but as I turn I see my wife sitting next to her. Awkward.

'Hey.' Maddie blows me a kiss. She knows Georgie well enough to know that anything more would not go down well.

Both women are silent. Either they shut up the moment I walked in, or they hate each other. I've always found women's friendships to be a mystery; they appear to like each other even when they don't. I ask Maddie how she is and we do a small-talk catch-up.

I open the fridge and whistle at the sight of about ten bottles of champagne. 'What the . . .'

'I know!' Maddie says excitedly. 'And there are canapés on a platter just under the champagne.' She points to a huge plate covered in film.

'So, champagne, ladies?' I pick out a cold bottle of Moët from the fridge.

'Did someone say champagne?' Lauren appears in the doorway, running her fingers through her wavy chestnut hair. Georgie prickles at the sight of her.

Still holding the bottle, I edge towards Lauren and we half-embrace.

'I thought you'd be in Hollywood making your next film,' I say.

'She isn't a *film-maker*, she's a *writer*,' Georgie snaps at me, then rolls her eyes in Lauren's direction in an attempt to pretend she's on her side. She stands up to hug her, when I know she'd rather slap her across the face.

They both tell each other how great the other one looks, with lots of smiles and fake compliments. Women are so fucking *strange*.

'So, champagne?' I reach for a glass.

Georgie looks doubtful.

'What?'

'I think we should wait.'

'For what?'

'You know what I mean,' she replies tightly. 'I feel uncomfortable. I mean, champagne? What are we celebrating, exactly?'

I put the bottle and glass back down on the counter, disappointed. 'Mummy' says I can't have the nice food and drink. 'The celebration is Daisy's life, isn't it?' I offer, hoping she'll buy this and I can drink the champagne without her disapproval.

'We're celebrating the life of a *murder* victim.' I think Georgie is trying to frown, but the fresh Botox is kicking in so it's hard to tell. 'You have to admit it's *weird*, Dan,' she adds, wrapping her arms around herself.

'No one is *celebrating*, Georgie,' Lauren says, in a sanctimonious schoolteacher voice I know will grate on my wife's every nerve. 'We are all here because a podcast is trying to leech off old headlines by trying to prove Professor Montgomery didn't kill Daisy. It's all about increasing listeners and making money.'

'Well, they've got their work cut out trying to prove his innocence,' I say. 'A bloodied hammer with his prints on, found next to Daisy's body, in his beach hut?' I shake my head. 'Call me old-fashioned, but they haven't a hope in hell of clearing his name.'

'Exactly,' Lauren replies. 'And they must know that. It's just a ruse to get listeners and make money. Where can they even *go* with this, and apart from the damning forensic and circumstantial evidence, he was the only one with a motive. Who else other than Professor Montgomery had any reason to want Daisy dead?'

We all look at each other.

'We all may have said it. People *say* it, don't they? "I wish you were dead" or "I could kill you". But no one here had a reason to go through with it,' Maddie says, in that charming, slightly jumbled, childlike way of hers. 'None of us *really* wanted her dead, did we?' She's staring at me. Why do I feel like she's looking right into my soul?

'I agree, Maddie,' I say, trying to shake off the idea that she's smoking me out. 'She wasn't always perfect, but who is? And just because she could sometimes be a bit selfish, or thoughtless, doesn't mean anyone would want to *kill* her.'

Lauren backs me up. 'I agree. None of us would even *think* in those terms.'

'Unless they were a psycho?' Georgie offers, sliding her eyes over to Lauren. After all these years, I'd hoped Georgie had forgiven her and moved on, but there's nothing my wife enjoys more than a long-held grudge.

'I can't stay here,' Maddie suddenly announces into the silence. She's standing up now, a determined expression on her face.

'You can't go. It's late, and the weather's getting worse. Wait until tomorrow?' Lauren suggests.

Maddie's standing against the table in a strappy party dress that shows off every curve of her body. I think about her full, naked breasts, the way they sway when she moves, and have to distract myself.

'I don't like it, I'm not used to being away from home. I miss my cat . . .' She looks almost tearful.

'Come on,' soothes Lauren, putting an arm around her. 'Let's make the best of it. It's a chance to catch up over nice dinners and some drinks. Some people would give their right arm for a weekend like this.'

Maddie's about to protest, but I'm bored of waiting and need a drink, so I open the champagne. It pops and Maddie does that cute little squeal that she does, and I try so hard not to think about her lying on her bed, groaning with pleasure, as I take the champagne flute from the counter to catch the fizz.

'They've thought of everything,' I say, trying to focus on pouring the bubbles into the glass, and hand the first to Maddie with a wink.

'Champagne is a nice touch, but I feel like I'm in an Agatha Christie play,' Lauren says, then her face goes dark. 'It's just us, isn't it – the housemates?'

'The killer question,' I joke weakly, handing her a glass of fizz.

'I won't stick around to find out the *answer*.' Maddie takes the weak joke and runs with it. At least this time she *got* the joke.

'I think Georgie and I will stick around, won't we?' I glance over at my wife.

Maddie and Lauren both give me an enquiring look. Her confused act is a bravura performance.

'Oh . . . I just realised, you two probably don't know – Georgie and I are married. Yeah, we got back together, about ten years ago.'

'Shit, that's freaked me out, but it's really great!' Maddie enthuses, giving me a little smile.

'Belated congratulations.' Lauren looks Georgie up and down. '*Lovely* news.' She so doesn't mean it.

'Sorry we didn't invite any of you to the wedding,' Georgie replies, embarrassed. 'But we never stayed in touch, did we?'

'Under the circumstances, it was probably best we all went our separate ways,' Lauren replies, always the voice of reason.

'It feels odd getting together to celebrate Daisy's birthday,' Maddie mutters.

'I agree. After all these years, we meet again for this.' Lauren sighs.

'But what is *this*?' I ask. 'Have we walked into some kind of trap?'

'I think it's obvious,' Lauren replies. 'David Montgomery's suicide has reawakened all the savvy armchair detectives desperate to find a scapegoat.'

'I need a drink.' I pour champagne into another two flutes, and the four of us move from the kitchen area towards the battered old leather sofa and chairs. 'I feel like an intruder from the past coming back here,' I say. 'I wonder if students still live in this apartment?'

'No, I saw on the website that some old halls are now used for visitors, which explains why they're empty and so clean,' Georgie remarks, circling the sofa like it's a dangerous beast.

'Is this the same sofa we had twenty years ago?' I ask.

'Ugh, wipe-clean pleather.' She recoils, perching on the edge.

'A prerequisite for any student accommodation,' I joke. 'These sofas have seen life.'

'Ugh, revolting.' Maddie almost mimics Georgie's face, which I find amusing. People are chameleons; they adapt quickly to the places and people around them. And now Maddie's back in her old habitat she's doing the same thing she did twenty years ago: trying desperately to fit in. 'So, what about Alex?' she asks. 'He told me he was definitely coming this weekend. Where is he?'

'Alex is tied up with company business,' Georgie says. 'He's flying in from San Jose tomorrow.'

I'm shocked. How does *she* know? 'How do *you* know?' I try to cover my irritation with a smile.

'I know because he *told* me.'

This makes my hackles rise. I have to leave it, or we could end up having a full-blown row in front of the other two. Is that who she's been speaking to on the phone, at night, in the garden? It would tie in with the time difference over in California.

I watch her as she sips her champagne neatly, like butter wouldn't melt. What I'd give to know my wife's deepest, darkest secrets.

9

Lauren

Not sure what's going on between Georgie and Dan, but there's definitely some tension. I had no idea she was close enough to Alex to keep in touch; I was surprised Maddie was still in contact with him too. He's quite the dark horse, always was. As attractive as he was, I never trusted him. Mind you, what about Maddie in that rare vintage Hermès scarf that's identical to mine? I reluctantly let Daisy borrow that scarf from me, and never got it back. It was my grandmother's, and I wondered where it had got to. I even looked in Daisy's room for it after she died, which is terrible, I know. But those things fetch about £400 these days. I can't believe Daisy would have given it to Maddie, but I wouldn't be surprised if Maddie was a bit light-fingered, saw it in Daisy's room and fancied it for herself. It's ridiculous, because Maddie is not vintage Hermès; *her* style is more *Love Island*.

Suddenly all our phones ping.

'It's a voice note on WhatsApp!' Maddie's staring into her screen, and her face pales.

'What is it?' I'm trying to see her phone. She taps the screen and we hear a woman speaking.

'Hey guys, it's The Killer Question *– Tammy here. Thank you all so much for attending this special weekend.*

'So, don't be nervous, just cast your minds back to the early 2000s, when everyone was using flip-phones and MySpace, and you were all students here at Exeter Uni. I was just a young girl in first grade back home in Southern California, but for you guys, this was the beginning of the rest of your life. The friends, decisions and choices you made here affected your future, and the people you became.

'This weekend, we will be recording everyone, and will clip your conversations for the episodes, dropping them in to give the listeners a real feel for who you are and how you roll. We want you all to feel comfortable and try to forget the mics around the place. Just be yourselves, say exactly what you think, how you feel. But, most of all, remember – if you didn't do anything scary, there's nothing to be scared of.'

'I don't feel I can talk, knowing it's all being recorded,' Maddie says in the silence after the voice note ends. 'I might say something dumb!'

We all smile indulgently at her, but before anyone can respond, our phones are pinging again.

'Tammy here. So, this weekend is a celebration of what would have been Daisy Harrington's fortieth birthday, but it's also something else. We are starting our investigation at the beginning – those early days of friendship and communal living, when your beer was my beer, your cigarettes were mine, and sometimes so was your lover.

'What we hope to uncover this weekend is what happened in those fourteen months you all lived with Daisy. Did you love her or hate her? Did you know her, or was she a mystery? And the ultimate killer question we hope to answer this weekend is: "If David Montgomery didn't kill Daisy, who did? Who wanted Daisy dead?"

'Since our podcast was launched, we've solved many cold cases, new cases and old cases, but this weekend is going to be something else. Set up in memory of Professor David Montgomery, head lecturer in creative

writing here at Exeter, our aim is to clear his name and find Daisy's real killer. Over the next three days, we hope to sift through the evidence and solve the mystery – through the recollections, conversations and theories kindly shared by you, our guests. Thank you in advance for your input and your help in finding the answers.'

I shift in my seat. There's nothing 'kindly' about it. I've only come here because *The Killer Question* threatened to tell if I didn't.

'Then, on Sunday night, at the final dinner, we'll present our findings. My sister Tiffany, my producer, is here as always, and I can assure you that we get answers 'cos we fight for them.'

After an initial stunned silence, we all look at each other in shock.

'Our *input* and our *help*? Fuck that!' Georgie slams her glass on the coffee table. She has no control.

'They aren't asking for our input,' I say. 'They're hoping one of us slips up, and drops themselves in it, so they can accuse whoever that is of killing Daisy.'

'But they can't *do* that.' Dan is even more outraged than Georgie. 'Apart from it being a violation of our privacy, it's *illegal* – they can't just record and then broadcast our conversations without consent, and accuse whoever they think is guilty!'

As horrified as I am by this whole prospect, I'm also conflicted. Whoever sent the invites knows what I did, and the last thing I want to do is risk that getting out. If anything does get out, that's it for me. I long to just grab my weekend bag and run but, at the same time, if I'm going to write another book and save my family from being homeless, I have to stay.

My name is still well known from my book, and there's a chance that, if I do leave, these podcasters will broadcast what I did.

I'm panicking slightly, my heart's beating fast, but as long as I stay calm I can work this out. How can this podcast, this weekend, *prove* I did anything? It's not like I *told* anyone; even in moments of terrible guilt or fear, I've kept the promise I made to myself all those years ago – that I'd take my secret to the grave. If anyone has an inkling of the truth, then I'll just deny, deny, deny, because no one can prove a thing.

A voice in my head reminds me that denial didn't work for poor David Montgomery. It got him locked up for life with a minimum of thirty years. I swallow hard and try not to think of the worst-case scenario.

Yes, I have to stay calm, and make notes while treading *very* carefully. I'll be taking a huge personal risk, but *this* could be the book. The former friends and suspects in Daisy Harrington's murder are lured to their old university for the weekend. What they don't know until they get there is that there's a podcast judge and jury of listeners listening to their every conversation and working out who's guilty! Who will drop themselves in it? Who will drop their *friends* in it? I'm excited, but not 100% committed yet because of my own risk of exposure. Meanwhile, the others look horrified, and Maddie's a flight risk and likely to disappear. But for this to work as a book, everyone needs to stay and take part.

Across the table, the girls are already throwing their toys out of the pram.

'No way – no way am I *fucking* staying here,' Georgie's saying, her language as fragrant as it ever was.

'Me neither. This is stupid.' Maddie stands up, and smooths her long blonde hair around one shoulder, just like Daisy used to.

Suddenly, our phones ring on WhatsApp.

'Our phones are ringing!' Maddie cries, like no one else has heard, and she picks up her phone and puts it on speaker, laying it down carefully in the middle of the table.

Then we hear Tammy's voice again.

'Hi everyone. We're just taking a little break from recording to deal with some admin. So I'm handing you over to my producer, and sister, Tiffany.'

'Hey guys! Tiff here. So, as my sister says, there's some paperwork to deal with before we carry on. Before we go ahead, everyone must give their signed permission to be recorded.'

'Ugh, they're too much,' I murmur to Maddie, who's sitting next to me.

'The documents giving permission to be recorded can be signed online, and have been sent to all your emails. So, for those of you who genuinely want to know who killed Daisy, please check your email and sign on the dotted line now!'

'I'm not signing *anything*.' Georgie looks terrified. How *interesting*.

'Thanks, Tiff. So . . .' We all stop muttering as Tammy takes over the call. 'For those who don't want to find Daisy's real killer, please leave the campus now.'

'I'm going.' Maddie starts. Not again. This is becoming quite attention-seeking.

'But just one thing, guys . . . If you walk out of here because you don't want to know who killed Daisy . . . is that because you already know?'

This hangs in the silence.

'The choice is yours. I just ask you to think how it will look to everyone else, including the police, if you leave now, Maddie.'

Poor Maddie seems to shrivel up, and sits back down wordlessly.

'Look, you all had your reasons for wanting Daisy dead,' Tammy continues, 'and that's the only reason you all turned up tonight, because we threatened to tell everyone those reasons. And I hate to be that girl – but if you leave, the threat still stands.'

I look around the table, but no one meets my eye. So it isn't just me? It seems all of us have something to hide.

'Every single one of you has a secret,' Tammy adds dramatically. I imagine her dropping the mic and waiting for the fallout, but there's just silence until Dan opens his mouth.

'Secrets?' He looks at each of us with a surprised expression on his face, obviously trying to make out he didn't have a reason to want Daisy dead. But I see the lie in his eyes.

'Looks like we *all* have them, Dan,' I reply quietly, a gentle shot across his bow. Dan's always had his secrets, and I won't allow him to play games and pretend otherwise. However, I'm more suspicious of his 'lovely' wife Georgie, who looks even more anxious than usual. She's in her default position of arms wrapped tightly around herself, but in addition she's rocking slightly, like a runner waiting for the starting gun, desperate to leave, but something seems to be stopping her from *actually* going.

'So, does anyone want to leave?' Tammy's saying down the phone. 'You're all free to go, we can't keep you here against your will. It's your choice.'

With that, the call ends and we all try not to react, which makes everyone look guilty.

'Christ, I mean, it's not like I have anything to hide,' Georgie says, 'but things might get twisted. They could say *anything*.' She looks at each of us.

Then Maddie joins in, simply repeating what Georgie said. 'They could say *anything* about any of us, guys.'

Dan keeps running his fingers through his hair and is now pacing around the small square living area like a caged animal. I'm conflicted too – it would be great to have a bestselling book, but at what price? Not if it means ending up in prison.

'I'm going to take a look at the document,' I announce, and, grabbing my phone, I open up my email. The paperwork is very formal, obviously written by a lawyer, and everything seems to be nailed down.

'*Guests need to be aware of the areas where they may be recorded,*' I read aloud. '*There is a detailed list with diagrams at the bottom of the document stating exactly where the recording equipment is situated.*'

'It would have been easier to have a diagram stating where there isn't recording equipment. It's everywhere!' Dan says, reading his own email. 'I can't do this.'

'Yeah, but what's the alternative?' I say, raising my eyebrows, wondering why he's suddenly so panicked. There was a lot of talk about Dan and Daisy in the weeks before she was killed. I've always dismissed it, but his reaction is interesting, and I'm fascinated to know the truth.

'So . . .' Georgie goes down the list. 'The recording equipment is only in the communal areas – the dining hall and open-plan kitchen and living room all have hidden mics. Only the bedrooms and bathrooms are safe. What the fuck?'

'It's like some sick game show on TV,' Dan says.

'Not even – it's audio, no pictures, just us talking,' Maddie adds.

They're like trapped animals, and I feel the same, obviously. But I need the others to stay the weekend or I'll have nothing for my book. So, in an attempt to seduce them into remaining, and at the same time make myself look innocent in front of the hidden mics, I give a rather hypocritical speech.

'I loved Daisy like a sister,' I start. 'And I came here this weekend to be here for her. I want to tell her story, bring her to life again – she went far too soon.' I give a little sniff. 'We all had private feelings regarding Daisy, as we did for each other, but they weren't necessarily dark *secrets* – just our way of keeping her alive inside, *preserving* her. As much as *The Killer Question* wants to prove Professor Montgomery's innocence, we want to prove *ours*. So, as I have nothing to hide, as I'm sure none of you do, let's stay and fight it out – prove our innocence to two million listeners. I for one will be happy to stay the weekend, remember her, and try to help work out what happened.'

'And what if, over the weekend, these lunatics discover that *you* had a very good reason for wanting Daisy dead, and accuse you of murder?' Georgie asks rather challengingly. I hear the catch in her voice. She's scared. She's also ruined my speech, but I don't bite.

'Like everyone else, I'll just have to prove my innocence, Georgie.' I smile, hoping no one can hear the fear in my voice.

10

GEORGIE

We walk into the old café bar, now decorated and transformed into a dining room, where a table has been laid with several bottles of wine and champagne on ice. There are four name tags at the place settings. I'd feel better if Alex was here – but hopefully he'll arrive tomorrow.

Dan starts pouring drinks, and Maddie and Lauren gratefully take a glass from him. He's always the life and soul, which is another marital irritant that chafes after ten years – something else I once loved about him that I now find unbearable. He's forcing champagne on everyone like he's the bloody host and it's all on him. I fancy another glass of champagne, but I go for apple juice just to piss him off.

Suddenly our phones ping, and Dan rushes to grab his but Lauren beats him to it with her own. She's so competitive. 'Voice note!' she sings, pressing play. Tammy's voice rings out into the room.

'So, is everyone sitting comfortably? Then I'll begin.

'Here at The Killer Question, *we have always believed without question that David Montgomery's conviction was a miscarriage of*

justice. His life was ruined, and he finally saw death as his only escape, and took his own life. But now it's time to clear David's name, and hopefully reveal who really killed Daisy. We are convinced that someone at your table watched an innocent man go to prison, and did nothing. So, not only did they kill Daisy, they now have David's blood on their hands too. But which one of you was it?'

This hits me like a punch. 'So this *is* a trap,' Dan blurts, clutching the table.

I shush him and discreetly glance around the group, but no one is giving anything away – including me.

'Insiders have been spilling secrets and telling tales, and hopefully we will know by Sunday evening who the killer is, but not before you've enjoyed a nostalgic trip down memory lane.'

'Who says it was a wrongful conviction?' Dan sounds like he might burst, the panic and outrage in his voice evident.

'Dan,' I admonish him. He's making himself look guilty.

'So please take your seats and let's celebrate your old friend Daisy.'

'I'm scared,' Maddie's saying, and despite his own panic Dan gives her a reassuring smile. It makes me want to spew.

'Oh, wait, guys.' Lauren's holding up her hand like a fucking schoolteacher. 'The message is still going.' She turns the volume up.

'Daisy Harrington was a second-year English student at Exeter University when her life was cruelly taken. She was young, intelligent and pretty, with the rest of her life stretched before her . . . until on November 22nd 2005, after a night out, she never returned to her student accommodation.

'Daisy was missing for six days, four hours and seventeen minutes – and, according to police files, all her friends, fellow students and housemates tried to help the police in any way they could. Along with everyone else, one of you combed the nearby fields, searched empty buildings and wandered the river and the beaches looking for a sign. And all the time you knew exactly where she was, didn't you?'

She pauses. This is awful. I feel like she's speaking directly to me, and can't look at anyone. But then I glance up briefly, expecting all eyes on me, and realise that every single one of us looks guilty as *hell*.

The voice note resumes, echoey in the hard silence.

'Daisy's body was eventually found in a beach hut on Exmouth Beach. Her head had been battered by a blunt object, later revealed to be a hammer. And it seems from forensic records that the frenzied attack on her face and skull weren't the only injuries inflicted. Ligature marks were found around her neck, most probably antemortem wounds, which suggested this occurred before death. And her underwear had been removed.

'Once Daisy's body was found, the police seemed interested in a member of the university faculty. Professor M, as he was known to his students, was a handsome and charming English lecturer. At forty-four, this sophisticated older man was popular with the young female students, and Daisy was no exception. She had attended Professor M's creative writing lectures and tutorials since her first year at Exeter. The professor lived in a beachfront home in Exmouth with his wife and children, and, like many other faculty members, he'd been interviewed when Daisy first went missing. However, on that occasion he rather stupidly hadn't revealed his relationship with Daisy, which the police discovered soon after the murder inquiry was launched. When questioned again, he admitted they'd had a relationship, and he'd met her on the night she died, and she'd told him she'd met someone else. She'd said she still loved him, but if he didn't leave his wife she would go away with her other lover, and never see him again. Consequently, he'd never really believed she was missing, and thought she'd turn up, which is why he hadn't admitted their relationship to the police. 'I didn't want to cause any more problems for my family,' he said. But his problems were only compounded by the circumstances of Daisy's discovery, following reports by Exmouth locals of an unusual smell near

the Montgomerys' beach hut. When police investigated, the hut showed no signs of being broken into, so whoever had gone into the hut with Daisy that night must have had a key.'

Suddenly, a door opens at the far side of the room, and two figures dressed in black emerge carrying trays, each with two silver-domed cloches. The man and woman walk to the table, lay down their trays and place a cloche-covered plate in front of each of us.

'Enjoy your starter,' the waiter says. 'It's chicken liver parfait with wholegrain toast. It was Daisy's favourite!'

They then lift the cloches in unison, with a flourish, and leave.

'Was it something we said?' Dan asks the table. My husband's trying to hide his nerves by behaving like a cocky idiot. I'd almost forgotten how good he is at that. The other two giggle nervously. They don't find him funny either; they're obviously just humouring him.

The starter sticks in my throat. The others are eating and chatting like they're at a bloody wedding, but it's *not* a wedding.

'Yes, they're definitely getting off on playing a cat-and-mouse game with us,' Lauren agrees.

'You even *talk* like a writer,' Dan says admiringly. 'I loved *A Day in the Life and Death*, by the way. Just brilliant writing.'

'Thanks.' She smiles, batting her eyelashes, loving my husband's attention.

'My father wrote a book.' Not this again. I yawn, pointedly.

'Really?' Lauren says, but I doubt she's listening.

'Yeah, he was a royal physician, treated the Queen once.' I'm watching him watching her. *He can't take his eyes off her.*

'From what I remember, he was practically royalty himself,' Lauren says. Dan beams, presumably taking this as a compliment, but Lauren's always been sarcastic. How dare she take the piss out of my husband? That's my job.

Poor old Dan – he still brags about his father, but when he was alive he hated being in his dad's shadow. He flipped between loathing him, loving him and wishing he *was* him. So conflicted.

'I always knew you'd be a writer.' He's still fawning over Lauren.

'I think we *all* knew that,' I add. She looks up, smiling, waiting for the accolade, so I go for the kill. 'I remember you wandering around our apartment in halls clutching your notebook like Virginia Woolf.'

'I wouldn't compare my work to Woolf's,' she says graciously.

'Neither would I!' I gasp, genuinely surprised at her arrogance. In what fucking world does she think her name would ever be associated with one of the greatest and most influential writers of the twentieth century?

But Dan moves the conversation along at a pace, developing his eulogy on her first novel. I cringe at his excited enthusiasm and her feigned modesty. Lauren really needs to get over herself. And my husband needs to back off.

'I'm working on my novel,' she used to say, holding notebook and pen like they were surgically attached to her. But one day she left her notebook in the kitchen, and I couldn't resist taking a look. When I opened it, I was genuinely shocked to see page after page of doodles. Not *one* single word was written in there. I was flicking through thinking *WTF?* when she ran into the kitchen all anxious and accusatory, which was usually more my style than hers.

'Were you looking at my *work?*' she screeched. And that's when I *saw* her. Lauren was a chameleon, a pretender, and she'd not been writing anything, just copying Daisy and the way she wrote everything down, leaving scraps of paper around with her thoughts on. Lauren just took Daisy's habit, and formalised it with a notebook and pen. I wanted to slap her.

My irritation for Lauren is building all over again, just remembering how fake and pretentious she was . . . Is. Then our phones suddenly ping.

Everyone flinches.

'Honestly, I feel like I'm standing on the edge of a cliff,' Maddie says. 'And every time I hear that noise I'm going to fall off,' she adds with a heavy sigh, as she plays the voice note on her phone.

'So, the starter is finished, and we're gonna give you a little palate cleanser. The new evidence, which our team are compiling for the police, proves so far that David Montgomery is clean as a whistle.'

The sharp, invasive sound of a whistle intrudes upon us and we all wince.

'So what's the new evidence?' Dan asks. He's looking up at the ceiling like he's talking to God.

The voice note continues. *'We are getting closer to finding the answer to the killer question!'* Cue a few bars of dramatic music, which was used in the previous notes like a full stop.

We look at each other with puzzled faces, like we're all thinking: How can the podcast find the answer, because we all know David Montgomery did it – don't we?

'But this weekend isn't just about finding the killer – it's about remembering Daisy, and who she was to each of you. She was the friend, lover, frenemy you lost on that cold November night, and you'll all have your own special memories of her.'

At this, the waiter reappears and walks around the table, placing a card, an envelope and a pen in front of each of us. As he does, the voice note continues.

'So, what did you love about Daisy and what is your favourite memory of her? Write two short answers on the cards in front of you and put them in the envelopes. Answers are anonymous, which is why the cards and envelopes are identical, as are the pens. If you think someone might recognise your handwriting, then disguise it. We want you to be honest and know you're in a safe space.'

I tremble slightly as I pick up my pen.

I nudge Dan for some kind of support, and he turns to look at me, but there's an extra glint of nothingness in his eyes tonight.

I turn away from the dying embers of his gaze. 'This is such a waste of time,' I mutter to myself. 'Why are we even doing this shit?'

Not missing a golden opportunity to patronise me, Lauren sets off, in *that* voice: 'Georgie, it's just a podcast. They can sell it as "finding a killer", but it's entertainment. Pure cat-and-mouse, and we're the mice, sweetie.'

Fuck you, Lauren. And don't call me sweetie.

'Entertainment? Two people *died* for this "entertainment", *Lauren*,' I say, echoing her own voice back at her. I push my plate away. 'And that parfait was too fatty!'

'Ooh, steady on, girl.' Dan's chuckling. He sounds like his father undermining his mother in those upper-class tones. 'Don't start on the defenceless parfait.'

'Fuck *off*, Dan.'

He looks at the others with a pantomime shocked face, hoping for allies, but they choose to ignore him. It is never my intention to publicly embarrass my husband, but if he insists on playing the village idiot, he leaves me no choice.

It's all very tense, but like good schoolchildren the others start to fill in their answers obediently. I need to play the game too, or risk being singled out, so I start to write.

'Gosh, it's easy to think of things I loved about Daisy,' Maddie's saying in her childlike voice. I don't agree, and I'm not sure I believe her.

'Yeah, for me too,' Lauren replies, climbing on the bandwagon. 'So many happy memories with her. Too many to choose.'

Is now the time to remind Lauren about the night she pulled a clump of hair from Daisy's head when they had a fight? Perhaps not, so I go for something more subtle.

'She wasn't as perfect as you guys are making out,' I say. 'Sorry, but someone has to be honest. Daisy could be a pain. She'd steal food from the fridge and blame it on Maddie . . .'

Maddie gasps at this.

'And she'd flirt with other girls' boyfriends and cause no end of problems – didn't she, Lauren?'

'I don't remember,' Lauren says through gritted teeth.

'I remember. You used to fight all the time over boys. And she'd sometimes bring strangers back at three a.m. and have noisy parties in our apartment.' I turn to Dan. 'That drove *you* mad.'

'No, it drove *Alex* mad.'

'Alex? No, he'd forgive her anything. I reckon Alex is the only one who *didn't* have any issues with Daisy.'

Maddie squirms in her seat, starts twirling her pen. 'I think Alex had a few issues too . . . She owed him money.'

'My point is – Daisy was just as flawed as the rest of us, and we don't have to pretend she was perfect just because we're being recorded and don't want to sound suspicious. We can be honest – we all had a reason to dislike her at some point, but it doesn't mean any of us *killed* her,' I add bluntly. Dan gives me a look, which I ignore.

'Bit harsh,' Lauren mutters.

'I know what Georgie means,' Maddie offers, reluctantly. 'We all loved her but she wasn't perfect. She was quite mean *to me sometimes*.'

Lauren pulls an awkward face at this. She's compromised, because when Daisy was being mean to Maddie, Lauren was usually cheering her on.

'Exactly!' I say. 'Like I said, she was as flawed as the rest of us.'

Dan's fidgeting next to me, and whispering in my ear. 'We're being recorded, be *very* careful what you say.'

'Calm down, your dirty little secret's safe with me.' I turn to look at him. 'For now.'

11

Maddie

What did I love about Daisy? She could be kind, and fun, and she'd sometimes come into my room to watch my TV and eat my chocolate. 'Let's have a sleepover!' she'd say, and we'd watch daft films like *Freaky Friday, The Princess Diaries, Bridget Jones*, stuff that made us laugh. We'd watch Disney films too, and take the Princess Test – to see which Disney princess we were. Daisy was always Pocahontas: *spirited, open-minded, and longing for adventure.* I was always Aurora: *shy and reticent, but brimming with passion.* I have often thought how accurate those silly teenage quizzes were, and I smile to myself. She once said, 'With you, Maddie, I don't have to be cool.' Being oversensitive, I wasn't sure if that was a compliment – did she mean I wasn't cool? But now I realise she meant she could be herself with me, and I felt the same.

'Do you still drive fancy cars?' Lauren's asking Dan. Those two seem to be bonding. I never saw a connection before, but perhaps it was there all the time?

I'm not great at reading people; I think that's why I'm taken advantage of sometimes. Mum used to say I never see the bad in anyone, but that's not true – I can sniff out evil.

'Ooh, our phones pinged, let's listen!' Lauren says, holding up her phone. I've put mine on mute, because every time it pings it makes me jump. I'm smiling, but inside I'm a wreck.

Lauren's still clutching her phone, waiting for our attention so she can play the voice note. I get the feeling she's actually *enjoying* this torture. Did she really hate Daisy so much that she can find pleasure in this rehash of her death?

'So, your answers on the cards will now be collected as dinner is served. The main course this evening is pizza, topped with heirloom tomatoes, artichokes and buffalo mozzarella. Daisy loved pizza. Apparently she met Alex for pizza on the day she died.'

We all raise our eyebrows at this. 'What was she doing with Alex? I don't remember hearing that before,' I say.

'They were good friends – they often went out together,' Lauren adds. 'It was mentioned in court, but only because he was the last one of us to see her.'

'Oh, I was in Dubai by the time it went to court,' I say, but no one's listening.

'They're about to serve us her last supper. Bloody hell, that's a bit much.' Dan grits his teeth.

'This course doesn't feel quite so appetising,' Georgie says half-heartedly, as the waiters bring in platters and lay them on the table. 'And pizza after parfait? Yuck.'

Georgie groans, lifting her crust with the end of a knife like it's contagious.

A messed-up menu is the least of our problems, and it doesn't seem to offend Lauren, who's soon tucking into her food. She only stops eating to fill everyone's glass, including her own, which she downs quickly. Lauren always liked drinking; she could drink all night and never get really drunk. I wonder fleetingly if she struggles with her appetite for wine as I do with food?

'I can't face that.' Georgie pushes hers away, and I look longingly at the untouched vegetables and tangy cheese atop the sweet tomatoes and sourdough crust. Despite the nature of this dinner (or perhaps *because* of it), I'm feeling the irrepressible urge to eat, and wonder if one pizza will be enough. I adore pizza, and attack mine with gusto – and regret. I knew this weekend would be an emotional roller coaster and lead to a binge. I just wish I'd brought extra food with me to eat alone later, in private. Why do I play these games with myself? I should have known I'd lose control.

Even with my mouth full, and a huge pizza in front of me, I'm fully aware that Georgie's pizza is still there, untouched. It's taking all my willpower not to reach over, take that pizza in my hands and stuff it into my mouth until there's nothing left.

'I *hate* this,' I hear myself say, surprised at how angry I feel. It's been bubbling under all evening, and my lack of control over the food is making me feel worse. I hate feeling like this. I'm away from home and have no control over anything.

'You okay?' Lauren asks gently.

'No, I feel under pressure. I want to be at home on my own with Minty.'

'You have a partner?'

'No, it's my cat.'

Lauren smiles indulgently. 'Oh, Maddie, you are so sweet. Look, we're only here for three nights. You'll be on your way home to your cat by Monday morning. I know it's hard, but we all need to push through this and come out the other end. It will make us feel stronger, like good therapy – trust me.'

'I already have a therapist,' I confess. 'He says I'm self-destructive, insecure, and find reality hard to cope with.'

'I think we all have those emotions at times.'

'I smash things to pieces, Lauren. It's self-sabotage. I did the same with my ballet career, my degree and even my relationships – they all came to nothing. I had this fear of failure, and I turned it into reality. It was me who made myself the failed ballet dancer, the failed daughter, the failed lover . . .'

Dan and Georgie look up, surprised. I got carried away. I have to be careful this weekend, and not blurt out a list of the failures in my life at the dinner table.

'I didn't know you felt like that,' Lauren says quietly.

'Why *would* you? We aren't close, we haven't kept in touch.' The thing is, the people gathered around this table knew little of my life even when they *lived* with me. Daisy, Lauren, Dan and Georgie were the stars of the show; Alex and I were merely extras in their drama. They were all so busy performing, and playing their parts, that they weren't interested in the bit-part players. But they'd be surprised if they really knew me, if they knew what I'd *done*, or discovered what I *do*.

'So, have you ever been engaged, or married?' Lauren's asking. I guess the writer in her loves a life story, and the (failed) actress in me loves telling mine. Even if bits are deleted here and there.

'Yes, actually I was married, but I ran away.'

'I see,' Lauren says. 'There's a pattern, isn't there? You abandoned your uni course too. You literally ran away the night Daisy was . . . found.'

'Yeah, I . . .' Do I continue with this? I have to – if I don't it will look suspicious. 'I guess I just hoped that the week she was missing, that's all she was – missing. But when they discovered her . . . body, it felt like the end of everything, so I left. I realise now that I was probably in shock – well, we all were.'

'And we all respond differently. No one is right or wrong.' Lauren reaches her hand across the table to mine and squeezes it. I squeeze back, and her kind gesture warms me. 'I remember the police interviewing us all, and though you were only missing for a night we were concerned that you'd gone the same way as

Daisy – that's when the Campus Killer headlines started. Everyone was terrified, thinking there was a serial killer at large slaughtering female students.'

'Yeah, but I was still on the train when Alex told the police where I was. I'd only told him – I just had to get away. I was angry with him at the time, but he did the right thing.'

'Yes . . . Then of course you had the finger pointed at you. Everyone was asking why you'd left suddenly – and did you know something.'

'God, Lauren, it was obvious that I ran away because I was upset at the news. What kind of person would say I left because I knew something? I didn't! I ran away *because* they found Daisy's body, not because I killed her!'

'No, no, I wasn't suggesting for a moment . . . I just meant people were talking.'

I bet the only people talking were my housemates. I'm sure their natural instinct was to try to pin it on me or Alex, the outsiders.

'So what happened in Scotland? We never talked about it.'

Lauren is hilarious. She and I never talked full stop. She wasn't interested in me; she was too busy having an obsessive-possessive relationship with Daisy and keeping me out. Only now does she want to know what happened. I bet she's writing another book.

'Nothing happened. Two police officers were waiting at Edinburgh station for me when I got off the train, and the next day they took me home. I don't even know why I went, I had no family or friends there. I'd never been to Scotland before in my life. It just seemed far away, another country . . . The police were very understanding. They realised that me jumping on a train wasn't an act of guilt, but one of grief,' I add, driving my point home.

Running away had been a knee-jerk reaction; it was stupid and it made me look guilty. They're all being sympathetic now, but I know at the time they questioned my innocence, because Alex told me.

Lauren is looking at me just like my therapist does. 'So, after the police found you in Edinburgh, why didn't you come back to uni, continue your course?'

Her single-mindedness, her search for answers, astounds me. 'I . . . I couldn't. I found it too distressing. Were *you* okay? After all, she was your best friend,' I say, throwing the spotlight on her.

'Yeah, obviously I was devastated,' she says, unconvincingly. 'But I had to finish my degree. It's what she would have wanted.'

I almost laugh at this. What a cop-out. I know how Daisy felt about Lauren – their friendship had deteriorated to the point that they were barely speaking when Daisy died. And, alive or dead, she wouldn't have given a toss whether Lauren finished her degree. That just wasn't Daisy.

'So, where did you go instead of uni?' Lauren is asking. She really can't leave it alone.

'I stayed at home with my mum, tried to stay under the radar, but then, after a few weeks, a friend offered me work dancing in Dubai.'

'Running away again,' Lauren sighs. I wish she'd drop it.

'Yeah, but being somewhere completely new and away from all the hate helped me move on,' I reply defensively. 'But I never settled, and until recently I was moving around, working in bars, living in caravans.' The truth is, I've been scared to stick around anywhere in case I get close to someone and they start asking questions.

'So, have you met anyone else? Do you have a man in your life now?'

This is difficult, and I'm not sure what to say, especially now Dan and Georgie have completely stopped their own private conversation to listen in to ours.

'No, I'm single. I just bought my own home. I love being alone . . . I'm . . . happy.'

'Good! I'm proud of you.' Lauren is beaming.

'So what do you do?' Georgie asks.

'I . . . have a yoga studio . . . I teach dance too,' I lie, my cheeks burning.

I want this to be over. I can feel their eyes on me.

The other phones ping, and I unmute mine and place it on the table so we can all listen to the voice note.

'So, when formally questioned, David Montgomery admitted he was having an affair with the deceased. On the night she was killed, Montgomery's wife and children were away, and, according to him, he and Daisy had a secret liaison earlier that evening. Consequently, some of his DNA was still on the body, but did that mean he was the last person to see her? The jury thought so – but we're not convinced . . .'

We sit in silence while we take that in.

'Your answers were collected just before the main course, and now Greta, your waitress, will return those answers. They will still remain nameless, and you will all read someone else's to keep your identities secret – but then again, you might be reading your own!'

Everyone looks at each other nervously, including me.

'Four people answered questions tonight, as Alex isn't with us yet.'

Greta hands us each an envelope with our name on it.

'Please keep your envelope sealed until it's your turn to read an answer out.'

We all do as we're told. 'This must be what it's like being in a cult,' I offer, but everyone seems so nervous they just ignore me.

'So, let's go round the table. What do you love about Daisy, and what's your favourite memory? Dan, would you like to read yours first?'

'Okay,' Dan says, and despite his relaxed demeanour I notice he's all fingers and thumbs opening the envelope. 'Okay,' he says again, more confidently, and clears his throat. '*What I loved about*

Daisy was her optimism, and her kindness. Ahh, that's nice,' he adds. Georgie rolls her eyes and glares at Lauren. '*My favourite memory of Daisy is when we used to eat a large tub of ice cream together and watch TV.*' Then he turns to me. 'Maddie, you go now.'

I'm already holding the piece of paper. '*She was my favourite housemate, she was fun and sexy, and my favourite memory is being in bed with her,*' I read, then feel myself flushing. God, I didn't expect *that* one.

Georgie gives Dan a filthy look. 'It wasn't me!' he's muttering, but she obviously doesn't believe him – and neither would I.

'Lauren, you're up next!' Dan says. He's obviously taken it upon himself to be 'quiz master'.

'*Daisy was fun, and I loved her laugh. Favourite memory – Daisy making great cheese on toast when she was drunk!* I love that.' Lauren beams.

'*And finally, Georgie?*' Dan turns to his wife, but she doesn't look at him. She just rips the card from the envelope, unsmiling.

'*I loved Daisy because she was a brilliant writer and one day would have been a famous novelist,*' she reads without much enthusiasm.

I assume this is Lauren, and give her a smile, but she doesn't look at me, just shifts uncomfortably in her seat.

Georgie looks pale. 'I don't want to read the rest.'

'Go on.' Dan nudges her. 'What's the favourite memory? Don't be a spoilsport.'

'Dan, I'm not being a bloody spoilsport!' she hisses under her breath.

'Not like you to break the rules.'

This seems to change her mind. 'If you insist, Dan, then I'll read it. *My favourite memory of Daisy is seeing her lying on the floor, trickles of blood coming from her head, her beautiful blue eyes wide in wonder.*'

12

Dan

'Well, that was awkward!' I try to joke, but no one responds.

Everyone gasped when Georgie read out the last favourite memory.

'Which one of you wrote that?' I ask. 'It's presumably a joke?'

'A *sick* joke,' Georgie mumbles.

'Yeah, but someone at this table wrote it,' I say.

Still recovering from the shock of reading it out, Georgie rolls her eyes. 'It's *obvious* who wrote it.'

'Is it?'

'Yes, it's *you*, taking the piss, but it's not funny, *Dan.*'

I shrug, but before I can continue to irritate her, our phones ping.

'Okay. We didn't expect a full confession so early – but I suspect someone might have been serving us a red herring,' Tammy trills.

There's a long pause, nobody looks at anyone else, and we all find something very interesting to look at on our plates.

'So, a final question, and it's a little deeper and darker,' Tammy *continues, over dramatic music.* The tension is unbearable. It's now deathly quiet, and none of us dares speak. We're on tenterhooks,

but I think deep down we all know what the final question is going to be.

Even I don't want to make a joke because I feel like we're back to being suspects again. It's just like before, when they realised Daisy had been murdered – the police and the public just went for us . . . especially *me*.

Then, after several torturous seconds that feel like hours, another voice note arrives.

'Tammy here – please write down your answer to this question. If David Montgomery didn't kill Daisy, which of the five housemates did? We won't make you read these out – even we aren't that cruel. We want you to feel secure enough to be honest. And if you know one of your ex-housemates is guilty, we're hoping you will say who and why without worrying about repercussions.'

'No, no, I'm *not* going to put anyone's name on this piece of paper. It's not for *me* to decide who did or didn't do it,' Maddie's saying, almost in tears. I can see her distress – she doesn't want to upset anyone – and I want to get up and give her a hug. But if I do, Georgie will probably flay me alive, so I resist, and offer her a get-out instead.

'Look, Maddie, if it really upsets you, just put *my* name down. I really don't mind.' I give her a reassuring smile. I'm genuinely trying to make it easy for her. I hate seeing women distressed, and, if I'm brutally honest, it won't do me any harm when the podcast goes out. Two million listeners will hear me trying to appease Maddie, and sacrificing myself. If I were the killer, would I do that? I guess me offering my name is a good double bluff.

'That's kind of you, Dan,' Maddie replies, 'but I *want* to put David Montgomery. His DNA was all over her and—'

'Yeah, he had *motive*,' Lauren adds, nodding. 'And though most of the evidence was circumstantial, it was pretty damning.'

Georgie's agitated. 'But the question was "If David Montgomery didn't kill Daisy, which of the five housemates did?" So we have to put one of *our* names down. That's the rule!' Georgie's a stickler for rules, and can't bear the thought of someone not adhering to them. Perhaps she has her own suspect and wants to play cat-and-mouse with *her*? Then there's the possibility that my wife knows more than she's letting on, and wants to stay under the radar. Well, if she really wants us to stick to the rules and say who we think killed Daisy, I'll put *Georgie's* name down – see how she likes that.

'I'm not happy putting one of my friends' names on here,' Lauren's muttering as she picks up her pen.

'You can put my name down – I'm not your friend, Lauren,' Georgie says. She means it.

'You still have that cruel streak, don't you, Georgie?' Lauren shoots straight back.

'Georgie didn't mean she isn't your friend. She just meant you haven't kept in touch,' I offer, trying to pour water on the flames.

'Don't you *dare* apologise on my behalf. I'm stating a fact! Lauren and I are not friends, and we've *never* been friends,' Georgie yells as she hurls her pen across the table.

'No, Dan's right,' Lauren says supportively. 'We haven't kept in touch, probably because we don't *like* each other,' she says with a sweet smile, which I find quite funny, but I daren't react.

'Alex did the right thing coming late, didn't he?' I say, to remind the others of him in the hope they write his name down.

'Did you say he was coming tomorrow, Georgie?' Maddie asks. Georgie nods, deliberately avoiding my eyes.

Lauren and Maddie start talking about the food, but I'm confused about the Alex thing.

'Are you in touch with Alex then?' I ask. I mean, *what the hell?*

'I just called because I wanted to know if he'd be here.'

She continues to drink her wine as the other two chat to each other.

'But you didn't call either of *them* to ask if *they'd* be here?' I nod in Lauren and Maddie's direction.

'No, because I didn't *care*. I liked Alex, we were friends.'

'Friends? You were *lovers*,' I whisper in her ear.

'Before you, yes.'

I still feel a frisson when I remember I took her from Alex. He was a bit of a junkie, but a handsome, charming junkie. All the girls fancied him.

I'm aware my jealousy is hypocritical, considering the way I've behaved all these years. But this Alex thing makes me wonder how well I know my wife.

'Ooh, another voice note!' Maddie calls.

'Please can you hand in the answers to your question, so dessert can be served. Daisy used to love this dessert as a little girl, and we hope you do too!'

I don't know how much more I can take. It's stressful coming back here – I knew it would be, but I'd thought it was a celebration of Daisy's life. I assumed the whole blackmailing thing about 'everyone will know why you wanted Daisy dead' was more of a bluff to get us here, a sick joke. And it worked – I came because I didn't want to be exposed – but I never expected this.

'So, we've come to what we thought was a birthday party for an old departed friend,' I say, 'and it's turned into a murder mystery party, where we're the murderers!'

'Only *one* of us is,' Maddie corrects me.

'Allegedly,' Lauren corrects her.

I'm trying to be cool and light-hearted, but inside I'm screaming. I feel like everything I say is being monitored and analysed – either by the women on the podcast or the women at the table. Especially my wife! Then there are the two million 'armchair detectives' – or trolls, as I like to call them – and they'll take no prisoners. It's just a bit of fun to these people, something to while away a long afternoon. Even the podcasters have no real skin in the game; they have nothing to lose, but they'll pore over every inch of this weekend and presumably hurl accusations at one of us for the climax. This could ruin our lives, and the only reason we all came here was to prevent that happening.

'What if I write down someone's name and they *aren't* the murderer? They could end up in prison,' Maddie says, her eyes wide in alarm. Has this only just occurred to her? Probably.

'No, because no one here is the killer,' I point out. 'David Montgomery was tried and convicted. And unless his innocence can be proved, or someone else owns up to it, nothing changes. This is all a game, as Lauren said earlier – it's just entertainment.' I wave jazz hands at Maddie and she breaks into a slow smile.

'I remember seeing a documentary a few years ago,' Lauren says, 'and the forensic psychiatrist said Daisy's killer was someone close – someone who was emotionally involved with her.'

'He couldn't *know* that, it's just a presumption.' I shake my head doubtfully.

'Why do you assume the forensic psychiatrist was a man?'

'Shit. I walked right into that one,' I chuckle. Then I take a deep breath. 'All I was saying was the psychiatrist obviously didn't know the killer was emotionally involved. It's guesswork.'

'No, not necessarily.' Lauren is warming to her theme. 'She said that Daisy's body had been covered with an old child's blanket from the beach hut. It's called "undoing behaviour" – the killer wanted to cover the face or body because they couldn't look at what they'd done. It's like they wanted to symbolically *reverse* the murder.'

'Oh God, that's so creepy. Imagine . . .' Maddie murmurs.

'It's horrific,' Lauren continues. 'Killers sometimes position the body so it's face down, or they even wash it, or put a pillow under the head. It distresses me to even think about it.'

It can't be that distressing for her – she's still talking about it.

But the more she talks about 'the body' and 'the blood', the more uncomfortable I feel, and I have to stop her talking. 'Yeah, well, like I told Maddie, write *my* name. I really don't mind, because obviously I'm not the killer.'

'Don't feel bad, Maddie, I'm putting his name on my card,' Georgie smirks.

'What? But you're my wife.'

'Yeah, but not your alibi,' she replies, making it sound loaded. WTF is she doing to me? And at this rate, all three of them are going to write my name down as the killer. I mean, there's being kind and there's being buried, and I'm treading a fine line here.

'Yeah. Georgie, if you don't want to write Dan's name, you can use a name from my book, *A Day in the Life and Death*, if you like?'

A nice little book plug there from Lauren.

Georgie gives her a look of incredulity. 'Why would I use a fictional character from some book? We've been asked to name a real person, one of the housemates. Besides, I don't know any names from your book because I've never even *read* your book.'

I can't help but smile. My wife's an uptight, anxiety-riddled snob who comes out in hives if there's a towel on the bathroom floor. But tonight I'm actually enjoying her vicious takedown of Lauren. To add to the frisson, I'm winding Georgie up even more by pretending to be Lauren's biggest fan and constantly admiring her 'work', which I haven't read either. But that's how we roll, Georgie and I – we play twisted games with each other. We always have.

Georgie sees most women as a huge threat, but she's always had a big problem with Lauren, and I love it because it makes it so easy to get her back up. Lauren's good-looking, successful, intelligent, and obviously lives an exciting life of book launches and media glitter. Lauren was always receptive to my outrageous flirting in front of Georgie, and tonight is no different. Mind you, looking at Georgie now, in a red sleeveless dress, with her red lips and that dark shimmery hair, she'd even win over Lauren tonight.

I think the fact that Georgie might have a thing for Alex is making her even more attractive to me. I can feel a glimmer of something I haven't felt for years; it's more than lust, it's about being here and remembering how we were – who we were. I gently slide my hand on to her leg, feeling for the thigh-high split in the silk.

She's grabbed my pen and written her answer, put the piece of paper in the envelope, and is now licking the envelope slowly, looking at me from under her long lashes. I want her right now, here, on the table . . . and for once it looks like the feeling might be mutual, but I take a breath, and grab my piece of paper as a distraction. I fully intend to write *Kylie Minogue* or *Beyoncé* for a laugh, but instinctively I write someone else's name. Why waste the opportunity to throw someone *else* under the bus and take the heat off me?

We all hand our sealed envelopes to Greta and the other waiter, who then place exotic-looking desserts in front of us.

'I don't suppose it matters who or what we wrote on those pieces of paper. It's not like they're going to be handed to the police, is it?' Georgie says, which worries me slightly.

Tammy said our answers would remain anonymous, but they must have marked them in some way. I know the listeners will have heard me suggesting Maddie write my name, and the sane ones will understand that Georgie probably wrote my name as an easy way out. But still, the optics aren't good, and the crazies will be straight on it thinking there's a clue in the fact that my own wife doesn't trust me. Perhaps she doesn't? After all, I don't trust *her*.

13

LAUREN

'After all this time, do people still care who killed Daisy?' Maddie suddenly asks.

'Of *course* they care. There's still a lot of interest— concern,' I correct myself quickly, to sound more sincere. I don't want anyone here to know yet that the subject of my next book is them. When I've finally written my account of this weekend, I'm sure they'll be pissed off. Georgie will probably attempt to kill me, and I'm only half joking about that.

Looking at them as we sit around the table eating dessert, I reckon Maddie is the only one who might be coerced into doing interviews to support the book launch. I could pay her a fee – she probably needs the money. Though Dan might help out too.

'Maddie – and the *thing to remember is this* – we all know this is just an exercise,' I say. 'Professor M did it, none of us did, and hopefully that will be proven this weekend. And when it is, that's our opportunity to *finally* clear our names once and for all. This thing has haunted us for years.'

'So true,' Dan says. 'I can't go through that again. I was hounded by the press, and now, with social media so much bigger, it would be even worse.'

I nod vigorously. 'Exactly. Let's use this weekend to show the listeners that we're real, that we're good people. We know that none of us killed Daisy, so let's prove it by sticking this out until the end of the weekend. We can all walk out of here with our heads held high.'

This is a call to arms – and I'm scared and excited. I want everyone to stay the weekend, and I want those two million people to read my book. But I don't want them to know what I did.

What I've just said about us all being innocent does not justify the hate emanating from Georgie across the table right now. She sips her wine through tight lips, and her bitterness taints the chocolate mousse we're having for dessert (Daisy's favourite, apparently). I wonder again what Dan sees in her. Their sex life must be so vanilla; he probably has to disinfect himself before and after because she's such a germophobe. She and I never bonded, but then she never *bonded* with anyone except Dan, and sometimes Maddie – but then Maddie's easy to bond with, she's such a people-pleaser. Georgie was a loner – too obsessed with playing house to join in with the rest of us.

Tonight, the look on her face if anyone even *mentions* my book is enough to curdle milk! She's so jealous of what she thinks I have, and loves to take me down. I was glad she read the note I wrote: *My favourite memory of Daisy is seeing her lying on the floor, trickles of blood coming from her head, her beautiful blue eyes wide in wonder.* I smile to myself. It was brilliant, though I say it myself. I was going to say that my favourite memory was watching *Mean Girls* on her laptop together. But that would have been boring; real life often is. This was so much better – after all, I am a writer of fiction. And when by chance Georgie was the one who had to read it out – well, that was the icing on the cake, and a gift to moi!

To Georgie, I'm the human embodiment of success, and a reminder of her failure, her lack of career and her disappointing marriage. She believed her degree in business studies would turn her into a millionaire entrepreneur, but she doesn't have the talent or the ideas. All she can do is stalk her husband and scrub their home, and I'm no expert but that's not a recipe for success.

'Where are you living now?' Georgie's asking Maddie.

'Dagenham.'

'Oh, you're not too far from us then?' She glances at Dan, but he ignores her.

'I'm not far from you,' I say. 'I'm in Crouch End.'

'It's quite the celebrity hub there. I bet you fit right in, Lauren.' Dan gives me a wink. He's been fawning over me all evening; it's quite uncomfortable, especially as Georgie seems to flinch every time he speaks to me.

'Is that your *real* home, or the one you use for TV interviews?' Georgie asks, unable to hide her resentment.

'Oh, you saw the TV interview then, at my home in Sandbanks?' *Gotcha.*

She bristles. 'No, I just saw a picture of it somewhere.'

'Yes, we have the house in Sandbanks, the one in London and one in LA. I hate listing them. It sounds like I'm bragging.'

'Yes, it does,' she replies.

God, she brings out the worst in me. She's assuming I still live in that big house overlooking the sea in Sandbanks that was featured in all the magazines. Presumably she also thinks I hop on planes to my place in LA every couple of days, but that couldn't be further from the truth. It's my fault, because I can't bring myself to tell anyone, even Dan – who I'm sure wouldn't judge – but it's all long gone. This weekend I leased a new Mercedes, hired my designer clothes and bought a few second-hand. Despite *A Day in the Life and Death* earning me more money than we'd ever dreamed of, there's nothing left. We assumed I'd write more and the gravy train would continue. But I couldn't write any more, we made some bad investments, and then Richard lost his job. That's why I *have* to turn this weekend into something Finty can sell. But the closer I get to the flame, the more I realise I might get burned.

After dessert we all leave to go back to Apartment 101. Georgie goes into her room, and Dan into his, while I make coffee for me and Maddie.

'Bit weird, their marriage, don't you think?' I say to her.

She shrugs. 'I don't know.'

'Well, I don't either, but just from being with them tonight you could feel the tension.'

She smiles. 'I guess.'

Maddie obviously doesn't want to bitch about our fellow guests, which is fair enough. But I wonder if she doesn't trust me because of who I was back then? 'Why do you and Daisy beat up on Maddie all the time?' Alex once asked me.

'Because she's boring,' was all I could offer. I didn't really know her, just followed Daisy's lead. And that's when I decided I wasn't going to even try to be friends with Alex. He *saw* too much; he was always watching, and judging. Dan told me once that Alex said Daisy and I were mean girls. But Daisy always picked on Maddie, who just seemed to take it, and I let it happen. Later, though, around the time Daisy was killed, she and Maddie seemed to have bonded, and I was the one out in the cold. Mum always said three didn't work, that there was always someone left out – it was never Daisy, though.

Maddie seems quiet now, so as I make our coffee I try to make conversation. 'Do you sometimes wish you'd stayed at ballet school, and chased the dream? You didn't have a great time at uni, did you?'

She shrugs, which she does a lot – it's irritating, like she's pushing the conversation away.

I join her in the seating area, where she's flopped on to the sofa, and hand her a mug.

'Your book is great,' she says, presumably trying to shift the focus from her.

'Thanks.' I smile, but I know she hasn't read it. I can tell because she's flushed, a sign she's not telling the truth. Daisy used to tease her about that.

'You can never tell a lie, Maddie, because your face gives you away,' she would say, which would just cause Maddie's blush to deepen. 'Are those your chocolate wrappers hidden at the back of the cupboard, Maddie?' she'd ask. 'You are a Miss Piggy, aren't you?' Then she'd poke her in the tummy and I'd laugh; it all seemed quite harmless, affectionate almost, but Maddie's face would redden. 'Ooh, look, Lauren, she's lying again,' Daisy would say, and fall about laughing. To me and Daisy it was harmless teasing, but I realise now that Maddie was fragile and neither of us realised the harm we might have been causing.

'If you ever need someone to talk to, I'm always on the end of the phone, Maddie.'

'Thanks. Same here, if ever *you* need to talk.'

Oh, I see. So she doesn't appreciate my offer of help, and thinks I might need it too?

Suddenly Dan's bedroom door opens, and without addressing us he storms into Georgie's room. We both widen our eyes questioningly at each other.

'I wonder what's going on there?' she says.

'The same that was going on there twenty years ago. Can't live with each other, can't live without each other.'

'Do you think Dan *loves* Georgie?' she asks.

'Hard to imagine, eh?' I shrug. 'I doubt it. I always thought she was a convenient girlfriend. Now she's a convenient wife.'

'She went out with Alex before Dan, didn't she?' Maddie says.

'Yeah, until she was seduced by Dan's car.'

'Was she?' She seems surprised.

'Don't you remember his car?'

She shakes her head.

'He drove a cherry-red MG Convertible – he was a student and he drove an MG.'

'Oh, is that fancy?'

'Yeah. Weren't you with us? Maybe not. We'd only been at uni a few weeks. I'll never forget Georgie's face when she saw the car. "I'm riding shotgun," she said, and basically knocked everyone else out of the way to sit in the front with him. She carried on seeing Alex for the first term, but once she got her claws into Dan, Alex was unceremoniously dumped. I bet she regrets that now.'

'Why?' she asks.

'Where have you been, Maddie? Alex is a hot-shot tech guy – he's a billionaire.'

'Oh, *that*.'

'Yeah, *that*. He's not some hapless junkie anymore.'

'He never was,' she says defensively, like a lovesick teenager defending her boyfriend.

'No wonder Georgie's still in touch. Probably wants to rekindle the old flame. She'll be all over him when he arrives.'

'But she's with Dan, and Alex is married now too.'

'Is he? I didn't realise. That won't stop her. I heard she once slept with Alex and Dan at the same time.'

She doesn't seem surprised by this. 'Daisy always said they were the two best-looking men on campus.'

'Yeah, Alex had that lovely long, dark curly hair, and Dan was good-looking, in a boyish way. Still is. God, it was all a bit free and easy back then, wasn't it? A pint of cider and a couple of tabs, someone would have a big row and split, only for a new couple to emerge from the ashes the next day,' I recall wistfully.

'Yeah, Georgie and Dan were always breaking up and making up. Then there was the time he and Daisy got together without Georgie knowing. She was so angry.'

This is a surprise to me. 'I bet Georgie was raging, but I didn't realise Daisy and *Dan* . . . ?'

'Yeah, just before she died.'

'But . . . I thought Daisy was seeing David Montgomery then?'

'No . . . I . . . think she was seeing them both for a while, but she was definitely seeing Dan.'

'How do you know?'

'She told me.'

She never told *me*, but that was probably because we weren't really talking by then. 'I don't remember this. I must have missed it in the fog of student weed. I thought she only had eyes for Professor M.'

'I don't know, she kept a lot to herself those last few months.' Maddie pauses, as if she's thinking, then says, 'I think David Montgomery killed her because he loved her too much, and he didn't want anyone else to have her.'

She makes it sound almost romantic with her dreamy faraway look.

'My understanding from the trial was that Daisy was too much in love with *him*,' I say. 'I mean, she sent his wife a letter telling her about the affair. I know Daisy denied it, but who else would do that?'

Maddie shrugs. 'All I know is that David was angry about the letter. I think he broke up with her, and she started seeing Dan.'

'That sounds like Daisy, but I just can't imagine her with Dan. He was rich, but not very sophisticated back then – not compared to Professor Montgomery, anyway.'

'I think Dan was there for her. She didn't tell me much, but I remember seeing him sneak into her room once when Georgie was asleep, and when Georgie went home for weekends they'd spend a lot of time together. I think Georgie must have found out, because she and Daisy stopped talking to each other.' Maddie leans closer to me and lowers her voice. 'And then, a couple of nights before Daisy died, Georgie and Dan had this big row. There was only me at home, so they just let rip, they didn't care that I heard it all. Georgie was screaming at him – she said horrible things about Daisy.'

'Shit . . . Did you ever tell the police?'

Maddie shakes her head.

'That's pretty damning, Maddie. You should have told *someone*.'

'Dan and Georgie were always arguing.'

'Yeah, but if Georgie was saying terrible things about someone and a couple of nights later Daisy was dead . . . I mean, that sounds like a motive.' I make sure I say this loud enough for the recording.

'There was no point telling anyone. It wouldn't have changed anything.' She's still talking quietly, but I'm sure the mic will pick it up. Those two million armchair detectives will *love* this scoop. 'Lots of people were angry with Daisy. That doesn't change the fact that David Montgomery was the one who battered her head in with his own hammer that night.'

She says this so matter-of-factly, I wonder if we've *all* become desensitised to murder?

But I'm still surprised that Dan and Daisy had a thing.

Daisy loved older men. Hearing about her and Dan makes me wonder what else I missed that was staring me in the face.

I'd hoped that this weekend I could lay some ghosts to rest, but all it's done so far is open up the wound, and posed more questions. And what's fascinating and terrifying is that we all know different things about different people, and have different perspectives on what happened back then. Having been apart for so long, we're remembering things differently, and stuff is coming out that we didn't all see before. Perhaps that's what the podcast keys into – it unlocks the past, releases the jumble of our memories into this confined space, and waits for the truth to emerge.

14

Georgie

'Reminds me of when we were first-years and trying to hide from everyone else in the apartment,' Dan says.

We're in my bedroom after dinner; I called him in because my mum rang to say the girls wouldn't go to sleep until we FaceTimed with them. So, as late as it is, we chatted to them for a few minutes, and it seems that talking to our girls has softened things between us a little, because he's still here, talking about when we were first together.

'It was so stressful. You were always sneaking in here in the middle of the night and convincing me to have sex with you,' I say, pretending to be cross.

'Was it like that? I don't recall having to convince you that much.'

'Our night-time adventures ended a long time ago, didn't they?' I murmur, almost to myself. 'Funny, isn't it – when we were first together you didn't want to be exclusive, and if anyone asked I had to lie and say we weren't having sex. Now, if anyone asked, I'm sure you'd like me to lie and say we are!'

'Yes, I would. It's weird. We're married and we haven't had sex for months now. Let's get together now, shall we?' he asks, ever the optimist.

I'm on the bed and he's on the floor, lying on his back looking up at the ceiling.

I can't deny I'm vaguely tempted, but I'm not standing down so easily. He's still in the 'no sex' punishment block after his dalliance last summer.

I lean over the bed to look at him. 'No. *You* were supposed to be going back to your room after our call with the girls.'

'Can't I stay with you? Our old halls of residence have made me feel nostalgic . . . Romantic.'

I snort at this. 'You only want to be with me because you think I still fancy Alex.'

'Well, do you?'

'Depends. Who do you fancy this weekend?'

'You,' he lies. 'Anyway, I'd steer clear of Alex, he's looking pretty dodgy to me. He hasn't turned up yet – is that to avoid any awkward questions?'

'I doubt it – Alex doesn't have anything to hide.'

'How do you know?'

'I just know, Dan, Alex is a nice guy.'

He's gazing at me, and I know that look. 'I remember, during the very first term when we lived in this apartment, I used to watch you go into Alex's room and wish you were coming into mine.' He always loves to say that he *took* me from Alex – but I *chose* to leave Alex. Dan loves imagining me with other men, and in the past, on a couple of occasions, we invited other people to join us, but it was fucked up. Now he's just hoping the conversation will lead to sex, but I don't want sex. 'So, why did you leave Alex for me? Was it my boyish charm and good looks?'

'Well, Alex was gorgeous, very sexy, but I chose you because you seemed less complicated.' I love winding him up.

'For "less complicated" read "less *interesting*".' He pulls a sulky face. 'You forgot to say how clever and handsome and charismatic I was. Still am,' he jokes.

'No. I didn't forget.'

He thinks I'm playing around, but these days I don't see my husband as clever or handsome or charismatic. He's loud and stupid and annoying, and I've realised after too long that I'm with the wrong person. The only reason I'm not walking away and taking the kids is because I still have this little bit of love left. I know that I can't walk away until that's gone, because I'll just come back. It makes no sense to me.

We've just been together so long, we can't operate independently.

When we first met, I was impressed by his car and flattered by his attention. He was the confident one, popular with his peers, always invited to parties and at the centre of things. And when he finally asked me to be his girlfriend, a door was opened. I was afforded the same kudos, and people assumed that because I was with him I must also be sociable, fun and charismatic. Er, no. I was the plus-one, always in his shadow, and I still am. Dan's the star of our show, he gets the laughs and applause, while I take care of everything backstage. My reward when we first got together was to be wherever he was. Dan was everything Alex wasn't, and I guess it was the thrill of the new for me.

Alex had a difficult childhood, and it messed him up. Despite being cool and quietly confident, Alex struggled to get through most days; he was just incredibly sad and scared. Sometimes he found it hard to leave his room and make it to lectures. I used to hold him in the night after he'd taken pills that seemed to make him even sadder. So Dan was like a ray of sunshine after a dark storm, and I thought I'd found what I was looking for, but Dan was more messed up than even Alex.

Thinking about Alex makes me sad. I entered his life and led him on, made promises I had no intention of keeping, and I still feel bad about that. I feel bad about a lot of things that happened at uni. So when he called me a few months ago, I was really glad to hear from him, and before he even started talking I said: 'I just want to clear the air and apologise for the way I treated you all those years ago.' I'd imagined he'd still be hurting, but I had obviously overestimated my impact on his life, because he made it clear he'd got over me pretty quickly back then. But the other big reason I wanted to talk about that time was to find out if he'd seen me creeping back into the apartment the night Daisy died.

It's always bothered me, because I lied to the police, told them I was in bed with Dan – when in fact I wasn't, I was down on Exmouth Beach that night.

'Do you remember?' I asked him.

'Yeah, I did see you that night,' he said.

'Did you tell anyone?'

'No. I just hoped it had nothing to do with Daisy.'

'It didn't,' I lied. 'Thanks for not telling anyone.'

'I just figured you'd had enough with all the Dan and Daisy shit going on. They were playing you, and she was playing him . . . You weren't a killer, were you, Georgie,' he said. It was a statement, and not a question. I didn't respond.

Then, when I got the invitation, I was glad we'd broken the ice a few months before, and I called him a few times. I was feeling disillusioned with my marriage and I just wanted to talk to someone who'd once had feelings for me. It was innocent on my part, and nice to reconnect with Alex – he'd always been kind to me regardless of how I'd treated him.

Now I move my mind away from Alex, turning my attention back to my husband, who's still lying on the floor of my room.

'Anyway, I think Lauren's more dodgy than Alex,' I say. 'Tonight she was unintentionally hilarious, saying she wasn't bragging about her three homes, but she so was!' He doesn't respond, so I continue. 'I mean, she's only written one book. I doubt she's the millionaire author she makes herself out to be.'

'Oh, right,' he says, a smile playing on his lips.

'She's always had a strange relationship with the truth. And that Gucci handbag is a fake.'

'You're *kidding*, right?'

'No . . . Her handbag's fake and she's fake . . . I bet her outfit tonight was "pre-loved".'

'No . . .'

'Oh yes, or it might even have been hired.'

'Stop! She's a pre-loved fake-handbag-wearing braggart who hires her dresses?'

I'm getting so carried away I only just realise he's taking the piss.

'Oh, you think you're so funny.' I'm deflated. 'I thought for once you were seeing what I see. But how could you, because you only ever see women as sex objects? Anything more than bra size is beyond your comprehension.'

'Ouch, you're extra-salty tonight, Mrs Levine.'

'I'm not *salty*, I'm frustrated because you aren't *listening*. And stop trivialising my feelings. I'm not just being mean about Lauren. I think she's hiding something. I have a theory . . .'

'Go on then, Poirot, give it to me.'

'Do you remember when we first realised Daisy hadn't come home the night before and that she was missing?'

'How could anyone forget. It was the beginning of a nightmare . . . I was so scared and—'

'Okay, this isn't about *you*, please stop talking and *listen*. So, later that day, you, Alex and Maddie went out looking for her, while Lauren and I stayed at the apartment, supposedly in case Daisy came back. But as soon as you'd all left, Lauren said she'd check Daisy's room *again*. I didn't think anything of it at first, but after a few minutes . . . I went to see if she'd found anything.' I glance over at him, to make sure he's still with me.

'And?' He's looking at me intently now.

'So I went to Daisy's room and stood in the doorway, but she didn't realise I was there because she was too busy on Daisy's laptop. She was glaring at it intently, like she was looking for something. I dunno, she looked really anxious, and that's what first intrigued me. Lauren doesn't do anxious.'

He pulls his mouth down on either side, in grudging agreement.

'I assumed she was checking emails, trying to find clues as to where Daisy might be,' I continue. 'So I said something like, "Is there anything interesting there?" And she looked up and seemed really surprised, and almost threw the laptop in the air, which was an odd response. I'd definitely caught her doing something she shouldn't.'

'What? Looking through someone's laptop to help find them?' I knew he'd defend her. 'No, she wasn't doing that.'

'How do you know?' he asks challengingly.

'Lauren's shiny red memory stick was in the laptop. I knew it was hers because just the day before she'd joked about how it looked like a lipstick.'

'So what do you think she was doing?' He's still convinced Lauren is an angel, but he's coming round to the alternative.

'She was *copying* something from Daisy's laptop! I reckon she was taking advantage of Daisy going missing to copy her coursework. You remember what they were like – Daisy really clever and Lauren always struggling because she was always late with assignments, usually in tears over the essays.'

'That *could* make sense, I suppose? But wouldn't we all do that in the situation?'

'No, Dan, we wouldn't! I certainly wouldn't copy someone else's work, especially if they'd gone missing. It's wrong on so many levels. It's *stealing*. She was copying or removing something that didn't belong to her. Think about it: Daisy had only *just* gone missing, and instead of trying to find her, Lauren's on her laptop. What kind of best friend *does* that?'

'It's not necessarily *bad*, Georgie. She may have been deleting emails that Lauren knew Daisy wouldn't want anyone to see?'

'Perhaps . . . But at that point we didn't know Daisy was dead, we thought she was just missing.'

'Yeah, well, we'll never know.'

'Well, I think we will. Lauren was jealous of Daisy. She'd been whining for weeks before that Daisy had an unfair advantage on the course because of the extra "help" she had from David. Perhaps Lauren thought she would check out Daisy's notes and steal them? Or maybe she was looking for emails between David and Daisy?'

'Why would she do that?'

'I don't know, but what if Lauren was stealing Daisy's files because she was the one who killed Daisy?'

'Hang on.' Dan sits up. 'You can't say that.'

'Well, it would explain why she felt it was okay to wander into her room and start taking stuff off her laptop. If she *knew* Daisy wasn't coming back.'

'So, you're saying it might look like Lauren *knew* Daisy was already dead, so she was getting rid of evidence?'

'Possibly? Either she's a psycho killer, or just a straight psycho stealing her missing friend's work.'

'She might have been deleting sex tapes they'd made or something . . .'

'Your mind went straight there, didn't it? What a surprise,' I monotone. 'AND . . . AND . . .' I start, sitting up now, moving to the edge of the bed. 'A few days before Daisy went missing, she and Lauren had a really nasty fight.' I make a mental note to remind everyone of this when the podcast is recording.

'Yeah . . . That fight wouldn't look good for Lauren,' he says, frowning.

'And Lauren once had that scratch from Daisy's nails down her face for weeks,' I remind him. 'Their friendship was intense – they were both so competitive. If Daisy had been given a really high mark, or been praised for some writing, Lauren wouldn't speak to her!'

'I still can't see Lauren *killing* Daisy. Yeah, they were a bit feral at times, but this murder was brutal – I remember one of the detectives describing her body as one of the worst things he'd ever seen in his career . . . And don't forget, Daisy's underwear had been removed.'

'Mmm, I'd almost forgotten about that, Dr Watson. I guess my theory still needs some work.'

'God, what a waste.'

I hate when he mourns for her; I feel so *excluded*. 'Well, Dan . . . if Tammy whatever-her-name-is has any proof at all that David was innocent, you are fucked. The underwear, the crime of passion, the way she was attacked . . . It looks like a love affair gone wrong. And the finger could so easily point at you. God, Dan, you're such an idiot. Why did you even get involved with her?'

'It wasn't just me who *got involved* . . . and you *know* it.'

15

MADDIE

Alex should be here today; I'm dying to see him. When Lauren was going on about him being a big success, it wasn't news, but he's just Alex to me. We got back in touch a few months ago when he called out of the blue, and it was wonderful to hear from him. I'm not sure if he's quite a billionaire, as Lauren said – she's a writer, she exaggerates – but he's doing okay. I always take what Lauren says with a pinch of salt; no wonder her book did so well – she's good at fiction.

I'm enjoying a rare moment of peace alone in my room when my phone pings with another voice note. Honestly, it's like torture; I'm totally triggered.

'Hey guys!'

Tammy's voice is friendly and upbeat, but it's starting to depress me.

'Are you all enjoying the weekend so far? Hope so.

'Today over breakfast – which is waiting outside the apartment door – we're doing an interview. It drops in fifteen minutes, and we'd really love for you to take a listen while you eat together in the kitchen.

'Later we're taking you all for a walk on the beach at Exmouth. Remember the bonfires on golden autumn evenings, when life was sweet, the moon kept watch and stars hung like lanterns in the sky?'

I feel sick. Yeah, we had some great times at Exmouth Beach – until Daisy *died* there. I try not to think about that night because I will never be able to comprehend what happened. I need to get out of this room; it's like a prison cell of memories. Every inch of this place reminds me of her. I leave my room and walk into the bathroom; I need a few moments to gather myself. Some rooms in the halls have an en-suite, but not mine. The en-suites cost more, so students like me, Daisy and Alex had to use the cramped shared bathroom, and if the others had mates round they'd use our bathroom too. At the time it never occurred to us to feel deprived, resentful or in any way lesser than the others. That came later.

I stand here now, looking in the bathroom mirror, and something seems to move behind me. I freeze, unable and unwilling to turn around, imagining it's Daisy. Was it an illusion, or the swish of her long blonde hair?

I don't hang around to find out, and open the bathroom door, heading quickly into the kitchen, where Georgie is manically wiping the surfaces with antibacterial cloths.

'Morning!' I say, still a little shaken and unsure. Georgie turns slightly, throwing a smile over her shoulder. 'There's a podcast interview in fifteen minutes.' I try to sound happy about it.

'Yeah, so I heard. Dan's just in the shower.'

Georgie's *always* stressed, but this morning she seems worse than usual, scrubbing a small area on the kitchen counter like her life depends on it. She's wearing full make-up, and has blow-dried her hair like she's off to a party. It's 8.30 in the morning.

'Hope you don't mind me asking, but are you and Dan okay? It's just that . . . I thought I heard you arguing last night?'

She stops scrubbing the counter for a moment and I can see she's upset. 'Were we?' She sounds flustered. 'I don't remember, we argue most of the time.'

'Do you want to talk about it?' I ask, gently.

Her eyes fill with tears. 'Thanks – you were always so lovely whenever I'd had a row with Dan. You'd let me cry on your shoulder.'

'That's what friends are for.'

'Yeah. I just hate . . .' She pauses. '. . . being away from the kids. My mum's with them, but she lets them stay up late and gives them too much sugar; they'll be tearing around the place . . .' She leans against the counter, looking exhausted. I reach to turn on the coffee machine, and she wipes where my hands have been, then sees that I'm watching her. 'Sorry, I'm a bit . . . Well, you know.'

'I know.'

'I drove you all mad back then, right?'

'I always felt like it was *us* driving *you* mad. I once left toast crumbs on the counter – I thought you were going to kill me.' I chuckle.

Suddenly the half-smile fades. 'I'd never harm *anyone*, Maddie.'

'No, no, I wasn't saying . . . It was a turn of phrase, but in the circumstances it was . . . I just remember you standing there. You were chopping peppers and you raised the knife . . .' I know this is incriminating, but she did.

She's staring straight at me now, her eyes wide with horror or hate. I feel threatened.

'Sorry, I made it so much worse by mentioning the knife,' I say, mentioning the knife. Again.

'We have to be so careful what we say here, Maddie.' She's wiping again. 'The mics in the communal areas are recording everything, and everyone is looking at everyone else,' she whispers, her eyes wild. Then she says loudly for the recording: 'The slightest thing you say without thinking could get someone who's innocent in big trouble, Maddie.'

I pull an apologetic face and mouth. 'Sorry!'

Tactless and socially awkward. That's what Daisy called me. I can still hear her saying it, like the lines of a song forever in my head. I guess they all think I'm like that.

'Hey, I just remembered, there's breakfast out here.' I open the apartment door to find a huge wicker hamper sitting in the hallway. I carry it back in, and place it on the counter – an offering to appease Queen Georgie.

'Don't put it there, it's in the way,' she grumbles. I know the drill, so move it to the table, keeping out of her way until she calms down.

Fortunately, it isn't long before Lauren and Dan join us. By then I've made coffee, and laid the table with the muesli, croissants, Danish pastries, fresh fruit and cheese from the hamper. Georgie's disapproval permeates the air like the smell of bleach, but it fades into the background once we're all around the table.

'I don't remember breakfast ever looking like this when we were here the first time,' Lauren's saying as she takes a croissant and a spoonful of bright-red strawberry jam.

I already ate two croissants while putting the food out on plates, but that doesn't stop me taking a pastry and cutting it into tiny pieces to make it last. I hate eating with other people. In fact I hate doing *anything* with other people.

Suddenly there's the sound of our phones pinging throughout the apartment. This time it's an audio file.

Dan puts his phone on the table and we all shush each other expectantly, waiting to hear Tammy's voice. I don't speak. I feel like Georgie hates me and the others tolerate me. It's like I'm eighteen again at university.

'Hey guys! Just doing a recap for our listeners for when the episodes drop next week . . .

'So, it's more than twenty years since Exeter student Daisy Harrington was brutally murdered, and the man convicted of her killing took his own life six months ago. Today is Daisy's birthday, and if she'd still been with us she would be forty years old. We're spending the weekend with the housemates of Daisy Harrington, and the fifth housemate, Alex Jones, is flying in from the US today.

'So, on with the story. All Daisy's friends came under the spotlight when she went missing, and more so later when her body was discovered. They were interviewed by police at the time, who believed these teenagers had nothing to do with Daisy's death.

'Meanwhile, the police discovered that Daisy had been having an affair with her lecturer, who may have had a motive to kill her . . . but more on that later.

'So, our next guest has spent eighteen years campaigning tirelessly to keep David Montgomery in prison. While the "Free David Montgomery" campaign continued, and appeals were fought and lost, she kept Daisy's story alive by speaking with the press. Constantly reminding the public who Daisy was, she believed strongly that David was guilty of her murder, and that his was not a wrongful conviction.

'But recently, some incredible information has come to light that has changed everything she so fiercely believed. This shocking new evidence could prove once and for all that Professor David Montgomery was not Daisy Harrington's killer . . . but someone here is.'

16

Transcript from *The Killer Question* Podcast

Episode 3: Interview with Daisy's Mother, Teresa Harrington, Part One

TAMMY: So, today we're talking to someone who believed for a long time that David Montgomery was guilty of Daisy's murder. But then, six months ago, she met with his family, and along with them now wonders if the police and the courts may have got things wrong with David's case.

Here at The Killer Question we've always doubted David Montgomery's conviction. We believe it was unsafe and based on prejudice and assumptions about forensic evidence. We've also heard from a close source who says that, at the time, other people in Daisy's orbit had stronger motives than David Montgomery. But as police interviewed David early in the investigation, and he was arrested and charged quite quickly, they assumed, like everyone else, that David was guilty.

So, a big welcome to the woman who has helped us to move forward on our journey to clear David Montgomery's name, and find Daisy Harrington's real killer.

Teresa Harrington, Daisy's mother, has kindly agreed to join us to discuss the impact of her daughter's death, and how a meeting with David's family has changed her perspective. Does she now think that the killer may have been closer to home – perhaps even a friend and housemate of Daisy's? Welcome, Teresa Harrington.

TERESA: Thank you . . . I'm a bit nervous but . . .

TAMMY: Please don't be, Teresa – you are among friends. We SO want to help you find your daughter's killer, and hopefully this weekend we're going to do that. So, let's begin with you. A bright young woman, from a poor family, and despite doing well at school, you left at sixteen, when you discovered you were pregnant with Daisy.

TERESA: Yes . . . I didn't have much, but did the best I could for my girl.

TAMMY: So despite economic hardship, your daughter Daisy thrived. In fact she was the first in your family to attend university. You must have been very proud.

TERESA: Very, very proud . . . Yes. (Teresa sniffles.) I was on my own, and it was hard. We lived in a damp bedsit for ten years, then in 1996 the council finally gave us a house and Daisy had her own bedroom for the first time in her life – she was ten years old. I painted it purple; she said she was too old for pink. (Teresa chuckles softly.) Daisy grew up fast – she had to as I was out working two jobs and she had to look after herself. She was proper grown-up, she was, but still kept her Furbies and all the My Little Ponies, and she had a Tamagotchi too . . . Oh, and she loved the Spice Girls.

TAMMY: Tell us about Daisy as she was growing up, Teresa. Did you have a good mother–daughter relationship?

TERESA: We did. She told me everything, and even at university she called me most days to tell me what was happening, who she liked, who'd annoyed her, what she was having for her tea . . . It had always been just the two of us, you know?

TAMMY: And you worked several jobs to try and give her everything she needed?

TERESA: (A pause.) I was a cleaner for two different companies. It was bloody hard work . . . Oh, sorry for swearing. I tried so hard to give Daisy what she wanted, but as it was just me it was twice as hard. Like, when she was twelve, Daisy asked me if I'd take her to see the Spice Girls for her birthday. I said yes, but when I checked the prices the tickets were twenty-three pounds each – that was a lot of money then. A lot of money to me, anyway. So I started putting money in a piggy bank, saving up every last penny, doing without food myself so I could give Daisy the birthday present she wanted. She was so excited, she'd go around the house singing 'zig-a-zig-ah' and she invited her friends over to be Spice Girls. They were all so envious that she was going to see them on stage and kept asking if they could come too. (Teresa pauses.) Then, one day, I was telling this woman I worked with all about it, and by then I had forty pounds saved and only needed another six pounds to buy the tickets as soon as they went on sale. She said she knew someone who worked at the venue and she could get me the tickets cheaper, and I could have them now. So I gave her all the money I'd been saving for weeks – she took the money, and I never saw her again.

TAMMY: I'm sorry that happened to you, Teresa – that's appalling.

TERESA: Daisy was upset, of course, but she took it well. She was used to disappointment. (Silence for six seconds before Teresa continues, her voice cracking.) But you know what? When they called me to say they'd found her body, that was the first thing that came to mind. All I could think was 'She never got to see the Spice Girls.' Weird what grief does to you. It plays tricks.

That woman stealing my money almost blocked out the horror of what they were telling me. And instead of wanting to find out who'd done that to my girl, I wanted to find the woman who'd robbed me of giving her that gift. Our Daisy had never had much, and now her life had been taken too . . . (Teresa starts to cry.)

TAMMY: *Please, don't get upset. (Tammy pauses.) Let's talk about the good things, the happy times in Daisy's life – I'm sure you gave her some wonderful things. Daisy was a popular girl, and bright too. Did you ever imagine she'd attend university?*

TERESA: *It was a dream and she made it come true . . . Not many working-class kids went to university where we lived. But she was bright, and at school she was top in her class for English. I remember going to parents' evening when she was about fourteen and the teacher said, 'One day she'll be a writer.' I think she would have been too.*

TAMMY: *If you could say anything to the murderer now, Teresa, what would it be?*

(Silence for three seconds.)

TERESA: *They took a girl from her mother, and they took a young woman's future. If it wasn't David who killed her, then I don't know why it happened, what the killer wanted. I've tortured myself, Tammy, trying to work out why. I ask myself that all the time – why?*

TAMMY: *I'm sure it's awful for you: the constant wondering, the what-ifs. We've dealt with a lot of victims' families – and a lot of killers too – and sometimes you never know why, or what someone wanted from a killing. It's often something petty, something that mattered only in that moment. It could be money, jealousy, lust? I don't know. But those few minutes of revenge or sexual pleasure – or hate – end with them taking away someone's life. And trying to work out how or why is impossible and won't help you . . . That way madness lies.*

TERESA: *I agree, Tammy. I think I need to try and remember the good times, and how lucky I was to have our Daisy at all. But now David Montgomery has taken his life, leaving his children without a father.*

TAMMY: *Yes, and his conviction all those years ago meant the real killer could breathe a sigh of relief and move on. They continued on with their own life, but the horror of Daisy's death echoed down the years, and had an impact on those left behind.*

TERESA: At the time, I thought the right man was in prison. It wouldn't bring my baby back, but it was the best I could hope for. Once the trial was over, I just existed, and only the campaign to keep him in prison kept me going. It gave me something to fight for, a reason to go on.

TAMMY: But recently, your opinion has changed?

TERESA: Yes. Earlier this year, I met with David's wife and family, for the first time, and just talking with them, realising we're all victims . . . it's helped me, it has.

TAMMY: In what way?

TERESA: Well, I used to think that Daisy was just trouble for David Montgomery, and when his wife found out about them he had to get rid of her.

TAMMY: Just to keep listeners up to date on this, the police report stated that David Montgomery was angry with Daisy because she'd told his wife about the affair. He ended their relationship, but just a few weeks later they arranged to meet down on the beach – and that was the night Daisy died. So it was assumed the murder was premeditated.

TERESA: And I thought the same, because I'd listened to the police. I'd been in court and heard David's testimony, but I didn't believe him. But now I'm not so sure . . . Now I think that someone else killed Daisy . . . and that the killer was one of her housemates.

17

Dan

Well, that was awkward. I bite into my pain aux raisins, and try not to catch the eye of any of my former housemates.

Shit, this is uncomfortable. I should say something, break the tension. I'll try to be subtle.

'So, it was someone who lived with her – which one of you was it?' I joke.

'Not funny, Dan,' Georgie monotones.

I guess I don't do subtle very well.

'I don't believe it. Teresa's just making wild guesses. She's *wrong*. I'd trust you guys with my life.' Maddie, as ever, is blindly optimistic, and doesn't seem to have lost her faith in human nature – or woken up and smelled the coffee. 'We were her friends, and we loved her,' she continues.

Georgie looks at me and rolls her eyes imperceptibly. When you've been married for ten years you don't need words, you communicate in micro-movements. That's why marital sex is boring. You know each other's every move.

'I mean, they keep saying it, but no one actually wanted Daisy dead – did they?' Maddie's now looking around at each of us like a child needing to be reassured by the adults. Maddie's a love, but she really doesn't have a clue what's going on. Don't get me wrong, I admire her optimism, and she's got a great body – especially when she's naked and begging for it. But she really believes that we're all good people. She's too naive for this world.

Our phones ping with another voice note intrusion and I leave mine on the table, press play, and we continue to endure this torturous trip back in time.

'So . . . hi again, guys, Tammy here. I have some notes here from the Free David Montgomery campaign that I'd like to read to you . . .

'David Montgomery never confessed to killing Daisy Harrington, and his DNA was found on Daisy's body because they'd made love before she died. David's DNA was also on the murder weapon – the hammer – and this informed much of the prosecution's case against him. But the hammer belonged to David. He'd used it around the house and therefore his DNA would have been on the handle.

'Also, if he did kill Daisy, then why did he leave her body in his beach hut to be discovered? David had plenty of opportunity to move the body, as back in 2005 there were fewer CCTV cameras, and in the dark he could have carried Daisy's body to the sea unseen.

'But he didn't. He didn't move the body, because he didn't know it was there.

'And think about this . . . Would he really use his children's Disney blanket to cover up his lover's dead body?'

Everyone is quiet. No one knows what to think or say, so we sit in silence and consider this for a moment, until the voice continues.

'In his suicide note, David Montgomery said he couldn't bear the thought of being locked in a prison cell until he was seventy, for something he didn't do. He also said that not seeing his children was the most unbearable part – his wife had refused to visit him, or let him see their young daughters, Cordelia and Cassandra.

'Six months ago, unable to take another day, David Montgomery twisted a pencil inside a bed sheet, and tied the sheet around his neck. He slowly twisted the pencil at his throat, with each twist tightening the pressure. It was a slow and agonisingly painful death, but in his suicide note he revealed that he'd found some sense of freedom. "After almost twenty years with no control over my own life, I am finally taking it back and choosing when to die."'

The voice note ends and we all look at each other. Georgie is crying, and I put my arm around her. 'That was hard to hear, wasn't it?' I say gently, my own tears not far away.

'Yeah . . .'

Even Lauren seems shaken, and Maddie reaches out a hand to her across the table.

For a few moments we just let it all sink in, then I jump slightly as our phones ping with another voice note. Tammy is speaking.

'This isn't about the lurid headlines, the endless interviews with fake friends, the outpouring of grief from people who hardly knew her, or the many books that were spawned, from those in the true crime genre to works of fiction that sold only because the writer happened to know Daisy Harrington.'

We all instinctively glance at Lauren, who keeps her head down. I feel sorry for her; that was pretty harsh. But she did write a book and make a lot of money by shamelessly using Daisy's death for self-promotion.

'This is about the grieving mum, a father in prison for a crime he didn't commit, and the tragedy of a young girl taken too soon.'

I feel sick. I don't know how much more of this I can take.

Then there is the very real threat of a visit to the beach this afternoon. I honestly thought I was going to throw up when I heard about the trip. Too many memories – and not all good. I used to take everyone to Exmouth Beach with the top down on my convertible. I'd drive fast and the girls would let the wind rush through their hair. It was great fun, until Georgie banned me from taking anyone but her. So I'd ask the others to wait outside for me, and I'd tell Georgie I was going to the library. It was always so much better when Georgie stayed home and cleaned or did her coursework. I just felt so free sitting on the beach talking into the night with Daisy, Alex, Maddie and Lauren. We'd meet up with other students there too – just drinking and smoking and flirting. Everyone was there for fun, no nagging, no demands, and sometimes, if we got carried away, I'd break open a beach hut and take a girl in there. I had some of my best times in those beach huts, and on warmer nights I'd have sex in the sea, or behind the rocks with whoever was willing. I was excited by the idea of just doing it there in the sea or on the beach, in plain sight, yet it was still secret.

But now we're almost forty and it's freezing, and December . . . and Georgie will be there. There's also the other aspect, that this was where she died, and I don't know how I'll react to seeing beach hut number thirteen. I just hope I can hold it together. It has a red door and a little ceramic picture of a yacht attached to the outside wall. I remember it so clearly because Ali West, the TV documentary woman, forced me to stand in front of it for an interview. It was so triggering. I was upset, and in shock – and I was trying to impress Ali West, and sound like I cared, which I did. But I came over as besotted with Daisy, like I had some kind of obsession with her. That's when the world decided I was Daisy's murderer, and the messages on MySpace were so damning, I was scared I'd end up in prison. I still am.

18

Transcript from *The Killer Question* Podcast

Episode 4: Interview with Daisy's Mother, Teresa Harrington, Part Two

TAMMY: So, we're back for part two of the interview with Teresa Harrington, Daisy's mother – if you missed part one, check it out now!

Teresa was a staunch critic of the Free David Montgomery movement, and actively fought for him to stay in prison. She campaigned against his appeals and was often interviewed by the press about her biggest fear – the possibility of David ever being free.

So, Teresa, after campaigning for all those years to keep the man you referred to as 'the beast' in prison, you agreed to meet with his family. And am I right in saying this meeting had a profound effect on you?

TERESA: Yes, I met with Louisa, his wife, and their – now grown-up – children, who all said they'd never believed David was capable of killing anyone. They insisted he was a kind, gentle man, and though they had no actual proof, they knew he wasn't guilty. But I'd always been convinced that he was the killer, that the 'evidence' stacked up and he should stay in prison. But when we got talking, I mean really talking, I told them what I knew about Daisy's friends, and it turned out that David had expressed concerns about every single one of them.

TAMMY: Wow! Was that enough to convince you of David's innocence?

TERESA: No, because for me there will always be doubts, but talking to Louisa and her kids made me think it might have been someone else. It was the first time I'd even entertained that idea, but the more I thought about the things she told me about the different housemates, the more I could see that there might be something I'd missed.

TAMMY: Agreed, and something that perhaps the police had missed too? Here at The Killer Question we have concerns about the way the police proceeded. David was arrested soon after the body was discovered, and the press and the public were baying for blood. The public had been avidly watching, listening and reading about 'the missing girl' for a week, and in that time they'd hoped and prayed she'd be found safe. So by the time Daisy's body was discovered, the public felt that they knew her – 'Exeter's daughter', one of the newspapers at the time called her. Consequently, with all this frenzied interest, the police were under a lot of pressure to find Daisy's killer. There was a huge spotlight on the case, and when someone was arrested, everyone was relieved that there wasn't a campus killer on the loose. On discovering that the killer was Professor David Montgomery, the victim's lecturer – the police, public and press had found their bogeyman. But even then, there were those who wondered if David was innocent. And if someone else was the killer . . . someone closer to home?

TERESA: I can't deny that even back then it crossed my mind that Daisy's housemates were a bit too keen to be on screen and seemed to love talking to the press. Barely a day went by when one of them wasn't in the paper telling the world how much she meant to them, but it felt a bit fake to me. And I knew Daisy had her problems with some of them.

TAMMY: *What sort of problems?*

TERESA: *Well, her first year she seemed to have fun. They were all new, and everyone got along – so well, in fact, that they all moved into a house together in the second year. But it seemed in those few months of the second year the problems started. I knew she'd been seeing her lecturer, I knew he was older and married and I wasn't happy about it. But it was her life and she said she loved him, and I knew she wasn't going to listen to me. But one day she phoned me and she sounded really low, and said he'd ended things. I was angry – he'd hurt Daisy, and she was still my little girl. (Silence for three seconds.) Always will be . . . (Teresa crying.)*

TAMMY: *Would you like to take a break, Teresa?*

TERESA: *No . . . No . . . Thanks. I'm fine.*

TAMMY: *So, at the beginning of year two, she and David split?*

TERESA: *Yeah, but it wasn't for long. She said she couldn't live without him, and I presume he felt the same. But in the few weeks they were apart, her housemate Dan started to really harass her. She told me he was always buying her chocolates and flowers, and he'd begged her not to tell Georgie, his girlfriend.*

TAMMY: *Wow! And did she tell Georgie?*

TERESA: *I don't think so. She said Georgie scared her – she had a foul temper, apparently. Anyway, she said she and Maddie shared the chocolates, and she tried not to encourage him. She said she didn't want the hassle with Georgie. 'If she knew Dan was chasing me, I might wake up one night to see her standing in my room with a knife,' she said.*

TAMMY: *Was she joking?*

TERESA: *I thought so at the time. Now I'm not so sure.*

TAMMY: *And did you worry about Dan taking such a shine to Daisy?*

TERESA: Not at first. She called him her 'hero' because if ever there were spiders in her room – she was terrified of spiders – he would get rid of them. 'He's the best spider catcher,' she used to say, and as her mum I was glad there was a boy around to look after the girls. But that was in the first year. By the second year she said it was sometimes uncomfortable being alone in the house with him. He'd find an excuse to come into her room, or somehow get close to her, touch her . . . You know? And on more than one occasion she said he'd tried to kiss her, and could be quite forceful. She said she'd had to push him away.

TAMMY: Do you think she was scared of Dan?

TERESA: I think she was . . . uncomfortable, but she'd just bat him off, said he was a lech. I think she was more scared of Georgie, who was very jealous.

TAMMY: Do you know if Georgie knew her boyfriend was trying to seduce Daisy?

TERESA: (Teresa gives a soft chuckle.) It seemed like Georgie knew everything Dan did. She controlled him, never let him do anything on his own without her if she could help it. Daisy said that, when he was home, Georgie was his jailer, and when he went out she was his stalker.

TAMMY: Georgie was just another nineteen-year-old girl. Surely Daisy wasn't really scared of her?

TERESA: Daisy didn't scare easily, and she didn't want me to worry – so she didn't tell me everything. But Georgie could be pretty unpleasant, and hinted once that anyone who got between her and Dan would get hurt. There was also an incident with a knife . . . I can't remember exactly what happened, because Daisy didn't say too much. But I know she felt threatened by Georgie.

TAMMY: Yet, according to our sources, in spite of Georgie's threats Daisy and Dan did have a fling.

TERESA: Yes, I got the feeling he just wore Daisy down. She was so fed up of him constantly harassing her, she gave in. For Daisy it was also someone to be with while she was getting through her time without David, I suppose.

TAMMY: And eventually she dumped Dan and returned to David?

TERESA: Yes, she loved David, she was young and stupid, and I couldn't talk her out of it. As for Dan, he thought he could have anyone, and he usually could – but Daisy was different, she played him at his own game. She didn't want a commitment, and for once he didn't like it. And when he found out she was going back to David, she said he was angry – he begged her not to, said he'd even finish with Georgie if she'd stay with him. But Daisy wanted David, she didn't want Dan.

TAMMY: So do you think now that all this was more significant than you thought?

TERESA: Yes, I do. When Daisy died I just put it down to David Montgomery. I didn't think too deeply about all the issues at the house. But I remember Daisy calling me one night saying she felt like everybody in the apartment hated her. There were the issues with Dan and Georgie, and apparently Lauren had physically attacked her because Daisy had accused her of copying her work. And Maddie was annoyed with her for going back to David, she said she'd lost respect for her, which obviously upset Daisy. Maddie tried to talk sense into her, told her it was a mess and that, either way, people were going to get hurt. It was good advice – I told her the same. I said, 'If you won't listen to me, please listen to Maddie,' but Daisy never listened to anyone.

And then there was Alex, who was also critical of her relationship with David. He gave her some money to help her out, but she said she felt beholden to him. I'm not sure what that was all about, but he was a funny one. Daisy liked him, but said he could be moody, and didn't mix with the rest of them much, kept himself to himself.

TAMMY: So those first couple of months of the second year weren't happy for Daisy?

TERESA: No, she wasn't happy. I think in her final days my daughter was very lonely. She called me a lot in the weeks before she died . . . I often wonder if she mentioned something and I didn't pick up on it. I was always listening, but did I hear her? It just hurts so much to think she had no friends to turn to, and the people she saw as friends all seemed to have something against her. But I never expected . . . Sorry, I just need a moment.

TAMMY: Take as long as you need, Teresa.

(Silence and muffled crying from Teresa for seven seconds.)

TERESA: Sorry! . . . I just hate to think that Daisy may have lived in the same house as her killer . . . and . . . I just want to find out who did it. I'm not saying it wasn't David – but what is it they say in court, something about reasonable doubt? I now have doubts that David was the killer, and I just want whoever killed Daisy to be behind bars. If it wasn't David, then it has to be someone. I have my own theory as to who that might be, and they don't get to end my daughter's life and go on to live theirs. That's why I've now joined the campaign to have this case reopened.

TAMMY: We share your concerns, and your desire for justice, Teresa. (Tammy pauses for seven seconds.) Teresa, just one more thing. You mentioned to me when we first spoke last week that Daisy had a laptop?

TERESA: Yes, she did. I was told the police had seized it.

TAMMY: Well, we've done some digging, and it turns out the police did take the laptop for analysis. But, according to their records, that laptop was returned – not to you at Daisy's home address, but to the house where she was living while at university.

TERESA: I didn't know that.

TAMMY: Presumably this was the address the police had for Daisy, and it was assumed it would be returned to the rightful owner. And did anyone other than the police ever contact you to tell you that the laptop had been returned?

TERESA: No, no one ever mentioned it, and it was never returned to me.

TAMMY: Would it surprise you to know that police records show that, when it was delivered to the house, one of Daisy's housemates signed for it?

TERESA: Yes, it would . . . (Silence for nine seconds.) Who signed for it, Tammy?

TAMMY: It was Lauren Pemberton.

19

LAUREN

Shit! Oh. My. God!

Everyone is looking at me, waiting for my explanation. The interview on the audio file has finished and I stare ahead for a moment, then go into a surprised reaction. I haven't a clue what to say, but know I have to at least aim for *some* truth.

'Yes, I was there when the laptop was returned. I opened the door and signed for the delivery from the police,' I say. 'But I don't know what happened to it after that. I just left it around and someone must have started using it, thinking it was a spare?' I suggest. It's not ideal, but no one can argue it, though I'm sure Georgie will try. Mind you, Teresa pretty much just accused her of being a knife-wielding bunny boiler, so she'll be too busy worrying about how she looks to start heckling me.

I'm exhausted. This virtual accusation from Daisy's mother was right off the back of Tammy singling me out, by making reference to 'works of fiction that sold only because the writer happened to know Daisy Harrington'.

'I have a headache,' I murmur into the thick, accusatory silence, and leave the breakfast table.

Should I just forget this second book, go now and risk being found out? Or do I stay, gather more information, and just hope nothing more about me comes out? I have to consider the life-changing money the book would bring. We could move to a bigger place, buy another holiday home to replace the one we lost. We could send Clementine to private school and I could have *real* designer handbags again instead of the fake shit I have to have now. And God, what I would give for a neck lift.

Yes. I need to stay. I lie down on my bed, traumatised from that bloody podcast, and drop off to sleep. When I wake I feel slightly better because I know that no one can prove I kept the laptop. It lay around the house, and someone picked it up. End of. It's a lie, but a good one, and I'm completely covered.

So I collect my notebook and head back into the communal area. I need to face them all and get all the information I can, but no one's there, so I sit down and make some notes. It isn't long before Georgie walks in – the last person I want to see right now. I don't look up, but I can see her slim legs in designer jeans on the sofa. I'm not sure how long I can ignore her, so I look up. But just as I do, she begins to leaf through the book I left on the coffee table. *A Day in the Life and Death. My* book.

'That was a difficult listen,' I say.

'Who for?' She looks up, frowning.

'Erm . . . Both of us, I guess?'

'Not for me. I wasn't jealous of Daisy, and she wasn't scared of me. Her stupid mother got it all wrong – it makes me so fucking angry. Because she doesn't know what *really* happened, she's making shit up and I'm a sitting target.'

'Yeah . . . Me too. I mean, that laptop was just left around, but she made out I stole it.'

Georgie's looking at me with this incredulous expression on her face, then she says, 'You and I both know you did a lot more than steal Daisy's laptop.' Her voice is icy, and I'm chilled to the bone. She knows.

I'm trying not to react to what she said, because whatever my response is, I know my guilt will show itself.

She's stuck the metaphorical knife in my chest and is now ignoring me. My whole body is tingling with fear; this could be it for me. She's flicking erratically through the book, and the air seems to prickle and spark. She isn't reading it, she's just working out how to twist that knife and hurt me some more. Georgie's always watching, listening, like a wild animal waiting to pounce.

I think she's jealous of other women's looks, their careers, their lives. She was so negative about my success, whereas the others were kind and supportive. When my book was first released Maddie sent flowers, and Dan sent champagne. But nothing from Georgie.

'What's your new book about?' she suddenly asks without looking up.

'It's another crime book.'

At this she lifts her head, and I brace myself. '*Crime*. Like this one?' She lifts the book up.

'Yeah, but this time it's non-fiction. A true crime, murder . . . sort of . . .'

'*Murder?* Seems to be your speciality . . .'

We hold each other's gaze too long. I'm the first to look away.

Our phones ping and I open up my WhatsApp for the inevitable voice note.

'Get your buckets and spades, we're off to Exmouth Beach for ice cream and sandcastles. A place for old friends to unwind and chat, just like you once did as students – wandering the beaches, sharing stories and memories, good and bad.'

First Teresa's implied accusation over the laptop, then Georgie's vileness, and now this weird, fake-fun message about revisiting the place where Daisy was hammered to death. I don't know what stops me from just bursting into tears.

'What's happening now?' Dan appears in the doorway with his hair all mussed up.

'Have *you* been asleep?' Georgie asks, disapprovingly.

'I have, my princess. I was hoping you'd come and kiss me awake.' He winks at me.

'Fuck off!' she says. She's obviously still angry about Teresa, and I take a moment of sadistic pleasure imagining her anger if she finds out what her husband's been up to. But my dark pleasure is fleeting, and a heavy mass of dread creeps into my mind.

Half an hour later we all reluctantly set off for the car park, where apparently our carriage awaits.

Georgie and I end up walking together through the halls and, as the other two take the lift, she refuses, insisting on going down the three flights of stairs. I feel obligated to join her.

'So, do you enjoy crime?' she asks. Again, I know what she's doing. She's trying to torture me, and like all victims of torture I just want her to stop, but I try to sound strong.

'Yes, as much as anyone can *enjoy* crime.'

'You can't fool me, Lauren. I *see* you.'

'What . . . what do you mean?' My heart's pumping, and it isn't because of the stairs.

What does she *know?* There's a sting in my chest. I feel like my ears have suddenly filled up with water.

'What have you done since you wrote the last book?' she's now asking as we walk into the freezing car park. I feel like she knows the lie that is my life.

'I've been working on the *next* one.'

'For *eighteen* years?' She turns to me, doubt in her eyes.

I pull my fleece jacket tighter around me, to protect against the questions as much as the cold. Even I can't lie about this; it's bloody obvious I haven't had a book out since the first one, and Georgie's not stupid. I'm now bracing myself for the vicious comment that might destroy me.

It's suddenly all too much, and I feel tears spring to my eyes, and to my own surprise I start crying. Georgie doesn't deem this significant enough to acknowledge, but just then Maddie and Dan appear and, within seconds, Maddie is by my side.

'What is it, Lauren?' she says gently, as Dan and Georgie reunite. He's asking her if she upset me and she's quietly but angrily defending herself as we walk along together.

'Sorry.' I grab a tissue from my pocket and wipe my eyes. 'I'm being silly, ignore me.'

'You okay, Lauren?' Dan asks, concerned.

'Yeah, Georgie was asking about my next book, and I just started thinking about the deadline, and felt overwhelmed,' I lie. I see him shoot a look at Georgie, who turns away and starts to walk on her own. Good! It's about time she was called out. I'm beginning to think she's truly *evil*.

'I'm sure you'll be fine,' Maddie offers. 'You'll get there, Lauren. You did it before, you can do it again.' Dan is nodding in agreement, and I genuinely appreciate their kindness.

'Thanks, guys,' I say as we approach the minibus. Georgie's leaning against it, waiting, arms folded, her face like thunder, obviously having expected Dan to run after her.

'God, it's freezing.' Dan's stamping his feet to try to keep warm as he opens the bus door and stands back to let us on. But Georgie's already slipping in ahead, securing the best seat for herself and Dan.

'Sorry . . . You know what she's like,' he whispers in my ear, his hand on my waist. He's pretending to help me up, but his hands move up and under my jumper, touching bare flesh so briefly I barely register it. I don't react, and Georgie's too busy pouting in her powder mirror to catch it.

'Can you put the heater on, mate?' Dan asks the driver, and soon we are thawing in the little bus as it trundles along to Exmouth Beach.

But within the first few minutes of pulling away, Georgie obviously wants to continue my public shaming. 'You wouldn't get me slaving over a second book if I'd made the money you have. You have *three* homes – do you really need any more?'

'It isn't about the money. It's about the creative fulfilment, Georgie.'

'Oh, right,' she mutters, gazing out of the window.

'Have you read the book, or seen the film?' I ask.

'God, no, not my kind of read.' She frowns and opens the *Hello!* magazine she's brought with her from the apartment.

'Yeah, Georgie only reads high-brow, academic stuff,' Dan jokes, taking his life in his hands.

She doesn't respond, but I know he's going to suffer for that later. I look out of the window, glad she hasn't read my book or seen the film. I don't want her analysing every sentence and destroying me with her cruel critiques.

By the time we arrive at the beach there's a wind beginning to whip along as we climb from the bus. The sting of sand and sunshine is a stark reminder of the times I came here with Daisy. It makes me so uncomfortable.

'You used to drive us here,' I say to Dan. I'm thinking of the time we came alone, just the two of us. It was too hot, and I drank too much, and we stayed too long, our faces and shoulders pink.

'Yeah, we had some good times down on this beach.' He puts his arm around Georgie and I'm suddenly jealous. Richard and I barely touch anymore.

We walk in a gaggle along the beach, throwing stones, teasing the ripples of icy-cold water then skipping away as they chase us back up the beach. Dan and Maddie walk on ahead, and start to run along the edge of the water, and she screams when he catches her, and they play-fight. I glance over at Georgie, waiting for the tight lips, the jealous flame, but all I see is hurt.

I have this weird urge to comfort my tormentor; she's all teeth and nails and fire, but underneath I know she's as vulnerable as me.

'This is fun,' I say as we walk along together.

'It's not fun, though, is it, Lauren?' She looks at me, and pain shines in her eyes. I never realised before, but I think it's always been there. 'I wish I was the kind of woman men chase along a beach,' she murmurs, staring wistfully at Dan as he puts Maddie in a headlock.

She clearly isn't comfortable with their physical closeness, and can't bear to watch anymore; she picks up speed, jogging on ahead. Daisy was right, she was Dan's jailer and his stalker, and that hasn't changed – she's clearly still concerned about her husband and other women. She should be. I feel for Maddie, though: she's no match for Georgie on the warpath. There's a reason we called Georgie Scary Spice and Maddie Baby Spice.

I can't help but notice Maddie's wearing the Hermès scarf again. Is it just a coincidence that we both have one and mine went missing? Unless my first thought was correct, and Maddie took it from Daisy's room, because the last time I saw it that's where it was. Daisy *definitely* never gave it back to me.

I feel quite angry and frustrated, because I *know* it's my scarf but can't prove it, so I just try not to look at the beautiful soft silk in pale chocolate and turquoise.

I keep walking in the same direction, watching Georgie ahead of me as she jogs even faster now to break up the party of two. What does she think she can save? Dan? Their marriage? Her sanity? Looks to me like that train left some time ago.

The wind is nipping at my face, but the sunshine's bright and crisp and the beach is pretty. Not many people around today, and the cold is biting, but it's calm and quiet save for the constant, soothing hiss of waves. Then something makes me turn around and look behind me. The hairs on the back of my neck prickle. *She's here.* A teenage ghost in shorts and a crop top, dancing along the beach, excited to be here, excited to *be*. I smile, and relief washes over me. I can explain everything to her. She'll forgive me, won't she? But then suddenly a cloud crosses the sun, and the beach is plunged into greyness. When I look back, she's gone.

In the far distance now, Georgie is approaching Dan and Maddie, who are still locked in flirtatious combat. She reaches out, takes Dan's hand and removes him from temptation, staking her claim. I watch from my safe distance as they circle each other, moving uncertainly in the still grey light.

Suddenly, I feel sharp little clusters of ice on my face, and look up to see hail falling dizzily from the sky. The others start to run back to where I am, and when they get to me we run together, laughing and calling just like we used to. We moved into and out of and around each other's lives, sometimes on the edges, sometimes in the middle. I realise in that moment that, whether we like it or not, we will always dance like this, together and apart – Daisy tied us to this place, to each other, forever.

◆ ◆ ◆

Once back at the apartment, we shed wet clothes and I go to the student prison cell I once considered my sanctuary. I lock my door and sit on the narrow bed, feeling the same as when the world was younger and hope lingered in the air like the scent of spring.

Now, I sit in the dark wintry afternoon knowing this weight I carry will only increase as time goes on. I still see her, hear her voice calling me, echoing through the years. I'm overwhelmed by guilt and grief. I feel a sudden chill run through me, and something makes me turn and look through the window. The sky is dark; bare trees move in the wind like black skeletons against the dusky backdrop. And my heart almost stops at the face staring through the window. She's there, outside, staring through the glass, her hands flat on the windowpane. I gasp – her eyes are filled with terror, her mouth opening in a scream. But there's no sound. My heart thumps loudly in my head. I hear a whimper coming from my mouth, then, silently, I scramble off the bed, unlock the door and, my whole body now electric with fear, run from the room.

20

GEORGIE

We just got back from the beach trip. Feelings from long ago have been dredged up. Watching Dan chase Maddie along the shore reminded me of the other times, with Daisy. I was surprised how much it hurt, and it sucked me back until I was drowning in the past. I haven't gone to my room because Dan will follow me in there, and I don't want to be alone with him. I don't want to have to dredge over everything Teresa said about Dan harassing Daisy and me scaring her. I hated myself back then, and there's no justification for what happened. I came to sit in the living area to escape him, avoid talking. But he's followed me in here and is now lying on the sofa.

'Where are the others?' he asks.

'Maddie's gone for a shower. Lauren's in her room, I think. Why are you lying across the sofa like that?'

'Sorry, is it affecting your feng shui? Does my untidy body bother you?'

'You *know* it does, so just indulge me, Dan, and stop being a mess.'

He rolls his eyes at this. 'You okay after what Teresa said?'

I shrug. 'I feel pretty numb. I'm not sure who I hate most, her, you – or me.'

'Yeah, it wasn't easy to hear any of that, was it? But Teresa wasn't there, she doesn't *know* anything.'

'I hope not.' I take a deep breath. 'In other news, Lauren's notebook fell out of her pocket on the bus. It landed on the floor by my feet.'

He looks at me doubtfully. 'Are you sure it just fell? I reckon you took it out of her pocket.'

'I didn't. I wouldn't dream of rifling through someone's pockets.'

'Liar. You go through mine all the time.'

'That's because you can't be trusted. Anyway, shut up. I jumped down and picked up her notebook before she could, and it fell open, and guess what?' I move to the edge of the sofa, and speak even more quietly, so he *has* to listen. 'On the page it said "Daisy" in curly writing . . . and there was a picture of a face, a *girl's* face – like Daisy's.'

'We're all remembering her in our own way, Georgie.'

'You don't think it's creepy?'

'No, and I think you need to calm down. I'm still pissed off with you for the way you spoke to Maddie on the beach. I don't want you taking this into dinner and having a pop at Lauren too.'

'Oh, I'm sorry if I spoiled your beach romp with Baby Spice,' I snap.

'Shh. Remember we're in a communal area, we're being recorded.'

'I don't care, Dan, I'm trying to tell you what I saw, and what I say next will shock even you.'

'Go on then, try me,' he says, sounding bored.

'The girl's face . . . in the doodle, the one that looked like Daisy?' I pause to make sure he's with me, and speak slowly and clearly – because I *want* this to be recorded. 'It was on its side and . . . and what looked like blood trickled from the *mouth*!' Just describing this makes me recoil inside. 'I don't care what you say, that is fucking *insane*. Lauren is obviously—'

'Sorry, guys, I didn't realise you were in here.' Maddie's soft, girlish voice oozes into the damning words I am about to spew across the living area.

'That's okay, Maddie, join us,' Dan says.

'No . . . Don't want to disturb you.'

'No, do come in, Maddie, we're just chatting.' I don't want her to feel bad after me being a bit rude on the beach. Damn – I managed to talk about the drawing for the recording, but I wanted two million people to know my *theory* about Lauren. I can't now say it in front of Maddie – she might tell Lauren and give her a chance to get her story straight.

'I just had a lovely hot shower,' she's saying. Her hair's wet, her face is pink and she's in a short towelling robe.

Dan starts patting the sofa next to him. 'Come and tell Uncle Dan all about it.' *Too far.*

'Uncle Dan? What the *fuck*?' I say, unable to hide my disgust. He can be such a dick sometimes – really puts himself in the firing line. After what Teresa said about Daisy feeling uncomfortable when she was alone with him, you'd think he'd be careful saying predatory things to the women he lived with.

'What? I'm only joking. Maddie knows that, don't you, Maddie?'

'Please keep "creepy uncle" out of your comedy repertoire,' I say, trying to smile like it's a joke, but my heart's beating hard in my chest. He needs to watch it or he's going to move straight to the number-one-suspect slot this weekend, and take me with him. Stupid bastard.

Meanwhile, poor Maddie shifts from one foot to the other; she doesn't want to sit with him and anger me, but he's still patting the sofa and she doesn't want to offend him either.

'Sit with me,' I say. 'Ignore him.'

Dan isn't smiling now. He doesn't like being made to look stupid in front of a pretty woman. So he stands up, mutters angrily about going for a nap and storms out of the room. I'm relieved. The mood he's in, he's safer on his own, away from female company.

'So, how's your day going?' I ask Maddie, without acknowledging his departure.

She sits down next to me as I suggested. 'Okay – yours?'

'All fine.' I smile, but it isn't genuine. I doubt Maddie realises that. We sit in silence, and I remember the awkwardness I always used to feel around her. She's a lovely person, but so quiet, and doesn't really contribute much – never did. She isn't funny or clever, or even mean. As Daisy used to say, 'Maddie's just . . . *nice*.'

'I can't believe how young you still look, like time hasn't passed and the rest of us got all the wrinkles,' I say.

'That's kind of you, but I have fillers and Botox,' she admits, like she's confessing to a terrible sin.

'You can't tell, it looks *very* natural. Though I never expected you to have Botox.'

'Why?'

'I don't know, it's just that you're so wholesome. You still vegetarian?' I ask, for something to say.

She shakes her head. 'Not anymore. If I was I'd have fallen off the wagon with that chicken liver parfait last night.'

'Oh . . . Yes, of course.'

'I gave up being veggie when I got my cat, Minty. She eats meat and fish, and it's difficult to be a vegetarian when you live with a carnivore.'

'Yeah, right,' I say, nodding, like this makes sense.

I glance down at my magazine, trying to think of what to say next. I don't know anything about her life now – didn't know much about her back then, come to think of it.

'I remember we all came to watch you in a play . . . What was it now?'

'*Macbeth*.'

'Oh God, yeah, I remember now – you were amazing, not at all like you.'

She laughs. 'That's what they call acting. I'm not really like Lady Macbeth.'

I smile at this, but before we can talk any more there's a thumping sound and Lauren dashes into the doorway, hair on end, eyes wild.

'Has something happened?' I ask, alarmed. She looks absolutely *terrified*.

'Yes . . . I . . . I saw her . . . at the window, she was staring at me through the glass.' She shudders at this. 'She was standing there, her face pressed against the window. It was *her*.'

'Who?' asks Maddie.

'*Daisy*, of course!' Lauren's actually trembling.

'No!' The blood drains from Maddie's face.

'It *isn't* Daisy.' I shake my head dismissively. Lauren always has to be the centre of attention. She's probably been sitting in her room for the past half-hour trying to work out how to create a drama.

'I'm not making this up, Georgie,' she says through gritted teeth, clearly irritated.

'Well, you *did* make it up, because she's . . . *dead*,' I say, looking at her like she's stupid. Which she is.

Maddie's hugging her, and two accusing faces turn to stare at me.

'Sorry, I know that sounds brutal – but . . . she is!'

'I miss Daisy.' Lauren's sniffling through the sobs. 'I miss her *so* much.'

'Me too.' Maddie is now joining in.

I'm confused at the sudden emotion unravelling in front of me. Surely Lauren isn't *crying* about Daisy after all this time?

This tableau before me is reminiscent of life before Daisy died. Girls constantly huddled in twos or threes, sharing secrets, crying, laughing or arguing. I always stayed detached and avoided the emotional mess of the young and hormonal sharing a living space.

'Would it make you feel better to have a lie-down in your room? I'll come with you if you like?' Maddie's saying.

'No . . . No. I'm just tired from writing, and thinking . . . Being back here, remembering *her* again – it's so unsettling.'

This is turning into mass hysteria, and I want no part in it.

'I'll go get ready for dinner,' I announce, and return to my bedroom, where I'm disappointed to see Dan is taking up the bed. He's fast asleep, and I kick him gently, but he doesn't move so I kick harder.

'Ouch, Georgie, what the hell?'

'Why are you sleeping in *my* bed?'

'Because I fancy Goldilocks . . .' he mutters.

'Ugh. You have your own room, Dan.'

'Yours is warmer. It's over the boiler for the building.'

I give up trying to remove him when I realise that at least he's someone to bitch with. 'Honestly, the performance that's going on out there,' I say, climbing over him and plonking myself on the bed.

'What?' he mumbles through sleep.

'Maddie and Lauren sobbing over Daisy.'

He stirs. 'Well, Lauren was her best friend.'

'More like best *frenemy*, and Maddie and Daisy weren't that close, except for a few weeks when we all started in the first year, and whenever Daisy and Lauren fell out. Daisy soon dumped her when more interesting people turned up. And, hello, it was twenty years ago, get over yourselves!'

'Freshers' week was the best week of my life,' he says sleepily.

'I know Maddie's daft, but why has she got caught up in Lauren's drama? God, Lauren's so fake – she pretends she's this big author, making notes . . . "Deadlines, deadlines." *What* deadlines?'

He's still half-asleep, rubbing his eyes. 'Why are you so *bothered* about her?' He slowly sits up, leaning on his elbows.

'Because I still think she knows more than she's letting on. She's hiding something, Dan.'

'Mmm, now you're the one who's being dramatic. In this febrile atmosphere I'd stay under the radar if I were you. Don't go accusing, because it could put the spotlight on us and—'

'I *know*, I'm not an *idiot*, Dan!'

'Are you just jealous because she had all that success and money with her book?' He's teasing me, but we both know there's some truth in it. 'When her book was released, you refused to even send her a congratulations card, and told me if I sent her anything you'd file for divorce.'

'I didn't think it was appropriate that *either* of us stayed in touch, given Lauren's closeness to Daisy.'

'Why?'

Do I really have to spell it out? 'Everything that happened between us and Daisy – she was best friends with Lauren, she *must* have told her.'

'No . . . She didn't.'

'How do *you* know?'

'I don't.'

'So why say it? Daisy more than likely told Lauren *everything* – and now with this podcast it's even more risky. Lauren could totally drop us in it . . .'

'All the more reason for you not to be so vile to her – to everyone!' he says, irritated, his face flushed with anger.

'I don't have to put up with this shit,' I say, and, grabbing my towel and toilet bag, I head out of the room to take a shower. My room has a small cubicle with a sink and toilet and shower, but I'm not going in there because he might invite himself in, and I'm not in the mood. So I leave my room and head for the shared bathroom, and have to pass Lauren's room to get there. It's then that I notice the door is still wide open from when she fled earlier, having apparently seen 'Daisy's ghost'!

I check behind me to make sure she and Maddie are still engrossed in their conversation about 'grief' in the living room. They are – so I go in.

Once inside, I'm straight to the laptop and quickly scrolling through her files, checking the door every few seconds. I can hear Maddie and Lauren still talking, so I just keep going; this is my chance. I browse several documents in a folder titled 'BOOKS', and see one called 'Daisy Harrington'. On opening that document, I start to skim-read, and within seconds so many questions are answered. Lauren's behaviour, her attitude, her secrecy, now make sense – obvious, horrible sense.

21

MADDIE

I was terrified when Lauren came running in saying she'd seen Daisy. The way she described her, face pressed against the window, her mouth moving but no sound. It really got to me. It's obviously tough for Lauren, she was her best friend, but Daisy and I were close at the beginning. We met on the first day at uni, and spent freshers' week running around Exeter. It was the most fun I'd ever had, and in our own way we remained close, despite Lauren crashing in and becoming her bestie.

I make us both a cup of herbal tea and she seems calmer as we sit together on the sofa talking.

'Where did Georgie go?' I ask.

'She disappeared. Georgie doesn't do emotion.'

'I know, but we were having a nice chat when you came in.'

'Really? Are we talking about the same Georgie?'

'Lauren, she's *okay*.'

'I know, you just need to break through that crust of ice to see that there's . . . another, even thicker one underneath,' she jokes. 'Did you see her on the beach earlier? She didn't like you and Dan chasing each other.'

I feel embarrassed. 'You know what he's like.' I take a sip of my tea. Georgie has always been jealous where Dan is concerned, but I wonder if Lauren's trying to stir things up.

'Yes, I do, and I know what she's like too. Georgie sees women like you as a threat – women like you and Daisy.'

'What do you mean?' I ask.

'Well, you were both the pretty girls, with long blonde hair, just his type back then – well, most men's type.'

I hate it when people say stuff like this, so I just shrug. 'I used to feel sorry for Georgie. Still do, really.'

'Oh, Georgie can look after herself. I feel more sorry for Dan having her control his every move,' she says. 'She told me once that her father had affairs, and that's why she sees other women as a threat.'

'You'd think that would make her mistrust *men*, not women,' I muse.

'You're probably right, Maddie. She doesn't trust anyone, never gives anything of herself. Georgie has always hidden who she really is.'

'Don't we all? I've done a lot of therapy and I'm only too aware of how much I hide – even from my therapist!'

'Maddie, you're an open book, so sweet and pretty, and you've never been one for gossip. You just get on with life, don't you?'

'I'm not interested in gossip, and I hate it when people call me sweet and pretty,' I add, without explaining why.

So sweet, pretty girl, gorgeous woman, beautiful lady . . . The words unravel in my head, becoming random, meaningless letters on a screen. I imagine the accompanying voices – gruff old men, overly eager young ones, and the men who make you do things you don't want to do.

'I'm sorry, I didn't mean to offend you. It was a compliment, Maddie,' Lauren says, like I should be grateful.

'I know, and thanks,' I hear myself reply. *Gratefully.* 'You and I were so different,' I say. 'You smoked and talked about books, carried a notebook, always planning your novel. You seemed so . . . sophisticated,' I add, avoiding the word 'pretentious'. 'I'd never met anyone like you. I remember you joining me and Daisy in the student bar, and when I asked what course you were on, you said, "English literature. I'm going to write a bestseller one day."'

She smiles at this. 'God, I was a brat, wasn't I? Funny, I don't remember that. I can't recall even meeting you . . . I just remember Daisy.'

'Yeah, well, I was the quiet one, no one ever noticed me with Daisy around,' I say good-naturedly. 'In fact, no one ever noticed me full stop.'

'I'm sure they did,' she replies insincerely. 'What I do remember about you is that you were always happy. We all used to say that.'

Happy? As if I needed proof that no one really saw me.

'I envied you your sunny disposition,' she continues. 'I still do, but not like Georgie, who envies *everyone*. She can never be happy because she's always looking over her shoulder.'

Lauren just had to bring Georgie back into the conversation. She's *obsessed* with her.

'I think Georgie's doing okay,' I reply. 'Her gourmet catering start-up sounds like it's doing really well.'

'Yeah, I give it a year. Georgie never wanted the hassle of work, that's why she married Dan. She knew his hedge fund career would keep her in designer handbags and shoes for life.'

'We mustn't forget the recording, Lauren,' I say quietly. I'd forgotten until she started getting really personal about Georgie's marriage.

'Oh, Georgie knows what I think of her. She's too controlling. That's why she was with Alex in the first term. He was easy to control. I reckon that was down to the dope . . . Georgie encouraged him to take drugs too, because she liked to keep him compliant.'

'I don't think that she—' I really wish she'd shut up; this is all being recorded.

'Oh yeah, she *did*. She actually said that once. We were all having a few drinks and he started arguing with her, and I'll never forget she said, "Quick, give him some more downers, he's coming round."'

'That was just Georgie's dark sense of humour.'

Lauren bristles slightly at my refusal to be sucked in. 'I'm not saying she's a bad person, Maddie. I just think she thrives on control – putting everything and everyone in their boxes. I have never understood the dynamic between her and Dan. They're chalk and cheese.'

'Are you okay now, after your scare?' I ask, in an attempt to change the subject.

'I'm okay. I know Daisy wasn't *actually* there, Maddie. I'm not crazy. I resented Georgie's implication that I was making it up. But she looked so *real*.' She takes a sip of tea. 'This weekend has totally disorientated me. The suspicion, the mistrust – I felt it this morning over breakfast, and later at the beach. It was obvious on the drive back we were all checking each other out, and when I dropped my notebook Georgie swooped on it to try to see what I'd written. I feel like she's watching me, and I'm worried she might say things about me . . . that aren't true.'

'Let it go, Lauren.' She's obviously deliberately saying what she wants to be heard on the podcast.

'I can't. Georgie's held on to her grudge all these years. Someone told her that when she went home one weekend Dan and I had sex. She went absolutely crazy . . . Threatened to do all kinds of terrible things to me . . . and him too. All because someone said we'd slept together.'

'Did you?'

The look on her face tells me it was true.

'But they were a couple, Lauren. I don't blame her for going crazy.'

She seems surprised at me pushing back on this. 'Yes, but we were all kids, and it wasn't like they were married. Daisy told me stuff about Georgie – she was so twisted, jealous of everyone. Still is. She's probably even jealous of *you*.'

'Wow, even *me*?' I say, trying for sarcasm, but I can never carry it off.

'Yes,' she says, 'even *you*.'

I rest my case.

Her eyes suddenly slide across the room, like she thinks someone might be listening, then she leans in. 'It was Georgie who killed Daisy, I know it was.'

'Lauren, shhh, keep your voice down – we might be being recorded.'

'Okay, I'll whisper,' she whispers.

'Why do you say that?' I ask under my breath, and for once I'm eager to know her thoughts.

'Well, I shouldn't tell you this . . . and I didn't say anything at the time because . . . I didn't believe it. But Daisy told me Georgie had threatened to kill her.'

Given Lauren's dubious track record of exaggerating the truth, I'm not sure I believe this, but everyone's fighting for their own innocence this weekend. Lauren doesn't care who she takes down, but she'd *love* for it to be Georgie. And she isn't whispering as quietly as I'd hoped, which would suggest this is being staged.

'Georgie was always volatile. Back then she threatened to kill someone every day. Hell, she probably still does.' I'm joking, but again my delivery falls flat. Besides, Lauren isn't listening; she's too intent on putting Georgie right in the frame.

'No, no, you don't understand. Daisy said the threat was for real, but at the time I didn't realise the significance, until it all came out in the court case.'

'What do you mean?'

'Well, the fact that, when she died, Daisy was pregnant. I think Georgie threatened to kill her because she'd guessed the baby was Dan's.'

22
Dan

No one is happier to see Alex than me. Except perhaps my wife, who is currently clinging to him like a limpet. He's just walked into the apartment, and the four of us are standing round him, all wanting to say hi, but Georgie won't let go.

'You haven't aged at all,' she's saying as she hugs him, then she rests her head on his shoulder. It's weird to see Georgie cuddly and affectionate with anyone, and I confess I'm jealous.

I catch Lauren's eye, and she smiles; like me, she sees what's happening here.

I have to admit that Alex looks really good – still slim and tall, his hair a little shorter, but still thick and curly. He looks young, but I imagine with his money he probably has a bit of help.

He's obviously doing well. His coat is a floor-length wool trench with brass buttons, presumably designer – Georgie would know. The US seems to suit him. He's my age, almost forty, but he's still got this trendy air about him, what the kids would call 'cool'.

'So, how are you, mate?' I ask as he loses Georgie and turns to me with open arms.

'I'm good, mate. Flew in on the red-eye from the West Coast.'

I bet he flies first class. I think about those air stewardesses, all sleek and shiny like expensive racehorses.

'You shag any stewardesses in first class on that red-eye?' I whisper in his ear as we embrace, patting each other on the back.

He doesn't answer me, just chuckles awkwardly and moves to Maddie, hugging her and nestling his face in her neck. I'm surprised she isn't pushing him away. I wonder if there's something going on there? They were quite good mates at uni. he *Does he know* about Maddie? I'll mention it to him subtly. I mean, if he's hoping for something there he needs to know. I'll wait until I get the chance. I can't say anything in front of Georgie – or Maddie, for that matter.

We're all standing in the kitchen asking him questions like we're in the presence of greatness.

'Tell me all about your company.' Georgie's straight in there. 'I just started a small company.'

'Oh . . . great. What do you do?' He's as polite as ever, but still a bit out of it. And I don't mean drugs, though it wouldn't surprise me. He was a bit of a dealer as a student; he said selling drugs was the only way he could afford to be at uni. I wasn't complaining, as having a dealer for a housemate meant we didn't have to leave home to get high.

Georgie's looking up into his eyes like he's some kind of rock star, and it's really winding me up. I'm not even able to enjoy Lauren in that tight white dress that pulls across her breasts, because my wife's flirting with a billionaire.

'Most of the money I make goes into my foundation,' I hear him say. Wouldn't you know it, not only is Alex a rich, handsome bloke who looks ten years younger than me, but he's a one-man climate-saving, environmentally aware, kitten-loving philanthropist. And my wife's drinking him in.

'You have a foundation?' Lauren gasps. It's almost orgasmic.

'Yeah, we do a lot of work for education and world peace. One of my personal goals is to establish free public libraries in the Global South. I want to make self-education available to everyone.'

He's a saint too.

'Oh, I love that – don't you love that?' Lauren's now looking at him like he's Jesus.

'Hey Alex, this is all a bit weird, but it's the podcast, they keep sending voice notes and we're being recorded, so be careful,' I joke, slapping him on the back.

'So I gathered. They emailed me a document I had to sign about privacy and recording.'

'Yeah, we've all had to sign it too. God, I felt like I was giving away my first-born. Made me wonder if I should have come here.'

'Yeah.' He isn't really engaging with me. Back in our student days he would have been keen to chat. He always laughed at my jokes, but I guess he's changed, got a bit above himself.

When we arrived last night I was really self-conscious, and aware of the recording, but today I'm more used to it. Georgie seems to be embracing it, and I notice she's constantly trying to incriminate Lauren. I noticed she was speaking really slowly before so the podcast would have all the details about Lauren's drawing of Daisy, with blood coming from her mouth. Ugh. Thinking about it, that *is* weird, and it's made me look at Lauren in a slightly different light.

Then our phones ping, and a new voice note from Tammy interrupts everyone.

'As pleased as everyone is to see Alex, he isn't here by choice. He came because we threatened to expose his secret, just like everyone else.'

The voice note ends, and we all look questioningly at Alex, who holds up his hands and says, 'I don't have any secrets as such . . .'

'Go on, we've all got secrets, mate,' I say, slapping him on the back again.

'I guess what they're referring to is . . . I've been to prison.'

Everyone seems suitably shocked at this revelation.

'You all know I made my money selling drugs at uni – no secret there – but after Daisy's death I kind of hit a wall. And instead of the odd bit of weed, I made more and more money from drugs. What can I tell you? No excuses. I paid my dues, and during my time in prison I took a computer science course, and on release I started to work in IT . . . and wiped any mention of my brief prison history off the internet. Hey, there has to be some advantage to being a computer nerd,' he adds, and everyone laughs. His smile lights up the room, and he still has that boyish charm, the quirky, self-deprecating humour, and great hair. Am I jealous of the billionaire? Hell yes!

'So that's *my* secret, I'm an ex-con,' he's saying, 'and after this weekend it won't be a secret anymore. And you know what, guys, I'm okay with that. I want people listening to know that whatever hand life deals you, you can get up and get out and make a good life for yourself.'

God, he even makes his stint in prison sound like he volunteered for a bloody charity. And the girls are lapping it up!

'But what the podcast is threatening to expose is your secret about Daisy . . .' I remind him. 'It's why you wanted Daisy dead.'

Silence. That went down like a lead balloon.

Alex turns to look at me. He isn't smiling anymore; his eyes are cold. 'But I didn't want Daisy dead – *mate*.'

I feel instantly diminished. Alex the messed-up little junkie who me and my friends paid to bring drugs to whatever pub we were drinking in has just publicly humiliated me. Who does he think he is?

Georgie is giving me daggers. 'Alex, what were you saying before you were so rudely interrupted by my husband?'

I shrink a little more. We all had a reason for wanting Daisy dead, and I'm sure Alex did too. A short prison sentence for dealing doesn't count; it must be something else that *The Killer Question* threatened to reveal. So what is it?

'So I worked and worked and along the way I had some good timing,' he continues. 'I had a lot of luck and the business flourished, and I'm finally proud of where I am and who I am. But my greatest gift has been my wife, who is the kindest, sweetest, most supportive – and, yes, most beautiful – woman I've ever known. She went through hard times too, and overcame the odds to make a good life for herself, and four weeks ago we got married.'

Everyone makes approving comments, and in an attempt to reintegrate I whistle, and make stag-night noises. But it doesn't ingratiate me with anyone, and the looks I'm getting from Georgie would suggest she may kill me with her bare hands.

'So, that's my story,' he says. 'I've nothing to hide and there's nothing to see here, so let's open the champagne.'

There's another ping and a collective groan as we all look at our phones. Alex turns the sound up on his so we can all listen to what Tammy has to say next.

'You each thought you were the only one who wanted Daisy dead, didn't you? EVERYONE has a secret. Some are embarrassing, some are incriminating, some just need to stay buried to save feelings – but some are DEADLY.'

'Well, that's got the evening off to a fun start,' I say, as Alex pours the champagne. No one laughs.

'In just an hour, dinner will be served, and between courses there will be some very interesting interviews. Drinks are now being served in the dining hall, same as last night.'

As they finish their conversation, I stare briefly into the faces of my old housemates to see if anyone is giving anything away. *Particularly* my wife.

She's glaring back at me, her lips tight, and she's wringing her hands. I know her so well – she's trying to be sophisticated and worldly, but in truth she's dying to start scrubbing surfaces. And after she's finished cleaning, she likes to yell at me. I'm always the focal point of Georgie's anger, but here and now, she can't scream and yell. She has to restrain herself in company. And this in itself creates tension. And I can feel it building from a few feet away.

But she's now moving towards me, her eyes warning and wild.

Standing too close to me, she hisses instructions in my ear. 'Do not say a thing. Don't even *joke* about anyone else's secret. Don't be a jerk and drop yourself, or me, in it. Okay?'

'I have no intention of being a *jerk*,' I reply wearily under my breath. '*You* obviously have a secret too.'

'I don't,' she snaps, unable to resist glancing over at Alex.

'You shouldn't be flirting like that. He's married,' I say smugly.

'So are you, but it doesn't stop you, does it?' She grabs a nearby bottle and splashes champagne into her glass. I need to fasten my seat belt. I reckon it's going to get pretty bumpy tonight.

I glance at my wife, who thinks she knows my secret, the one she prevented from getting out all those years ago. But sadly, there's more than one . . . Still, I need to stay on the right side of her.

'You okay, babe?' I ask, hoping to soften things. I need her in my corner in this rather threatening environment.

She shrugs.

'If it isn't David, it has to be Alex,' I murmur, looking ahead. 'God knows what's going to come out at dinner. I doubt prison is his only secret.'

She turns to me. 'You need to stop pointing the finger at Alex and look after your own interests. If the police come for you this time there will be no alibi from me. From now on, Dan, you're on your own!' She moves across the room, and Maddie offers her a glass of wine, and despite already clutching her half-full champagne glass, she snatches it and downs it in one.

My marriage is built on secrets, and thrives on the thrill of those secrets. But I have another one that not even my wife knows. And if she ever did find out, my marriage, and life as I know it, would be over.

23

LAUREN

I'm in a dining hellscape at a table in my old university halls with four former housemates, one of whom I never wanted to see again in my life. Georgie's in a man sandwich, looking lovingly at Alex one minute, then turning to hiss like a cat at Dan while he tries to get my attention. It's pathetic. I suddenly recall the rumour about them having a threesome with Alex, and want to throw up. I never believed it at the time, but now I see it. I have to look away.

I have to say, though, Alex has brought a real positive energy with him, and even Georgie's smiling, which is a first. But he seems to only have eyes for Maddie; they were standing together throughout the pre-dinner drinks, walked arm in arm to dinner and arrived after everyone else. I'm confused, because there's definitely some kind of connection, but he's just told us he met a kind, sweet, beautiful woman and married her. I hope Saint Alex isn't cheating already.

Everyone is at the table now, heading down memory lane – 'Do you remember when . . .' and 'I'll never forget the time that . . .' The stories we can only share with old friends who were there at the time.

I'm suddenly reminded of something, and I'm so keen to share this memory that I start telling the story before remembering what happened at the end.

'I remember being out with Daisy and Maddie in Exeter once, and this woman stopped us in the street,' I start, when there's a lull in the conversation. 'She was American, said she was a model scout, and she said, "Hey, you guys are so beautiful." And we all smiled and said thanks, and then she said, "Have any of you ever considered modelling?" We all looked at each other and she said, "My name's Eddie, I work for Models 1 and I just think you guys have got a great look, very *now*."'

I stop and take a little sip of wine, and they're all rapt, even Maddie who was there.

'Anyway, she goes on to say, "Please take my card, I promise you this is legit, and in a couple of years you could be on the cover of *Vogue*." But Maddie's like, "No thanks, I have to go home and feed my hamster," or something equally *classic* Maddie.'

Everyone laughs at this, including her.

'Then Daisy pipes up, "Can you make me rich?" This woman looks surprised. I think she was used to people just saying *yes*, but she says, "Yeah, honey, I reckon I could. You're young, tall and beautiful, so it wouldn't be difficult. I could get you on the catwalks of Paris." And Daisy rolls her eyes, and says, "Nah, can't be arsed."

'This Eddie woman looks a bit surprised, and walks away, but she only takes a few steps and then suddenly marches towards *me* and I'm so excited. I think she must have seen my potential . . .' They all laugh again. 'So, she pushes this card into my hand, and I say, "Thank you SO much, I'd love to be a model, you've made my dream come true." And she looks me up and down and says, "Sorry, honey, it's not for you, but could you make sure you give it to your friend, the one who *can't be arsed*?"'

They chuckle at this. 'Talk about an insult,' I add. 'She wasn't at all interested in me, but still wanted Daisy even though she couldn't be arsed!' We all chuckle at this.

'So did you give the card to Daisy?' Georgie asks, as if I wouldn't.

'Of course I did,' I reply firmly. 'As soon as we got back to our apartment, I handed it to her, but she threw it in the bin. I said, "Daisy, aren't you at *all* interested in being a model?" And she said, "Are you kidding? I'd absolutely love to be a model on the Paris catwalks or cover of *Vogue*, who wouldn't? But it was a scam – that woman was a con artist."

'I thought the woman had seemed pretty genuine, but didn't give it another thought, until, after Daisy died, I . . . I was in her room – I felt closer to her there . . . and I saw the card still lying in her bin. It must have been there for ages – she never tidied her room,' I say affectionately. 'And I don't know why, but I took it out of the bin, and called the number.' My voice is breaking as I continue, and you can hear a pin drop as everyone waits for what I say next. 'It was Models 1, and Eddie answered.'

Everyone's expectant face drops. They wanted a punchline, a happy ending, and all I gave them was more tragedy – and a reminder of a young woman's enormous potential, erased.

There are nods and murmurings, and after a few moments we all try to break the tension of sadness hanging over us, led by Alex who takes the white wine from the ice bucket and starts pouring. That's something that Dan would have done last night, and it's fascinating to see how the dynamic has changed since Alex's arrival. It looks like Dan isn't the alpha anymore.

Suddenly, the double doors open and in walks a woman – a stranger to me. She's middle-aged with blonde hair, and looks vaguely familiar, and Maddie stands up.

'Teresa, it's been a long time,' she says, and walks towards her. Both women open their arms instinctively and hug warmly. Then Maddie grabs her hand and walks her towards the table where we'll all sitting expectantly.

'This is Daisy's mum,' Maddie declares, and we all stand up, eager to make her feel at home with us.

We shake her hand or hug her individually, and all the usual things are said about how pleased we are to meet her and how much we loved Daisy, none of which are entirely true. 'Thank you,' she says graciously, and she takes her seat at the table.

Everyone makes small talk now, and it feels very awkward. Daisy's mum seems nice enough, and as a mum myself I can only imagine what she's been through.

'Your interview was moving, Teresa,' I offer, but just then the starter arrives, and she doesn't have a chance to respond.

I look down at my small plate filled with leaves and foam, and think of Finty waiting for my first draft. I have no appetite, but I nibble at the leaves and force myself to swallow. If I want to write the book, I have to keep them all onside and continue the façade. So, I smile at everyone around the table and try to look fascinated while talking about nothing.

The book would certainly benefit from an in-depth interview with Teresa. It would be worth giving the victim's mother her own chapter. So I give her a big smile, and start talking.

'Teresa, hi, we haven't had chance to chat,' I start. 'I'd like to explain a few things in context to you,' I say, referring to what Teresa said in her interview about Daisy accusing me of copying her coursework and me attacking her. 'I'm concerned you may have got the wrong impression of me from Daisy.'

She looks up. Her stare moves from the foam to my face. 'No, I think Daisy gave me a very accurate impression.'

I wonder how much Daisy told her about our arguments. Does she know that I pulled a clump of Daisy's hair out? It was in retaliation for her scratching my face, but still, now she's dead I'm on the losing side of *that* one. If Daisy told her anything out of context, Teresa might think I'm a terrible person. And the way she's glaring at me over her duck-and-pistachio terrine with cherry foam and nasturtium leaves would indicate that I was indeed misrepresented. But, being me, I don't give up – especially when I want something – and, imagining the great potential of Teresa in my book, I just keep going.

'I always envied her, having such a young mum.' I put down my fork. I'm now in creep overdrive; I need this woman to like me. 'You had a lovely relationship, just like best friends.'

'We were.' She spreads terrine on her toast, and speaks before eating. 'She used to phone me all the time. "Mum, how do you make spag bol?" and "Mum, how do you get red wine off the carpet?"' She smiles, then looks at me and says slowly, '"Mum, David told me that Lauren came on to him, tried to get him to give her higher marks."'

No!

Everything goes quiet around the table, and I feel like I'm underwater. My mouth is moving but there's no sound.

She then puts the toast to her lips and takes a dainty bite, and places the remainder neatly on her plate.

'I'm sorry, Teresa, but that just isn't true!' I say in my most assertive voice.

'Isn't it?' she asks, wide-eyed. 'And what about you tearing a clump of hair from her head in a rage? And stealing her course notes?'

24

GEORGIE

Oh. My. God.

As Mother Teresa utters her damning words, accusing Lauren of coming on to Professor Montgomery so he'd give her higher marks, I gasp. Audibly. No one expected sweet, bereaved Teresa to come out with *that*. The woman is officially my queen!

I want to laugh out loud, and shout 'Preach it, sister', but even I wouldn't do that; it would be rude. *And* I would be showing my hand. Something I can't do – yet.

It takes a few minutes for the embarrassed silence around the table to be gently filled up again by the mumble of voices. Teresa is soon back to tackling her terrine, and a distressed Lauren is grabbing her fake designer clutch and sprinting for the bathroom. *Run, bitch. Run!*

That's when I turn to Dan. 'Did you hear that? Teresa just accused Lauren of coming on to David Montgomery.'

He doesn't respond, but his jaw tightens and his eyes slide left to right in acknowledgement.

'Told you she's dodgy. *Now* do you believe me?'

He shifts in his seat. 'Don't get carried away, Georgie,' he sing-songs under his breath.

'I'm *not* getting carried away,' I hiss. But I am.

'Shhh.'

I will put up with a lot of things, but I will *not* be shushed. This is too important, and needs to be discussed. 'Dan, do not fucking shush me!' I'm keeping my voice low, and Alex is now charming the table with stories of his new Bernese mountain dogs – 'We have two, we call them the twins' – and everyone is just melting. Maddie is particularly enjoying his company and lapping it up, just like a little cat.

'Lauren lies about everything. She was Daisy's friend and she was coming on to her boyfriend. Always complaining about Daisy only getting high marks because she was sleeping with the teacher – and all the time she's trying to sleep with the fucking teacher, to get better marks!'

'Okay . . . Okay,' he's saying in a way that suggests more shushing.

'I *need* to talk to you,' I say through gritted teeth. As far as the rest of the table is concerned, I'm whispering sweet nothings into my husband's ear. But he's turning away from me, refusing to engage, and I hate him all over again.

I glance over at Alex. He's been so nice to me tonight, and he's promised not to say anything about me lying that I was in bed the night Daisy disappeared, but still – can I trust him? I get the feeling we're all ready to blame each other to save ourselves. Alex is no different, and if I'm the next one they're going to lay the blame on, who's to say he won't pile on with his *evidence* of my guilt? After all, I lied to the police, and I lied to Dan about where I was, and the only person who knows I wasn't in bed asleep the night Daisy went missing is Alex.

I watch him discreetly from across the table. He's still good-looking, and I can't help wonder, *what if?* The mind-boggling prospect of that sliding-doors moment, choosing between two different men, two different lives. Driven by naivety, hormones and a fear of being alone, my future was decided at the age of eighteen. A gorgeous billionaire with big brown eyes and a four-million-dollar stucco mansion in Saratoga Woods (yep, I googled him), or Dan?

Oh, to wind back that clock.

If I'd gone with the Alex option, my business would be making caviar canapés for ladies who lunch, not birthday tea for kids' soft-play parties. I know, I tell everyone my business is gourmet catering, but that isn't exactly working out. The business wasn't taking off, so when Candyland Kids Soft Play called to ask if I'd do a six-year-old's pirate party, I said yes. I thought it was a one-off, but it was only the beginning of the living Disney hell I find myself in . . . Let's put it this way, my upcoming events are two *Lion King* toddler teas, a *Little Mermaid* princess party, and a *Pocahontas*-themed finger buffet for tweenagers.

We're not short of money. Dan's hedge fund job brings in a good salary plus bonuses, but I hate being dependent on him; it makes me itchy. At the age of seventy-four, his father left his mother for a much younger woman, and Dan's inheritance is now being spent on a thirty-year-old Beyoncé lookalike. The fruit doesn't fall far from the tree, and watching Dan watching the young waitress right now, I don't need a crystal ball to see *my* future. So I do need a job.

But the priority right now is us both getting through this weekend without being arrested or exposed.

I need to stop focusing on the negatives and appreciate what I have, and my mind returns to its happy place – Lauren being handed the Bitchiest Best Friend of the Year Award from Teresa just now. It was delicious!

I give a great big beaming smile to Mother Teresa. I want to hug her. Meanwhile Lauren's back from the bathroom and attempting to explain why she ripped the hair from Teresa's now-deceased daughter's head.

'Dan,' I say under my breath.

'What?'

'I wasn't going to tell you this, I was saving it to confront her with, but I can't keep it to myself a minute longer – Lauren did a *lot* worse than stealing Daisy's coursework,' I blurt.

'Georgie, you can't start saying stuff. You don't *know*—'

'I do. I saw it with my own eyes. I was in Lauren's room earlier and—'

'Stop, now!'

'Don't you *dare* speak to me like that.'

I take a large swig of wine and slam my glass down to let him know how angry I am. Then I lean in to him, and whisper in his ear, 'Come outside with me a moment.'

'No. I don't want a scene.'

'Stop being such a dick and come outside with me. If you don't, I'll stab you with the butter knife.'

'Enough of the sweet nothings, my little viper,' he replies under his breath.

'Just going for a breath of fresh air,' I announce to anyone who cares. Nobody does.

He gets up and follows me out, and once we're in the hallway goes to the exterior doors and tries to open them.

'They're stuck. I can't get them open,' he's saying.

'Idiot. I don't want to go outside in the freezing cold. I just wanted to get out of there and into the men's toilets.'

'Is this a new kink or something?' he asks optimistically.

'No . . . I need to *tell* you something, and the toilets are a safe zone – there's no recording equipment in there.'

He rolls his eyes; the irritation has returned. 'I've just left a very nice starter and the champagne is flowing, but you've dragged me away because you want to bang on about Lauren in the gents?'

'It's *huge*, Dan.' I grab his hand and drag him into the doorway of the toilets.

'I don't *CARE* . . .' He tries to back out, but I'm clutching his lapel so he can't. He's terrified of tearing his suit.

'So you aren't interested in what I have to tell you?' I say. 'Even if it puts Lauren in the spotlight and saves you? Dan, what I've discovered about her gives Lauren a strong motive to kill Daisy. That's why I don't want it recorded now, because what I have to tell you will blow everything apart. I want to confront her with this when it's being recorded.'

'That's why we're in the gents' toilets?'

'Yes, because what she did gives her a motive and will take the heat off us . . . especially *you*!'

Suddenly, out of the corner of my eye, I see something move in the mirror in the gents, the reflection of someone moving past the door. I put my finger to my mouth to warn Dan, then I take a step into the corridor to see who it is. Someone is standing just around the corner – watching, and listening – and even from here, I can see exactly who it is.

25

MADDIE

I'm glad Alex came tonight. It's not been easy with this lot – the constant tension wears me down. Lauren's okay but a bit full of herself, especially when Georgie's around; they're both so competitive. Lauren stormed off earlier because Teresa seems to be on to her, then she came back, and when Georgie dragged Dan out of the hall Lauren left again. I get the feeling she followed them, and what's that about? They're all back now, but the atmosphere is so frosty I can't handle it. 'Do you fancy some fresh air?' I whisper to Alex.

'Yeah, definitely.' He's already standing up, obviously as eager as me to leave this ice palace.

'Just popping out for a vape,' I say, and we almost run from the room to make our escape, both giggling with relief as we reach the hallway.

'Fancy a spliff on the back step for old times' sake?' he says.

'You still doing that?'

'Yeah, now and then. Coming back here makes me want to smoke and forget. I may be the CEO of a multimillion-dollar company, but at heart I'm still a messed-up little junkie,' he jokes, referring to the way Dan once described him. These things run deep, and last forever.

We step outside into the freezing winter night, and sit on a step around the side of the building near the kitchen extractor. It's pushing out hot, savoury air, which stops us from freezing to death while he smokes and we talk.

'Jesus, it's cold out here.' I look up into the clear night sky, and an all-seeing full moon glares down at me. 'It's good to get away from them.'

'Yeah. The conversation is a constant middle-class carousel, moving around investments, property and long-haul luxury holidays.'

'Don't forget the cost of private schools.'

'And don't even *talk* about schooling in the US,' he adds. 'Lauren had to leave their place in Bel Air because they couldn't find a school for poor Clementine.'

'Fancy naming your kid after a fruit.'

He laughs at this. 'Meanwhile, Dan is desperately trying to bond with me by making lame sexist comments, while Georgie sits there all waspish, like she just sucked a lemon.'

I'm laughing at this. 'I'd forgotten how funny and bitchy you can be, Alex. I miss you . . . I miss this. Just you, me, talking under the stars.'

'Yeah, I do too.'

We sit and gaze at the night sky. There are no clouds, and the stars are twinkly tonight.

'I hope, if they do reopen the case, the police get it right next time,' Alex says.

'You think David Montgomery was innocent then?'

'I dunno, but I think someone in there knows more than they're letting on.' He looks at me intently as he hands me the spliff.

'If they do, I have no idea who that might be. I'm not convinced of his innocence. Just because he's killed himself, it's brought it to the fore and everyone's suddenly got an opinion.'

He shrugs. 'I often listen to *The Killer Question*, and they're a pretty slick outfit. They do their research, and have a great track record in quashing verdicts. If *they* believe David Montgomery is innocent, there'll be good reason. I've always believed that his conviction had more to do with him being a forty-odd-year-old lecturer having an affair with his teenage student. Jurors are supposed to subjectively evaluate the evidence, but if there were mums and dads on that jury, I reckon unconscious bias could easily have come into play. Throw in some DNA "evidence" and poor old David's banged up for life.'

'You seem very knowledgeable about the case.'

'I'm just interested, and feel for his family who've supported him from the outset. His parents are dead now, but they remortgaged their house to pay the legal bills. His brothers, his wife and extended family – *and* now the victim's mother – think he might have been wrongly convicted! I reckon the case'll be reopened, unless someone confesses first and it's open-and-shut.'

Alex has never struck me as someone interested in true crime, or legal issues, but he's obviously given this some thought.

'I guess, having been in prison myself, I know what it must have been like for the bloke. I was only there for two years, and that was long enough – but he was incarcerated for almost twenty. Imagine.'

'Alex, do you *really* think one of us did it?' I feel a shiver go down my spine.

'Yes . . .'

'Who . . . who do you think it is?' My mouth's dry. I don't want to know.

He's breathing smoke out and shaking his head. '*Don't* . . . We might be being recorded out here,' he says in a low voice.

'We're outside. It's a safe zone, isn't it? They can't record here.'

'I wouldn't be so sure. I think we should be extra-careful.'

'Yeah . . . Better safe than sorry.'

'So, what's it like being back with them?' Alex asks.

'Just the same. None of them have changed,' I say. 'And neither have we. We're still two outcasts sitting outside in the cold.'

'Yeah, that pretty much sums up uni for me. But I've come in from the cold now.'

'Yeah, you have,' I sigh. 'I'm still out there.'

Alex, Daisy and I were bright working-class kids who happened to get into university by the skin of our teeth. The other three were upper middle class with a good education, money and two parents, which created a huge invisible divide right down the middle of our apartment.

'It was the little things that got to me,' I say, 'like Dan leaving Post-it notes saying "Sorry I ate your cheese." He would eat everyone else's food – just help himself to whatever was in the fridge.'

Alex shakes his head. 'So entitled.'

'I know. It was nothing to him, and when I asked him not to take my food because I couldn't afford to buy any more, he said, "God, you look so sexy when you're angry."'

'Ugh, sounds like Dan,' Alex mutters.

'God, he was just a lecherous, selfish, inconsiderate pig. I couldn't believe it when Daisy started seeing him in the second year. I was like, "What the fuck, Daisy?"'

'Well, she wasn't looking for love with Dan, was she?'

'No, by then she just wanted a baby daddy with enough money to support her,' I reply. 'She could be so calculating and manipulative, but funny and bright and . . . I still miss her.'

'Me too.' He leans over and puts his arm around me. 'We all do in our own ways. I bet even Georgie misses her.'

'I doubt that. She was even more angry than I was when Daisy got with Dan,' I say as he hands me the spliff again. I take a long inhale, and hold the smoke in my lungs until I can't remember her, and if I do it doesn't matter. None of it matters, and that's where I like to be.

'Those two are so co-dependent. She plays mummy, and he plays her hapless kid, which means she can indulge in cleaning and nagging, and he can shag around and be naughty.'

'Nailed it. You've nailed it in one sentence, Mr Jones.' I breathe out, watching the smoke escape, dancing and curling in the darkness.

'I remember how they'd make a point of including us whenever we had what they wanted. I provided the nose candy, you'd provide the eye candy, but the rest of the time they ignored us.' He's shaking his head. 'All they ever did was complain about their wealthy parents and the government and how by not eating meat they were doing their bit.'

'I don't know what I'd have done without you and Daisy at uni. You especially kept me sane. And your little side hustle saved us all, Alex.' He gave me money for food and helped Daisy to get out of debt. 'Did Daisy ever pay you back?'

'Nah, but I never expected her to. You and D were like sisters to me.'

'Daisy borrowed off me too. I felt sorry for her – she was desperate and crying, said her mum was going to be evicted. So I took out an extra student loan and emptied my bank account. "We can stay in and eat cheese on toast together," she said. I felt like I'd done a good thing and really helped my friend. But when I couldn't go out because I'd given her all my money, she'd go without me – using my money.' I laugh incredulously. 'She never even bought me a drink, or invited me along.'

'Poor Daisy,' he says. Alex doesn't have a bone of resentment in his body, and I now feel guilty for sounding like a bitch.

'I guess I just expected too much from her.'

'You didn't have to pay me back, you know, Maddie. When I got that cheque last year I was going to return it.'

'I would have been so pissed off with you if you had. I'd owed you that money for years and it weighed me down. I feel like somehow I lost my dignity, and when I started earning good money, I had to buy it back, you know?'

'I understand, and I'm glad the yoga studio's doing so well. I'm proud of you!'

I nod, but can't meet his eyes. My financial success has given me back my dignity, but I need to work on the shame that hangs around my head like a festering mould. I long to tell someone the truth, especially Alex, but I've told so many lies over the years, they're part of me, and I have to live with them. Everyone here is worried about a secret being revealed. I have more than one, and they're pretty dark. I don't want anyone to know about me, what I am, or what I did.

26

Dan

It was all so stressful; Lauren must have heard everything. Georgie was saying that Lauren had a motive to kill Daisy. She said that by revealing Lauren's motive publicly it would take the heat off us, especially me!

I keep going over it in my head. Lauren isn't stupid, and I saw the look on her face – she was hurt and angry at the same time. Women do hurt and angry well.

I do wonder about Georgie. The way she was pointing the finger at Lauren while pointing it at me. Is Georgie trying to throw me under the bus too?

If she is, she'd better be ready for when I push back with my intel on *her*.

We're all back in the dining room now, and I'm sitting opposite Lauren, who won't even make eye contact with me. She's no doubt angry because she assumes I'm on board with Georgie's crazy idea that she had a motive to kill Daisy. I still don't know what the motive is, because when we saw Lauren, Georgie shut up. I'm done with it all – the whispers, the tension, the constant testing of each other. Tonight I'd just like to run away with the cute waitress and tell everyone else to go to hell.

'You need to try and keep stuff to yourself, Georgie,' I say as quietly as my anger will allow. 'You're dropping everyone in it, including me. I thought the whole point of coming here this weekend was to keep what happened *under* the radar, not recorded for two million people to hear.'

'Well, it's going to come out sometime, isn't it?' she hisses.

Suddenly there's a ping, and I feel a jolt in my chest. Is it my heart?

'Voice note,' Alex says, putting his phone in the middle of the table and turning up the volume so we can hear what Tammy has to say next. For him this all seems to be a novelty, a little weekend break, but for us every voice note is another layer of agony.

'Hope you guys are having a great time! So, while the rest of your dinner is served, I'd just like to give you a little background info. Here at The Killer Question, *wrongful convictions are something very close to our hearts. So far, we've worked on twenty-two miscarriages of justice in four years just in the UK, and next year we're hoping to expand and cover some US cases too. So, the odds are on our side this weekend, and we're determined to find out who wanted Daisy dead most.'*

Given that she's talking about us, I find her enthusiasm vaguely threatening.

I catch Alex's eye. 'This is difficult, isn't it, mate?'

He nods, and gives a slight eye-roll.

'Not nice that one of us might be accused of a murder that happened twenty years ago – that someone *else* did and was actually convicted of,' I add, trying not to sound too bitter or defensive. And failing.

He shrugs. 'He never confessed. What can you do?'

Classic Alex – cool as a cucumber.

I lift my glass at him resignedly, then lean in to Georgie. 'I'm sorry, but Alex is *too* bloody relaxed – he's either innocent, or on the Xanax tonight.'

She ignores me – something my wife excels at. Right now, though, I'm more concerned about Alex, as his non-committal shrug might be a sign that he's going to drop me in it. Mind you, this weekend is an exercise in paranoia; every word, every look, every bloody nuance between us is loaded. I had hoped, as the only other bloke here, he might be an ally, but I didn't consider his closeness with Daisy, and now I'm worried that she may have told him something and that's why he's being a bit off with me. Shit!

I'd better try again to be friendly with him, figure out the lay of the land. Is he friend or foe?

I lean across the table to Alex. 'Tammy keeps hinting at stuff, and I think they know more than us.'

'I'm sure they do.'

'Once the sad armchair detectives get involved, a dossier will be winging its way to the police,' I add. But now he's turned back to Maddie and they're talking. *He's deliberately avoiding me.*

And Daisy's mum is giving me the creeps, the way she keeps looking over. This weekend is making me really paranoid.

'Did you enjoy your starter, Teresa?' Georgie asks.

'No, I didn't,' she replies bluntly. 'I just want to know once and for all who took her, and get this over with.' Her voice cracks with emotion.

I look up, about to offer some solace, but the expression on her face is fury, and it's directed right at me.

I don't look at her, but lean in to Georgie. 'She seems hell-bent on finding someone guilty, but she isn't *qualified to make that call* – she's the victim's *mother*.'

'Shush, you're being loud. They're recording, remember?' she says, without looking at me.

But I can't stop talking. I want the recording to pick this up, for the listeners to question what's happening here. I hesitate, then lean in again: 'Is she just going to point the finger at whoever she doesn't like the look of tonight? And then on Monday the mother hath spoken, and the trolls and their mates online gather the "evidence" and make something out of nothing?'

'Dan, you're drawing *attention* to yourself, and you *really* don't want to do that.' Georgie speaks through her teeth while smiling vaguely in Teresa's direction.

I give Teresa one of my most boyish smiles, but she looks away.

I notice Georgie's hands shaking as she lifts her drink, and as the waiting staff lay down bowls of vegetables, platters of meat and our plates, her arm catches the waiter's and she almost knocks it from his hand.

'SHIT!' she declares loudly, and everyone stops talking.

'Calm down,' I'm saying under my breath, as calmly as I can, my voice betraying my own fear.

'Don't tell *me* to *fucking* calm down,' she says while aggressively spooning vegetables on to her plate. Her hands are shaking so much the peas are going everywhere, bright-green beacons on the pure white cloth, a warning as to her state of mind.

She's so tightly wound right now that there's no reaching her. Since she received this invite her anxiety has been off the charts, and she's been cleaning and washing her hands over and over again. I don't understand why she's like this; she says it's my fault, but what the hell have I done?

She seems determined to find something, *anything*, on Lauren. I wonder what she knows? Or is Lauren just an easy target for Georgie to put in the spotlight while flying under the radar herself? There's so much going through my mind, my head feels fuzzy.

Suddenly our phones ping. 'God, that made me jump,' I groan. 'You'd think we'd be used to it by now. But as most of the pinging happens around food, I reckon I'll develop a Pavlovian response after this weekend. Every time I get a WhatsApp in future I'll start to dribble!' They all laugh at this, and even old Teresa breaks a little smile.

'They don't have WhatsApp in prison, mate,' Alex 'jokes'.

What the fuck? I'm shocked at the implication, but manage to laugh along. 'Well, you've been there, you should know,' I reply with a fake chuckle. He's really pissed me off, saying that. Does he suspect me? Is he going to try and drop me in it?

I need to keep it up – the idea that I'm innocent and therefore not scared . . . *I'm not scared. I'm innocent. Not scared.*

Alex is now pressing play on his phone, like he's in charge, and that's also winding me up.

'As we always say, The Killer Question *is about crime, but it's also about the impact of that crime. We don't just report the lurid details in a sensational way . . .'*

'You could have fooled me,' I murmur, rolling my eyes.

It's the most sensationalised rubbish I've ever heard, but I don't say any more. Georgie's elbowing my ribs and Teresa is homing in on me like an Exocet missile.

'We also speak with those affected by crime. And we specialise in murder, the victim's story, their family and friends – anyone whose life has been impacted by, in our view, the worst possible crime: taking someone else's life.

'Through our listeners, our podcast has more time, more manpower, and more detective skills than the whole of the British police force. Families and prisoners come to us with suspected wrongful convictions, and we fight for those we believe in. We aren't exclusive or judgemental, and we talk to the alleged perpetrator's family, digging into their past to find out what makes them tick. But this case is different, because one half of the whole – Professor David Montgomery – isn't with us

anymore. He took his own life, and denied he committed the murder until his last breath.

'Shortly, we'll be chatting with Louisa Montgomery, the professor's widow. She's going to talk about something that, in the police investigation, was considered to be the catalyst for the lead-up to Daisy's death.'

I bite into my beef; it's slow-cooked, savoury and bloody. The voice note ends, and I pour myself a large glass of red in an attempt to imagine I'm at a normal dinner party. I'm telling myself that we aren't all potential killers, just old friends enjoying a weekend reunion. But who am I kidding?

My stomach clenches, threatening to eject the fleshy beef. I imagine it landing on the white tablecloth, messy with blood and wine, dotted with the bright-green peas my wife spilled earlier with her shaky hands. I continue to eat my beef and try not to think of the post-mortem, Daisy's body on the slab, the knife slicing into that perfect young flesh.

'I haven't slept for twenty years . . .' Teresa's saying, dragging me from my waking nightmare. 'And this is torture. All I want is for them to find the guilty person who's sat back all these years and watched a man rot in jail until he couldn't anymore. I'm her mother, I need closure – I can't move on or even die until I know the right person is locked up.'

'I agree, I completely agree,' Lauren gushes. 'Whoever killed Daisy *targeted* her. When I did the research for my first book, *A Day in the Life and Death*, about the rites of passage of a young, working-class woman in a world that didn't hear her, I obviously didn't base it on Daisy's story, it was a work of fiction, but—'

'Yeah, any resemblance to actual persons, even those based on real people living or dead, is purely coincidental,' Georgie chuckles. No one responds, except Lauren who shoots her a look that could kill, before continuing her weird schmoozing of Daisy's mother.

'Sorry I was interrupted, but what I was saying, Teresa, was . . . As I wrote the book, which may have been inspired by Daisy's love of life, her sense of humour, her—'

'What are you trying to say?' Teresa asks.

'Well – while I was researching, I realised that Daisy's murder was a crime of passion, and I believe that Professor Montgomery was the killer. Perhaps it wasn't an act of hatred, but an act of love – and he loved Daisy too much?'

Georgie starts to slow-clap, and my stomach dips. 'Bravo! Nice little book plug there, Lauren, and you got your innocent plea in that speech too – cos, let's face it, no one could accuse you of loving Daisy too much.'

And we're off!

Georgie's smirking, while Lauren glares at her with the coldest eyes I've ever seen.

'I think there are some crimes that begin with a small thing, then move into darker territories, like sex crimes and murder,' Teresa suddenly announces. We all take notice, out of respect, but also because she seems to have something to say. 'These perverts get a taste for it and have to go back, and once you've done something like that you could do anything.' She turns to me. 'Don't you agree?'

27

LAUREN

Teresa is glaring at Dan. Is this who she believes is the *murderer*? Everyone's looking awkwardly at everyone else, except of course Maddie, who's asking, 'What did she say?' Classic Maddie.

Meanwhile the blood's drained from Dan's face; no little jokes or witty repartee from him right now. I do feel a bit sorry for him, despite being annoyed at overhearing his wife telling him I had a motive to kill Daisy, and him not defending me.

'Teresa, I'm not sure what you're implying,' Dan eventually manages to say.

'Nothing. I just wanted to see your face when I said that.'

'Oh . . . It was a test?' he asks hopefully.

'You can take what you like from it. I have my views, and a right to air them.'

'Yes, of course, and we all respect your views,' he says in the patronising tone he always used with Maddie and Alex. 'But you *can't* implicate any of us without evidence or some kind of proof.'

'Who says I don't have evidence . . . on any of you?'

'This isn't a party game, Teresa. Whatever you say will be broadcast to a hell of a lot of people tomorrow evening!' Georgie's voice is raised, her face pink with fury.

'Good, then I can get my message across.' Teresa clearly feels attacked, and sounds like she's on the verge of tears. This is typical of Dan and Georgie: they would often form a tag team and gang up on someone. I think we all faced that ordeal at some point, and at the beginning of second year, just before she died, they seemed to target Daisy most of all. I wonder why?

'Yes, but being Daisy's mother doesn't give you *immunity*.' Georgie's so fiercely protective of Dan, it makes me wonder if the lady doth protest too much. 'I mean, you can't say *anything* about *anybody* in public, especially for broadcast. There are laws to protect people from this kind of thing – we could just as easily say *you* did it!' she snaps, and Teresa starts to cry.

'*Georgie*,' Dan groans.

Maddie's up off her seat, followed by Alex, both now comforting Teresa. Maddie has her arm around her and Alex is handing her napkins while Dan and Georgie sit there with faces of stone.

'I wouldn't harm a hair on Daisy's head. I'm her mother!' Teresa sobs. 'How could you even think something so horrible? She was *my* little girl.'

'Georgie didn't mean—' Dan starts.

'I'm sorry, Dan, but you can't defend your wife's behaviour this time.' I have to say something. 'As the grieving mother of a murder victim, Teresa should be treated with respect and kindness, not attacked by your wife!' I snap.

He doesn't respond. He knows he can't justify her behaviour to others. I can see what his life with Georgie is now – he told me himself, it's just one drama crashing into the next.

'Lauren, this has nothing to do with you!' Georgie's rage is gathering like a storm. 'She's virtually just accused my husband of sex crimes and murder – she can't *say* shit like that!'

'Suddenly you're pushing back on what Teresa's saying?' I yell back. 'I don't remember you stepping in to defend me when she said I'd stolen Daisy's coursework. Where was your outrage and your devotion to laws that protect people? No – you were licking your lips then.'

She's sitting there, arms folded tightly across her, mouth clamped down sullenly. If she were a cartoon, steam would be puffing from her head. She's furious that someone's called her out, and I'm so here for it.

When I overheard her earlier saying I had a motive to kill Daisy, it felt like she'd sliced into my flesh. I will never forgive her for pointing the finger at me, and in that sneaky way too – not to my face, but to Dan, and loud enough to be recorded, even though they were standing in the toilets.

I watch the candles flicker on the table, and decide to start a few little fires of my own.

'The thing is,' I start slowly, running my fingertip around the edge of my glass, 'I think Georgie may be being a bit hypocritical regarding unfounded accusations.' I give it a beat; timing has always been my strong point. 'Because only minutes before Teresa implied Dan may know a thing or two about sex crimes and murder, Georgie was – behind my back – accusing me of having a motive to kill Daisy!'

I wait for the reaction. Maddie does the usual confused gasp, Alex stays cool, and Georgie's body language shows her discomfort. So far, so students of Apartment 101 St Luke's Campus 2005.

I lean forward. 'Just wondering if it's time to roast you, Georgie.' I wink, and pick up my fork. It brushes against my glass, almost knocking it over, but Dan catches it. Sharp, devastating words sit on the tip of my tongue. But I must resist. I will watch and listen and work out how best to handle this, and when to strike the blow that will destroy her.

'Lauren, I agree, it must have sounded awful, what Georgie was saying . . . but . . . no one was accusing you of killing Daisy.' Dan's obviously so scared that I'm going to blow his cover.

'Calm down, Dan . . . I'm not going to drop you in it!' I reply.

Georgie's eyes dart from me to him and back again, questioning.

'You thought you knew everything about your husband, didn't you?' I pause, lifting my wine glass and raising it to her. 'Well, think again.' I take a long sip, smiling as I place the glass back on the table. Georgie's glaring at me like she's mesmerised – numb. She hasn't a clue.

Suddenly, our phones ping. 'Another audio file,' I announce, and I tap my phone screen and lay it on the table so everyone can hear. I'm glad the conversation was interrupted; I don't actually have the energy for a row with Georgie. And, given her theory on my motive to kill Daisy, I need to be careful: I don't want that secret split wide open here.

28

Transcript from *The Killer Question* Podcast

Episode 7: Interview with Louisa Montgomery, Professor David Montgomery's Wife

TAMMY: As promised earlier, we're interviewing Louisa Montgomery, widow of David – or Professor M, as he was affectionately known by his students.

LOUISA: Thank you for having me . . .

TAMMY: My pleasure. Is it true you and David were childhood sweethearts?

LOUISA: Not exactly, though we were eighteen when we met at Cambridge.

TAMMY: Oh, so it was a meeting of minds?

LOUISA: Yes.

TAMMY: So, tell me a little about your life with David.

LOUISA: It was perfect, or so I thought. We were both academics, had a good family life with our two children, enjoyed the theatre. We had dreams of retiring to France one day, buying an old farmhouse, doing it up.

TAMMY: You were happy?

LOUISA: Yes – very.

TAMMY: And then . . .

LOUISA: It was October 2nd, 2005. I remember it because it was the end of life as I knew it. That morning an envelope arrived at home, addressed to me, and I wandered into the kitchen opening it. David and the children were having breakfast, they were laughing and loud and . . . everyone was noisy and . . . happy. *(Louisa takes a breath.)* We were chatting about a half-term holiday, planning a trip to the Dordogne. And as I was talking, I pulled out the contents of the envelope, placing the letter on the table . . . and as the family had breakfast and laughed and joked, I started to read the letter.

(Louisa stops talking, then seems to compose herself.)

It was so cruel, revealing intimate details about David and her, but also about our marriage, things only he could have told her. That hurt more than anything else – to know he'd shared personal information about our relationship with a teenager. The tone was horrible – she mocked me, said he didn't love me and he needed someone younger like her.

I found it hard to forgive Daisy for that. It's one thing telling me my husband's having an affair – but the details, they were so unnecessary. The extra pain was . . . well, sadistic. She showed no remorse or empathy. Then she ended the letter by saying, 'I'm having his baby, he's leaving you and we're going to run away together.'

TAMMY: And you'd had no idea, of the affair or the pregnancy?

LOUISA: No . . . This was the first I knew. She told me in her letter.

TAMMY: And when you say 'she', you mean Daisy? She was definitely the one who wrote the letter?

LOUISA: It was signed, 'Love, Daisy.'

TAMMY: That must have been so hard.

LOUISA: Brutal . . .

TAMMY: So, can we just rewind a little, back to the morning the letter arrived. For you, was that the end of your marriage?

LOUISA: Yes. He'd thrown away our lives and our family for a fling with a student. He'd betrayed me, but he'd betrayed Daisy too, sleeping with someone so young who looked up to him. It was a different world, before #MeToo. The power dynamic was unhealthy, and no one was looking out for girls like Daisy Harrington. She was nineteen, and he was forty-four – twenty-five years older.

TAMMY: Wow.

LOUISA: I remember thinking about my own daughters, and how I'd feel as Daisy's mother. She was in his care . . . *(Louisa is struggling to find the words.)* David was a lecturer, a trusted adult, and Daisy's mum should have been able to trust that her daughter was safe in his care. I found it hard to get past that. I just felt disappointed in my husband, and as much as I resented her and was hurt by the letter, as a mother I also felt protective of Daisy.

TAMMY: Just a matter of weeks after you received the letter, there was even worse news – that Daisy was missing. Did it ever cross your mind that David may have had something to do with her disappearance?

LOUISA: I have to be honest, of course it did. But I never imagined for a moment he'd hurt her. I did wonder if perhaps she'd gone away, and he knew where she was. It occurred to me that he was planning to meet her, and they were going to run away together. But by then he was saying he didn't love her, he loved me and wanted to try again, and we had the girls and our home and our life – I thought it was over with her.

TAMMY: But then Daisy's body was found in a beach hut you owned on Exmouth Beach, very close to your home. There were no signs of anyone breaking into the hut – in fact the hut was locked, so whoever had killed her locked the door after themselves, and the police and prosecution said this could only have been David. Louisa, didn't you even think then that your husband might just be guilty . . . ?

LOUISA: Some days I wondered if he knew more about it than he was saying. And the police finding her body in our beach hut was pretty damning, I can't deny it. Then, of course, there was the trial, which I found incredibly hard. I was horrified that a young girl had died, but the humiliation of sitting in court hearing intimate details about their relationship was almost too much for me. And after his imprisonment, I'll be honest, I found it hard to even think about him without crying or feeling such anger. I wanted to punch walls. It took me a long time to get in touch, or even respond to his letters. I refused to visit him, and certainly wasn't taking the girls into a prison – they were too young. But his parents had fought hard for his innocence throughout, and when they died there was no one on the outside for him, so I continued with the campaign. I did it for my children, but also . . . I knew my husband, and I was never truly convinced that he was capable of murder.

TAMMY: Do you have your own suspicions who the real killer might be?

LOUISA: Yes, I have my suspicions . . .

TAMMY: Is the person you have your suspicions about someone who shared the house with Daisy?

LOUISA: Yes . . . Yes, it is.

29

GEORGIE

'Oh wow!' Lauren can hardly contain herself. 'Who is it?'

'It's still David, obviously,' I say quickly. *Too* quickly.

'Are you sure?'

'Of course I'm sure!' I reply, irritated.

'Christ, you're defensive this evening, Georgie – well, more defensive than usual.'

'I'm not defensive, Lauren. I'm just stating the bloody obvious,' I say, trying to stay calm, and give nothing away. I have to keep pushing the idea that it was David, even if it wasn't. 'I mean, Louisa can whitewash the past as much as she likes, and she's obviously managed to convince Teresa too – but I'm not buying it. David did it. End of!'

I can't stop talking. I could kick myself – I should have kept my fucking mouth shut.

'I disagree, I think it might be one of us . . . and perhaps someone covered for him, *Georgie*?' Lauren replies smugly.

What the fuck?

I feel Dan flinch next to me; he grabs my knee, telling me to shut up, but I push him away.

I look around the table, panicked, desperate for some support. I know I won't get it from my husband, but one of the others? Maddie? Alex? Surely Alex will confirm I'm not harbouring a murderer? But nothing.

'Lauren can't *say* that!'

'She just did!' Lauren pipes up.

'*You* have a bigger motive than anyone else here, Lauren, so I'd shut up if I were you,' I spit back. She looks like she's just been smacked in the face, and next time I'll do it for real.

'Calm. *Down*,' Dan's saying quietly into my ear.

'No, Dan, stop telling me what to *do*! It's rubbish, just malicious rubbish, to imply that you . . . and I . . .' I'm ranting now, and even Dan's looking at me with fear rather than concern.

'You're digging a deeper hole for yourself, Georgie,' Lauren remarks coolly. 'No one has accused you *or* your husband of *anything*. I just said I wonder if someone is hiding in—'

'You don't need to repeat it for the fucking recording, we all *heard* what you said!'

I'm clutching the table, aware I might be a little out of control, but what can I do? My therapist says I should talk to myself, say things like 'It's okay, this won't kill me' and 'I am good enough' or another line from a long list of meaningless shit. Like everything else my therapist suggests, it's totally impractical. Lauren's just implied Dan is the killer and I'm covering for him, which is *terrifying*. Everyone's staring at me open-mouthed. The horror on their faces suggests they might be thinking I'm slightly unhinged. To begin telling myself 'I am good enough' on a loop while at the table is probably not advisable right now.

I see Teresa out of the corner of my eye, and suddenly feel bad – we're talking about her daughter's murder, after all. 'Sorry,' I mumble in her direction. 'I'm just upset.'

Teresa says nothing while the others make soothing noises, like I'm a wild animal that needs to be calmed.

'You can imagine how all the saddos listening to this podcast will react,' I say. 'All they'll hear is *Georgie is hiding her husband, the killer*. There'll be no rational thought, no questioning, they'll drink it in blindly, like a baby taking a bottle. Mark my words, there'll be a bloody price on my head.'

I push away my plate, untouched. I thought I'd managed everything so well. Stupid me, I guess.

Lauren's sitting there smugly toying with her beef and making eyes at my husband while the others just stare ahead, embarrassed.

I take a large swig of Merlot and then, grabbing the bottle, fill my glass up.

'Whoa,' Dan warns from the side.

'Oh, fuck off, Dan.'

Teresa sits up in her seat, as if to assert herself. 'That letter to Louisa wasn't written by Daisy,' she says firmly. 'Daisy wouldn't have written a letter like that – it was cruel, and my daughter wasn't cruel. Someone *else* wrote that letter.'

Fuck!

'Why would anyone *else* write that letter?' I ask, knowing I should shut up now, but I daren't allow even the tiniest seed to be left out there to grow.

'*You* might?' Teresa offers, and I see Lauren's eyes sparkle with mirth and her hand fly to her mouth.

I almost throw up on the spot.

'I remember Daisy calling me. She said David was annoyed, he was surprised that she'd sent such a vicious letter to his wife. Daisy didn't know what he was talking about, and he kept saying "the letter you sent to Louisa". David was concerned that, now she knew, Louisa would go to the university, kick up a stink, get him sacked and Daisy thrown off the course. "I never sent a letter to his wife, Mum," she said. "I wouldn't do that."'

I'm trying to take deep breaths without the others seeing.

'I asked her, if she didn't send it – who did? And she thought about it, then said, "I think it was Georgie . . . She *suggested* I send a letter to his wife, to break up their marriage." Daisy said she'd been horrified at this suggestion and rejected it completely.' Teresa looks over at me. 'She said, for someone to suggest such a thing, they must be a psycho – that's what my daughter thought.'

She takes a sip of her wine, like she hasn't just been recorded saying the murder victim called me a psycho just weeks before she died.

'I reckon Lauren wrote it,' I announce, ignoring the sound coming from Lauren's mouth, now wide open in theatrical outrage.

'That's not what Daisy said,' Teresa replies.

'Daisy didn't know who sent it, you just admitted that,' I reply. 'She thought it might be me but it could just as easily have been Lauren. You see what I'm saying, Teresa? We can't just accuse anyone because someone "thought" it might be them.'

'And therefore you can't say it was me, hypocrite!' Lauren says, glaring at me.

'I can make an educated guess.' I just keep going, batting off everything they're throwing at me. 'Lauren was always whingeing about Daisy getting preferential treatment because she was sleeping with the course leader.' I'm addressing the whole table now. 'We've already heard how Lauren came on to David – it would have been very much in her interests to split them up, and that letter did just that. David finished with Daisy as soon as the letter arrived. He was angry and probably disturbed that she'd do such a thing. And that's exactly what she planned, didn't you, Lauren?' I add, fighting as hard as I can.

'Well, if it's an educated guess you want, Georgie, here's one,' Teresa starts. I dread to hear what's going to come out of this woman's mouth next. 'I asked Daisy if she thought Lauren might have sent it, but, as my daughter pointed out, Lauren's an English student. And according to Daisy, she wouldn't have written it like that, she would have been softer. It was a brutal letter – Louisa told me herself, it was nasty. My Daisy wasn't nasty – and she could spell. Daisy said whoever wrote that letter didn't even spell "Montgomery" right, and trust me, Daisy knew how to spell that. So would Lauren – after all, he was her tutor too. If Lauren was writing as Daisy, she wouldn't have made that mistake.'

Shit.

'Okay . . . Okay, so *Daisy* thought I wrote that letter?' I ask.

'Yes. Because you'd already suggested she do it, and she'd refused.'

'But why would I even *think she should do that?*'

'Daisy said you wanted to throw a bomb into her life, that you knew a letter like that could get her thrown off the course. And that would have suited you – because you realised by then that Dan and Daisy had become close. You didn't trust Dan, and you saw Daisy as a threat to your relationship.'

'*What?*' I look around at everyone, trying to show shock.

'She said you were insecure and couldn't bear to let him out of your sight. It drove you mad if they did anything together, even if it was going for a coffee or a walk.'

'That's just not true,' I lie.

But it is true, and as hard as I try to deny this, I know the others are doubting me. I used to be eaten up with jealousy and suspicion, always wary, assuming he was sleeping with others. And yes, I followed him, and Daisy, and I was tormented by jealousy. But how can I admit to that and not look guilty?

Mind you, if I continue to deny that I wrote the letter, I could incriminate myself and end up being accused of far worse than a stupid letter.

'Daisy told David it was you. But by then he was just so angry with her he wouldn't listen – he assumed she'd sent the letter to end his marriage, and deliberately misspelt his name so he'd think someone else did it.'

'Perhaps that's what she did?' I offer half-heartedly, but judging by the look on Teresa's face I'm wasting my time. She knows I sent that letter, and everyone's looking from her to me, waiting to see who speaks next.

This is mortifying, but there's only one thing I can do. I have to publicly own up to this.

'Okay, okay. I'm sorry, Teresa, I admit I sent the letter. I wanted her away from Dan, out of our lives and out of the house – so yes, I'm sorry, I wrote that letter, but that's *all* I did.'

The whole stupid thing backfired anyway. She and Dan were just friends, but when David dumped her, she was so upset, and like most pretty girls Daisy needed another man to turn to. She needed someone who'd massage her ego, be her puppy dog until she could get David back – enter Dan Levine, the rich, good-looking idiot-in-waiting.

'In my defence, I was an insecure nineteen-year-old in love for the first time,' I say, attempting to appeal to Teresa's better nature. 'I was crazy about Dan, very insecure – and Daisy was gorgeous and charismatic and a huge threat.' I turn to Teresa, and her face seems to soften slightly.

'But the letter was key evidence. It was used by the prosecution to prove that David had reason to kill my daughter,' she replies angrily. 'The prosecution said that's *why* he killed her, because the letter had shaken him, and he was scared of what Daisy would do next. If you'd come clean then, the truth may have come out, and whoever it is you're covering for might now be in prison – where they should be.'

'I admit it was stupid to send that letter, I was wrong, and what I did had far-reaching consequences. But how could I know what would happen – how could anyone? But I promise you, I'm not covering for someone else,' I say, realising this isn't strictly true. I've been protecting, forgiving and making excuses for Dan all my adult life. But I can't say that, not now.

'Look, Teresa.' Dan finally steps in, if only to protect himself. 'Regardless of who wrote the letter, if David thought it was Daisy who wrote it – then he'd still have motive to kill her. It doesn't make him innocent because Georgie wrote the letter!'

'Exactly. I haven't been protecting *anyone*. Teresa, believe me, I never meant to cause all this trouble. I was young and stupid and wrote that letter to try and keep my boyfriend. But when Daisy was killed, everything was suddenly under the microscope.' I turn to the others. 'I know you guys felt it too – we were kids and we behaved like kids, doing the stuff all teenagers do away from home. We slept around and drank too much and partied all night. We were young and free and it was like being at the fairground, having the time of our lives, when suddenly the ride stopped and the world went dark.'

'You should have told the police you wrote the letter, Georgie,' Maddie chides in a five-year-old's voice.

'I realise that now,' I reply coldly, and turn to Teresa. 'After Daisy had gone there seemed to be no point in telling anyone I'd written the letter; it wouldn't bring her back, and truthfully I didn't see the significance. Like everyone else, I just assumed David was her killer, and when the letter was produced as evidence in court, I thought *good, that will convict him.*'

Everyone's still looking at me, but one person is openly enjoying my distress. *Lauren.* She's half-smiling, her eyes sliding over to Maddie and Alex, then back to Dan, but while they all look serious and concerned, I feel like she wants them to join in with her and laugh at me. I feel foolish – I made that confession hoping everyone would understand what it took. And now she's humiliating and belittling me, and this has pushed me over the edge. My embarrassment has transformed into a boiling rage that can't be contained. Nothing and no one can stop what I'm about to do. I lower my voice and lean across the table.

'Are you *laughing* at me?'

She glares at me, and the smile fades.

'I *said*, are you *laughing* at me?'

She swallows, and without taking her eyes from mine, shakes her head slowly.

'That's *enough*, Georgie.' Dan reaches for my arm.

'Get *off* me!' I knock his hand away.

I continue to glare at Lauren. No one around the table dares move; they're all terrified of me, just like Daisy was. But then I catch her glimpsing anxiously at Dan, her eyes pleading with him for help. How *dare* she ask my husband for help?

Still holding my full glass of Merlot, I slowly move my chair back, and it grates in the silence that folds around us as I stand. Dan knows what's going to happen, and he knows he can't stop me, and he turns away in embarrassment like the coward that he is – and always has been.

I lift my glass, and see the horror on her face as the red liquid splashes on to her head and face and soaks into her pale-cream silk designer dress like warm blood.

30

Maddie

'God, I hate all this upset,' I murmur, as I help Lauren try to soak as much of the red wine as possible from her dress. Everyone knows Georgie has a temper, but watching her tip a full glass over Lauren was still shocking to witness. I saw it coming, and when it happened it felt like slow motion. For a few seconds after, we all just sat there open-mouthed.

Dan called Georgie 'an idiot', and she burst into tears and ran from the dining room. Then Lauren started swearing and whimpering about her dress and ran to the toilets. I followed her, and found her trying desperately to wipe off the red stain. It was quite chilling; she reminded me of Lady Macbeth.

I'm now on my knees pressing paper towels all over it to try to get the stain off. She's already shouted at me for rubbing at the silk, but how would I know you're not supposed to rub at silk with wet paper towels? I'm really trying to help her but, as is often the case with me, I think I'm just being annoying.

'Was it an expensive dress?' I ask.

'It's fucking Gucci!'

'Oh, Lauren, that must have cost a fortune – is it insured?'

'Is it *fuck*, it's *hired*.'

'Oh dear.' I press harder with the towels. 'I'm sure the hire company will be insured.' Red wine seeps into the paper like blood, but I try not to think about it.

'No, they'll charge me for the dress. Christ knows how much this will cost me.'

'It won't be that much, I'm sure.'

'But I don't have any money, Maddie!'

'What do you mean?' I look up enquiringly, but she obviously decides not to elaborate.

'Oh, forget it, forget I said that. What a bitch Georgie is. She's always had anger issues, that one. I'm not surprised everyone thinks she killed Daisy.'

I don't respond. I'm not getting involved in any of that; I'm staying under the radar. There are too many loose tongues around here, as Mum used to say.

'The dress is clearly ruined, there's no point in even trying,' she's saying hopelessly as I continue to kneel on the floor, pressing paper towels on to the fabric like my life depends on it. 'There's no *point*, Maddie,' she repeats, gently pushing me away.

I know this, but am compelled to keep going. I'm desperately hoping that if I do it for long enough the towels will eventually lift off *all* the red liquid. I need to see it gone.

'Just one more towel,' I say, like a gambler at a fruit machine. 'This one might just be the lucky towel.'

She laughs hopelessly at this, then stops and looks at me. 'Maddie, I'm sorry, I think I snapped at you then. You're always so kind, even if what you're doing now does feel a bit weird and ritualistic.' She's looking down at me and we both smile as I abandon the not-so-lucky towel and stand up.

'I wish we'd been friends back then,' she says with a sigh. 'My fault,' she adds presumptuously, like I had no say, it was her choice not to be my friend. 'I was very closed off,' she's saying. 'I only wanted to be friends with people like *me*. I never saw it then, but you're bright and funny – there's more to you than meets the eye . . . but I just wanted Daisy to myself. I wanted the best-friend experience. You know, secrets and gossip – just the two of us.' She pauses and, staring ahead, says, 'I still miss her.'

Daisy never shared secrets and gossip with Lauren; she didn't trust her. I was Daisy's friend, and we were always in each other's orbit one way or another, from the first day of the first year until she died. Our relationship ebbed and flowed, like her – hot and cold, happy and sad – but I was the consistent one, always there for her when she needed a shoulder to lean on. And before she died, Daisy and I drifted together again, probably because she and Lauren had fallen out, but I was happy to take the crumbs where Daisy was concerned.

I'd seen who Lauren was early on. I'd known girls like her at ballet school. So competitive, and driven by enormous ambition. But Lauren never felt good enough; she was always coveting someone else's clothes or work or boyfriend. And having targeted the beautiful, bright A-student Daisy, she hoped some of the stardust might rub off on her. Daisy was pursued by Dan, Lauren, and to a degree by Georgie too – they all wanted what she had. Daisy was just effortlessly cool; she wore second-hand clothes, and gathered her hair up in a loose bun and looked stunning. She was clever and funny and everyone just wanted to be in her company, but she was a social butterfly, always fluttering off. Perhaps it was her elusiveness that captivated them?

This was agony for Lauren, whose competitive nature hated to be constantly outshone by Daisy. Lauren was never able to focus on her own goals because she was too busy comparing herself to her clever, beautiful friend.

I'd seen this kind of overriding competitiveness, in ballet, when dancers literally fell during a move because they weren't focused. The teacher would yell at them, 'Eyes front', and the dancer would start by looking at the wall in front of them – some teachers even made a mark with a felt tip to look at. They would then hold their head high and maintain eye contact with that reference point while they started the turn. Once they'd turned so far that their head couldn't stay in that forward-facing position any longer, they'd quickly whip their head around in the direction of the turn and immediately face forward again, focusing on that same spot. However, if for a moment they broke concentration by glancing over at another dancer, they lost focus, and often fell to the ground. I always thought of this when I watched Lauren with Daisy – she was always looking around to see what she was doing, and if she needed to compete, or criticise, or copy her. She was obsessed with Daisy, and if Daisy received high marks, or someone paid her a compliment, or anything positive happened for her – it was quite chilling to see Lauren's reaction. Consequently Lauren was so obsessed with what was happening with Daisy that she lost sight of the spot on her own wall, and fell to the ground. I know she continued at uni after Daisy's death, but I heard she struggled, and no one was as surprised as she was at her success with the book. I watched an interview with her once on TV and she just seemed sad and angry.

'Did you see the way she looked at me?' Lauren is saying as we wash our hands. 'I saw such hate in her eyes before she threw that wine, and I thought . . .' She grabs my arm for impact. 'Is her hate the last thing Daisy saw?'

Again, I don't respond, not willing to partake in this pointless, damaging gossip.

Lauren is studying me now, leaning against the sink, just looking into my face, the garish red blot screaming from the cream silk dress.

'You still don't say much, do you, Maddie? You've always been loyal to us all, I think. You've never gossiped.' I think she's frustrated that I won't dish with her about Georgie, but who am I to criticise anyone?

'I just find it a bit uncomfortable, if I'm honest. I'm nothing special, just Maddie from the block,' I joke. 'I'm still addicted to Snickers, still love the Spice Girls. And I'm always out of the loop, never quite sure what everyone's on about.'

She laughs properly at this. 'I think the ballet might have stunted your emotional and social growth,' she offers, and smiles at me warmly, completely unaware of the massive insult she's just hurled. 'But you certainly have more self-insight than anyone else in there,' she adds, nodding her head in the direction of the dining hall.

'Thanks, I think.' It doesn't feel like a compliment; it feels patronising.

'Georgie really should have told the police it was her that sent the letter,' she starts, back on her favourite subject of Georgie-hating. 'Coming back to it now, twenty years on, it really makes her look like a liar at best . . . And at worst . . .'

Does she expect me to finish that filthy sentence? Because I'm not going to.

I just nod. I don't know what to say. I can hardly defend Georgie – by sending that letter she started something that ended in Daisy's death.

'Come on, let's get back in there,' Lauren says. 'We don't want them all talking about us in our absence.' She grabs me by the arm and ushers me through the doors. She's bloody paranoid – if I was her, I would have stayed in the bathroom longer, waited for everything to die down. But, for all her talk, I've realised Lauren lacks confidence; she's scared of being talked about – and even more scared of being left out.

'Don't you want to change your dress before going back in, Lauren?' I ask as we walk along the corridor.

'No . . . I'm going to keep it on all night, as a reminder to Georgie of just what she did.'

Classic Lauren. Why move on when you can hang on, and keep milking a situation?

There's a sudden ping, and I check my phone: a full audio file's been sent. 'I think it's another interview,' I say to Lauren, and I press play on my phone.

'Hey guys! My name's Ali West, you might remember I was a young reporter back in the day, and I covered a lot of the story around Daisy going missing and the subsequent murder investigation – including the court case. I'm standing in for Tammy in this next interview, and the reason for this will soon become clear.'

Lauren and I look at each other as we walk in and take our seats next to the others, and I stop playing the audio file as Alex already has it playing on his phone.

'In this recorded episode of The Killer Question: Who Wanted Daisy Dead? *I'd like to welcome Professor David Montgomery's two daughters. Welcome,'* says Ali.

'Hey Ali, thanks for standing in today to interview us,' says a familiar voice.

'Yeah, thanks, Ali!' says another.

'Confused? You will be. If you haven't already guessed, guys, today's interview is unique. The podcast host, Tammy, and her sister, the podcast producer Tiffany, are in fact Cordelia and Cassandra – David Montgomery's daughters.'

'Whaaat?' Dan's shaking his head. We're all feeling the same.

'What a plot twist!' Lauren gasps.

'Who?' I ask, just to play my part.

'The bloody podcasters are David's *daughters*!' Georgie hisses.

'Keep up, Maddie!' Dan adds good-naturedly.

'So the girls are actually called . . . Cordelia and Cassandra, but as they have unusual first names their relationship to David Montgomery might easily have been discovered on Google. So, when starting the

podcast, they decided to call themselves Tammy and Tiffany, giving themselves American backstories and American accents.'

'*We didn't want our story to overshadow anyone else's, that is, until we were able to reveal the truth – and that time is now,*' says Tammy.

Yes, I'm Cordelia, but on air I'm still Tammy – even before we started to fight for Dad's innocence, my 'podcast persona,' has always been, California Tammy. My sis and I had a tough time growing up, and this podcast has allowed us to escape from reality, to have a façade for the outside world, but keep our real selves hidden, safe from the spotlight. I hope you understand, and don't feel too deceived.

'*Okay, so let's start this story!*' says Ali. '*Tiffany, or rather Cassandra, you're the younger sister. How old were you when your father went to prison?*'

'*I was eight and my sister was ten. My dad went to prison in 2007, two years after . . . Daisy died.*'

'*That must have been so difficult for you both.*'

'*Yes. Despite us being so young, there was a lot of abuse, online trolling – not aimed at us, aimed at Dad, but it was tough – and our mum suffered a lot.*'

'*When your father was first imprisoned, you were involved with the campaign to get him released. Tammy, can you tell me, did you ever believe your father was guilty?*'

'*No, I didn't, and we worked with Mum and our grandparents – Dad's parents – to try and prove that. But back then everyone believed the right man was locked away, and the world wouldn't listen.*'

'*You were just little girls. How did your lives change as a result of the conviction?*'

'*A lot,*' says Tammy. '*Our grandparents sold their home and spent their life savings on lawyers, and this continued when we attempted to start appeals. Mum was later forced to sell our family home, and her mental health suffered – she couldn't work.*'

'We did have supporters, but we were constantly being attacked, both online and in person,' adds Tiffany. 'People sometimes shouted at us in the street, saying, "Hope your murdering dad dies in prison."'

'Yeah, it was a horrible time,' Tammy concedes. 'But then, about ten years ago, the TV news interviewed us and we talked about how much we'd been through, even though we'd never committed a crime. And since then people have been a bit kinder.'

'And you told me earlier that something else came from that TV interview?' asks Ali.

'Yes, after it aired, we received an anonymous donation,' replies Tammy.

'Was it a large donation?'

'Yeah. I don't like to say how much, but it was extremely large. So much that at first we thought it was a joke. Then we were worried it might be illegal to accept it, so we contacted the police and explained that it had arrived in our bank via a money order. They said, "Looks like you have a rich benefactor."'

'Wow!'

'Yeah. It's an annual payment, and apparently we'll have this for life.'

'And you've no idea who this person is?'

'No. It could be a complete stranger,' says Tiffany. 'We have a theory that it must be family on Dad's side who are keen to help us, but don't want to be involved in the scandal. We are so grateful, as the money helped us both through university, and we've been able to buy a home for Mum and put money away for our futures. We also started the podcast with some of the money, and pay lawyers' fees and researchers for the cases we're working on.'

'We do it for our dad,' adds Tammy. 'We're sad that he'll never be here, being interviewed, taking part. But these episodes we're making now are so important to us on a personal level, and we know he's listening. So now we're continuing in his memory.'

The recording ends.

Everyone around the table is stunned, and even Georgie has perked up.

'I'm shocked,' I say. 'I can't believe that his daughters have been interviewing us and—'

'Yeah, not sure how I feel about that,' Georgie says, 'and I know they're recording, so I want them to know. They should have told us.'

Lauren is shaking her head. 'I'm shocked, but unlike Georgie I'm not angry.'

Georgie rolls her eyes.

'No, I can't be angry – those girls have suffered. All they're doing is trying to get some redemption for their father, and good luck to them.' Lauren's deliberately trying to highlight Georgie's unreasonableness.

'Why would a stranger, an anonymous person, pay a load of money to those girls?' Georgie asks, ignoring Lauren's shady comment. Georgie's probably using this moment as *her* chance to leave the spotlight and start accusing someone else.

'As they said, it might not be a stranger, it could be their extended family,' Alex offers, totally redirecting where she's going with this.

'Yeah, but *if* it's a stranger, then why?' Georgie's determined to point the finger and turn this kind gesture of a donation into something sinister.

Alex shrugs. 'I dunno. They donated money because they're kind people?'

'No, what I *mean* is—'

'What Georgie's trying to say,' Dan says, talking over her, 'is it might be a *guilty* stranger. Someone who feels bad about Professor M doing their time?'

'The *killer*?' I ask.

'Could be,' Dan says, 'but his daughters said it was a *lot* of money, and who here could afford that?' He looks pointedly at Alex.

'Yeah, I reckon Lauren's done pretty well for herself too,' Georgie pipes up. 'I mean, *three* homes – gosh, you must be loaded after all your success with the book.'

Lauren is horrified and, sitting there in her wine-splattered rented dress, visibly shrinks away from this damning remark equating wealth with guilt.

Little do any of them know that after Alex I'm probably the wealthiest here. But no one's looking at me, because I'm staying out of the spotlight. How I got my money is my secret – and I intend for it to stay that way.

31

DAN

'Well, that was, I think, one of the worst nights of my life,' I say, back at the apartment. Everyone else stayed for another drink, but I got Georgie out of there quickly and now I'm making some strong coffee to sober her up.

'You want to talk "worst nights", Dan, try finding out your boyfriend's sleeping with one of your housemates, having promised he never would in your absence. Then keep calling and calling him, but he's told you he's out drinking with friends and not picking up.'

Here we go, she's going over the night Daisy disappeared – again – and trying to trip me up, as she has been for twenty years.

'Then think how it feels when you see the girl putting on her lipstick, fluffing her hair, throwing her scarf around her neck and skipping off for what looks like a date but saying, "I'm only meeting a friend." I didn't know it was David, I thought it was you.'

'Whoa, why are we going over this again?'

'Because I've been wanting to tell you . . . and before it comes out this weekend, you should know – I followed her that night.'

'You followed *Daisy* . . . the night she . . . ?'

'Yes. I followed her all the way to Exmouth – I thought she was meeting you.'

'What? Jesus, Georgie, sending that letter to the professor's wife was bad enough – and Daisy was right, it was psycho stuff. But now you're telling me you weren't home when Daisy was killed – you were out stalking her?'

Now I know I can't trust her anymore. She's always been fiery and unpredictable but I never realised she was so *unhinged*.

'But you told the police you were at home in bed. What the fuck were you doing, Georgie?'

'You needn't act so high and mighty. I was your alibi. Remember, I told the police you were with *me* . . . which you weren't. So, where the fuck were you, and what the fuck were *you* doing?'

'Georgie, shut up! We're being recorded!'

'Fuck, fuck, fuck.' She runs to her room and slams the door. A few seconds later I follow her in.

'Tonight's been the worst. That bloody Teresa, and *fucking* Lauren!' She's sitting on the bed, still in her glitzy red dress, taking off her high heels.

I'm about to say something, but without looking up, she lifts her finger to warn me.

'*Don't* start lecturing me, Dan.' One of her strappy shoes drops to the floor, and for a fleeting moment I remember when my wife dropping her heels on the floor turned me on.

'Lauren is so vile, sitting there *laughing* at me. I couldn't help it.'

'She *wasn't* laughing,' I say, all thoughts of sex wiped cleanly from my mind. 'Can't you tell, she's *scared* of you, she wouldn't laugh openly in your face – Jesus, who would, when you're like that?'

'Whatever she was doing with her face, it was smug.'

'*That* doesn't excuse you throwing a big glass of wine over her.'

She takes a long breath and considers this. 'I probably shouldn't have done that,' she admits, in a rare moment of reflection. Then she turns to me and I see the helpless little girl in her eyes. 'But I see this red mist of rage, and . . .'

'I know, I live with it, but other people don't *have* to. I was praying you wouldn't, but you were clutching the stem of that glass so tightly it was only going one way.'

'Over Lauren.' She closes her eyes, a pained expression on her face. 'You turned away, you didn't stop me. Coward.'

'Yeah, I probably am a coward, but you've made me that way. You scare me. I wanted to snatch it from you but was worried that, if I did, you'd hurl it over *me* instead.'

'That might have been easier. Now I have to apologise to that witch.'

I'm surprised and relieved she's even considering an apology. Her usual tactic is to push blindly on, being stubborn and defensive.

I plonk myself down on the bed next to her. 'I know this is stressful, no one wants to be here, and you and I . . . well, we're in a difficult position. There are things we did back then that I'm not proud of. And you writing a letter to Louisa Montgomery does kind of put the spotlight on you. All the years we've been together, why didn't you tell me?'

'Because it doesn't make any sense, but you of all people should understand why I did it. I was scared of losing *you*.'

My wife is angry and bossy and stubborn. But as her other strappy shoe falls on to the carpet, and she looks at me with helpless eyes, I'm touched by her vulnerability.

'I wanted Daisy out of our lives,' she explains. 'She was everywhere – at home chatting with you, at uni talking earnestly with you about her problems. I'd see you both in a café having lunch when you'd said you couldn't meet me because you had a lecture. So I sent the letter hoping she'd have to leave uni – and David would dump her – but instead of her fleeing, or losing her place on the course, in the following weeks she turned to you. And from that moment, not only was she in our house and at our uni, she was now in our bed.'

Tears stream down her face, and I gently put my arm around her. 'I couldn't bear to see you together, Dan.' She pauses. 'But when I found out about the baby . . . That broke me.'

I see the pain in her eyes, and not for the first time I wonder just how far Georgie was prepared to go to get rid of Daisy.

'She made out she wanted to keep the baby, but she was just toying with you, and you couldn't see it. I wanted to save us, save you, but you didn't hear me, you wouldn't listen. That's when I realised that, whatever I did, however much I tried to stop you leaving me, I couldn't trust you – I still can't.'

I take a deep breath. 'That's *your* insecurity. I may have had a wandering eye in the past, but not anymore.' I hate myself.

'Really?'

'Yes, I've changed, Georgie,' I say, knowing this isn't true.

'Promise me?'

'Yes, that's all in the past. When you threatened to leave me last summer, I realised what was at stake.'

She looks doubtful, but hopeful.

'It's just that I saw the way Lauren looked at you tonight – like she thinks she has a chance.'

'Please don't go down that road again, babe.'

'I can't help it. Since we got here she's been constantly seeking out your eyes.'

'No she hasn't, you're imagining it. Stop torturing yourself.'

'What happened with Daisy was traumatic. I've found it so hard to trust you.'

I soften again at this. 'I know, and I take some responsibility for that. But stop living in the past. We have a great future together, so let's put it all behind us.' Her spat with Lauren has made her vulnerable, and for all her bravado and bitterness I'm glad that sometimes she needs me.

'What about Maddie? I see the way you look at her.'

'Maddie's lovely, but I find it hard to have a conversation with her, let alone an affair.' Maddie's always been immune to my charms. A shame, because she looks so good naked.

Georgie smiles – something she doesn't do often.

'I know you and Lauren once had a thing, in our first year, when I went home for the weekend.'

'God, I barely remember it. I was a kid – it was nothing.'

'To you, perhaps, but I wonder if she thought it was more. You have to be careful with Lauren. I think she would definitely push us both under the bus if she could.' She pauses, and the vulnerability of a moment ago is replaced by something mean and hard. 'But here's the thing, Dan, if she ever tries to throw *me* under the bus, I'll throw *you* under too.'

It's not easy being married to someone who's pathologically jealous. She could lash out at any time.

'Tomorrow night that podcast goes out, and trust me, everyone is gearing up for their own defence. If that means betraying someone else, or lying to do it – they will.'

'You make it sound like an episode of *The Traitors*,' I joke, in an attempt to hide my unease.

'Trust me, Dan, it's far more treacherous than that. They are *all* looking for something – *anything*. And we both know they won't have to look too far to find dirt on you.'

It's a sobering thought.

'And her *mother* thinks you're guilty.'

'Yeah, that was a blow,' I admit.

'We were careful, with Daisy – weren't we?' she says, seeking reassurance.

'Yeah, but we need to get our stories straight if things start to fall apart and we're interviewed by the police again.'

'God, it constantly plays like a video in my head,' she says, looking around the room as if seeking an escape.

'Same. It's a video on a loop that I can't shut down. After they found her body, I couldn't eat or sleep. I thought my whole life was ruined, that my father would disown me.'

'It was a scary time, but you really lost it – you were hanging around the scene of the crime. I'll never understand why you did such a stupid thing.'

'I know.' My heart hurts, recalling how devastated I was. Alex had given me something, I felt high, and I had this feeling I could resurrect Daisy. I was so desperate to have her back.

'I was just grieving,' I say, unwilling to share any more with my wife. 'No one would even have known, except the bloody *News of the World* were staking out the crime scene twenty-four-seven!' My stomach churns at the memory – the photo of me on the front page standing by the beach hut, a shadowy figure in the eerie dawn light.

'*Daisy's housemate returns to the scene of the crime*,' she's saying, shaking her head. 'Just replace "housemate" with "murderer", and that's what the press were implying.'

'And I don't blame them. I might as well have confessed. I even unwittingly provided the creepy photograph. Any journalist worth their salt would snap that media package up.'

I see the fear still in her eyes; it was as dreadful for her as it was for me. I wonder if that's why we're still together – two terrified people on a life raft, clinging to each other to save ourselves. Both so scared that if we pull apart, we might drown.

'My father was so angry, but, worse, he was upset – I'd never seen him cry before.' I still feel his pain. As a father now myself, I understand. 'If it weren't for you giving me an alibi I might have found myself in David Montgomery's place. Did I ever say thank you?'

'No, but you're welcome,' she replies, unsmiling.

She lies back on the bed, her dress slides up a little, and I think about how we used to be. Georgie was always adventurous in our student days, and seeing her like this makes me want to touch her smooth thighs, slip my hands under the silky fabric of her dress. I begin to rub her feet, waiting for her to push me away. And when she doesn't recoil at my touch, I move next to her on the bed and we start to kiss. She's clearly aroused, probably stimulated by memories of Daisy, or the threat of Lauren creeping into my bed. Or the thought of Alex creeping into hers? We have our best sex when others are involved – if only in our heads these days.

'It's all fine,' I breathe into her ear. 'I will always come back to you.'

'I keep imagining you with Lauren,' she pants. 'She's on top.'

'She loves it on top,' I whisper. 'She likes it in the back of the car, the windows get so steamy . . .'

I describe our bodies, the sweat, the positions, the way Lauren's long legs wrap around me when I take her up against a wall. By now Georgie's desperate for me, she's kissing me, licking me, climbing on me, begging me to do the same with her that I do with Lauren. It's so twisted and dark; my imagined adultery is exquisite pain for my wife, and she sucks the blood out of it like a vampire. And afterwards, as we lie on tangled sheets in the student-sized bed, she rests her head on my chest. It feels good; she's finally calm.

'I love our fantasies,' she murmurs, 'because that's all they are.' I stroke her naked shoulder, and I think about Lauren and all the other women I've made love to while being married to my wife. And just thinking about Lauren right now I want her long legs wrapped around me as I take her against the wall – as I just described. Georgie thinks I imagine these scenarios with other women for her, but it isn't fantasy. I don't have the imagination to create erotic encounters; I need to experience them. Georgie thought it was fantasy when I said how Daisy liked it rough, and begged me to tie her wrists together. Georgie got off on that, because she thought it wasn't real, she had no idea I was already sleeping with Daisy and this 'fantasy' was real for me. But later it became real for both of us, when Georgie and I together ran our fingers through Daisy's long, silky hair and explored her soft, naked skin. Even now, in flagrante, we sometimes whisper about the silk scarf we'd tie around her wrists, and I imagine my hands around Daisy's soft, white neck . . . .

32

LAUREN

Maddie's on edge. She reckons a breakfast hamper will land any minute, and she keeps going to the door to check. She's like a cat on hot bricks, and after last night's dramas she's adding to my jumpiness. I had to stand under a hot shower for a long time to get the stench of the red wine out of my hair. 'Are Georgie and Dan still in bed?' Alex asks.

'I've no idea,' I lie, my stomach lurching. It was early morning, and still dark, when I woke to see someone standing by my bed, watching me. I screamed, but he put his hand on my mouth to keep me quiet, and that's when I knew it was him.

I was still angry about what Georgie had done, and even angrier that he hadn't tried to stop her. I told him to get lost, but he pushed his face in my neck, and whispered that he was missing me. Within seconds I could feel my anger, and my willpower, drifting away in the darkness.

'I can't bear for you to be just inches away and I can't have you,' he panted in my ear, and that was it.

I'm dragged away from this delicious memory by Alex asking if I want coffee.

'Yes please.' I flop on to a chair, exhausted from lack of sleep, but it was worth it.

'You okay? You tired?' Maddie says.

'Yeah, I didn't get much sleep last night.'

Maddie puts her head to one side in sympathy. 'Was it the thing with Georgie?'

'Yeah. I have to warn you guys, breakfast may be as unpleasant this morning as she was last night.'

'Yeah, we all ducked when that wine hit the air.' Alex smirks, which isn't quite the support I'd hoped for. My only consolation regarding what happened is that it will be in my book – and probably the podcast too.

'Try not to take things too much to heart,' Maddie says sweetly. 'I think Georgie was just feeling attacked.'

'I'm sorry, Maddie, but you can't justify the fact that Georgie *assaulted* me last night.'

'It was just a glass of wine,' she sing-songs, blonde ponytail swinging, smile big and bright.

'Maddie, it's a stressful situation for all of us, but you didn't see anyone *else* throwing wine over their fellow dinner guests last night. She's out of control, like a wild animal. Georgie's always angry with someone, and her rhetoric was violent and unforgiving. She scares me!' I add, just to drive it home. Maddie's so bloody slow on the uptake.

Alex smiles at this. 'Yeah, she hasn't changed. She used to overreact to everything. It always made me laugh,' he says like we're ambling down memory lane together. Do either of these zombies get how serious it was last night? 'Like, she'd come storming into the house threatening to *decapitate* someone because they'd pulled out in front of her on the road,' he says, still smiling.

Maddie laughs. 'Yeah, she once threatened to stab a waitress because her coffee was cold. Not to her face, but she muttered it as she walked away.'

I don't laugh; I want them to see that Georgie isn't funny, she's deranged!

'Christ, who *knows* what she's capable of,' I say pointedly, hoping these two pick up what I'm saying. 'Daisy used to impersonate her, you know – I can see her now, heavy frown, arms wrapped ludicrously around herself, pacing around her room wiping surfaces with a kitchen towel. So funny.'

'Oh yeah, I just remembered another one,' Maddie says. 'She yelled at the lady in the campus canteen, threatened to "smash up" the kitchens because they'd run out of cheese-and-onion tart.'

'Joking aside, though, she once took a knife to Daisy because she wouldn't turn the TV over,' I say, and wait for their shock and outrage.

But Alex ruins my proof of Georgie's violent nature by correcting me because, annoyingly, he was there. 'I don't think that's quite how it happened,' he starts, and my heart sinks. 'Georgie was chopping peppers, had the knife in her hand and wandered in to ask Daisy if she could watch another programme. Daisy was so scared of her she freaked out. It was so funny, but even Daisy laughed about it.'

'I remember it differently,' I reply. It bothers me that they're talking about her like she's harmless and hilarious. I need to impress upon them that she's dangerous and violent. But they're both so slow-witted they just assume we're reminiscing with affection about funny Georgie. Where are the others? *Bring on the adults, not the clowns!*

I refuse to let this go, and move the conversation back to last night. 'I'd done nothing, I was just having dinner, and . . . and she openly *attacked* me. It was *frenzied*,' I say, deliberately echoing a word the police used to describe Daisy's murder. I'm keen to push the idea of Georgie as a violent, out-of-control potential killer.

'I think you handled it very well, Lauren,' Maddie says, patting my shoulder. 'By the way, I googled it and apparently putting rice on wine stains can help. We could try that on your dress if there's any rice in the cupboards.'

'No, there isn't,' I say, just to stop her talking about this. It's boring. I'm so over the stained hire dress. I have no idea if there's any rice in the cupboard – and what's more, I'm not interested. I don't even care about the very expensive hire dress. What I am interested in is ensuring that everyone, including these two bozos, believes Georgie is capable of murder.

'I'm not angry with Georgie, I'm genuinely concerned for her and her mental health,' I say with a pious smile. 'The woman has serious anger issues.' I pause a moment, then lean forward and speak quietly. 'I think she needs help.' I'm nodding as I say this. 'I mean *professional* help.'

They look at me, then each other, but I still don't think they've bought into it. I have to remember I'm not talking to Dan or Daisy or even Georgie, and I desperately try to think of simple anecdotes that they can understand.

'She can be a bit crazy,' Alex confirms.

Finally! I'm seeing a chink of light, and want to yell, 'Hallelujah!'

'But not crazy as in kooky, I mean really crazy,' I add, just to confirm we're all in the same ball park here.

'Yeah. I find that wild-eyed craziness strangely sexy,' Alex announces.

I'm horrified. 'Alex, psychopaths are *not* sexy!'

'Nah, she's a pussycat,' he says, in an almost admiring tone. Unable to compete with Alex's apparently still-surging hormones, I bring out the big guns to get them onside.

'Guys . . . I'm writing a book – but not fiction, this time it's true crime. It's about Daisy, and us, and I'm going to include stuff about this weekend and—'

'*Everything?*' Maddie looks doubtful.

'Man, that's heavy.' Alex's eyes are wide in wonder at this, like he's suddenly woken up.

'Yes . . . A memoir of my time here, as Daisy's best friend. Then and now . . . Actually, I quite like that title,' I murmur.

'Wouldn't you have to ask permission from Daisy's mother?' Maddie asks.

'No. I won't be asking *anyone's* mother!' I snap.

Honestly, I'd forgotten how irritating Maddie can be. Then I realise by her face that I just snapped at her, so say in my 'kind teacher' voice, 'I would need some people's permission, and I'd have to be careful about what I write, of course. But as long as it's true and there's nothing slanderous, I'd just be giving my account of the weekend. And I hate to say it, but Georgie hasn't exactly covered herself in glory these past two days, and it's all going in the book.'

Hopefully I've done enough here to point them in Georgie's direction, and get any heat off me. After all, if I was guilty of murdering someone, I'd hardly write a book about it, would I?

'I need to call Richard and my daughter,' I lie. 'I won't be long.' I stand up.

'Oh, but the breakfast should be here soon.' Maddie's clearly still dealing with her eating disorder, and I stroke her ponytail affectionately, but she moves away.

'Sorry,' I say, unsure what I'm apologising for.

'I just don't like . . . to be touched,' she says. I reckon there's a lot to unpack there; I hope one day she'll let me help her, but for now I have to call Finty with all the book news.

But before I can move from the kitchen, I'm suddenly face to face with my aggressor. She's in full make-up and a red jumper, with matching tight red lips and her arms folded. Ready for battle?

We face each other in silence, both standing our ground.

'Duck!' Alex suddenly says under his breath, and for a moment we continue to stare. But Maddie and Alex are sniggering at his joke, and the implication that Georgie may randomly hurl more wine at me is vaguely amusing.

Her eyes are flashing fire, but then seem to soften, and a half-smile plays on her lips. 'Okay, Alex, you're a funny guy,' she concedes, and when she turns back to me her smile fades as usual, but she seems to be struggling to say something. 'Lauren . . . I . . . I'm sorry,' she blurts out, opening up her arms awkwardly.

'It's okay,' I mutter, stepping forward with caution to receive the coldest, stiffest embrace I've ever endured.

'I completely overreacted, it was a . . . tense evening, but no excuses. I lost control, and – I'm embarrassed.'

'Don't be – it's . . . it's okay. Just a shame it had to happen.'

'Yay! Breakfast has arrived,' Maddie yells, breaking into the awkward aftermath of the apology.

'How does she know the breakfast's here?' I turn to Alex as she skips to the front door.

'Maddie can smell baked goods from twenty miles away.' He smiles, watching her fondly as she runs to the door. I decide not to escape on the pretext of calling Richard; Finty can wait. Besides, it would seem rude to go now, after Georgie's apology. So, I sit down again to join them as Maddie returns with the hamper, her face pink with pleasure at the prospect of breakfast.

When Dan finally appears, Georgie and I are playing nice over maple pecan plaits. His hair is all mussed up, and I'm surprised again how good-looking he is and how attracted I am to him; it hits me every time. I watch discreetly as he plonks himself down at the table and takes a croissant, then looks straight at me, eyes on mine, a little secret smile. I get a flashback to this morning, his hands all over my body, silently pulling off my T-shirt and lifting me up as

I wrapped my legs around him. God, it was so good. The fact we had to be silent so no one would hear made it all the more thrilling.

And later, when we lay on the floor, my head on his chest, damp with sweat despite the cold morning, I felt such bliss.

'I can't wait until we can be together forever,' I sighed.

'Me too,' he replied huskily. And sitting at this table with him now, so near and yet so far, I feel warm and fuzzy and girlish. I haven't felt like this in years, and I hold his gaze, licking my lips suggestively. After what happened just a few hours ago, and his reassurances about our future together, I feel brave. I don't care if anyone sees me flirting so openly; he's got my back and I've got his. We've been seeing each other in secret since I bumped into him in London just a couple of months ago. It was late September. He suggested we go for drinks, and told me he and Georgie had had a difficult summer – he didn't say why, but he didn't need to. I imagine being married to her is very difficult, regardless of the season. It wasn't long before we were meeting in hotels, and it wasn't the first time we'd slept together. We had a fling as students, and I've always had a crush on him, but now it's developed into something real.

I can't drag my eyes away from his laughing blue eyes and the mouth I long to kiss. Georgie's looking at me, I can feel her gaze from the side, but I'm not hiding anymore. She'll know soon enough, because when we get home I'm asking Richard for a divorce, and Dan's asking Georgie.

33

GEORGIE

I knew it! I fucking *knew* it. I woke up in the night and he wasn't there, and I naively assumed he'd gone to the bathroom. After a while I decided he must have gone to sleep in his old room, and perhaps I'd been restless and I'd woken him. But now a third option has formed in my brain, and this idiot – me – is returning to familiar territory I swore I'd never go to again. I'm numb with shock and realisation, as not-so-discreet eyes meet across the table and . . . *Oh. My. God.* She's licking her lips just for him.

Given my marriage, you'd think I'd have picked up on this sooner; it obviously hasn't just started this weekend. The past few months of late nights, overnights, the stench of perfume in his car – it's so bloody obvious it's almost boring. And suddenly I think about the way the passenger seat has recently been moved back each time I've climbed into his car; it was clearly moved to accommodate *someone* with longer legs than me. The same long legs he describes in such intimate detail while panting in my ear during sex.

So last night, after we'd made love, he left me in bed and went to *her*, just as he used to with Daisy.

As the others talk over breakfast, my mind whizzes back to the past, and how I fell for him the moment I saw him. I was with Alex then, but secretly in love with Dan, who hadn't even noticed me, he just saw me as a friend. He was gorgeous, quite tall and slim, with floppy fair hair and a posh accent he tried to hide but I adored. He was funny and charming, and I knew we would be perfect together; I just had to convince him. But he was young, and it was his first time away from home, and there seemed to be a constant line of pretty girls heading for his bedroom. I'd be there at the apartment in agony, watching him take them to his room, my heart heavy with grief.

'Dan and his one-night stands,' Alex once said. 'He introduces them like they're his girlfriend so they'll sleep with him, uninhibited.'

Meanwhile, I'd lie in bed with Alex, hearing the sounds of pleasure coming from Dan's room, and cry quietly in the dark while Alex slept.

Eventually, when he'd run out of girls, Dan and I let Alex down as gently as possible and started seeing each other officially. It was just before Christmas in the first year and the happiest time of my life. At first he was everything I thought he'd be. I was in love, it was new and I was terribly insecure, but by the time we started our second year I was feeling more settled and comfortable in the relationship. We'd been together for almost a year by then, and the only shadow on my horizon was Daisy. She'd started to hang around with Dan, and I knew at that point they were just friends, but I saw the way he lit up whenever she was around, and I wanted her out of his life. That's when I sent the letter to Louisa Montgomery, revealing her husband's affair and pretending it was from Daisy. I saw Daisy in tears only the day after the letter, and assumed the fallout had started with David and it would only be a matter of time before they were both sent packing from university. Just a few days later, Dan said he had something to tell me, and he took me to a bar and bought me a beer and I honestly thought he was going to tell me he loved me.

'It's about Daisy and me . . .' he started. 'I've always liked her, but she told me she feels the same. I'm really sorry, Georgie, but I think you and I should go on a break,' he said, clumsily.

Was this some kind of joke?

'I think I've always been a little bit in love with her,' he added, liberally sprinkling salt on to the fresh wound.

I can remember the feeling, like I was standing on the edge of a very high cliff and might fall. But it didn't matter if I did. Nothing mattered anymore. I didn't speak at first because I couldn't form the words.

The crazy thing about it was that Dan had just assumed I'd be okay with what he'd told me. But the casual cruelty, the clumsiness of his words, the 'little bit in love' with someone else floored me.

I actually thought I might die. I'd heard the word 'heartbreak' a million times, but I'd never really considered how real it was until that night. I honestly felt like my heart had broken in two; the pain was physical.

'But Daisy's in love with her lecturer,' I told him, assuming he didn't know about David.

'Not anymore,' he replied. 'She's dumped him for me.'

Of course, later we discovered that in fact David had dumped her because of the letter, and she'd found the nearest safe haven with Dan. But at that point I had to believe what he did – that she'd chosen Dan over David.

I'll never forget the look in his eyes – the very thought of winning her from a professor seemed to be an extra thrill. Just like when he'd taken me from Alex. He was so young and naive and insensitive to my feelings, he didn't even try to hide his excitement from me about his 'new' relationship. I *hated* her in that moment. More than I've ever hated anyone before or since. I really think he expected me to be happy for him – being with 'the most beautiful girl on campus', as he later described her to Alex. In front of me.

When I started sobbing openly in the bar, it dawned on him that this could be embarrassing, so he offered me a consolation prize.

'You and I can still sleep together if you like?' he suggested half-heartedly, to stop me making a scene.

'So you would do me the honour of sleeping with me while pursuing a relationship with Daisy?' I asked sarcastically through my tears, feeling the hurt and fury welling up inside me.

He nodded.

Oh dear. Until then, Dan had only ever seen the Georgie I let him see. My uncontrollable rage had been locked away for almost a year while I'd been with him. I loved him so much I wanted to keep him, and knew that revealing my other self would scare him off. I adored him, I lived and breathed him, and I would do anything for him as long as he stayed. At nineteen that kind of love is dangerous, because you'll do *anything* to keep it.

We walked back to the house that night, and all I could think of was the two of them together. It was as if a match had been lit and thrown on to gallons of petrol and I'd swallowed the flames. They crackled and roared inside me, and all the feelings I'd been suppressing – good and bad – came rushing to the surface. In the time it took to reach our shared house, I had become slightly unhinged; I screamed and yelled and I couldn't stop myself. I was totally out of control.

In trying to calm me down, Dan went to put his arms around me, to hold in the madness and stop me spiralling. But I fought him, shrieked at him to get off me, and all the time I was slapping his face and scratching him with my nails.

He was understandably terrified at my reaction. The fact he'd told me he was *in love* with someone else in such a matter-of-fact way showed he had no idea of the power he had over me. And when he tried to leave my bedroom to go to his, I begged for him not to leave me, falling to the floor and holding on to his legs as he tried to escape, dragging me along the floor with him. My legs were covered in carpet burns, but I felt nothing. I was immune to any pain other than the pain he was inflicting on me.

When even Dan realised that my mental health wasn't in good shape, and walking out on me wasn't a good idea, he reluctantly agreed not to break up with me. But I knew in my heart that it was only a matter of time before they got together, probably behind my back.

Dan felt they had a connection, and he wasn't going to let her go. They were *inevitable*.

Then, one day, I had this horrible idea, but it was all I could think of to keep him. 'What if we sleep with her *together*?'

I didn't want this, but I could see there was a kind of sense to the three of us. It appealed to my controlling nature – to know where he was, to actually *be* there when they were together, to take part, to *orchestrate* it, even? I could either let him cheat on me and lie to me, or share him openly – and keep him. It was scary, but at the same time it felt sophisticated and grown-up – like smoking, which can also kill.

And now, twenty years later, over a basket of croissants in my old halls of residence, I realise it wasn't just Daisy who was 'inevitable' for Dan. The truth is, I've never been enough for him, and even allowing him to share his fantasies about other women won't keep him home. I've endured the sheer agony of hearing his lecherous desires because I believed they were fantasies, that we'd found a place where we could both exist and be happy – together. But I was fooling myself; his fantasies are real, and last night, after talking about what he'd like to do with Lauren, he left my bed and went to hers. I feel like I did twenty years ago when he left me sleeping to go to Daisy. It happened before I joined them and after

– he was never honest with me about Daisy. And despite giving him an alibi, I still believe there's something he's hiding from me about that night.

I watch Lauren now as she stands up to make coffee. She's wearing a nightshirt, and my husband can't take his eyes off her long, bare legs as she strolls past. And then . . . as if I needed confirmation, her hand caresses his back. It's the lightest of touches; it could almost be accidental, and it's probably invisible to everyone else. But I *see* it.

How the fuck have I missed this?

'I'm making coffee,' she announces from behind the kitchen bar. 'Anyone want some?'

I don't want some, but bitch you're gonna get some. I hold on to the table, my knuckles white – I've held on to Lauren's secret since I discovered it in her room yesterday. I haven't even told Dan because I don't want him holding me back when it's time to let everyone know exactly what Lauren did to Daisy.

That time is now.

34

Maddie

Breakfast is wonderful – croissants, pecan Danishes, cherry jam, homemade sourdough, sea-salted butter and a basket of fruit. I've sampled everything, and as the others seem unaware of how much I've eaten, I go again and fill my plate. Dan has just arrived, but it looks like Georgie's not very happy with him. God knows why – I thought Lauren would be today's hate figure. But having only just apologised to Lauren, Georgie needs someone else to be angry with, and perhaps Dan fits the bill? He's desperately trying to find a safe harbour with Alex, but that feels a bit awkward too, because Alex remembers how invisible Dan made him feel when we were students. Meanwhile, Lauren isn't principled like Alex, and she's now trying to build on Georgie's apology and schmooze her. It's sickening to watch, and makes me quite angry; the woman threw wine over her last night, but because Lauren's writing a book, she obviously wants to keep in with everyone. It explains why she's been so nice to me and Alex, who she barely spoke to when we lived together. She no doubt saw him the same way Dan did, as 'a messed-up little junkie'. How wrong they all were.

I may be high on sugar, but even I can see that, despite her apology, Georgie isn't embracing Lauren's BFF vibe. They always pigeonholed me as 'the Phoebe', from the TV show *Friends*, just because I don't pick up easily on social cues, but who says I even want to? I sometimes find other people so boring that I have no interest in gossip or their opinion on others. I try to pretend I do and always have, just to fit in. I'm not stupid, or slow, which they have all implied at some point. They used to call me 'the quiet one', but that wasn't really who I was. I believe they made me quiet – I was of no significance to them, and if people ignore you long enough, you become invisible.

I nibble the edges of an almond croissant, and ignore them all for a moment, waiting for the hit. But the usual deep pleasure of the crisp buttery pastry and the sweet nutty topping is overwhelmed by the familiar tide of guilt and self-loathing. I'm out of control, and the stress of this weekend means the overeating and regretting has come in quickly. I have to make myself sick sooner than I'd planned this morning, so head for the shared bathroom and run taps and flush the toilet so they can't hear the retching, which goes on for a while. But once I'm purged, I feel like Maddie again – whoever she is.

When I eventually go back into the kitchen, everyone's still there, and, no longer filled with pastry and guilt, I take my seat at the table. The compulsion to binge has left me – for now, my head is clear and my senses are heightened from the purge. Consequently, I'm more aware of my surroundings and the people I'm with, because my compulsion isn't tugging at my sleeve like an evil toddler. As soon as I sit down, I sense a change in the atmosphere. There's a new tension in the room, and I try to work out where and who it's coming from.

Lauren isn't sitting with Georgie anymore. She's making coffee by the kitchen island in her nightshirt, and Dan has just wandered over to help her. Georgie is glaring at them with barely concealed hatred . . . or jealousy . . . So far, so Georgie. Lauren seems oblivious but, judging by the look on his face, I think Dan is aware he's breached one of Georgie's strict rules. Talking to another woman without her permission.

Alex is looking at his phone, and in the heavy silence Dan and Lauren continue making coffee with the odd little comment and chuckle, while Georgie continues to look on like some weird overlord. So I try to build a bridge across the kitchen, and bring Dan and Lauren back into the group, by asking if I can have a coffee.

Keen to keep in with us all, Lauren looks up from the cafetière. 'Of course, Maddie, yes . . . Coming right up.' She smiles.

Dan is now gathering the mugs from a cupboard, and Lauren takes the milk from the fridge and starts to open it, when Georgie says, 'Do you have a copy of your book here with you, Lauren?'

Lauren almost jumps at this, her usually confident mask slips, and she starts to stutter. 'N . . . no . . . no, I . . . d-don't.' She's unsmiling, uncertain.

Dan seems to pick up on this, presumably seeing the storm coming, and his panicked eyes are now darting from Georgie to Lauren.

'Well, you do, because I swear I saw it in the living room yesterday, but never mind.' Georgie smiles a cold, dead smile and turns to me.

'*You* have a copy of Lauren's book, don't you, Maddie?'

I'm suddenly in the spotlight. The air prickles in the silence as everyone waits for my answer.

'Oh . . . Yes, er, Lauren gave it to me.' I look at Lauren, who smiles uncomfortably, her eyes wide with alarm. *What the hell is going on here?*

'Where is it? The book?' Georgie asks, unsmiling.

'It's . . . er, in my room,' I say into the taut silence.

'Would you do me a big favour, Maddie? Would you fetch it in here for me, I need to check something.'

This doesn't augur well. Georgie's sitting with her arms folded, and Lauren's trying to open the milk, and Alex is looking at me with a 'what the fuck?' expression on his face.

What can I say? I can't refuse to let her see the book. 'Yeah, sure, I'll get it,' I say, and like a good child I go to my room and take it from my bed where I left it.

As I'm walking back in, Georgie is taking her laptop from her bag. 'Thanks,' she says. I've done what she needed, and she doesn't have to waste even a smile on me now. She grabs the book from my hands and plonks her laptop on the table.

'I was flicking through this book yesterday, and something . . . I don't know what it was . . . *bugged* me,' she says, scrolling through her laptop.

The only noise in the room is the clicking of the keys, and in the silence we're all looking at each other, dreading what's going to happen next. The atmosphere is electric, and not in a good way.

'As I leafed through the book and read the odd paragraph, I thought to myself, *this doesn't sound like Lauren.*' She looks up, turns to me and says, 'Know what I mean?'

I don't. But my attention is on Lauren, whose hands are shaking and she still can't open the milk. She turns quickly to Dan to open it for her, but I inwardly groan at this. Dan is not *that* guy. He's never there to take the strain; he's fickle, he goes where life is easy, and right now behind that kitchen counter with Lauren is *not* easy. So instead of being supportive and taking the milk bottle from Lauren, Dan steps back. Poor Lauren still thinks he's got her and releases the bottle into his hands, but as she does he lifts his hands away, like it's hot. The bottle falls to the ground, smashing into a million pieces.

'Shit!' Lauren says loudly, while Dan makes some stupid, lame joke about crying over spilled milk as the three of us at the table watch open-mouthed.

'I kept thinking about the book, and I had a theory, but I couldn't prove it, so I checked it out. I looked on Lauren's laptop, and I saw these files with Daisy's name on them, and I opened them,' Georgie's saying, pretending to ignore milk-gate going on in front of us.

Everyone's looking at her now, and Lauren is open-mouthed too. 'You looked on my laptop? How dare you.'

'No, Lauren.' Georgie lifts her eyes from her own laptop screen. 'How dare you.'

'What do you mean?' I say eventually into the silence.

'Before Daisy died, she asked me if I would read something she'd written,' Georgie starts, keen to tell this story. 'She told me that Lauren usually read her work and checked it over and vice versa, but they'd fallen out and she didn't trust Lauren anymore.'

Lauren can no doubt hear this, but she's choosing to stay behind the counter, on the floor, picking up pieces of glass. At one point she says 'Ouch!' but no one goes to help. Dan has now sneakily and silently moved back to the table to show his allegiance to his queen, leaving Lauren alone. She eventually appears from behind the counter, standing up to deal with the blood trickling from a cut on her hand. But also seemingly looking for Dan? When she sees where he is, tears begin to fall down her face.

'So, all those years ago, I read Daisy's manuscript,' Georgie continues, 'and it stayed with me. So evocative, and engaging, so real. I loved it. So, you can imagine my surprise, as I flicked through Lauren's book yesterday, when I had this sense of déjà vu. Yeah' – she's nodding – 'and when I checked Lauren's laptop, Daisy's original manuscript was there, the exact same one that she asked me to read all those years ago! But Daisy told me she hadn't given the manuscript to Lauren this time, because she didn't trust her. So how did it get onto Lauren's laptop, you may ask? Well' – she pauses for drama – 'I'll tell you. Lauren stole it, the day Daisy went missing – turns out Daisy was right not to trust her best friend.'

No one speaks. Lauren emerges slowly from behind the kitchen counter, her face a vision of horror at what Georgie's just said. But Georgie hasn't quite finished, and, resting her chin on elegant hands, she addresses us all, like a teacher concluding her lesson.

'Now, I'm not pointing fingers, but if Lauren did pass off Daisy's novel as her own, that's a very strong motive for wanting Daisy dead.'

35

Dan

Well, *that* was awkward.

After Georgie's little speech, there was this horrible, thick silence. I was waiting for Lauren to challenge Georgie's claim that she'd stolen Daisy's book; in fact I was willing her to. But she said nothing, and I was pretty unimpressed – if Lauren really did do that, then perhaps Georgie isn't so bonkers after all. I mean, stealing a dead person's work, taking the credit and making a fortune – who does that?

When Lauren realised that she'd been discovered, her face kind of broke up into fragments and she stood there clutching her injured hand, her face still wet with tears. We were all so stunned that no one made any attempt to comfort her – not even Maddie – and then it seemed to dawn on Lauren that she was on her own, and she ran from the room covered in blood and tears. Maddie is now on the floor mopping up the milk, and the blood from Lauren's cut, along with the shards of glass, while Alex and I sit with Georgie at the table. We're just silently watching her, waiting for what happens next.

Finally, she speaks. 'I told you I caught her in Daisy's room just after she went missing,' she says triumphantly, sitting behind her laptop, her arms tightly folded. Like the cat that got the cream.

'Just because she used some of Daisy's writing as her own doesn't mean she *killed* her,' I try vainly.

Georgie ignores this, but I know she heard me because I see her jaw twitch. She is the most stubborn person I know, and if she's decided Lauren did it, she'll make events fit her narrative. She's right even when she's wrong, my wife.

'I think you may be taking this and running with it. You can't accuse anyone of murder without proof.'

She whips round so she can yell properly into my face. 'First of all, Dan, don't fucking *speak* to me.'

'What?'

I can feel her fury thrumming through the table. It's that quiet rage that has a slow burn, but can take one's head off once it gathers momentum.

'I don't want to hear another word out of *you*, Dan, because you're biased!' she shrieks in my face.

She knows, she *knows*! She's found out that I've been sleeping with Lauren. Fuck. I barely hear what she says next as I try to think up excuses.

'And *for your information*, she didn't use *some* of Daisy's writing, she *lifted* the lot! She *stole* Daisy's novel! Even you can't spin this to make her innocent.'

'I'm not trying . . . I'm thinking of you. I don't want you winding yourself up and—'

'Winding myself up? Yes, I am! She's a thief, and the worst kind. She's lied and cheated all her adult life. She's lived off Daisy's talent. How can anyone defend her?'

'I wasn't . . . I'm not . . .'

Georgie turns to Alex. 'Daisy was so good. The work may have needed a little editing, but it's not like Lauren even added her own voice, or altered it in any way. It's about the daughter of a single parent, born into poverty in Thatcher's Britain, where everyone was striving, and she and her mum couldn't afford electricity. It's so well told, the writing comes from the heart and is so descriptive – you'd have to have lived through it to write about it. It's the book that Daisy wrote!'

She's now showing Alex the original, which she has on her laptop. 'I kept this and transferred it to every new laptop. I don't know why, I'm no writer – I can't even spell. But I was compelled to keep it – I wonder if Daisy made me do it? I wish I knew about publishing. I would have offered it to an agent on Daisy's behalf. She could have had success posthumously.'

'That's what Lauren should have done,' Alex says.

'Exactly, there's no excuse for it – she could have offered it in Daisy's name. But she didn't, and it's too late now. The newspapers will bloody love this!'

'Poor Daisy.' Maddie wanders over, clutching a cloth covered in blood. She looks so sad. 'I only started the book yesterday, and it was weird, but the voice was familiar. I actually thought I could hear Daisy in some of the words and expressions. It spooked me a bit, to be honest. The story too – about a girl who lives with her mother, the way she negotiated all the difficulties of being young and in love with an older man . . . I assumed Daisy had told Lauren all these things throughout their friendship. I guessed Lauren had been inspired by Daisy . . . but never this.'

Ping!

'Oh God,' Alex groans. 'That ping reminds me, this is a communal area, so everything that's happened this morning will have been recorded.'

'Yes it will, and the world will soon know all about Lauren Pemberton,' Georgie says smugly.

I lean on the counter for support, and Alex increases the volume on his phone so we can all hear.

Then Lauren walks back in, and she looks a mess, covered in blood and milk, her hair everywhere and her eyes swollen from crying. She's been drawn in by her phone – we're all like lemmings heading in the same direction when we hear the ping. She's now leaning in the doorway looking defeated, and I feel sorry for her, but it's embarrassing, and no one acknowledges her entrance. What can you say? Fortunately, we don't have to make conversation, as Tammy's voice soon starts up.

'Welcome back, guys. Well, it's been a fascinating couple of days . . . So let's look at where we're at: five suspects – but only one killer.'

I can feel us all weighing each other up. It's very subtle, but we are all trying not to look guilty. Which probably makes us look more guilty. The tension is tight as a rubber band as we wait in silence for the next voice note.

'So, what have we discovered so far about all you housemates wanting Daisy dead? We know that Georgie wrote the letter pretending to be Daisy, telling Louisa Montgomery that she and her husband were having an affair. We've seen this weekend that Georgie has anger issues, and there have been comments that she was also pretty free and easy with a sharp kitchen knife around Daisy. Into this mix of anger and sharp utensils, Georgie felt her relationship with Dan was threatened by Daisy. Another ingredient to add to this heady cocktail is sexual jealousy, a common motive for murder and a good reason for wanting Daisy dead.

'And what about Baby Spice – Maddie? She's a sweetie – but she has her secrets too. She was close with Daisy – until Lauren came along, and their friendship drifted. With Lauren as her best friend, Daisy made Maddie feel excluded and insignificant. They even mocked her

openly sometimes, which hurt Maddie deeply. But Maddie is kind, and was always there for her friend, cared about her friend, and begged Daisy not to go to David the night she died. If Daisy had only listened . . . So did Maddie feel unheard, and unseen, and had she had enough of feeling like the lesser person in this friendship? Did she want revenge on the mean girl? Was this her motive for murder, and her reason for wanting Daisy dead? And then there's the small matter of Maddie's chosen career . . .

'Now to Daisy's best friend, Lauren – the ambitious wannabe novelist who'd stop at nothing to achieve her dreams. She'd hitched her wagon to Daisy's star, but all it did was leave Lauren in the dust. Despite being Daisy's best friend, Lauren was jealous of her, and constantly complained about Daisy's high marks and accolades for her work. She would never acknowledge that Daisy was cleverer, more talented than she was, and attributed her achievements to favouritism because she was in a relationship with her lecturer. But today, Georgie has revealed that Lauren downloaded Daisy's unpublished novel and passed it off as her own! It's earned millions and a life of luxury for Lauren, who never told a soul that this was her deceased friend's writing and not hers. To gain so much from someone else's work – that's a pretty strong motive for murder, and Lauren had a good reason for wanting Daisy dead.

'Alex . . . He sold drugs to fellow students to pay his way through university, and by his own admission he sometimes pushed those drugs a little harder than he should. And, as a result, a few years later he ended up in prison. Our recordings reveal that Alex loaned Daisy a lot of money when she got into debt in the first year of uni. He discussed this outside with another guest, where he thought he wouldn't be recorded, but our inside mics picked it up. There's also some very interesting, if a little grainy, CCTV footage of Alex and Daisy walking through Exeter together on the day she went missing. At the time, Alex told police that they bumped into each other in the town and went for pizza. What did they discuss during Daisy's last dinner? Did Daisy ask Alex for

more money? Did Alex ask Daisy to pay back all the money he'd been giving her – and did Daisy refuse? Did he feel used, taken for a ride? Is money a motive for murder? Definitely, and a very good reason for wanting Daisy dead.

'Then there's Dan, the ladies' man – according to our source, he has used and abused women all his life, and it seems like Daisy was one of them. She apparently told her mother he harassed her in the house, and he could be quite forceful, even when she said no. He cheated on Georgie with, among others, Daisy, and when Daisy was pregnant there was some question as to who the father was. How did Dan feel about this? Daisy's mother said Dan wasn't happy about Daisy getting back with David. Did Dan feel used and jealous? He wasn't used to being rejected; he was the one who used and rejected. Sex could easily be Dan's motive for murder, and his reason for wanting Daisy dead.

'So, now we'd like you all to think long and hard about everything you know or have learned about your fellow guests this weekend. And if you have the slightest inkling, or know something we don't, please let us know – and you can do that by sending us a voice note before this evening. State who you think killed Daisy and why. You don't have to do this, but let me explain. Firstly, you haven't exactly stayed in touch in the last twenty years, so you can say what you feel – you're unlikely to see these people ever again. Secondly, you might be fighting to prove your own innocence, so don't hold back, because, trust me, your old housemates won't.'

36

LAUREN

I barely heard what Tammy said about anyone else in that bloody suspect round-up, I'm so devastated about my own situation. I could kill Georgie; she's ruined my life. I'm listless, my flesh is tender and I feel like I need to lie down. But I'll just start crying again. I stand in the kitchen doorway trying not to look at Dan, who's sitting close to Georgie, and as soon as the voice note ends I grab my coat and go outside.

I need to think, because it looks like I've lost everything, including my unreliable lover.

I wander outside into the freezing-cold, bright day, and spot Alex having a joint around the back of the bike sheds like he used to. I don't know him as well as I know the others, but I need someone to talk to and let off some steam with, so I go and join him.

'Hey Alex,' I say as I approach. I hadn't realised, but he's on his phone, and as soon as I'm up close he quickly pushes it into his pocket. He looks guilty, but perhaps we all do?

'You okay, Lauren? That got a bit rough in there.'

'Yeah, well, I deserved it. I've been waiting all these years for someone to point the finger. Had nightmares about it – I shouldn't have done it. Just wish it hadn't been Georgie, that's all.'

I watch him sucking at his spliff, holding the smoke in his lungs, then slowly releasing it.

'I never intended to steal her story. My plan was to submit it to publishers and if anyone wanted it I'd agree a deal, say it was Daisy and give the money to Teresa.'

'Why *didn't* you do that?' He offers me the joint. I shake my head. I'm no angel, I took acid when I was younger, but never dope; I always thought it would make me drowsy, and right now that's the last thing I need. With Georgie out to get me, I need to keep my wits about me.

'I didn't come clean because . . . well, because the editor just called me up and started waxing lyrical about what a talent I was. And I was young . . . I know it's no excuse, but . . .'

I turn to him, but Alex rarely looks at people; he seems to live in his own little world, always gazing into the distance, like he's sharing a private joke.

'I was going to tell them but then they offered me this huge advance, and I had no job, I'd just left university . . . I couldn't believe my luck, and I figured Daisy was dead, so it was no use to her.'

'Your parents had money, though, right? I mean, you weren't on the street?'

'No . . . But I wanted my independence, didn't want to stay living with my parents, and the advance would give me the opportunity to start my life.'

'How much was the advance?' He takes another puff. Then he finally looks at me. He's interested now.

I'm shocked that he'd ask, though. It's so impolite.

'Six figures?' he asks. He's quite pushy.

'Something like that.'

'*Shit.*' As he exhales, I breathe in the heavy herbal waft; it's not unpleasant. 'That's a lot of money for doing nothing.'

'I didn't do nothing, I changed the ending . . .' I say defensively. He's made me feel terrible; all the guilt is brimming just under the surface – it always has been. 'My agent helped me to rewrite the end, because of course Daisy hadn't finished her story . . .'

There's an uncomfortable silence.

'So they wanted the protagonist to be murdered . . .' I say, 'like . . .'

'Daisy.'

'I guess, but the heroine wasn't called Daisy. It was fiction.'

'Yeah, I know,' he says slowly, staring ahead. I think he hates me. I never have been able to read him. 'So you killed the protagonist – did you kill Daisy?' he suddenly asks, like we're talking about the weather.

I'm shocked. 'No, I didn't. Alex, I may be a plagiarist, but I'm not a murderer. So I stole my dead friend's manuscript and passed it off as my own, but it doesn't mean . . .'

'When you put it like that, Lauren . . . it sounds almost as bad as murder,' he chuckles, and holding the spliff between thumb and forefinger he puts it to his lips.

'No it isn't, it's nothing like murder. It wasn't a *frenzied* attack on another person, it was an honest mistake!'

'*Honest?*' He laughs, and I remember why I never bothered with him – he made me feel stupid, used my own words against me and twisted me into knots. Alex was very clever, cleverer than anyone gave him credit for.

'A mistake then,' I correct myself.

'A *big* mistake, and plagiarism is a criminal offence,' he says slowly, like it doesn't really matter but he thought he'd just mention it.

'You don't think I'll go to prison, do you?'

He shrugs. 'I dunno. You might?'

'I have a young daughter. I can't leave her.'

'You just have to make the best of it – write the book about how you wrote a book and got found out . . . You'll have plenty of time to write if you do end up in prison.'

'I suppose so.' I breathe in his sweet smoke, and relax a little. 'Finty will have kittens when I tell her the truth.'

'Who's Finty? Your cat?'

'*No!* My agent. I don't mean she'll literally have kittens.' I glance at him, wondering if the dope has addled his mind, but he's smiling, looking at me sideways. He's teasing me. 'I thought I was talking to Maddie for a moment,' I joke.

'Ah, Maddie. She plays you all. Always has. Everyone used to roll their eyes and say she was slow, but did you know her IQ is something like 140 . . . ?' He blows smoke high into the air.

I'm shocked. 'I *didn't* know – she's never said. If I had a really high IQ I'd want everyone to know.'

'That's because you haven't got a high IQ. You have to be a genius to appreciate the value of keeping your IQ to yourself.'

'Oh, I see.' Is what he just said really profound or really stupid? I'm sure he's high, and I'm not convinced that Maddie's a genius.

He continues to gaze out on to the misty playing fields, exhaling another thick cloud of cannabis into the cold air.

'I just hope to Christ that Teresa doesn't sue me for the money, the big advance, the royalties even. I don't have anything left.'

'What, nothing left after six figures?'

'Well, it sounds more than it is. I mean, once you've bought a house and paid for your child's education there isn't any change, even out of six figures,' I point out truthfully. 'But for a while we had even more. The film and investments – it just kept pouring in. That's when we bought our place in LA. But then Richard and I took risks, made some bad investments. The sharks saw us coming, and convinced us wet-behind-the-ears millionaires to buy hundreds of thousands of pounds of stock that was apparently "a dead cert".' I look at him and he knows the punchline. 'It wasn't. And, between us, now we *literally* have nothing.'

'Shit,' he says, without much feeling.

'Yeah, it's been a roller coaster. In August I was forced to sell the last of my designer handbags.' He doesn't react, so I explain. 'It was a Balenciaga Bel Air medium leather tote in ebony.'

'Right.'

'My heart literally *broke*, Alex.'

'I bet.'

I think he's being sarcastic. I was never sure if he was laughing with me or at me, and now I know it was at me. Still, I'd rather be here breathing in weird Alex's expelled smoke and feeling mellow than anywhere near violent, vindictive Georgie and her cowardly husband.

'Richard had to sell both his cars. We've moved to a poky little house. Oh God – I never told Richard the truth about the book, and it's all going to come out now, she'll make sure of that. He's going to be so upset.'

'You even told your hubby you wrote it?' Alex chuckles at this.

'I met him around the time it was first published. He was impressed, and I thought he might not like me if he knew the truth. I was suddenly very popular with a lot of people – strangers, really – who suddenly started inviting me for drinks, wanting me at their parties. Richard became my plus-one, then he became the only person I could really trust.'

'That's sad, Lauren.'

'Yeah, well, it's all gone down the toilet now. I guess that's my retribution. Everything has a price,' I add, reaching for the joint. 'I never took his name, I always kept mine, Pemberton,' I say slowly, feeling the plum of the 'P' in my mouth.

'You don't have to take your husband's name,' he murmurs vaguely.

'No . . . But for me it was more than that,' I say, aware that just breathing the smoky air is making my tongue loose. 'I wanted my teenage name on the book, that's who I was in the newspapers and TV at the time . . . It's associated with Daisy and her . . . death.'

'It was our fifteen minutes of fame, I guess?'

'Well, I wouldn't call it that.'

'I would.'

I look at him; he isn't joking, he's just staring ahead. I didn't have him down as judgy – what's he trying to say?

'I just feel more *me* as Pemberton,' I reply, holding the spliff between my finger and thumb. I tentatively take a great big puff, and after a bit of a cough I do it again.

'Whoa, Lauren, mate – you need to take it easy, man, that stuff is strong, and you're not used to it.'

'I'm fine, it isn't even making me feel anything. I'm still angry and uptight and ashamed.' I hand back the spliff. 'Weird, isn't it?' I say.

'What?'

'We lost Daisy twenty years ago, yet it turns out that in all those years she never left. She's been with each one of us, keeping our secrets, reminding us all who we are – I didn't always like her, but I *always* loved her.'

'Yeah, me too.'

I glance over, and see something unfathomable in his eyes. I wonder if Alex is deeper than any of us give him credit for?

'Did it bother you that Daisy never paid you back? Was Tammy right when she said it was your motive for murder, Alex?'

He pauses a while, then, shaking his head, says: 'I was happy to help her out, I never wanted her to pay me back. I cared about her, she was my friend, but she made some stupid choices over stupid men, and she wouldn't listen.'

I hear a flicker of irritation in his voice, and feel a chill as I remember that the supposedly calm, affable Alex was the last one of us to see Daisy alive.

37

GEORGIE

'How have I held on all these years?' I hear myself say to Dan in the silent aftermath of breakfast.

Everyone has left the room, and we're sitting at the table, just the two of us, and Dan has his head in his hands. A litter of croissant crumbs, screwed-up napkins and sticky coffee circles are all that's left of Apartment 101's breakfast.

Dan reaches his hand along the table and touches mine, but I recoil and snatch it away.

'No, Dan, living in the past this weekend has helped me see the future, and it isn't pretty.'

'If you're talking about Lauren then you're being silly. Yes, she's been after me all weekend, but nothing happened.'

'We both know that's not true; when I told everyone about Lauren stealing Daisy's manuscript, I was preparing for act two – the "you two are having an affair" monologue. And before she stomped off, I tried really hard to gather the energy to do it. I focused on the two of you having sex in *our* car, her on *my* seat, and *you* promising you weren't cheating. I really tried to get angry, an emotion I've never had an issue conjuring up from nowhere – but guess what? I'm not even angry. You've finally managed to numb my feelings, and all I feel now is sad – for *you*.'

'What do you mean, *sad*?' He seems offended.

'Because I've wasted too much time on you – on us. All the nights I've cried myself to sleep over the past twenty years, telling myself I need to be sexier, slimmer, a better wife, less angry, more understanding, a better *person* – when all the time it's been *you* who needs to change, not me. I've always known who you are, but I just told myself, *he's a good father, a good provider, he's funny, he puts up with me*. But is that the kind of love to build a marriage on, to pin a life to? I'm almost forty, and if I'm lucky I have at least another thirty years of this, and I can't do it anymore. I live on the edge, not knowing where you are, who you're with, and pretending to myself that your "fantasies" are enough to keep us together. But they aren't, and they never will be, because you want the real thing. I'm sure you believe that running home and telling me everything not only gives you a thrill but also legitimises your betrayal.'

'Betrayal?' He scoffs at the word, thinking I'm being dramatic. He really has no feelings, no empathy. And he says *I'm* the psychopath. Dan thinks and cares only for himself, and I've immersed myself so deeply in this life with him that I've lost myself. I'm overwhelmed. But I don't want him to see me cry – I *never* cry.

'I saw the look on everyone's face when I confronted Lauren about the book earlier, and I felt *ashamed*. Have I really become so cruel, Dan? Am I now reduced to getting my kicks by hurting other people just because *I* live in a permanent state of hurt? What Lauren did was bad, but I can see how she got caught up in a world that flattered and fawned, and who am I to criticise? I've done a lot worse.'

'I don't want to talk about this . . .'

'You don't have to talk about it – but for once you will *listen*!'

We glare at each other across the table, and he's the first to look away, so I continue.

'When I found out that Daisy was pregnant, I was so hurt, I tried to finish with you. It was late September. You said she'd only just found out – "a missed period" was how you described it. I didn't believe you then, and I don't now. You must have been sleeping with her long before I knew. You'd made out that I was always involved, but you'd obviously already slept with her when you tried to finish with me . . .'

'Look, you begged and begged me to stay – I didn't know what to do.'

'So I'm right. You were sleeping with Daisy in the summer?'

'I slept with her once, in the August. You probably remember, I went to Exeter and moved some of my stuff into the house. She was really down because David had gone on holiday with his family. She'd hung around Exeter all summer to be with him, and said she felt used. She was lonely, and so was I because you were at home with your family.'

'Yeah, I was at home with my parents – it was the summer holidays. How like you to somehow make it my fault that you slept with someone else in my absence. You've never been honest with me, Dan. You haven't changed – you never will. You convinced me that Daisy was pregnant from sleeping with her at the beginning of term, when I was with you both. You see, even when you'd done terrible things, you could always persuade me otherwise. You'd tell me lies, flatter me, make all kinds of promises you'd never any intention of keeping. But this weekend, something has finally clicked, coming back here to where it all happened, where you gaslighted me, betrayed me and used me; now I realise it wasn't your persuasive charm or seduction techniques that kept me with you, it was my *low self-esteem*. I never understood what you saw in me, and I was so grateful for any crumb this handsome, intelligent boy could throw my way. And you did, you threw me crumbs for a long time, nothing more – and my friends would tell me you were a cheater, but I wouldn't listen. I thought I loved you, but it wasn't love. I'm not sure I've ever truly loved anyone, because you've always stood in the way of real love for me. You were *familiar*, and with you I felt this strange comfort I was accustomed to but couldn't quite understand. Now I know – it's because men like you are all I've ever known. My father and later my stepfather were both unfaithful men who had no real regard for my mother, just used her and betrayed her. I realise now that subconsciously I'd soaked it up, thinking that was what love looked like. Just like the men who took my mother for granted, for you I was convenient.'

'Not true,' he monotones dismissively, like he's bored.

'It is. It began at uni – I cooked for you, and cleaned your room because my obsessive cleanliness couldn't ignore the mess and dust. I even did your washing.'

'I never asked you to.'

'No, you didn't, but that's not the point. I'm not blaming you for my obsession with cleanliness, but I think it's become worse over the years. We both enabled each other in different ways. I enabled you to be unfaithful and you enabled me to turn myself into your mother – and your rescuer.'

'What are you *talking* about, Georgie?' He has this way of looking at me that makes me feel stupid.

Not anymore.

'I was the person you ran to when you were in trouble, and I never let you down. I'm tired of saving you. And I know what will happen now. Having led Lauren to believe she's more than a fling, she won't let you go. She'll call you and beg you, and ultimately I'll have to deal with it, and sort your mess out, because you've no intention of leaving me. I don't flatter myself – it isn't about me – but why should you leave someone who looks after your kids, keeps your home spotless, does everything so you can do nothing? And I pretend not to notice when you come home late, smelling of another woman's perfume.'

'I won't leave you, Georgie, I love you.'

'You really don't listen, do you? I'm leaving *you*. I hate who I've become and I have to try and be a better person. I have to start by letting go of the past – and you're part of that.'

We sit in silence, and I think about everything that's happened, while he no doubt replays his own version.

When he discovered Daisy was pregnant, Dan was a mess. He was in tears when he told me, more scared that his dad would cut off his allowance than anything else. And, believe it or not, as devastated as I was, I felt flattered that he'd told me and touched that he wanted my help. He was desperate for Daisy not to have the baby, as was I – and we assumed she'd want the same. So, I arranged for the three of us to meet up in a bar in town, and he offered her the money to have an abortion.

'No way,' she said. 'I'm having this baby whether you want it or not. My mum was almost made to have an abortion when she was carrying me. I couldn't even think about it.'

I hate myself for this now, but I really tried to convince her to do it. 'Look, it's the best thing for you and the baby. You won't be able to continue your studies – you won't be able to even *afford* a baby.'

I didn't care about Daisy's baby; I only cared about my future with Dan and how this inconvenience would impact that. He was the same.

I *hate* who we were. And I hate who we are now.

I was seeing a very different life than the one I'd envisaged for Dan and me. A life Daisy and her child would always be part of, and when she got bored or was in between boyfriends she'd weave her magic and lure Dan back. We'd never be free of her: she'd emotionally blackmail him, seduce him whenever she wanted anything, and demand his support.

We all walked home that night, and I knew we couldn't just leave it, so when Dan came to my room later, we talked into the small hours about what to do.

Less than two months later, Daisy was dead.

38

MADDIE

I had a shower after breakfast and returned to the kitchen later to find everyone gone, so checked in the bread bin and the fridge for leftovers.

I'm on the sofa spooning bright-orange marmalade on to a leftover croissant when Georgie wanders in and flops down next to me. 'I was just writing up what I was going to say in my voice note condemning Lauren, stating that she killed Daisy because she wanted to steal her work and make loads of money – but I'm not sure I can do that.'

'Okay. Why?'

'Because it probably isn't true.'

'Fair enough. I think right now we all just need to calm down and be kind to each other.'

She turns to me. She seems engaged for once, interested in what I have to say. 'You know, Maddie, I envy you – no partner, no kids, you live a happy life teaching yoga. You never seem to get wound up or fall in love with the wrong people – and look at you. You're gorgeous, and you don't have to watch your figure.'

My mouth is full of buttery croissant and tangy orange and I want to laugh at her perception.

I finish my mouthful and say, 'Don't look at me and see something that isn't there. It will only make you unhappy – because you'll think I've found the answer, and I haven't, Georgie. I'm probably as unhappy as you – I just don't show it.'

She looks surprised. 'Don't take this the wrong way, Maddie, but that's deep . . . I didn't expect to hear that from you.'

'Which is my point. We all have these perceptions of people, even our friends, and some people might see you as an angry, bossy, controlling person, but I just see frustration and sadness and . . . disappointment.'

Her eyes suddenly fill with tears. 'You're right. On the surface people can't see why I'm unhappy; I seem to have everything, but I have nothing.'

'You just have to find what's right for you, listen to yourself and work it out. Just knowing that another person can't bring you what you crave is a start – and don't be fooled by the phrase "you complete me". It's a con. It's co-dependent drivel.'

'Wow. You don't need anyone, do you, Maddie?'

'No – in fact I crave solitude more than I ever have. I listened to myself and discovered that's what I need more than anything. I don't need other people, and there's no shame in saying I don't have any friends, and I don't want any either. Stop forcing yourself into other people's ideas of what you are, what you should be – it's such a positive energy when you let go and just do you. People think because I'm childless and single I'm unhappy, but it's the opposite – I have my career, and my memories, and Minty my cat . . . and that's enough.'

'Did you have a happy childhood?' she asks, proving once more that these people really never took the time to get to know me.

'Not really. I loved my mum, but my dad died when I was very young. I barely remember him. Like Daisy, it was always just Mum and me, and it was a struggle – that's why she and I bonded as soon as we got to university, we could relate to each other. But my memories before university are mostly sad, and the saddest are still from my days at ballet school. Mum always loved dance, and was delighted when I got a scholarship to ballet school. It was near London and we moved house so I could go there.'

'How good of your mum to do that.'

'Yes, it was, but it also put pressure on me to succeed. And it wasn't quite the Angelina Ballerina world I'd dreamed of.' I smile. 'The training was gruelling, and starting as a six-year-old, most of my childhood was swallowed up. One of my earliest memories there is being told by my ballet teacher I was "too fat for a ballet dancer",' I say, looking at my croissant. 'See, even now, eating brings on guilt and shame . . .'

'Maddie, that's awful. I knew you'd been to ballet school, but I had no idea.'

'It was brutal. I remember a teacher standing me in front of the full-length studio mirror and telling me, "If you don't get those hips down, you'll never be a ballerina." So when I say ballet school shaped me, I mean it both metaphorically and literally – because crap like that gets in your head and sits there forever.'

'I'm sorry you had to go through that,' she says, sincerely.

I take a sip of coffee. 'It wasn't just the teachers; there was this competitive bullying culture which really became ingrained in an institution like that. By the age of nine we were openly body-shaming our friends, and privately body-shaming ourselves.'

'Christ, I have two girls, it horrifies me.' Her eyes are kind, and she's genuinely concerned. Perhaps beneath the anger and sadness there's a warm heart in Georgie – I just never saw it before. 'So, what happened . . . ?'

'Eventually I was given an ultimatum. "Lose a stone, or lose your place at ballet school" . . . And by then my breasts had started to grow. They were full and cumbersome and one teacher even suggested binding them with bandages . . . At eleven I was ashamed and embarrassed by my breasts.'

'Shit.' She's shaking her head.

'They suggested Mum put me on diet pills. I lost loads of weight and everyone was pleased. For a few months everything was fine again, I had huge amounts of energy, my body felt right, my training was going well. The teachers were thrilled, constantly telling me how great I looked now, which made me think I must have looked horrible before. I didn't tell anyone, but the pills made me jittery, unhappy, like I had this huge emptiness inside, and though my dancing was the best it had ever been, I lost *me*.'

'That sounds horrible, and you were only a kid . . . What, about twelve?'

I nod. 'I told Mum how I felt and she immediately took me off the pills. But they were speed – I'd been on them for months and was now coming down and feeling hungry again. Starving, actually. That's when I began to self-medicate with doughnuts and crisps and chocolate, all the things I hadn't been allowed to eat most of my life.'

'That explains the mountain of crisp bags and chocolate wrappers I used to find hidden in the bottom of the bin. I was the only one who ever emptied the bins, and no one would ever own up to the wrappers.'

'Yeah, that was me.' I remember we're in a recording area, and whisper, 'I'm . . . bulimic, and I tried to hide what I did, but it still lives with me, controls my days and my nights. It's like having a demanding partner – I can't go out or do anything without checking in with my bulimia first.'

'Maddie, is this your secret?' She takes my cue and whispers back. 'Because if it is, you need to start sharing it, and getting help.'

I nod, ashamed of myself, and she reaches out, hugging me warmly, and I want to cry.

'I've never told anyone . . . Please don't . . .' I say into her neck.

'I won't.' She lets go and, holding me by the shoulders, searches my face. 'As long as you promise you'll get help,' she says quietly.

'I will,' I lie, knowing I'll never do that. It might kill me, but I'd rather die than live without it. I guess that's how love feels.

Suddenly Dan appears in the doorway. 'What are you two doing?' I think he's surprised to see Georgie hugging someone.

'Nothing,' I say tearfully, and go to my room, where I continue to think about the past, and it all floods back. I left ballet school at twelve for a very different world at the local comprehensive, where I was a novelty. The girls asked me questions about my life as a ballet dancer like I'd just floated in from another planet. The boys just looked at my breasts. At first the girls were friendly, not competitive and mean like my ballet friends, but because I'd had to *live* ballet for most of my life, there wasn't much left of me. It was the late nineties, and though I'd heard of the Spice Girls and Madonna, I'd never listened to their music. My new friends loved someone called Ricky Martin, and I asked if he went to our school. I'd never heard of him, and that's when they realised I wasn't a novelty – I was different.

That's when the bullying started. I simply didn't fit in, and instead of fighting it and trying to be someone I wasn't, I stayed true to myself. I was seen as a loner, and when the boys grabbed me and touched me in places I didn't want to be touched, no one believed me because I was 'weird'.

I think that continued when I got to university, but doing drama I used to hide behind characters. This weekend has brought it all back: the not belonging, the lack of acceptance, and Daisy, the only one who really knew me. She could be mean, she sometimes picked on me publicly, but that's because she didn't want anyone else to know we were friends.

I remember her in freshers' week: she was standing in the student union, long fair hair, perfect skin and a soft, curvy body. A light from the DJ booth was shining behind her, and she looked like an angel sent from heaven. I'd been flirting with religion around this time, and I saw it as a sign that she had been sent from God.

We just got each other, and I can't believe I'll never see her again – in this life, anyway. Even now I keep expecting her to come running out of her room in high heels, tugging her short dress down, with dark lipstick and those smoky eyes. She just made me smile, and I wanted to spend every moment with her. I wanted to *be* Daisy.

I could see she was heading down a dangerous path, sleeping with a married lecturer, but she wouldn't listen. Then Dan came into her life. The night she went to meet David down on the beach, Dan called and asked if they could meet, and she said no, she was going to see David. She was angry; she told him to stop calling her or she'd tell Georgie. I told her that neither of them were good enough for her, that she should just tell them both to get lost and give herself time to work out what she wanted. But she wouldn't listen to me. No one ever listened to me. And that night she went out, and never came home.

39

Transcript from *The Killer Question* Podcast

Episode 9: Interview with Alex Jones, Daisy's Housemate and Friend

TAMMY: Hey guys, welcome to the final dinner. Hope you're all enjoying your pre-dinner drinks. We chose the Gin Daisy cocktail for obvious reasons. Because he arrived late, Alex Jones hasn't had the opportunity to take part and tell us his side of things. Do we really know him? What was his relationship like with Daisy? How does he feel about his friends and former housemates? So, we've prerecorded an interview with him so he can share his perspective.

Hey Alex. Now, we just want to clear a few things up – for our listeners, mostly. On more than one occasion this weekend, you've been referred to by your old housemates, and yourself, as a 'junkie'. Is this true?

ALEX: Nah, I was just a dealer who dabbled a bit. *(Alex gives a faint laugh.)* I never had a problem with drugs.

TAMMY: Okay, so we've cleared that one up. Now, you and Daisy met on the day she went missing?

ALEX: Yeah, yeah we did.

TAMMY: Wanna talk about it?

ALEX: It was talked about in court – nothing to see here. I bumped into her in Exeter city centre and she seemed a bit lost. So I took her for pizza, and we talked. She'd told me she was pregnant a few weeks before, and the baby was David's. 'I'm meeting him tonight in Exmouth,' she said. 'We're going to talk about the baby, and what we're going to do.'

TAMMY: Okay, and did she seem nervous? Happy? Unsure? What was her mood?

ALEX: Yeah, I'd say happy about the baby – but a little nervous and uncertain about David's intentions. She hoped he'd just agree to be with her, but she knew he'd been upset about her supposedly telling his wife, and she worried he'd blame her for losing his family.

TAMMY: Yes, because after Louisa received the letter about the affair she went straight into divorce mode.

ALEX: Apparently, yes.

TAMMY: We also revealed earlier today that you loaned Daisy a lot of money during her first year, which she never paid back. Was this mentioned at the lunch?

ALEX: No. Look, I didn't expect the money back. For God's sake, it was Daisy – she never had any money.

TAMMY: Did Daisy's death affect you, Alex?

ALEX: Of course it affected me, Tammy. What kind of person do you think I am?

TAMMY: Sorry, it's just—

ALEX: I loved Daisy, and her death sent me into a spiral. I still wonder even now if there was something I should have said or done that day that might have made a difference.

TAMMY: You were the last to see Daisy, weren't you?

ALEX: Yes, of all of us here – but the last person to see her was her killer.

TAMMY: That wasn't you?

ALEX: No, no it wasn't. I had no reason to want Daisy dead! *(Silence for four seconds.)* Apologies if I snapped at you then, I just feel guilty . . . like I should have protected her, I dunno.

(Sound off, as there is a four-second pause in the recording.)

TAMMY: So, you told your secret on arrival yesterday – that you've done time in prison.

ALEX: Yeah. I earned a lot of money dealing drugs at uni. Something I'm deeply ashamed of now. I didn't understand the implications. I was just trying to make money, and I will always feel bad for that. There are no excuses, but I had no parenting, no moral code, if you like. I was young and poor, and my childhood spent in children's homes wasn't exactly inspirational, and though I got into uni, I still found it hard to shake the other side of me. If I hadn't had that short stint in prison for drug dealing, I wouldn't be where I am today.

TAMMY: And where's that, Alex?

ALEX: Well, Tammy, I'm happily married to the love of my life, I have a fascinating career, and I'm involved in charity work, which is what I love. And despite being a bit snappy today – apologies again – I'm a lot calmer and less anxious about life these days.

TAMMY: You earn a lot of money. But you don't use it to buy cars and houses, you use it to help people?

ALEX: Yeah, I've set up several charities. I guess I'm trying to redeem myself – for the mistakes I made selling drugs when I was younger.

TAMMY: Now, back to Daisy . . . You say when you met up for a pizza that day, you talked about the baby. Did she explain that, at the time, there was some question over the paternity of that baby?

ALEX: I . . . No. It was David's, she'd presumably worked it out and was sure.

TAMMY: Really?

ALEX: Oh yes, but David was still angry with her, and she was scared he was about to reject her once and for all. This would be devastating emotionally, but also she couldn't afford to bring up a baby alone.

TAMMY: So she was definitely going to have the baby, even if David didn't want to get back together?

ALEX: Yeah. You know, I think people might be surprised at that. Daisy sometimes gave the impression she just wanted to party, but she was so much more than that. She wanted a home, a family; she and Maddie and I didn't have traditional family units, so we envied our rich friends with en-suite student bedrooms and two parents. We thought the grass was greener. I guess we all wanted the white picket fence, and Daisy wanted her child to have a better life than she'd had. That's why she'd told Dan that the baby might be his.

TAMMY: And Dan bought this?

ALEX: Yeah, he totally thought it was his. She knew it was wrong, but his family were wealthy, and Dan would look after her and the baby financially, and give them a good life. She told me she would marry him or do whatever was necessary for the baby if David rejected her.

TAMMY: Do you think she had feelings for Dan too?

ALEX: No, she said she could never love someone like Dan, she was just playing him. What can I tell you, Tammy? Daisy was a survivor, and she used what she had to get by. As for Dan, he'd used enough girls in his time, and now someone was using him – it's only what he deserved.

TAMMY: And what about you, Alex? You said earlier you loved Daisy. Were you in love with her?

(Silence for five seconds.)

ALEX: Yeah. In a way, but I saw her completely for who she really was. By that I mean I understood and accepted her flaws because she was a hustler, like me. I didn't like that about her, but I also didn't like that I sold drugs. We just did what we did. But, in the end, I believed in her and me. I knew we could both be fixed, and we would thrive if we found someone who made us feel safe. But not each other.

TAMMY: Teresa, Daisy's mother, has told us that Daisy talked of you fondly in her calls home. She respected and trusted you. Is that because you saw beyond Daisy's beauty and appreciated her talent and intelligence?

ALEX: I'm glad to hear that – I didn't know she talked about me to her mum. So many people used Daisy: David played with her, Lauren stole her work, Dan used her in his usual way, and Georgie – well, she was so messed up she'd have done whatever Dan asked of her. I'm glad Daisy knew she could trust me and felt I was there for her.

TAMMY: Did you try and advise her on her situation over pizza that day?

ALEX: Yeah, I did. I said I thought she was being unfair to Dan. I mean, even he didn't deserve that. Besides, his father was a piece of work, and may have demanded a DNA test to prove the baby was his. But she wasn't listening, she only wanted my approval.

TAMMY: And when she didn't get it, was she angry with you? Did she hate that you'd called her out?

ALEX: No . . . I think I know where you're going with this. I'm not answering any more questions.

(The recording is silent for seven seconds.)
Episode ends.

Transcript from *The Killer Question* Podcast

Episode 10: Tiffany Reveals Tammy's Secret

TIFFANY: Hi. Just a little reminder, I'm the producer of *The Killer Question*, and also Tammy's little sister. And I'm here to tell you something, because we don't usually keep anything back from our listeners. So, for this weekend to work, we've had to conceal one or two things from both our guests and our listeners. Apologies, this isn't something we would ever normally do, but if you'd known, it wouldn't have worked, and as you now know, this particular series of podcasts is extremely close to our hearts, and we wanted to find the killer even more than we ever have before, to clear our father's name.

So, a couple of years ago, Tammy joined a true crime chatroom, and started chatting to a guy called Alex. They got along really well, through a shared fascination of complicated, true-life murder cases. Alex was in the US and Tammy was here in the UK, but they discovered straight away that their interest had been inspired by one big case from 2005, and both had their own reasons for feeling close to the case. It was the murder of Daisy Harrington by her lecturer Professor David Montgomery.

Tammy's interest was obviously down to David being our dad. We believed he was innocent and we were desperate to see justice done. Tammy was pleased to hear her online friend Alex also questioned the verdict. He said he'd always felt it was 'too neatly packaged up', and that one or two of his housemates should have been looked at more closely, because they probably had reasons to want Daisy dead.

What are the chances of these two people randomly meeting on a true crime chat group? Tammy says it was fate, and that Alex was meant to come into our lives, and they just kept talking and talking about the case and how they could get more information.

The podcast was already up and running, but we needed IT support and financial support too. Alex said he'd help us, and give us the resources to research and hopefully discover the truth about Daisy's murder. It's taken two years to get to where we are this weekend, and we couldn't have done it without Alex's support, and his company's expertise.

But, most of all, Alex is an ideas man, and last year he suggested we do a 'special'. He offered to reconnect with a couple of our guests, the ones he had his own friendships or relationships with. He didn't call Dan or Lauren because he had never been close to them, but he started chatting online and on the phone with Maddie, who he'd kept in touch with since uni, and Georgie. And the more Alex chatted and rekindled his friendships with those two guests, the more he learned. Within a relatively short time, Alex's theory that one or two of the housemates might have had a reason to kill Daisy changed to all four of them. From researching online and talking to these two key housemates, Alex now knew that each one of the four former friends had a reason to want Daisy dead. That's when we started to set up the weekend, send out invitations, and plan this series of Who Wanted Daisy Dead? So, which one of you is it?

But there's one more little surprise for you guys having dinner right now. Alex and Tammy remained friends throughout the investigation, and this friendship deepened across the miles. Just a month ago, my wonderful sister Tammy – aka Cordelia Montgomery – and Alex Jones were married, in a beautiful ceremony at Alex's home in San Francisco. I'm Tiffany – Cassie Montgomery – and my family and I have been through so much pain. But today I'm the proudest sister, sister-in-law, and soon-to-be auntie the podcast world has ever known!

40

Dan

Wow! That was a twist. Well, more than one, actually. Firstly, *WTF*? I thought I'd got Daisy pregnant, and for twenty years I thought that baby was mine, but it turns out it was David's all along. And secondly, *WTF* 2? Turns out Alex is behind all this? I dislike him even more now he's trying to put one of us in jail to clear his father-in-law's name. I'm looking over at Alex and finding it hard to believe that he has this amazing life that I could only dream of, and I googled those sisters and both are hot. They're English too – the flirty SoCal girls I'd imagined, sunning themselves on the beaches of Malibu were just an illusion, a rather nice one, but not real.

'Hey Alex, you could have told us,' I say, which is an understatement.

'If I had, it wouldn't have worked. We needed you all to be honest.'

'I guess that explains why you've been in touch with my wife again this year. Just wanted to find some dirt, did you?' I ask, wondering what the fuck Georgie's been saying to him.

'Don't be like that, Dan. I wanted to reconnect with a couple of the people I was fond of – and along the way I got a picture of their lives now, and their feelings about Daisy. It's all cool, man.'

I don't respond. I'm still humiliated that Daisy told him she was basically just using me as a cash line for her and the baby if David dumped her. What a bitch she was. Georgie was right all along.

We're down to the serious stuff now, and as great as it all is for Alex and his new bride, it feels like the Last Supper to me.

I was hoping, as it was our final day, we might all spend it together. Who knew what would happen at dinner, and I felt the need for company. But earlier everyone took to their rooms, and Lauren locked her door – I know because I tried it. I might attempt to make some amends there, but I think that's over now. It's a relief, actually; she wanted more than I could give.

But I'm worried that this has pushed Georgie too far. Earlier today, she told me she was leaving me. At first I thought I could talk her round, convince her that Lauren was just a one-off here last night – and how could she break up our family because of a one-night stand? But she really wasn't receptive to anything I had to say. In fact, she became more and more angry with me.

'Dan,' she finally said, 'I want a divorce.'

I was shocked; I'd never expected that. In all the time we've been together, no matter how angry she's been, she's never asked me for a divorce.

I'm still trying to process this, and I'm concerned she might actually mean it.

I guess my takeaway from the weekend is to make sure the woman I'm seeing on the side isn't an old college friend. Or someone from my wife's book club, or a mother at our kids' school – yeah, that was a tricky one.

But Georgie will come round; she always does. When we get home, we'll see the kids and I'll take us all out for pizza and everything will be back to normal, and I'll try to be faithful – for a while, anyway. If, on the other hand, she means it, a divorce will cost me a fortune. God, I hope I can convince her otherwise once we're home . . . If we go home? If they reveal tonight that Georgie did it, I might be asking *her* for a divorce.

This weekend has been so tense, and despite the threats from Tammy and Tiffany that they will discover who did it, I doubt they will. We all have our stories and secrets, and our own individual relationships with Daisy, be they good or bad.

What no one knows, even Georgie, is that, just the day before she went missing, Daisy asked to talk with me alone.

'Come to my room later,' she whispered in the kitchen. 'Don't bring her!'

So, that night, when Georgie was asleep, I crept into Daisy's room. There, she told me she wanted to be with me, and that I was the love of her life. I was surprised at this sudden love-bombing, because Daisy, Georgie and I had, a few weeks before, had a very difficult conversation about the baby. We wanted Daisy to have an abortion, but Daisy had completely rejected the idea. I have to say I wasn't as *against* the baby as Georgie was, but I *was* scared about telling my dad I'd got a girl pregnant. Sticking with Georgie and letting her sort it all out was the easiest and kindest thing for me to do. But there I was, in the bedroom next to Georgie's, with this beautiful girl telling me she loved me and wanted to keep my baby. I kept looking at her and thinking about coming home to her every night, with these little fair-haired kids running around. Daisy was calm and chilled, rarely lost her temper and never tried to control me – in fact I was the one trying to control her. I wanted to *keep* her. And that's when I really started to change my mind.

'Shouldn't a baby have a mother *and* a father?' she said.

'Absolutely. I want it too,' I said, and I felt so happy.

But now I know that it wasn't my baby, it was David's all along, and Daisy was just using me. And *she would have gone on using me. Georgie said that's what she was doing, and she was right – she's always right. How am I going to survive if she divorces me?*

I never told Georgie about this encounter with Daisy; she would have gone through the roof, caused the biggest scene, and probably dumped me straight away. I wasn't going to tell Georgie and wreck what we had before seeing how things might be with Daisy. I mean, you don't give up your job without securing another one first, do you?

So the next day I called Daisy, to try to plan our escape, but she burst into tears as soon as she picked up the phone. She said she still felt the same, but she'd also been talking to David and felt very mixed up. I realise now that Daisy was doing the exact same thing to me as I was to her – checking everything out before making a choice.

I tried not to put too much pressure on her over the phone. But I wanted her and the baby even more now, and I knew if I saw her in the flesh I could convince her to be with me. So I asked if I could meet her.

'Not tonight, I'm going to Exmouth to meet David,' she told me. 'Perhaps tomorrow?'

I may be a bit of a hypocrite, but there was no way I was waiting for her to see David and then choose *him*. I had to get to her first. So I told Georgie I was popping out for a few drinks with a mate. She was pissed off, but by then I didn't care, I just wanted to see Daisy. I got in the car and waited outside our house for about half an hour, and then she eventually appeared. She wandered off down the road to get her bus for her romantic reunion with David. But I wasn't having that.

I stayed a safe distance from the bus all the way, and eventually pulled in near the beach, a few hundred yards from the bus stop.

It was dark and cold, and no one was about. I didn't really know anyone in Exmouth anyway, so I was pretty safely tucked away. I could see her, but she couldn't see me.

I was there a while, and then I saw someone walking along the front. At first I thought it was Daisy – they were about the same build – but then the person disappeared. I couldn't really see from where I was, but by the time I got out of the car, there was a figure on the beach, and it looked like Daisy. I decided to have a discreet stroll – see if it was her, and if so I'd go and talk to her, try and convince her to be with me.

But before I could get down to the beach, I saw the figure of a man walk down to meet her, and immediately I realised it was David. Trying to keep out of sight, I moved nearer to where the couple were, and it was definitely him and Daisy, as by then some of her long blonde hair had escaped her woolly hat. My heart stung seeing her with him, and it was painful to watch as they embraced for a long time. I didn't want to see this, but at the same time I couldn't leave. I felt rooted to the spot, just watching them and wishing it was me with her, down there on the beach. I hung around for a while, and eventually watched them disappear arm in arm towards the beach huts. I assumed they were heading inside one to talk, or make up, and they did – they had sex in the beach hut, which was revealed later through the DNA tests.

They were gone for about half an hour, and eventually I realised there was no point me hanging around, so I started to walk back to my car. But as I turned to go, I suddenly became aware of a figure standing on the beach, looking back at the beach huts. It was odd for someone to be standing there alone and still, in the freezing cold in the dark. I couldn't see clearly, but was still close enough to know they were there, and it creeped me the fuck out. I felt *so* uneasy. In retrospect, I was right to feel uneasy, but it was hard to get a good look; I didn't want them to see me, and so I began walking away. But as I did, I turned one last time, only to see David and Daisy emerging. They embraced, had a long, lingering kiss, and the person who'd been watching moved behind the beach huts. Then David and Daisy parted, and he went one way down the beach and she started walking the other way in my direction, so I quickly jumped in my car.

I started the car, feeling sad and jealous, and I realised that I loved Daisy. I'd never felt like this about anyone before, and I'd certainly never felt this horrible jealousy in the pit of my stomach. I remember thinking this must be how Georgie feels, as I drove away down the road. But as I approached the beach huts something made me drive slowly past, and under a street light I saw the other person, the one I'd seen before, crouching. It was as if they were waiting. It was dark, and I didn't get a good look, I just saw this figure loitering in the shadows. It was so weird, and by now I thought it was probably some weirdo, a peeping Tom, and, aware that Daisy was walking back along the beach alone, I thought twice about leaving. But then I considered how it would seem to her if I suddenly pulled up in my car as she stood at the bus stop. She'd know I'd been following her and probably freak out. So I just drove back home, but as I did, something in the back of my mind was niggling. I thought about the figure waiting by the beach huts. There'd been something familiar about the way they moved, the crouching, the posture. That's when I started to have the most horrible feeling that I knew who it was – so horrible I had to stop and have a drink.

I never told the police I'd been there; it would only have made me look guilty or weird, and Georgie had already covered for me by saying I was with her. So I kept quiet, kept myself out of the spotlight, and never told a soul what, or who, I'd seen that night.

41

MADDIE

The *Killer Question* dénouement dinner feels very grand, and everyone's chattering away.

'Have we forgiven Alex for not telling us the truth about his involvement with the podcast?' Lauren says quietly. She must still be reeling from this morning's revelation about her stealing Daisy's book, and is probably looking for a distraction.

'There's nothing to forgive Alex for,' I lie. 'But I'm sure Georgie was far more useful to his research than I was. She had more insight into the group.'

'You could say that, but for "insight" read "blame" and I bet she spent a long time bad-mouthing me over the phone to Alex. It explains why I'm getting such a bashing.'

I think any bashing Lauren gets for what she did is justified. 'I just feel a bit sad because I thought Alex and I had a special bond, like me and Daisy did,' I say.

We'd kept in touch over the years, but in the months before the invite he definitely called me more. I'd assumed it was because he liked me, and missed our friendship, so it's disappointing to find out our more frequent chats were only instigated by him because he wanted information to use in the podcast.

'I wonder if he really believes one of us did it, or did he just say that for the podcast – and to give Tammy some suspects?' I say, throwing it out there.

'Well, they're married now, so if it was for Tammy, it worked,' Lauren replies, raising an eyebrow.

Thing is, now I don't trust him, and as we all sit with our pre-dinner drinks, I watch as he chats with Dan, suddenly both very chummy.

Dan's showing him something on his phone. Alex looks horrified, and by his body language it's obviously inappropriate for the dinner table. I know they think I'm slow getting jokes, but I deliberately never get Dan's because they aren't funny and are often crude. I can see now the same reaction to Dan in Alex, and I lean over to give him some support. If this is offensive, I might just tell Dan exactly what I think as it's the last night. I don't care if I upset him – he's upset everyone else at this table one way or another in the past.

Alex has moved back now and is engaging with Georgie and Lauren, but Dan's still watching whatever it is on his phone. Then he suddenly looks up at me and a strange smile forms on his lips, and he gives me a slow, knowing wink. In that moment, the world around me seems to stop, and I realise what he's watching.

'What the fuck, Dan,' I hiss, and reaching across the table I make a grab for his phone.

Laughing, he lifts it up in the air. 'Nothing to be ashamed of, Maddie,' he's saying in a horrible, creepy voice.

'Turn it OFF!' I hear myself whimper, trying not to draw attention to what's on his phone but desperate to stop it before anyone sees. But the rest of the table is surprised at my raised voice, and now intrigued as to what's on his phone. 'Great body, eh, Alex?'

And there I am, lying on my bed, naked except for a G-string, holding my own breasts up to the camera and pretending to have an orgasm.

I get off my chair and run around the table to where he is. 'Dan, please,' I beg quietly, leaning so close to him our faces are almost touching. 'Please, Dan, don't.' But he's just watching me on his phone, mesmerised. He isn't hearing me, he never has; I'm insignificant to men like Dan, unless I'm naked and pouting.

Tears spring to my eyes as he finally looks up at me, but even my tears don't seem to touch him. 'I'm one of your men,' he whispers in my ear. 'I get you to do all kinds of stuff.'

I want to be sick, but more than that I want to take the knife from the table setting in front of him and stab him through the heart.

I have always felt anonymous, and the men who pay me are too. I don't want them to know me; I want to be a bunch of moving pixels they send money to while they pleasure themselves. I am so stupid, but it never occurred to me that any of the men who pay me so much money to strip and fake-orgasm on my own bed might be someone I know. Might be someone I dislike, someone's dad, someone's husband – or my old housemate from university. How did I *ever* think I could keep this to myself forever?

'What's that, Dan?' Lauren finally asks on behalf of everyone else who's now watching us.

'Please, no . . .' I whisper to him. But still he doesn't hear me. None of them do. Even Alex is looking the other way as Dan waves his phone in the air and turns up the volume so they can hear me panting, winding a silk scarf around my neck and telling strangers to 'choke me 'til I come'.

'What the hell?' Lauren's open-mouthed.

'I remember the first time I saw her on this OnlyFans menu and I thought, *that woman looks like Maddie – oh shit, it IS Maddie,*'

Dan says, raising his eyes for a second to address the table. 'Honestly, I couldn't believe my luck . . .' He turns back to his phone to gaze at me. He's licking his lips and smiling, and talking about me like I'm not even in the room.

Lauren's looking at me incredulously; it's only a matter of seconds since he brandished the phone but it feels so much longer.

'Is that the vintage Hermès scarf you're playing with?' she asks, seriously.

'Who's looking at the scarf?' Dan's saying. 'She's amazing.'

'Dan, what the fuck are you . . . doing?' Georgie sees what he's doing, and looks from the phone to me. As this registers with her she immediately starts screaming at him to turn it off.

'Fuck you, Georgie. We're splitting up. I can do anything I like now. I won't be controlled by you anymore.'

'Turn it off, NOW!' she's yelling, and even in my worst moment I'm touched by her support.

'Fuck off. I'm glad we're getting a divorce, because you're a psycho, and by the end of tonight everyone's going to know what you did.'

Lauren's just sitting there telling Alex it's *her* scarf that I'm now weaving between my breasts in the video, as Alex looks helplessly on.

I can't bear another moment, and I smash Dan with my fists to grab the phone off him. I can hear my pixelated image groaning and moaning and saying the vilest things as I walk back around the table.

As I sit down in the weight of silence, all that can be heard in that big, echoey dining hall is me making animalistic sounds of pleasure for profit. And the others just sit there quietly with the backdrop of me panting for cash.

I'm trying desperately to turn off his phone while crying with shame and self-loathing. Dan isn't smiling anymore as, unable to work out how to turn off his state-of-the-art iPhone, I hurl the phone to the ground, then stamp all over it in high heels, like it's a swarm of cockroaches.

'Maddie, that's my new iPhone, I paid two grand for that . . .' He's moving towards me, but he's too late. The phone is now chewed up under my stilettoes, powered by my incandescent rage.

'This is MY life, it's MY job. I don't have wealthy parents, or a private income like you. That . . . that is all I have!' I yell in his face. I've had drama training, and no one expects the lungs of Lady Macbeth from the little blonde who's slow on the uptake. 'At least those faceless men saw me, they watched me. I had some significance, for a few minutes at least. None of you even see me!' I yell.

No one responds. They say nothing, just stare at me, apparently stunned, and after a few seconds Lauren speaks into the silence.

'I don't understand – I thought you taught yoga?'

Dan's on the floor now picking up the bits of his phone, not listening, not interested in me. 'You've ruined my phone, you sad little . . . you . . . !' Then he's standing up, thrusting the trampled metal right in my face. The look in his eyes is pure hate, and it chills me.

Suddenly, Georgie's standing next to me. 'Back the fuck off, Dan. Leave her *alone*!'

'Oh, I see, Mrs Angry is here. Hide the wine bottles, she's on the rampage!'

'At least I take responsibility for my behaviour,' she replies, guiding me back to my seat and sitting next to me.

He's always played the cheeky chappie, the affable guy, the joker. But he isn't funny. He's a bully, and he's spent twenty years winding Georgie into a tight little ball that can't function with him, and can't function without him. I feel for her.

'Don't talk to me about taking responsibility,' he snarls at her.

Georgie sits in her seat, her head down, and just as she lifts it, presumably to respond, our phones ping.

And the audio file begins:

'Hey, Tammy here. Welcome again to the final dinner, and the final recording, where we reveal who we at The Killer Question *believe is responsible for the 2005 murder of student Daisy Harrington.*

'But first – earlier we invited you all to make your own voice notes with your theories about who killed Daisy. Yes, we asked you to drop your former university friends in it, but only if you had good reason, and you've come up with some good reasons. No one has held back . . . But first the starters. Scallops, chorizo and paprika oil.'

The plates arrive – sweet white scallops with spicy chorizo and a drizzle of bright-orange paprika-hot oil. It's so delicious I almost forget about the podcast, but then there's another ping.

'So, the starters have arrived, and we will now play your voice notes and we'll be recording your reactions, and any discussions that may arise from the notes.

'We have only four voice notes, as Maddie declined to offer up a suspect. Her choice – and that's okay with us, Maddie. So, in no particular order, we're starting with Lauren.'

'Okay . . . Erm,' says Lauren's voice. *'I really thought at the beginning of the weekend that if it wasn't David Montgomery it had to be Georgie. I had no proof or anything, but for me she was the obvious choice – she hated Daisy, she was always jealous because of the Dan connection, and Daisy told me she was scared of her. Like, really scared . . . And witnessing her rage this weekend, I haven't changed my mind. So . . . yeah. I think Georgie killed Daisy.'*

This accusation must hurt Georgie, but she continues to sit coolly eating her scallops, not flinching, just staring at her plate, while Lauren mumbles, 'Sorry, no one else came to mind.'

Georgie shrugs. 'If it's what you think, then it's right that you say it for once. You've always been two-faced, so good on you for finally being honest. Don't spoil your new-found courage by apologising,' she says, then goes back to her food.

God, it's mortifying.

'So, our next voice note is Georgie . . .'

'So, I don't think anyone will be surprised that I think there's still a chance David Montgomery did it – but as that seems to be unfashionable I'm going with my husband, Dan. I thought it was Lauren – the book was a great motive, and I'm not saying she didn't kill Daisy – but I just think it's more likely that Dan did it. He thought he had Daisy in the palm of his hand, but she wasn't weak like me – or in love with him. The night Daisy died, he told the police he was home with me, and I covered for him – but he wasn't with me. What else . . . Erm, yeah, her underwear was removed, and the ligatures around her neck have always worried me. Dan has this fantasy about strangling women. I've never let him do it to me – what does that tell you about the trust in our marriage? So, yeah . . . Dan did it.'

'Bitch,' Dan mutters under his breath.

'I've been covering up for you for years. Not anymore,' she mutters back.

'So, that's Lauren and Georgie, and now we're going to play Dan's voice note.'

'Okay, it's er, Dan . . . I need to explain that I did follow Daisy down to Exmouth Beach that night. I wanted to try and speak to her before she got to David. Earlier, when I'd asked if I could see her, she'd told me to leave her alone, said I was a bit intense and she felt under pressure. I only wanted to talk to her, but Georgie was home as always and watching me. So I followed Daisy to Exmouth Beach, hoping I'd get the chance to speak to her before she met David and I lost her to him.'

'Lost her to him?' Georgie laughs. 'You are such a misogynistic prick, Dan. Women aren't football cards to be traded between men!'

He doesn't acknowledge her; he makes a thing about straining to listen to the voice note over her voice, as it continues.

'... I wanted to catch Daisy getting off the bus but I missed her, and ... then David was there. It's a long story, but what's really sinister is that there was someone else on the beach that night. The weirdo was crouching down by the beach huts. At first I couldn't see them, but there was something about the way they moved ... It was very dark, and I couldn't be sure, but now I know it was the person I thought it was – I saw Daisy's murderer.'

There's an audible gasp, and then absolute silence, waiting for more.

'I know this person is capable of smashing someone's skull in with a hammer; but until this weekend I thought Daisy's killer was asleep in their room the night she was killed. Daisy's killer was my alibi. But looks like I was their alibi all along, because today I discovered they'd lied to the police about being home that night, and they'd also followed Daisy to the beach thinking she was meeting me. That's when my worst fears were confirmed – and I knew the small crouching figure in the darkness that night was my wife. That's why I've never told a soul before that I saw her that night, but I know it was Georgie, I've always known it ...'

42

LAUREN

'No surprises – Georgie's rage makes her capable of anything,' I whisper to Maddie, who still looks pretty shell-shocked about being exposed as an online stripper. Not sure I can use her on my book tour now, which is a shame.

'No, it wasn't Georgie,' she replies. In spite of what she does for work, Maddie lives in Disneyland – she refuses to believe the bad about anyone.

Our main course arrives, but I'm not very hungry. When Georgie mentioned Dan's asphyxiation fantasy in her voice note, my stomach churned because he's asked me before if I'd like him to choke me. I said a firm no, but now I'm wondering about Daisy's injuries and if Georgie had a point about the ligatures round her neck.

I'm toying with my coq au vin when our phones ping, and Alex turns up the volume on his phone and places it in the middle of the table.

'Hi again, guys, Tammy here. Hope you're enjoying dinner – and now back to the voice notes you guys made earlier. Maddie chose not to do a voice note, so we'll go straight to Alex.'

'Hey guys, Alex here. I . . . To be honest I'm not sure about any of this. I've changed my mind so many times about who it was. Even before this weekend, just talking to Maddie and Georgie online and on the phone, I tried to get a feel for things, see if any clues were dropped. Maddie hadn't kept in touch with anyone, but I learned enough from Georgie to see where Dan was at. I'll be honest, I wasn't inclined to call Lauren because we just never gelled, and I thought it might seem odd to her, receiving a call from me. As we were keeping my involvement on the down-low, I didn't want to alert anyone. But Lauren has always had a rep for gossip, and I never thought she was a suspect – not for a second, even though she'd physically attacked Daisy. Of course, I'd no idea then about the book, and that has, over the weekend, concerned me, and I have flip-flopped slightly over Lauren. As Georgie put it yesterday, "There's your motive right there." But, you know, we aren't detectives, and this isn't a courtroom, it's a podcast. And because you guys were all good enough – or blackmailed enough – to come this weekend, we've had the luxury of watching and listening, and talking. So, for me, it's not about proof, it's about instinct, and that's all I have to go off, and I think it's either Dan, or Georgie, or both. He was jealous of David; Georgie was jealous of Daisy . . . and they may have done it together?'

'Wow! Thanks, Alex. Well, that's pretty conclusive. We have two people thinking Georgie did it, one for Dan and one for both of them.'

'I want to respond. It wasn't me – I didn't kill Daisy,' Dan says.

'I know I didn't,' Georgie's saying, but she seems on the edge of tears. I actually feel sorry for her, and wonder if I chose the right person when I said I thought she was the murderer.

'I'd like to respond too, please,' Maddie says, and she stands up. After everything that's gone on tonight with her OnlyFans being broadcast, followed by her jumping on Dan's ridiculously expensive phone, I'm surprised she's found the courage to speak. But she did drama, after all, and she's quite the actress. 'I need to say something,' she starts. 'Almost twenty years ago, the wrong person was jailed for a crime he didn't commit, and at the time I couldn't come forward. I was grieving, and my mental health was extremely fragile, and by the time I'd realised what was happening, David Montgomery had gone to prison. By then I felt it was too late – but of course it wasn't, and another life was lost as a result of me keeping quiet.'

I'm not sure where this is going. My mind's whirling through the weekend and all the 'suspects'. Does quiet, slow-on-the-uptake Maddie have some real juice on someone? Is she going to be the star of my story and accompany me on my book tour after all? She might wow the audience with her courage, beauty and strange career. What a story she'll have to tell.

Alex has stood up now. What's going on? 'Go on, Maddie,' he says. 'It's okay to say what you know . . .'

I'll be disappointed if it's Alex after all. I was just getting to like him.

'So, tonight it's looking like Georgie or Dan or both look guilty of being Daisy's killers,' she says. 'But it's neither of them. I can't let the wrong person go to prison again; I can't allow another person's life and another family to be ruined.'

Dan chokes on his wine, and the young waitress has to come to his aid. Meanwhile, I'm looking at Maddie and I'm thinking: *Is this a joke, or is it a trick to smoke someone out, or . . .*

Alex puts his big arms around her as she rests her head for a moment on his chest.

'I think about the way things were, and still ask myself how it happened, and why it happened,' she starts, gently pulling away from Alex to address us all.

'So tell everyone what . . . what happened?' Alex says, and she takes a seat and rests her head on her arms for a while.

We're all looking at each other, and both Georgie and Dan look terrified, but Alex urges Maddie to speak.

'All he wanted was a pretty young girl on his arm, but she loved him, she saw him as this amazing professor who was brilliant and handsome and . . . I told her David was bad news . . .' She pauses a moment. 'He'd promise to take her out to dinner or away for the night, and she'd get all excited and plan her outfits, and talk about it non-stop. I remember resenting the excitement in her voice, because it told me how much she trusted him, how she believed he'd be there for her. But so many times he'd invite her for drinks or to dinner and not turn up, and when he'd done this a few times she finally told him she didn't want to be with him. As I pointed out, he was married, he was never going to sit in a bar or restaurant in the city with her in case someone saw them. But then one night she called me from a posh hotel in Exeter. He'd booked a room and said they would spend the whole night together, and she'd been so thrilled. But now she was sobbing, saying she wanted to end her life because he'd just called to say his wife was home – and he'd let her down again.

'She was so upset, I jumped in a taxi, and when I arrived I found her in the hotel room in bed, distraught. I sat with her and stroked her hair, and when she turned over and lifted her bed sheet for me to get in, I did. That was the beginning . . .'

Maddie starts to cry.

'After that night, I wanted nothing and no one else but her. I'd always loved her from afar, always known I was gay, but I'd kept it to myself, and I wasn't ready to tell anyone. But that kiss with Daisy opened up my world – I knew this was who I was, and who I wanted to be, and I even started to like myself for a while.

'I'd found the love of my life, and I knew I'd never love anyone as much as I loved her. I remember holding her that first night, and I shared my feelings about her, and she said she'd often wondered if she might be gay too.'

I am agog. I didn't think there was anything that could shock me about Maddie after the cam-girl revelation, but this is all starting to make a kind of sense to me. She was never far from Daisy, always in the background of our friendship, waiting to step in if needed. It sounds like it was the same with Daisy's romantic relationship too – as soon as David let Daisy down, she called Maddie.

'The thing is . . .' Maddie continues, 'I genuinely cared about her. I didn't want to use her, or parade her around campus like David Montgomery did. In fact, Daisy was vulnerable and in need of protection, especially from men like Dan and David Montgomery.

'No one took any notice of me, so they didn't realise I was watching all the time. And I was – still am – a better actress than I was a ballerina.

'But Daisy's pregnancy at the start of our second year was such a shock. I helped her in those early days when she felt sick and wretched and didn't know what to do. By then she and I were sleeping together regularly, though no one knew; they just thought that, as her friendship had cooled with Lauren, I was spending more time with her. "Don't ever tell anyone about us, will you, Maddie?" she used to say. That's why she'd make fun of me and tease me in front of Lauren. She didn't want anyone to suspect anything was going on between us. But I wanted people to know we were a couple. I was proud of being with Daisy, and wanted to shout about it.

'I was fully prepared to leave uni and get a job and look after the baby together . . . as a couple.' She takes a breath. 'But then I noticed her and Dan were spending time together in the house and also around uni. It was all very discreet, probably so Georgie wouldn't know. But I knew. I understood Georgie's hurt, and the two of us would sometimes talk about how painful it was to have a partner who you couldn't trust. But Georgie thought I was talking about a boy I was seeing in my drama group. She had no idea I was talking about Daisy.' She turns to Georgie. 'Thanks for those late-night chats, and for being there. You saved me so many times.'

Georgie smiles the warmest smile I've ever seen from her.

'But then, one evening, out of the blue, Daisy told me she was meeting up with David. He'd been in touch and she'd realised she loved him. This blindsided me. I thought we were a couple. I knew it was still a secret, but to me it was real. But I should have realised, because it wasn't the first time she'd treated me as nothing, and it wouldn't be the last – I was never safe with Daisy. I was just someone else on a list of people that she called to keep her warm on a cold night.

'I begged her not to go, told her she was going to get hurt and that she'd regret getting back with him. "He's happily married with two children, is he really going to give everything up for a nineteen-year-old knocked-up student?" I said. But that wasn't what she wanted to hear, and it made her angry. She told me to piss off and mind my own business, and off she went.

'But I couldn't let her go like that, and I followed her, through the streets in the dark, heading for the beach, to meet David. I sat in a bus shelter on the promenade, waiting. I had my hood up and my head down so she wouldn't recognise me. There were one or two people out on the beach, walking their dogs, but no one saw me watching from my vantage point. And from where I was I could see her on the beach, kicking stones, looking up at the sky. It was a clear night and there were millions of stars – Daisy loved stars – and I watched her lift her head and twirl around and around. I think I loved her more in that moment than I ever had, and I was determined she would never go back to David.'

We are all rapt. This is a story to end all stories, and I hate myself but I'm already imagining the cover of the book I'll write – Maddie's story? Possibly.

'David eventually turned up, they soon disappeared into his beach hut, and I knew what they were doing. He was using her again, and she'd fallen back into the pattern – it was so destructive.

'Eventually, after an agonisingly long time, they emerged from the beach hut, kissed, and parted. So when he'd gone and she started walking up the beach, I caught up with her and, as I'd expected, she freaked out. "What are you doing here, you're being weird, Maddie," she said, which I suppose was understandable.

'"Can we talk?" I asked her, but she was like, "No way, just leave me alone, Maddie." I was running alongside her trying to keep up, and I wanted to go somewhere private and out of the cold so I could talk to her, explain my feelings. I begged her again to talk to me, only this time I lied, saying I had a photo of David to show her. I implied he'd been cheating with another student – which wasn't true. Eventually she agreed and we walked back to the beach hut, which was now locked. But it turned out Montgomery had had a key cut for Daisy, so she unlocked the door while I tried to get my head around the fact that he'd used his family beach hut for their affair.'

She almost breaks down at this, but is clearly so determined to tell her story after almost twenty years of keeping it inside that she carries on, her chin trembling with emotion.

'Once inside, I offered her a garden chair, but she shook her head, she wouldn't even sit with me. I reached for her, but she recoiled, like she couldn't bear to be near me, and that hurt me, a lot. "Show me this photo then," she said, reminding me why we were there, and the only reason she'd agreed to come to the beach hut.

'I didn't answer her, I just said, "Please don't go back to David. He already has two kids and a wife, he doesn't deserve you – or your baby." And that's when she got angry. She probably realised I'd lured her there under false pretences, and she accused me of lying. I realised in that moment that she was likely to run, so I said, "Daisy, let's just move in together, live in another town, somewhere far away, just you and me and the baby . . . ?" I waited for her to respond, to be emotional, to hug me, to say "Yes!" I thought she'd be relieved that she didn't need David or Dan, she had me.

'But I'll never forget the look on her face. It was pure horror, and yet her eyes were dancing, like she wanted to laugh, you know?

"I'll love the baby like my own – we can be a family," I told her, but by now I was beginning to feel unsure.'

We're all still listening, but she's mostly addressing Alex, who's now gently encouraging her to continue.

'Yeah, she just kept staring at me in horror, and then . . . then she started laughing. I thought she'd never stop. "I can't be with you . . ." she said, like I was repulsive. When I asked her why not, she said, "Because I'm not gay." I wanted to die. I'd never loved anyone like I loved her. And that's when she said, "Maddie, I enjoyed my time with you, and I did love you in my own way, but I can't live a life like that – I want a proper family, I want my kids to have everything I never had, but most of all I want them to have a dad."

'I started to cry. I knew she wasn't being true to herself; she'd loved me as much as I'd loved her, she just wasn't strong enough to face the world as a gay woman. But I was so hurt, and so disappointed in her – in who I'd thought Daisy was. She was denying me, denying who she was, who we were. I looked at her as she walked to the door, and saw no kindness in her eyes, just a desperate need to get away from me as she turned the handle to leave. I went to hug her, but she recoiled and pushed me away with such force, and tried to get out of the hut. But I begged her to listen to me, threatened to tell everyone about the two of us. "Everyone will know who you are, even if you don't know yourself!"

'"Maddie, you really are pathetic," she said, and that's when she started laughing; I could hear nothing but her laughter, and something came over me. I instinctively picked up the hammer by the door, and still she laughed. I held it high. "Stop laughing at me!" I was yelling, and I was waving the hammer, to threaten her. It was just a warning, I never meant . . .

'I just lost it, and only stopped hammering when I realised what I'd done, and by that time Daisy was lying on the floor of the beach hut, blood everywhere.'

Epilogue – A Year Later

Transcript from *The Killer Question* Podcast

Final Episode: *Young, Beautiful and Dead* – Interview with the Author

TAMMY: Today is a year since *The Killer Question* hosted a special weekend where five suspects, and old friends, were invited back to their university for a weekend to celebrate the birthday of their late friend and housemate, Daisy Harrington.

The recently released *Sunday Times* bestselling book, *Young, Beautiful and Dead*, tells the story of what happened that weekend. When old rivalries, passions and guilt came to the surface, the electric and febrile atmosphere climaxed in an unexpected confession from the real murderer.

In this final episode we're talking to the bestselling author who knew both the victim and the killer, and attended that fateful weekend.

The book has been sitting at the top of the bestseller list since the day of its release four weeks ago, and a film of the book has been optioned by a big studio in Hollywood.

Tonight we're back at the university, and it's amazing how much has happened in the twelve months since we were all last here. So, I'd like to welcome new bestselling author, and former student of St Luke's Campus, Exeter, the very talented Georgie Fraser.

GEORGIE: Hi, and thanks for having me on the podcast. Have to say I got chills just walking back in here.

TAMMY: Yes, from *The Killer Question*'s perspective, we were all a little freaked out to return after such a surprising weekend. I don't think any of us expected the killer to be Maddie.

GEORGIE: It was the biggest shock ever. *(Georgie giggles.)* Thing is, Maddie being the murderer was such a twist, because she always seemed the sweetest. And I have to add – she IS the sweetest. She's the loveliest, kindest girl, and it's such a shame that what happened happened. But believe me when I say most of us are capable of something like this, given enough heartache and pain.

TAMMY: Yeah, I'm sure you're right, Georgie. Alex says it now all makes sense, and, like you, he can see what Maddie must have gone through, but even as her friend he says he had no idea it was her. In fact, Tiffany, Alex and I all thought it was Dan, your ex-husband.

GEORGIE: Yeah, well, I had my doubts about Dan too, but I was also suspicious of Lauren Pemberton. And when I discovered she'd stolen Daisy's book and passed it off as her own, I was pretty convinced she was the murderer. But I feel bad for even thinking that now.

TAMMY: For any listener who's been living under a rock for the past year, Lauren Pemberton is the former housemate and author of *A Day in the Life and Death*, who was at the centre of a row involving accusations of plagiarism. After it emerged on the

Killer Question weekend that her 2007 prize-winning novel was actually written by murder victim Daisy Harrington, a civil lawsuit was begun by Teresa Harrington, Daisy's mother.

GEORGIE: Yes, it was shameful. I heard Lauren settled out of court, and had to sell everything, including the family home, to pay Teresa. I heard she's in rented accommodation . . . Very sad.

TAMMY: So, you took the baton, and began working with her old agent Finty Dole on this new one, which has sold a million copies in just four weeks?

GEORGIE: Yes, Finty called me after she parted ways with Lauren – she felt, as I did, that the book just had to be written. This case has remained in the collective consciousness for more than twenty years. Daisy Harrington is the every-daughter, and every parent and every teen can relate to the girl going away to college with her life before her, only to be slain by her lover on a lonely beach.

TAMMY: Her lover, Maddie Parr, was sentenced to a minimum of twenty-five years in prison. Are you still in touch with her?

GEORGIE: Yes, I spoke to her only the other day. Obviously we worked closely over the phone while I was writing the book, and I visited as often as I could. Maddie was so honest and open. I refuse to paint her as a one-dimensional killer – she's so much more, and I wanted the reader to know the kind, lovely, fragile person she is. I hope that comes through in the book. Maddie still doesn't fully understand her own actions, and will never come to terms with what happened that night.

TAMMY: In the book you use an interesting phrase, that she 'cowers in the face of her own brutality'.

GEORGIE: Yes, it's like she's two people. Under extreme duress, Maddie was capable of a violent killing. But the prison staff and psychiatrists she works with agree: it was an aberration, a moment, it will never happen again. Maddie was faced with a particular set of circumstances, and because of the emotional roller coaster, the stress, and her inexperience in matters of the heart, she cracked. Maddie had spent her childhood in a ballet school where training was all-encompassing, rigorous and intense. Add to that the hothouse setting of a competitive, mostly female environment, laced with an underlying toxic culture of body-shaming and bullying . . . It's really no wonder that, once she entered the real world of school, then university, this shy, quiet girl couldn't cope and rebelled against the world. She'd loved Daisy with all her heart, and the hurt was too much. The prison staff say she's an exemplary prisoner, kind and caring, always helping others, and it's just crazy that she has to stay there – but she has acceptance, she wants this, her punishment. 'It just feels right to be here now,' she told me.

The only thing she misses is her cat Minty, who my daughters insisted we adopt and who now lives with us – she leaves fur everywhere, but I don't care about stuff like that anymore.

TAMMY: Sounds like you're a changed woman, Georgie.

GEORGIE: Yes, and happily divorced too! I couldn't take any more of Dan's cheating, and after that weekend I realised my unhappiness, my obsessive cleanliness, my deep mistrust and dislike of most people – it was all down to my relationship. I take some responsibility, but my marriage was a dysfunctional mess, and I couldn't stay a moment longer, or allow my daughters to witness any more of it. Dan's now living with a much younger woman called Greta – she was one of the waiting staff at the podcast weekend.

TAMMY: Wow!

GEORGIE: Yes indeed, but I've let it all go. Dan was constantly looking for someone, and it wasn't me. I hope this one finally makes him happy.

TAMMY: Let's hope so. But, moving on, you might recall that Tiffany and I have been in receipt of anonymous donations from someone, and were disturbed to discover recently that that someone is Maddie.

GEORGIE: Yes, she told me about that for the book – she said that's why she started the online sex work. It was the only way for her to make enough money to try and make it up to you both. Another example of her selflessness.

TAMMY: Tiff and I struggled with this – she essentially took our father away from us . . .

GEORGIE: Yes, and as her own father died when she was young, it's something Maddie finds very hard to come to terms with. She's horrified that, because she didn't confess, your father was taken away from you. It's the reason she wanted to give you the money: she knows it will never compensate, but she told me she had to do something.

TAMMY: We couldn't accept the money anymore when we discovered who it was from, and we now redirect it to a charity we set up for young women from poor and difficult backgrounds. The aim is to give them the same chance of education and career as those who are more privileged. At least something good can finally come of this.

GEORGIE: What you're doing is wonderful, and I sincerely hope it goes some way to better lives for bright young women who need help to get to where they should be.

TAMMY: That's the plan. And, despite having mixed feelings, I do hope Maddie's time in prison will be as positive as it can be.

GEORGIE: I just hope my book will help people understand Maddie. I don't want to seem like I'm supporting a murderer, or enjoying the spoils of that murder. There have been lots of reports regarding the money this project with the book and film will make for me, but it's my job. I've worked hard, Tammy, and if the press snap photos of me in glitzy dresses at premieres – it's only work.
(Silence for four seconds.)

TAMMY: Yeah, but nice work if you can get it. *(Tammy laughs nervously, followed by silence for six seconds.)*

GEORGIE: I'd rather not talk about this in terms of my success. What happened in the beach hut that night was a terrible thing, let's not forget that. Now I'd just like to read a few lines from my book if that's okay, Tammy?

TAMMY: Oh, er, yeah, I guess?

GEORGIE: *(Clears her throat, then reads dramatically.) She'd been missing for a week when they found her, and by then everyone felt they knew her. People who'd never even met her declared their love for Daisy, and left flowers and soft toys by the oak tree outside our place. They sobbed at her funeral, wore black, made daisy chains out of plastic daisies. It was like they wanted to own a piece of her, a slice of grief that they wore like a fancy scarf.*

TAMMY: Thanks for joining us tonight, and congratulations on writing an original page-turner that really keeps the reader on the edge of their seat.

GEORGIE: I may have written this book, but I take little credit for the success, Tammy. People still can't get enough of Daisy Harrington. Her story, her life and her legacy will live on in our hearts – like Princess Diana . . .

Maddie

It's strange to find myself here, but there's a weird symmetry to being jailed for murder. My father was a murderer too, he killed a man in a drunken fight. Dad was an alcoholic – and I guess addictive behaviour isn't the only thing I inherited from him. It was 6 a.m. when the banging on the door started and the police came running in to take him away. I never saw Dad again. I was six years old. Mum said I must never tell anyone my father was in prison – I had to say he'd died. This was a lot for a child to take on, the shame of knowing my father was a bad man, fused with the guilt and sadness I felt in telling the lie that he was dead. My father gave me nothing – just a burning shame and the feeling I wasn't good enough, and never would be.

I thought being with Daisy would change that, erase the shame and the self-loathing, but now I realise that loving Daisy was the best and worst thing of my life. I think about her all the time. She's still beside me, and I talk to her in my head. I'm rarely alone in here, so I can't speak openly to her like I used to when Minty and I lived with her in our little house, just the three of us. We were like a little family – she was always there, a beautiful ghost, brushing past me on the stairs, wandering our home, climbing into my bed at night, a constant, comforting presence.

My therapist, Cara, says that when Daisy laughed at me, my mind couldn't take one more rejection, one more indifference . . . or another person walking away. I wasn't just lashing out at Daisy that night, I was erasing all the times I'd been made to feel like nothing. Daisy represented all the people who'd never bothered to find out who I really was, who left me when I needed them most. Including my father.

Cara tries to tell me in her therapist-speak that Daisy is dead. 'You need to come to terms with loss, Maddie, and take accountability for that,' she says. 'Only then can you face what you did, and move forward in a healthy way.'

'Yes, I realise I need to take responsibility,' I say. But I don't. I know exactly what I did, but I choose not to think about it, to imagine an alternative ending with a happy-ever-after. I have to believe Daisy's still here with me, and that night never happened. I didn't make her scream in terror, eyes wide, blood spattering everywhere as I hit her with the hammer over and over. And I didn't tie her beautiful scarf round her neck and pull it tighter and tighter until she finally stopped twitching. No, instead of going into the damp, dark beach hut, where she met her bloody death, we walked hand in hand back home along the beach. And then I tell myself we cooked dinner, and lived happily ever after, because I can't do goodbyes.

Cara sees me every week, usually Tuesdays. Everything here in prison has an intensity – emotions are heightened, cruelty is sharper, hurt is keener, and kindness breaks you. Consequently, my Tuesdays talking to Cara are like Christmas and my birthday rolled into one.

She listens, she cares, and her eyes meet mine as her clean, manicured fingers play with the crucifix at her throat. Cara wears her silk shirts open at the neck, and even though she's at the other side of the desk, my senses are sharp in here. I can smell her perfume. The delicate sweetness of lily of the valley and tuberose cuts through the smell of stale piss and smoke. Cara's fragrance takes me into a sun-filled garden – something I'll never experience again. But this is my punishment and I deserve it, and confessing that weekend was like cutting out a cancer I'd lived with for twenty years.

After that night, I just existed. I left uni, lived with Mum, then ran away to Dubai. But I was drawn back here, and I created my own prison, rarely leaving the house, just staying home with my cat and my memories. Finding solace in my addiction, I'd eat and purge and know Daisy was there, comforting me, loving me in a way she never could when she was alive.

Cara tells me I shouldn't be scared. 'You've never been able to trust yourself since that night, but you must learn to do that now, to know that you have choices. And you can learn to trust yourself again.'

I listen to her and always pretend I agree, but deep down I'm worried that, if I ever fall in love, the same thing might happen. But I can't tell her that, because if I do she won't like me anymore.

My sessions with Cara always go on a little longer than they should, and she makes me feel special, because she trusts me. And when the prison officer asks if she needs someone in with us, Cara says, 'No, this is Maddie's private time, I'm perfectly safe with her.'

She gives me hope that, despite being locked in a prison for the next twenty-five years, I'm not a lost cause. Cara wants me to 'open my heart and mind' to the possibility of love and friendship. I love our weekly sessions, and count the days until I'm escorted to the room where she waits for me with a cup of coffee and my favourite lemon cake. She gets my coffee from the machine, but she makes the cake at home, just for me. The first time she brought it, she asked for a plate and the officer brought a paper one.

'Could Maddie have a proper plate for her cake, please?' she asked. 'She's not a child.'

He said it was against the rules, but Cara told him firmly to bring me a proper plate and she'd take full responsibility. Ever since that day, my cake has been waiting on a nice, shiny white plate. I feel like a human being, not an animal as we are so often made to feel in here. Cara is the only person who's shown me any kindness or respect since I came to prison. It's only a slice of cake, but to me it's everything.

I know Cara makes that cake with love, and she ices it so beautifully, adds the little sugared lemon slices on top of the rich, citrusy, pale-lemon buttercream. It's the most delicious cake I ever tasted, and talking to Cara as I eat the exquisite cake is quite beautiful. Last week I heard myself ask if I could touch her blouse, fully expecting her to recoil, or reprimand me in some way. But instead she stood up and walked towards me, pulling the slithery silk that was tucked in her skirt, and holding it out to me. For a year

I've only felt the thick coarseness of prison garb, or the scratchiness of an officer's uniform against my skin. But she stood there, offering me the luscious silk, and as I slowly reached out and touched it, I gasped a little as it slid through my fingers like sand. I looked into her eyes as I caressed the cool blue fabric, and she looked back at me, sparking an electric current through my whole body. It was then that I realised my feelings are reciprocated. Cara loves me too.

This week I've spent counting down the minutes to our next session. Time goes so slowly in here, I've been in agony, but at last, today I am escorted to the therapy room. The lemon cake sits on a plate on the table as always, next to the coffee, and Cara smiles, and welcomes me into the room. But something feels different. As I sit down, my eyes seek hers for reassurance, but for once they don't meet mine. There's a tightness in the air as Cara fidgets with her pen. I feel awkward and uncomfortable as panic rises in my chest.

'I need to talk to you, Maddie,' she starts, and my heart cracks. It always starts like this, the ending.

'Next week will be our last session. I've spoken to my boss about our progress and she feels it's time for you to work with someone else. He's very good, a colleague of mine who specialises in cases like yours . . .'

Cases? Is that all I am to her, a case?

'Why?' I ask, my eyes stinging with unshed tears.

'We feel that it will benefit you to work with someone different,' she says, like she rehearsed this. Like we don't have a special relationship, like she doesn't make me lemon cake and give me loving looks throughout our sessions.

We go through the motions, she asks me questions and I answer them, but I am devastated. The light has gone out, plunging me back into darkness. All I can think is *how will I live without her?* I'll be left alone in my cell with tiny windows and no stars and no Cara. I'm lost and helpless. I'm losing everything, again. That's what love is, isn't it? Feeling lost and helpless, with moments of heightened euphoria and lemon cake, until the inevitable end.

'Do you think, if I ask to keep you as my therapist, they'll let you stay?' I ask, desperately.

'No, that won't be possible.' She's dismissing me, like they always do. I don't hear what she says next, I just watch her pick up her notes and tell me again what a great person I am, even though I'm obviously not 'great' enough for her to fight to stay. And as she stands to go, I feel a familiar thrumming in my head. I see Daisy lying on the floor, her blood jam-red, oozing from the wounds in her head, her beautiful face ruined for anyone else except me.

It's been good to love again, to escape these dank prison walls, fly briefly through barred windows and imagine another life with Cara. But now Cara's leaving me, I don't feel safe anymore. I have nothing to live for, and Daisy is everywhere. My nerve ends tingle, and the familiar aching has returned, and tonight I won't sleep. I'm terrified of what I know I must do. I hate to feel like this, but when you live in a cell with one window it's a relief to feel something . . . Even fear of myself, and what I might do.

In the same way I couldn't let Daisy go, I can't let Cara go. She has one more visit, and next week, like clockwork, she will arrive on time in a silk shirt, with my final slice of cake, and she'll think it's goodbye. But since being here I've learned to be resourceful, and plates that hold cake can also be broken and become sharp objects. So, next Tuesday, on our final session, when she's dismissed the officer, and once we're alone, I'll find a way to keep her. Cara won't leave me. I'll make sure she stays with me forever, just like Daisy . . . and we'll live happily ever after, because I can't do goodbyes.

ACKNOWLEDGEMENTS

Writing a book involves so many people, with so much talent, who give so much time, and there are always so many of those people, I worry about leaving someone out. But, as always, my editor is first. Vic Haslam listened as I shared my stream-of-consciousness embryo of an idea for *Wanting Daisy Dead*. And, despite my rather garbled thoughts, had enough faith in me to say 'go for it', and so we did. I'm grateful for her guidance, her input and her belief in me and this book.

Thanks to the wonderful editorial team, Celine Kelly and Gemma Wain, who teased and untangled, and finally made some sense of my ramblings. Thanks also to the cover designer Lisa Brewster and proofreader Silvia Crompton, who gave my work the polish and packaging!

Huge thanks to Anna Wallace, for another brilliant read, and the biggest hugs and thanks to Harolyn Grant, my friend and secret weapon, whose eye misses nothing, and whose side notes make me laugh out loud!

A big shout-out to my lovely friends Jan Newbold, Sarah Robinson and Jackie Swift for allowing me to take over our book club evening of food and wine with a brainstorming session for this book. Each one of them came up with something profound and inspirational, as always. Their support, their cooking, their cocktails and their friendship are wonderful, and very much appreciated.

Hugs to my family and those who ride this journey with me. Special thanks to Louise Bagley for dragging me from my laptop for much-needed lunches, retail therapy and cake. Thanks to Lesley McLoughlin, my oldest and dearest friend, for gifting me a special charm for every book I write; it means such a lot, and I treasure every single one. To my husband Nick, who is always there when I'm in desperate need of the right word, phrase or hot beverage, and who came up with the podcast name, *The Killer Question*. And finally, thanks to my mum, Patricia Engert, and my daughter, Eve Watson, who encourage, support, make me laugh, cook great food, and cheer me on in their own special ways. I'm so lucky to have you all in my life.

ANOTHER PSYCHOLOGICAL THRILLER BY SUE WATSON

Loved *Wanting Daisy Dead*? Here's a sample chapter of Sue Watson's incredible psychological thriller, *His First Wife*. Available now.

Prologue

Have you ever met a stranger who accurately predicted your future? I have.

It was my first summer in Sicily, and I was standing on a lonely road after work, waiting for a bus to take me back to my apartment. The bus was late, my phone was out of battery, and dusk was slowly creeping in.

Then, suddenly in the silence, I heard a rustling behind me, and turned to see a dark figure in the trees.

'Hello?' I tried to sound calm, while inside I was freaking out. I tried to make out who it was – was it even human, or was it just the shape of the trees? But then I heard the voice.

'Lady, lady?'

Was it male or female? I couldn't tell; the sound was high-pitched, mean and scratchy.

'Lady?' the rasping voice repeated. I was terrified, and clutched my backpack to my chest. 'I tell your fortune?'

Despite the heat of the day still holding on, I remember shivering as the disembodied words emerged from the darkness. I really tried to focus, but it was impossible to see a face in the shadows of the trees.

'I tell you who you marry? Will you be reech, and happy . . . or sad and poor? Will he love you – or will he lie?'

Was someone playing a joke?

I was cursing myself for staying at work so late – for being in this area of the town in the dark and not considering my own safety. I looked around to see if I could hail a taxi or just run into the road shouting 'Help!' But everywhere was deserted, I hadn't seen a car for ages, and there was probably no one stupid enough to be walking through the wrong side of town at night. I was in flight mode, ready to run, but what if they ran after me? What if there were more of them hiding in the trees?

Where was the bus?

'You want to know if your love, he's true? Will he be your husband?'

A branch cracking, a shuffling sound, they were approaching. I braced myself, ready to make a run for it.

'Give, give.' The voice was much closer to my ear. I could now see the person was wearing a shawl around their head, concealing most of their face. Dread prickled my skin.

'Who are you?' I asked, keeping my eyes on the figure as I slowly opened my bag to take out what little money I had.

'I tell you your future. Your hand. Geeve me your hand. Come, come.' The voice was urgent, irritable. Long fingers beckoned. I reluctantly stepped forward.

'Your name?'

'I'm . . . Sophie.'

'And you are in the love, yes?'

I immediately thought of him, and a fire rushed through me. I felt my hand opening up.

'I show you . . .' Their grip was strong as they pulled me towards them, their face now down in my palm, a scratchy lace glove on my wrist, hot eager breath on my skin. 'I see a man, very handsome?' Gloved fingers pressed clumsily into the lines and swirls of my flesh, pushing and kneading.

'Oh?' My heart was pounding.

'Yes, a very beautiful man but . . . I see danger, dark secrets. You have to leave here.'

Shit. I tried to get my hand back, but the hand holding mine was surprisingly strong, pulling me in. I was about to scream when I felt a whisper close to my ear.

'Beware, *teste di moro*, too many dark secrets . . . someone lies and someone dies . . .'

That's when I ran . . .

I'll never forget the first time I saw him.

1

I'm drinking coffee at a pavement café in Sicily with an English girl called Abbi. We've been having a conversation about our plans to travel to Rome. Both too old to be backpackers, we have the kind of wanderlust that sometimes hits in your thirties, when you realise one day you will die.

Like me, Abbi is fairly new to Sicily, and despite loving the place, her job working for a car hire company isn't her idea of *la dolce vita*. I love my summer job teaching art, and took it in the hope that the university might extend the contract to autumn, but talking about Rome with Abbi has given me itchy feet.

The teaching work isn't as I imagined it anyway. My students consist mostly of the teenage offspring of rich Americans. They are fun and lively, but their interest in art is minimal and it is clear they'd rather have sex, smoke dope and party than learn to paint.

I enjoy the work, and love being in Sicily, but my life is a mess. Two years ago, at the age of thirty-four, I left my home in England when everything started to unravel. I had to get out. But running away is never the answer, and guilt etches itself on to your soul; it nestles in your organs and becomes part of you. The guilt I carry is like the freckles on my face – a fundamental part of me.

So, still seeking some kind of escape from the past, I talked about travelling to Rome with Abbi for a few weeks in the naive hope that another escape might finally exorcise the past. But today, as I sit at a pavement café drinking coffee, I suddenly see this man – and I can't explain it, something shifts inside me, so much so that I wonder if, instead of travelling all the way to Rome, I should stay here, on Sicily. I've never seen him before, but there is something about him, the way he walks, not swaggering, just quietly confident, strolling through *his* town. I assume he's from here; he has the dark, brooding good looks, the easy sophistication of the Sicilian male who knows where he's going. I smile at my own assumptions – he might not be like this at all – but something deep down tells me this gorgeous man strolling through town might just be the person to help me forget. For a little while, at least? Perhaps I simply fancy him, but it's weird, I feel drawn to him in a really primal way, like the stars have collided and created this bright flash of recognition, of familiarity: *Ah, here he is, this is who I've been waiting for.* After flailing around in the wilderness, I finally see a chink of light. I know it sounds crazy and weird to be mooning over a total stranger – and it is! And even as I'm drinking in his dark good looks, and well-cut suit, I'm inwardly reprimanding myself for being so stupid. Unable to stop looking, the sight of him gives me this overwhelming rush – I'm slightly out of breath and agitated. What's wrong with me? My tummy is swirling, and as much as I tell myself to stop being silly, I can't. I love the sensation, the sheer madness of this, and I'm already addicted.

I continue to watch from behind my menu as the object of my affection stops to gaze into the Dior window. Taormina, the town in Sicily where I'm living, is rich in history, but also shiny with wealth and luxury. Chanel and Versace compete for attention on the high street, while billionaires' yachts wait in the harbour, ready to move to the next Mediterranean haven when they grow bored of this one. But this is an island of contradictions, and the high-octane glamour and hedonism is always overshadowed by Etna, the brooding volcano – waiting, threatening, unpredictable. It grounds me.

'So, I've planned our route,' Abbi is saying, as she unfurls an over-large map and waxes lyrical about the Pantheon and the Colosseum. I tune her out as I watch him wander into the designer boutique.

'Are you listening?' Abbi rips into my daydream. 'I said, I planned our route.' She brandishes her phone, with 'Be Kind' emblazoned across the case in gold lettering. 'I've kept all the receipts for the maps and stuff, so I'll work out how much you owe me.'

'Great,' I murmur, already having second thoughts about the trip. Abbi can be quite pushy, bossy even, and I don't always have the energy to stand up to her. 'Do we really need all those maps? I mean, it isn't the Victorian era, we have Google?' I suggest.

'Mind you don't spill coffee on this,' she says, ignoring my comment and unfurling the concertina of stiff paper on to the table, glasses on the end of her nose, like some despot planning world domination. 'The Basilica, Santo Stefano Rotondo, and, ooh, Chiesa di San Carlino alle Quattro Fontane,' she gasps. As my doubts about this trip and Abbi are growing by the minute, her ecclesiastical word salad isn't exactly selling it to me.

I gaze at the long, narrow high street, studded with achingly cool designer boutiques built into the ancient stonework. But having no savings, paying off debts from my previous life, and with only a temporary job, I always have my face pressed against the window of life.

'You have to be rich to be here,' I remark, staring at the wealthy tourists from behind the expensive coffee menu. Abbi isn't listening, too engrossed in her takeover of Europe, starting in Italy, one pope's tomb at a time.

The man is now emerging from the boutique with a white paper bag – 'DIOR' written on it in gold. I can only imagine what delicious designer gorgeousness is inside that hallowed bag. As he begins to walk up the high street and nearer to where we are sitting, I feel my tummy flip – he is even more handsome close up. His furrowed brow and expensive-looking jacket suggest class, and enough money to shop at Dior, and yet his shoes jar slightly. They are more like walking boots, dirty and worn. *How intriguing.* He has an air of mystery about him. I've always had a weakness for unfathomable men.

Abbi continues on about train times and student hostels, conjuring memories of cramped bunkbeds and the stench of overcooked cabbage. I'm suddenly distracted, my heart skipping a beat as the man wanders over to where we are sitting and pulls out a seat at a table close by.

'Imagine running your fingers through that dark hair, and unbuttoning that crisp white shirt,' I murmur, mesmerised.

'What?' Abbi has her finger pressed on the map, her phone in her other hand.

'Him – he's gorgeous!' I flick my eyes over to where he is sitting. For a moment, she drags herself away from dead saints to take a sidelong glance.

'Mmm. Good-looking, but isn't he a bit old for you?' She screws up her nose.

'I like older men.'

Her eyebrows raise momentarily before she returns to her map.

'*Un caffè e un cannolo, per favore,*' I hear him say to the waitress. His voice is like a warm summer by the sea, and my shallow heart thumps in my chest. I don't know this man, he could be anyone, I'm being silly, but when the waitress returns with his order, I see the way she looks at him and feel a tiny pang of jealousy, like a cocktail stick in my heart.

I think I may have imagined this, but when I catch his eye and smile, his eyes smile back, and I let my eyes linger a little too long on his.

Watching him take a bite of the crisp, sweet cannolo, I study his lips and wonder what he would be like to kiss. I also wonder if a man like that could erase the dark shadows that loiter in the corners of my life.

ABOUT THE AUTHOR

Photo © 2024 Nick Watson

Sue Watson was a TV producer at the BBC until she wrote her first book and was hooked.

Now a *USA Today* bestselling author, she has sold almost 2 million books exploring the darker side of life, writing psychological thrillers with big twists. Originally from Manchester, Sue now lives with her family and Cosmo the cat in leafy Worcestershire, where much of her day is spent writing – and procrastinating.

Follow the Author on Amazon

If you enjoyed this book, follow Sue Watson on Amazon to be notified when the author releases a new book!
To do this, please follow these instructions:

Desktop:

1) Search for the author's name on Amazon or in the Amazon App.
2) Click on the author's name to arrive on their Amazon page.
3) Click the 'Follow' button.

Mobile and Tablet:

1) Search for the author's name on Amazon or in the Amazon App.
2) Click on one of the author's books.
3) Click on the author's name to arrive on their Amazon page.
4) Click the 'Follow' button.

Kindle eReader and Kindle App:

If you enjoyed this book on a Kindle eReader or in the Kindle App, you will find the author 'Follow' button after the last page.